Devil's Redemption
Book Three of The Chosen Chronicles

Sirena Robinson

Supposed Crimes LLC • Matthews, North Carolina

www.supposedcrimes.com

This book is typeset in Goudy Old Style, licensed by
Ascender Corporation.

Amaya was awake. She lay in the dark, staring at the ceiling, listening to her parents. Their phone had rung several minutes earlier, and she knew by the hushed voices and whispered urgency that they were leaving again. She heard the flutter of wings seconds after the door slammed and she turned on her bedside lamp. Gabriel turned when the light came on and wagged his finger at her.

"You, young lady, are supposed to be sleeping."

"So are Mom and Dad, and they just went down the stairs. What's going on?"

"They've been called away."

Amaya huffed. "No shit, Sherlock. I'm not an idiot. I'm twelve years old now. I hear them when they leave and I see how they always come back bloody and bruised. What are they doing when they sneak out in the middle of the night?"

Gabriel crossed the room and perched on the side of her bed. "Your parents are helping people. There are wars being fought, and they are doing everything within their power to keep those wars away from you."

"It's drugs, isn't it? They're drug dealers?" She threw back the covers and climbed over him to stomp to the window. "Why won't they tell me anything? They sneak out in the middle of the night and leave you to watch me. They come back with cuts and bruises and don't talk about it. They call each other 'Mom' and 'Dad' but never by their real first names. When I ask, they just tell me I'm not old enough to know. I'm twelve! What is old enough?"

Gabriel stood and reached out to lay a hand on Amaya's head. "Your parents are not dealing drugs." He sighed deeply. "This is not a conversation that I should be having with you."

"You tell me stories that would make an adult blush." Amaya crossed her arms and glared at him. "Seriously, Uncle Gabe, I learned what sex was from your bedtime stories."

Gabriel made a strangled noise. "It would seem my storytelling may leave much to be desired. Does your mother know?"

Amaya couldn't help but giggle. "No, silly. She hasn't talked to me about that yet." Her face fell into another glare. "That would mean they would have to let me in the same room as a boy, and God knows *that* isn't ever going to happen."

"You're smart enough to realize by now that the stories are more than stories."

"Duh. I know that demons are real. You have wings." She lifted her eyebrows and stared at him as if he were a very simple child. "I'm also smart enough to figure out that some of these 'characters,'" She made air-quotes with her fingers, "are my parents, though we both know you aren't about to tell me which ones, or even if those are their real names."

Gabriel was silent for several moments. "You will eventually know everything, Amaya. It will not be tonight, and it will be left up to your parents to choose when they reveal things to you about themselves. It is not my place to make that decision or to provide you with that information. I cannot do that, no matter how much you desire to know."

Amaya tugged on her curly hair in frustration. "I'm not a little kid anymore, Uncle Gabe! I'm old enough!"

He reached out and cupped her cheek gently. "It is not my decision to make, child. I wish that I could give you what you ask, but I cannot. I can only promise you that the time will come that you will receive the answers that you seek."

"When?" She squealed in frustration. "Seriously. I wake up in the middle of the night to my literal Guardian Angel standing in my room, which has been happening since I was three! This is creepy! You're an adult, and a boy, and I'm a girl."

Gabriel's eyebrows drew together. "Do I make you uncomfortable?"

Amaya shook her head so hard her curls bounced. "No, you don't make me uncomfortable, but it still seems creepy. Do you spend time in many girls' bedrooms?"

"No. I watch over you because your parents are my friends and because they need to be certain of your safety while they are doing their jobs." He looked at her with a long-suffering expression on his face. "I fear you are beginning to enter puberty."

Amaya shuddered and blushed. "You're so gross, Uncle Gabe." She stared out her window for a long moment. "You promise they aren't criminals?"

Gabriel chuckled. "I promise that your parents are not criminals." He efficiently made her bed and drew back the blankets. "Back into bed with you. It's much too late for children to be awake."

She slipped between the sheets without argument. "I'm almost too old for stories."

He looked at her fondly. Amaya was beautiful, caught between being a little girl and a young adult, wanting a story and unwilling to ask for it lest it make her seem younger than her years. He toed off his shoes and climbed into the bed with her. "Would you like me to tell you a story, Amaya?"

She pretended to think it over before nodding slowly. "Maybe, if it's a good one."

"I haven't yet told you what happened after Laelia was killed." He smiled when she snuggled against his side. "Do you remember what the six were to do after killing Laelia?"

Amaya yawned. "They had to kill Garrick. He's the wizard that got the gate open."

"Very good. Garrick was a very powerful wizard. He was human long, long ago and made a deal with Beelzebub that he would serve Lucifer for eternity in exchange for immortality."

"Where did Garrick's magic come from?"

"Magic is energy. It is in and around everything and everyone. It can be good or bad, the same as people can be good and bad. In the purest sense, God created magic when He created Earth, and He created witches and wizards when He created Adam and Eve."

"How do people use magic?"

"They learn to find the energy and manipulate it to do what they want. That is how Greer heals people and it is how Aradia helped Greer and Alaria form their link. Magic, in and of itself, is neither good nor evil. It simply is. However, when those who sought to use it for evil did so, eventually magic twisted and became black. Black, or evil, magic is almost limitless. It is what Garrick uses. Aradia uses white magic, or magic from nature. She is only allowed to access as much as she can handle."

"Can she kill Garrick using white magic?"

Gabriel patted her knee. "That's a huge part of the story, my dear. You don't want me to ruin it for you, do you?"

Amaya giggled and shook her head. "I guess not." She snuggled down into the blankets. "Will you tell me one thing?"

Gabriel leaned back against the headboard and draped the blanket over his legs. "Maybe. It depends on what that thing is."

"Does Alaria ever figure out what she wants? She just seems so torn between the two men." She looked up at him. "I'm assuming the Gabriel in the story isn't you."

He didn't respond to the statement. "Alaria finds her path. That is not the story for tonight. Tonight I am going to tell you about Aradia and the power that flows through her and how she used that power in an attempt to stop Garrick."

"What about Javal?"

"Javal is a powerful demon. His ability, which stems from his existence as a human, is that he can take on any form that he wishes to. He can appear as a child or an old man, a dog or a dinosaur. He has the ability to change what he looks like to fool those he wishes to kill. When not inhabiting a body, however, he is weaker and able to more easily be killed. In a corporeal form he is nearly as strong as the Devils, and his abilities made him one of the most feared in all of Hell."

"Did Aradia have to fight them both?"

"Aradia was not fighting on her own. Remember, there were six, and they would either succeed or fail as one. She had plenty of help."

Already interested in the story, Amaya pushed herself to sit back up. "I think I'm going to like this one. How does it start?"

"It starts as all good stories start, my darling girl. Once upon a time, in a land far from here and in a time long forgotten, there was a magnificent Queen who was also a very talented Dreamweaver named Graciela..."

Chapter One

Atlantis

The woman knelt at the altar. Her hair—a curtain of spun gold—fell down her back, and the rich purple of the gown she wore betrayed her royal status as much as the crown upon her head. In one hand she held a wooden staff worn smooth from centuries of use. Her other hand, the one adorned with the rings signifying her marriage and her station as Queen, rested upon the bulge of her belly, swollen with child. Her lips moved, the words muttered under her breath so quiet that she was the only one who could hear them. Her grip tightened on the staff as she worked as hard as she could at channeling all of her power into it and out into the city.

"My Queen!"

Graciela's eyes snapped open as her servant charged into the chamber. She forced herself to continue with her spell work despite the interruption. "How dare you disturb me?! I'm working!" She groaned with exertion at the magic she was weaving. "You're supposed to be guarding the door, Atlas." She fell silent when she saw the look of terror on his face. "What's happened?"

"My Queen, you must leave. They have breached the walls, and they're in the castle. The battle is lost. We must go to the portal right this instant if we are to have a chance of living."

"I'll not leave my people." She stood, regal in her gown, her posture straight and proud. "What kind of a queen would I be if I left my people to die?"

Atlas grabbed at her arm, trying desperately to tug her to the tunnels. "Queen, they have already perished. The Dark Ones bathe in our blood in the streets. The city has fallen! You must protect the babe you carry. You know that your daughter is the only hope that we have of ever avoiding this fate. You must get to the tunnels and leave this time. "

Both of Graciela's hands went to her stomach protectively. "My husband?"

"King Liam is amongst the dead."

Graciela ignored the pang in her chest. She had failed. "If they are taking down Atlantis, then I will put them all at the bottom of the ocean with those they have killed. No one will survive this siege."

"My Lady, there is no time! They are coming even as we speak! You must flee to the portal immediately!"

Graciela pinned a look on him that could have frozen lava. "There is always time for a Queen to avenge her people. Prepare the passage. I require only a minute."

She picked up her staff, folded both hands around it, and slammed it into the floor. A loud crack sounded throughout the chapel, and a green light engulfed her. She smiled as the warmth closed around her and she felt the baby inside her kick strongly. Closing her eyes, she released the staff, willing it to stand on its own and channeling her magic. It hovered several inches above the floor, spinning slowly in a circle and glowing blue within the green light enveloping Graciela. Her eyes turned dark, and she threw back her head and thrust out her arms. When she spoke, her voice was deep and strong.

"Winds howl, waves crash. God of heaven, God of sea, heed my words, hear my plea. Free us from this endless night, raise the sun, bring the light. Walls crumble, city sink. God of sky, God of Earth, take the Beasts, preserve our worth. By the power given to me, as I command it, so shall it be!"

Magic swirled through the air like fog. She heard the roar of the waves as they crashed against the walls. Within seconds, the fog had dispersed to cover the entire city. The sky blackened, and rain began pelting the buildings relentlessly. The clouds shifted from black to red, and the raindrops turned to flames. The blood that had been spilled caught fire, and it seemed as if the entire city ignited with the strike of one single match.

Graciela sank to her knees, exhausted from the power she had expelled. Around her, the city began to shake as if the very foundation of it was cracking. Atlas raced to her, grabbing her by her arms, heaving her to her feet, and wrapping his arm around her to support some of her weight. He grabbed the staff from the green light and dragged her through the chapel and into the secret passage hidden behind the priest's confessional.

"Majesty, we must hurry." He half-dragged, half-carried her down the secret tunnel that led to the portal she'd had encased there as soon as she had ascended to the crown. Atlas placed her on the stone altar and laid her staff next to her. Chunks of stone fell from the walls and crashed to the ground, littering the floor with debris and filling the air with dust.

Graciela looked at the portal helplessly, trying to muster enough strength to activate the large stone dial with the intricate carvings. "I don't have the energy to control it. Not when or even where. I'll be at the mercy of the magic. There is no way to be sure of where I'll land or when it will be."

Atlas began pushing random symbols until the gate began to glow. "Anywhere is better than here. Your child—your daughter—must live. She's the only one who can stop the darkness. The Gods have a plan for her, and you must keep her protected." He rushed to her and fell to his knees, pressing his face against her skirts to sob into the fabric. "Go, my Queen. Keep the child safe from the darkness and make her see that she is the key to all worlds."

Graciela forced herself to lift her upper body, framed his face, and kissed his forehead. "You have served me well, Atlas. I could have asked for no more from anyone. Go in peace."

With that, Graciela sank to the stone, unconsciousness taking her. Atlas ran back to the console, pushed the button to send her through the portal, and watched as Graciela disappeared into the eerie blue light. As she faded, as the waves crashed against the walls that had protected them for millennia, he fell to his knees and began to pray. Not prayer, not the magic that lingered in the air from Graciela's spells, not even the protection of the tunnels could stop the crushing weight of the ruthless waves that came to kill him.

\#

Graciela screamed. Sweat beaded on her forehead and dripped down her face as she struggled to push her daughter from her body. The midwife between her legs looked tired, her face drawn and pale. For more than two days Graciela had labored. She had tried to work up enough magic to aid her in giving birth but had found that her pain was taking all of her energy.

The midwife moved quickly around the bedroom, the only light emanating from the crackling fireplace barely enough to illuminate them both.

"It is time to push, my lady."

Graciela bit down into her lip as she pushed with every ounce of strength she had. She felt a gush of fluid from between her legs, and black spots swarmed her field of vision. The midwife, whose name Graciela didn't even know, looked panicked and fumbled for dry cloths. She sank into the pillows and took a gasping breath. The bed was soaked with blood and amniotic fluid, and she knew the feather down would have to be replaced.

"What's wrong?"

"There is too much blood. I fear the after-birth has torn from your womb before it was meant to."

"Pull her out. Cut the cord. Do something!"

The midwife reached down and felt in the birth canal for any part of the baby. Feeling nothing, she withdrew her hand. Graciela caught a glimpse of the blood before the woman could wipe it on the towel and paled.

"I'm going to die."

The midwife looked up, her eyes betraying the truth. "My lady, there is a lot of blood."

Even as she spoke, Graciela could feel herself weakening. Blood flowed from between her legs, and she felt life slipping from her. Her magic was not that of a Healer. She stared up at the ceiling. "Cut her out."

"What? No! I cannot do such a thing!"

"I'm going to die. If I die, my daughter will die with me, and I cannot allow that to happen. Tie my wrists to the bed and cut her from my womb. She must live."

The midwife, Diane, moved around the room efficiently. She

gathered a sharp knife and tied Graciela to the bed, using her teeth to help knot the ropes. She stuck the blade of the knife into the fire to sterilize it and wrapped the handle in a towel so as to not burn her fingers.

At peace, Graciela closed her eyes and willed her magic to take away her pain. "You'll have a daughter. You'll name her Aradia. It means 'goddess of the witches.' She will be the most powerful witch that has ever, or will ever, live. Do you have magic, Diane?" She used her magic to find out the midwife's name.

"I have a wee bit of kitchen magic, my lady. No more than darning socks and having a special hand helping babies be born."

"This child is important. You need to listen to me very carefully. I can feel my strength waning and I need to say this before it is too late." She took a deep breath. "Death is not the end. I will be here to guide the child and to teach her. I am a powerful Dreamweaver, and I have the power to remain on the dream plane after death. I need you to promise me that you will raise her as your own and teach her all that you can about magic. There will come a day when she is called from this time, and she will leave you, never to return. You may be asked to give your life to ensure that she answers that call. Do you understand?"

Sensing the urgency of the moment, Diane nodded. "Yes, my lady."

"Will you do that? All that I have asked, without hesitation, and without fear?"

"Yes, my lady. I will care for your baby."

Graciela gripped her hand tightly. "Our baby. Your baby. She'll call you mother and your husband father. Do not fail in this task. All the worlds that ever have been and are yet to be depend on this one child." She closed her eyes in a meager defense against dizziness. "Our time is up. Quick! Cut her out before it is too late!"

Diane folded a strap of leather and placed it in Graciela's mouth to give her something to bite into. With a deep breath and a quick prayer, Diane sliced into Graciela's bulging belly.

The baby was ripped from her mother's womb screaming and angry. She was slippery with blood and white mucus and was still connected through the cord when Diane laid her on Graciela's chest. Blood flowed from her body, soaking into the mattress. She weakly spat out the leather and laid her hand on the baby, her waning magic the only thing keeping her alive.

"Breath of life, breath of death, my child resting on my chest. Breathe in life, feel it grow. My magic, my breath, I give to thee. Fight the dark, embrace the light. My precious daughter, born to fight. With dying breath, I give to thee, all my magic, all I see. With all I have and all I am, all I was, and will not be, all of this, I give to thee. By the power of what was given to me, as I will it, so shall it be."

Her eyes rolled back in her head, and her body clenched in a seizure. White smoke poured from her mouth, her nose, and her ears. It filled the room with a pungent, fragrant scent. Slowly, with every breath the baby took, the fog entered her until there was no more left. As the last bits of smoke entered the child, Graciela's heart stopped and her body went limp.

Hesitant and scared, Diane took a step forward and quickly cut the cord to sever the child from her dead mother. She wrapped the baby in a blanket and rubbed all of the remnants of birth from her skin until it was pink and warm. Her hair, red and rich, framed her round cheeks in curls much too long for a newborn. She opened her eyes and stared into Diane's, stormy blue locking onto plain brown. Diane—her voice thick with tears—called for her husband.

"Richard, you need to come in here!"

Richard, a big man with a full beard and rough hands, appeared at the door. He took in Graciela's body on the bed and the infant in his wife's hands. "Good Goddess. What do we do?"

Diane placed the baby in his hands. "We need to find a wet nurse. This is Aradia. Her mother has asked us to raise her."

Chapter Two

Aradia woke from the dream drenched in sweat, her heart pounding in her chest. She could hear her mother calling for her, even as she broke through the barrier of the dream plane and into consciousness. She knew in that instant that the time had come. She hadn't ever truly believed it would happen. Gabriel, an Archangel sent by God, had been promising her for years that her time would come, and after more waiting than she had thought possible, it had.

It was time. Twenty-five years of planning, of training, of sweating day after day while her guardians taught her everything she needed to know would finally come to an end. Spells, potions, healing charms, and medicinal herbs had all been among her lessons. They had taught her how to use nature and her surroundings for their power and to use those things to help herself, making her magic stronger. She had spent many years learning languages. She knew Greek, Latin, Aramaic, and English. Greek so that she could speak in her current time and English both so that she would still be able to communicate in Atlantis when she was finally able to return to the land of her mother and for her journey into the future to stop Satan.

If the dream was any indication, the time for her to leave Greece and travel to the future had finally come. Quietly, so as not to disturb the other women sleeping in the temple, Aradia crept back to her pallet and gathered her things. One leather bag was all she had been allowed to bring with her. Personal belongings were not tolerated in the service of the Gods. A change of clothes, two pairs of sandals, and the small leather bound journal she had snuck in were the only items she had brought from Richard and Diane's home.

She'd been chosen for the temples nearly a decade earlier when she'd reached eighteen. Since then, she'd been training and praying—spending days in worship and nights trying to learn what she would need to know. Leaving her duties at the temple would ensure that she could never set foot in the city again, so misinterpreting the dream would have serious consequences.

The woods were quiet, and she moved through them quickly. Her white gown was the only spot of light in the pitch black night. Small slivers of moonlight broke through the canopy and she could hear the stirrings of the nighttime creatures. Her red hair flowed behind her, streaming down to her waist in waves as she weaved her way through the trees, comfortable with nature and in her environment. There wasn't an animal living that scared her. Not even in the dark.

Soon the woods thinned into a clearing, and she was able to pick up the path that would take her to the cottage where she had grown up. It had been months since she had seen the familiar thatched roof and the roughhewn fence keeping in the animals. She easily worked the latch to the gate and unhooked the front door. Not surprisingly, the couple who had raised her were already awake and in the small kitchen. Diane was preparing breakfast at the fire, and Richard was perched at the table, a steaming mug between his hands. They both looked to the door when it opened, and their faces mirrored expressions of surprise and joy.

"Aradia! What on earth are you doing here?" Diane rushed to the door to envelop her in a tight hug.

Aradia spared enough time for a hug from each before dropping into a chair and waving Diane off when she began fixing a plate. "There's no time for that."

Richard sat his mug down, his brows drawing together in concern. "Something's happened. Are you ill? What is it, child?"

"I'm fine. I had a dream last night. It is time for me to go to the Angel gate. The time has come for me to leave this time and place and join the other five who share my task."

Diane twisted a cloth in her hands nervously. "You're positive it was not just a dream?"

"Gabriel told me that I would know. He told me one day I would hear the call and I would only have to answer. I've heard it. They need me."

"You know you cannot go alone. If you have heard the call, there will be others trying to stop you. You are the only one of the six in this time. The other five are together in their time. It is much too dangerous for you to make the journey to the gate by yourself. I'm not a witch, my power is limited to kitchen magic and a touch of healing, but you will be safer with me at your side for this journey." Diane rose and stroked her hand over Aradia's head, her mouth set in a stubborn line and worry clearly evident in her eyes. "I'll be going with you."

Aradia squeezed Diane's hand gently and bent to kiss the much shorter woman on the cheek. "This is my task. It is for me to do alone. If I allowed you to come, it would be asking you to risk your lives for what is mine to do alone. You've given me everything I needed, and now it is time to trust in my magic and let me go."

Richard shook his head and stood, everything about his stance declaring his intention to go with her. "I don't like the idea, Aradia. We were charged with the task of protecting you from harm. Do you want us to simply send you off without any assurances as to where you'll end up? That's not meeting our duties. No, we'll be going with you to the portal, and we'll be going through with you. This may be our home, but you are our daughter, and where you go, we will go also." His hand drifted to his hip to check that his knife was in its scabbard and he began clearing the breakfast dishes from the table.

Touched, Aradia blinked back tears. Though her guardians were growing old, their hair graying and their gait slowing, they were still loyal and willing to die to save her. After twenty-eight years, they would still rather put their lives in danger than see her embark on her mission alone.

"Have you seen my mother?"

Diane smiled softly. "Queen Graciela is rarely quiet for long, child. She died giving birth to you, pouring her magic into your tiny body, but not even death could keep her from you for long."

Death was not as black and white as most presumed. Graciela had managed to retain some version of herself within reach of Earth, trapped on the dream plane—never able to leave but able to stay close enough that she had, from time to time, visited Diane and Aradia, guiding, instructing, and helping them. The dream plane drained Graciela more each time she accessed it, and it had been three years since Aradia had seen her mother.

"What did she have to say to you?" Aradia smiled up at her father as he brushed his hand across her shoulder while moving through the kitchen and into the small bedroom adjacent.

"That there is much left for you to learn. The next months will be hard, and you must not give up."

"Three years of nothing and that's all she has to say?" Aradia stood and paced the small room. "I was apparently born for this huge thing. Time traveling, different worlds, monsters, what have you, and no one, at any point in my life has ever been able to tell me what exactly it is that I am going to be fighting. Demons? Witches? Warlocks? God? I don't know what to expect! I know that the other five have been battling already. I helped forge links amongst them, but I am trapped here, apart from the others and forced to wait idly while they risk their lives doing what I am to also be a part of."

Diane squeezed Aradia's hands reassuringly. "I know. We don't have any of the answers either, but we have to trust that your mother knew what she was doing. If you've truly heard the call, then we have very little time to get you to the portal. Beyond that, your absence from the temple will be realized soon, and this is the first place they will look." Diane placed a hand on Aradia's shoulder and smiled comfortingly. "Go now and pack what you'll need. Books and potions and such. I'd wager most of your ingredients will be available wherever you go. I'll put out the fire, see to the animals, and then we'll be on our way."

"What should I wear?"

"Your chitons will not be out of place in Atlantis. You'll be adequately dressed in what you have on. Take a cloak in case the weather is different."

Light was barely beginning to pierce the thick canopy of greenery as the trio began down the path to the portal. They had guarded the location of the altar since it had appeared nearly two decades earlier, rising out of the dirt and forming a stone platform and arch. The trees themselves seemed to be stirring, and Aradia sensed the magic in the air. There seemed to be a universally held breath as they walked, undercut by an inescapable feeling of evil.

"We're being watched." Aradia's voice was little more than a whisper as she spoke.

Knowing not to question Aradia's intuition, Richard's hand went to his scabbard, resting on the hilt of his sword. "Where? How many?"

"Six." Aradia's eyes darkened from fog gray to thunderstorm black in a heartbeat as she used her magic to look beyond what her eyes could see. "They carry knives but not because they need to. They're for show, to make us more scared. Their eyes glow red and their teeth are more like animals. Sharp and long. They're trying to surround us and to block us from getting to the portal."

Richard grabbed her shoulders and turned her so that their eyes met. "Listen to me, child, and for once, you cannot argue. If they're trying to keep you from the portal, they're trying to keep us from getting to Atlantis to save it, or to the others, if that is where your task lies. There is nothing more important than getting there and stopping this evil from happening." He pressed a dagger into her hand. "Use your magic if you need to, and this if you can't. I want you to run. Run fast and don't look back. Cast the spell and go through the portal. We'll hold them off as long as we can."

Aradia shook her head, unwanted licks of fear rising up within her. "You'll die."

"If you stay, so will you. You're as much my daughter as any I might have sired, as any Diane might have birthed. Let me do this. Trust me, and run."

Diane hugged her hard and pressed a small bag into her hand. "In case Atlantis is not where you go. There is enough gold in here to get you by for a while." She smiled softly. "Go with the Gods, Aradia, and always remember that we love you. You're my daughter in every way that matters."

Tears streaming down her face, Aradia turned and ran. She heard the forest explode with movement as the monsters saw what was happening and burst from the trees to attack. Richard and Diane were stubborn, and Aradia was fast. She raced down the path, darting between trees, leaping over bushes, and winding her way through the heavy underbrush. Once she had vaulted onto the platform that contained the altar, she pulled a skin full of salt from her bag and drew a circle to keep any sort of demons from getting in.

She walked to the altar, under a stone archway studded with gems. Using the dagger to score her palm, she let her blood drip to the altar, giving the Gods the sacrifice they required for the right to pass through the portal.

"Hear my words, hear my cry, bless my Quest, help me fly. The time is here, the enemy close. We beseech the Gods to fly from this world to another. Walls of time, tunnels of space, take me from here, help me leave this place. Walls of time, tunnels of space, take me from here, help me leave this place."

Aradia pursed her mouth when nothing happened, though she knew she had the chant right. She threw out her arms and for the first time ever let her energy flow out through her fingertips, lighting up the circle and sending out a beam of light so bright that it lit up the entire forest. "God hear me! I demand entrance to the passages of time. I seek to do my duty, to accept my birthright. As I command it, so must it be!"

The sky split open—rain poured down on her and thunder ripped through the sky. The wind howled, swirling around her in a blue and black mist. The circle began to glow, the light becoming stronger and stronger until it was cerulean blue and almost painful to look at. Without taking the time to think about it and relying solely on instinct, Aradia grabbed her bag, took one look back at the world that had been her home, and stepped into the swirling mist, gasping when she fell through time and space.

Chapter Three

January 1, 2031 - Las Vegas, Nevada

Gage Windsor rang in the New Year standing in his casino, watching people run around from table to table, all trying to win money, and none accepting that the house always won. He stood at the bank of monitors, his stance wide. His suit jacket was flung over the back of a computer chair and his expensive silk tie hung around his neck with the knot loosened. His blue shirt stretched over his muscular frame and picked up the silver color of his eyes. He held a glass of whiskey in one hand and laid the other on top of one of the monitors. His eyes narrowed when he caught someone counting cards, and he watched carefully as he tried to determine whether or not it was serious enough to warrant interference.

The woman to his left, a blonde named Pam, cleared her throat. "Mr. Windsor, sir? You might want to check out monitor twenty. A very strange-looking girl has just wandered in off the street."

Gage's eyes shifted over the bank of cameras until he settled on twenty. Standing ten feet inside the entrance was a woman dressed in a Grecian gown, carrying a leather satchel, and looking extremely out of place. The moment her eyes found the camera and he stared into them, he felt a punch of power so potent it made him feel as if she had physically struck him.

"Should I have security remove her, sir?"

Gage patted Pam's shoulder. "No, thank you. I don't think that'll be necessary. Would you call Alaria and Braxton—their numbers are in my phone book—and tell them that their presence is needed here as soon as is practical? They should bring Damon and Greer."

Without waiting for a response, Gage stepped into the elevator and pushed the button that would take him to the casino floor. He felt the magic as soon as he stepped through the doors, and his eyes sought, and found, those of the woman winding her way through the crowd. His silver eyes locked onto her blue ones, and they glowed with such intensity he was amazed they weren't on fire.

He sidled up to her and placed one hand on her back, just above the rise of her bottom. "I'm the one you're looking for. Come with me."

Aradia looked up at him with trepidation. "Who are you?"

"Gage Windsor. I'm one of the six. I can only assume that's why you've been dropped off here. Come on, I'll take you somewhere that we can talk safely."

Aradia looked at him carefully. "I don't sense evil from you. I wasn't sure where I would come to. I had hoped that we would all be taken back to my home, but I see now that I was meant to join you for this battle. You aren't human."

Gage noticed it wasn't a question. He pressed against her back and guided her toward the elevator that would take her up to his suite. "No, I'm not. I'm a vampire."

"You drink blood and kill people."

The first seeds of irritation stirred. "There is a huge difference between drinking blood and killing people. I'll answer all your questions and tell you what you need to know, but first we have to get out of the casino where three thousand people can hear us talking about this."

Aradia studied him intently, extending her magic to push into him, trying to determine whether or not he was a threat. When she felt nothing other than a warm feeling of security and safety, she extended her hand to him. "My name is Aradia. I'll be happy to accompany you."

Gage took her hand and shook it firmly. The bolt of electricity that shot up his arm was a surprise. He looked down at her and knew from the way her eyes widened that he wasn't the only one taken off guard by the spark. She pulled her hand from his grasp and averted her gaze, her eyes flitting around the room to take in everything. He put a slight pressure on her back and led her into the elevator.

She squealed and pressed herself into the corner when the glass doors slid shut and the elevator began its ascent. Gage held out a hand. "It's okay. It's a machine that takes us from one level to another. It's an alternative to stairs. Come look."

Cautiously, Aradia slipped her fingers into his and let him pull her to the front of the elevator. She peered through the glass and shuddered when she saw how high they were. "This is more magical than anything I have ever seen."

He gestured to his penthouse when the door opened. "Welcome to the twenty-first century." He walked to the kitchen to get her a glass of ice water. "I've sent for the others. Braxton, Greer, Damon, and Alaria."

"I've met Greer and Alaria. I assisted them on the dream plane several months ago." She took in the sleek black leather and chrome. "This place is amazing." She went to the wall of windows and looked out at the lights and buildings. "Vampires can live a very long time."

"I'm fourteen hundred and some odd years."

"I've never known of one as old. In my time, vampires do not exist. I've read of them in my mother's journals."

Aradia dropped her bag and went straight to the window, gasping at how high they were and gingerly reaching out to touch the glass, as if expecting nothing to be there, jumping back when her fingers touched the cool surface. She looked over her shoulder at him.

"You're a warlock then? To do all of this?"

Gage walked over to her. "No. I'm not a warlock. I have some magic, but only what comes from being Immortal. This is called glass. It's made by heating sand until it's very hot and then using tools to create a clear, hard surface that you can see through." He reached for her hand and used his own to press it fully against the window. "It's cool because it takes on the temperature outside. It heats up in the summer."

Her fingers curled beneath his, gliding over the glass, and she smiled, half because of the technology and half because of the sensation of her warm flesh sandwiched between the cool glass and his cool skin. "This is amazing."

He was close to her, and she could feel him behind her, almost touching. She knew his presence should have been threatening, or at the least disconcerting, but it felt reassuring and comfortable. His fingers were bigger than hers and were firm and strong on her hand. Her breath created steam on the glass, and she lifted her other hand to draw a line through it.

"I can't believe things have progressed so far since my time."

Gage stepped back. "Try living through it and watching it evolve. That's downright terrifying." He crossed to a leather chair and dropped into it. "You'll see plenty more of this stuff, I can promise you that. Come sit, and we'll talk a bit."

Curious, Aradia tapped her finger on the coffee table as she sat on the couch. "This is more glass, isn't it?"

"Well, the books certainly aren't floating." He smiled and crossed one leg over the other. "What do you know about why you're here?"

Aradia leaned back and folded her hands in her lap. "I've been training for this my entire life. My mother was the Queen of Atlantis. She knew that I was going to have an important role in saving the world, and she believed that if we succeed, it would save Atlantis from perishing. She believed that what we have to do will affect all worlds, not just this one."

Gage leaned forward. "You're talking about alternate realities."

"No, I'm speaking of the fact that time is not a straight line as most would like to believe. It is fluid, flowing both ways and allowing for travel among past, present, and future for those who know how to access the portals. I've spoken with Gabriel at length, and the one thing that seems clear is that our final battle with Garrick and Javal will be fought in Atlantis."

Gage shook his head. "You know more about this than we do. All we knew was that you would come to us and that we have two more tasks."

"I understand more than you do about magic and time and how to do the things we must do. That is my job in this. My mother was a very powerful witch. There is very powerful magic in life and death, and it was all passed into me as she died. Because of my ability and the training I have received, I am qualified to instruct the rest of you. Honestly, I think you'll enjoy training with me more than with Gabriel. He is suspiciously absent when needed and rarely gives as much information as I would like."

"That's Gabe all right. How do you know so much about your mother?"

"She fled Atlantis when it fell to the vampires. She used a time portal that brought her to Greece in ancient times. She carried me to term and died there. I was raised by Diane and Richard." She dashed tears away at the memory of their last moments. "They were killed before I came through. They died protecting me so that I could come through to get to you and the others. We were attacked on the path by vampires. I believe they were sent there from Atlantis or from this time in an attempt to stop me from coming forward. I have never before heard of a vampire in Greece."

"Then they know you've come through. The only chance we have is if they are not aware of where—and when—you are. How is it that they knew long before this ever happened?"

"Time is more easily bent on the dream plane. For a warlock to be as powerful as Garrick, he must have a solid grasp on it. It is highly likely that he sought out his past self and has given himself the information necessary to try and stop me from coming through. Since I was meant to be here, it was inevitable that they would fail." She stifled a yawn. "Do you know the date of the battle?"

"We'll need the power of the solstice, so we'll fight on June twenty-first. We have a little more than six months to prepare." He stood. "It's late. I'll take you up to your room to get some sleep. I'll go out and get some clothes and other things that you'll need and start the ball rolling on getting you enough official identification to travel." He took mental stock of her proportions for correct sizes. Before Aradia could get to it, he picked up her bag and headed for the stairs.

He led Aradia to the bedroom next door to his own. He saw her eyes widen at the sight of the bed, and he chuckled as he showed her how to use the toilet and the sink. She flushed the toilet several times, a look of amazement on her face. Aradia's eternal curiosity ended up getting Gage sprayed in the face when she reached up and touched the shower head, making it move as he showed her how to use the different knobs.

As soon as the water hit him, she realized what she had done and jerked her hand, the motion causing the spray to shift so that she sprayed herself and the bathroom with ice cold water. Gage reached into the shower and turned it off, quirking an eyebrow as she wiped her eyes.

"Satisfied?"

Mistaking his amusement for irritation, she grabbed a towel from the sink and began dabbing at his face. "I am so sorry. It was an accident, I swear."

Gage closed his hands over her wrists. "I'm not angry with you. It's water. Doesn't hurt anything." He looked down into her face, meeting her gaze with his own. The electricity flowed between them again, and he struggled to keep his voice light and teasing. "People here don't apologize quite so robustly. Especially not for something so little."

Aradia tugged gently to free her wrists. He released them immediately, and she offered the towel. "Then I suppose you can wipe up the water yourself." She walked to the bed and untied her bag, withdrawing a small pouch. "Diane gave this to me before I left, in case I didn't end up in Atlantis. She said that it may act as currency here. If it is an acceptable form of payment, I'd like to give it to you for the costs of providing me with clothing."

Sensing that she would be insulted if he refused, Gage took the pouch, judging the weight in the bag. If the coins were as pure as he suspected, she had just handed him a small fortune. It was more than enough to live off until the battle. "This will be more than adequate. I'll have it exchanged for you and show you our money system tomorrow so that you know how everything works."

"Thank you. I appreciate what you're doing for me."

"My pleasure." He offered her a smile and headed for the stairs. "I'll be back shortly. Help yourself to anything here. I'll arrange for more food to be here in the morning."

Aradia waited several seconds, fighting between her curiosity to see the city and the pure exhaustion that begged her to go to bed. Shaking her head, she dashed down the stairs and across the apartment, catching Gage just as he was leaving. She laid a hand on his arm as he was opening the door, her heart pounding in her chest. Gage turned, lifting an eyebrow and silently asking what she wanted.

"I was wondering, if it isn't too much trouble, do you think I could go with you? The city fascinates me, and I didn't get to see anything, and you know what everything is..." She trailed off, crossing her arms over her chest. Gage couldn't help the small smile that crossed his lips.

"Let me see if I can find any clothes that you might be able to wear. It's chilly out there for humans, and you're already looking out of place."

Five minutes later, Aradia found herself wrapped in a leather jacket much too big for her that smelled distinctly like Gage and a black T-shirt over her gown so it appeared as if she was wearing a long skirt instead. Her hand was tucked firmly into the crook of his elbow so she couldn't get out of his sight as they stepped out onto the sidewalk outside the casino.

"What is the name of this city?"

"Las Vegas. It's in a state called Nevada, and the country is the United States of America."

She tugged on his arm, pointing to a building to keep his attention on showing her the city. "How do they make things that tall?"

Taking her lead, he smiled as he answered. "There's special equipment now to make buildings. The structures are called skyscrapers. They use massive pieces of equipment to build them. Cranes, bulldozers—all sorts of things."

Aradia looked up at all of them, wonder lighting up her whole face. She scowled when someone crashed into her and grabbed onto Gage to keep her balance, obviously upset that the person didn't stop. She looked up at him, her forehead creased. "I see manners have been bred out of people."

"They've been gone for quite some time." He chuckled deep in his chest, running a hand through his coal-black hair. "Believe me, even seeing everything evolve doesn't make it any easier to swallow. I was born in Ireland, fourteen hundred thirty-three years ago. Which is probably another fifteen hundred years after you were born." He grinned. "I've never met someone older than me before."

Aradia smiled and shook her head. "I'm twenty-eight. Just because I traveled through time doesn't make me older than you." She laid her hand on his cool flesh. "My heart beats and my blood pumps. I've not lived through it as you have. In that way, you are much older than I."

"You're powerful. I sensed it as soon as I saw you through the cameras. Have you tried to explore what you can do?"

Aradia shook her head, looking sheepish. "To a point. Diane did as much as she could, but she was a kitchen witch at best. I've tried to feel my way, but all I know is what I've managed to discover on my own. I only have one spell book, and I don't know many potions."

"I don't think you're going to need spells and herbs. The power rolls off of you. All you have to do is tap into it, and from what I know, you had to do that to get here. Only a strong witch could activate that portal."

"We'll see. These other women, do they have magic? Perhaps they could help me?"

"Greer and Alaria would both do whatever they can to help, though neither are witches." He lifted a brow when she yawned widely. "Sleepy?"

"Yes, but I wanted to see some of these buildings. The architecture is completely amazing to me." She laughed when she yawned again. "Sorry. I had to leave the temple in the middle of the night, and then the men chasing us and the drain from activating the portal. It's been an overwhelming day, but I do have a question, if you don't mind."

"Sure."

"The men—vampires—that came after us. They avoided the sun. Why?"

"Sun is fatal to vampires."

"You can't go out during the day?"

"I can. Most others can't. I spent the best part of five centuries slowly exposing myself to sunlight until I built up a resistance to it. It isn't the most comfortable thing in the world, but it's not painful, and I can enjoy a nice stroll in the daylight."

Gage pulled her into a store and steered her over to a clerk, a bubbly blonde in a sleek black suit and sky high heels. She squealed when she saw him, throwing her arms around his neck and kissing his cheek enthusiastically.

"Gage! It has been too long! When did you get back in town?"

"Last week. Erica, I'd like you to meet Aradia. She's visiting from out of town and is going to need some things." He nudged Aradia forward. "We don't really have time to try things on. Feel like working some magic?"

The blonde let her eyes rake over Aradia. "Five seven, about one-forty, size eight I think. A little bit top heavy, but I don't know a single man that's going to complain about that. Yeah, I can pull some things that are gonna look fabulous. How generous you feeling, Gage?"

"You know me. Set her up. Deliver it to my apartment by tomorrow morning. Stuff appropriate all the way through fall if you would."

"I'll have to call into some other shops for summer gear, but it is Nevada, so that shouldn't be too hard to find." She flashed him a huge grin. "I'll get it set up for you."

Aradia didn't speak until they were out of the store. "That woman likes you."

"I know. I'm very well-known in this city. My casino is one of the largest ones in Vegas, and I'm one of the richest men here. They want to impress me." He grinned wryly. "I've had a millennia to gather my fortune. People love when I spend a bit of it."

Her arm still tucked through his, they walked in silence for a while. Gage led her down the strip, letting her marvel at the buildings, the people, the lights and the noises. He patiently answered her questions about everything, laughing at her innocent excitement. Only when it was becoming apparent she was about to fall asleep on her feet did he gently lead her back toward his own casino, swiftly guiding her through the crowd and onto the elevator.

He stepped off the elevator and smiled at the groceries that had been brought in and neatly unpacked while they had been gone. It was amazing what one quick phone call could accomplish. Aradia slid his jacket off of her arms and hung it up neatly in the closet, putting it back exactly where she'd seen him retrieve it from. She turned, her eyes tired and her face starting to pale from exhaustion.

"Thank you for taking me with you. I enjoyed the walk and the company." She offered a smile, the flash of white teeth making his stomach clench. "I think we'll get along quite well over the next months."

"I certainly hope so."

Gage shrugged off his suit jacket, and pulled his tie over his head. Aradia started to ascend the stairs, Gage behind her. Halfway up, she tripped and would have fallen if he hadn't shot out an arm and locked it around her waist, yanking her up and keeping her from smashing her nose into the stair case by hauling her against his body.

In that moment, he had a flash of her, naked and beneath him, her legs wrapped around his waist, her head thrown back in ecstasy, his body pounding into her, his face buried in her neck, and her breasts pressed hard into his chest. He could feel her body surrounding him, the liquid heat of her, the flush of her skin as she writhed, even the softness of her flesh and the slightly rough skin of her nipples against his skin. One look into her eyes, at the shock on her face, and he knew she had experienced the same thing.

Her voice was weak and confused. "How?"

Gage shook his head. "I don't know. I don't even know what."

"We haven't—I wouldn't—"

"It must have something to do with the warlock we're going to be fighting. A distraction he's trying to use to get our heads muddled, maybe." He shifted her against his chest, guiding her feet onto sturdy ground, not wanting to release her but knowing he had to. Because if he didn't, she was going to feel exactly how his body had reacted to the image, and that would make an awkward conversation worse.

"Magic, you mean." She braced her hands on his shoulders, her eyes meeting his, traveling over the chiseled planes of his face, the curve of his lips and the dark slash of his eyebrows. "The image was—quite erotic."

He could hear her heart beat, slightly increased from where it had been all night and her breath was a bit shallower. He could smell the slight arousal that the vision had caused and inhaled deeply, letting the scent permeate him. He could not remember ever having been so attracted to a human since he had been turned into a vampire.

Before he could stop himself, Gage gave into his desire and leaned forward, tracing her lips with the tip of his tongue, barely tasting her. Her eyes widened, and she stiffened in his arms, the smell of her blood and desire intoxicating him, her fingers clutching at his shoulders. He knew if he didn't step back, he was going to fall into something that would hurt them both. He knew he couldn't let himself do that, but neither could he let her go without one good taste.

Quickly, he crushed his mouth to hers, sweeping his tongue into her mouth and tasting her groan—the sweet and spicy flavor of her mouth filling his senses. Just as she started to go limp, her fingers beginning to dig into his flesh, he released her, setting her back.

"Goodnight, Aradia."

Shaking, Aradia smoothed her hair with one hand. "Goodnight, Gage. Thank you for a nice evening."

He dashed back down the stairs and stopped at the bottom. "I won't do that again, but I had to do it once. If only to see if it's true."

"What?"

"The vision. Now we know it isn't a complete figment produced by whatever it is that sent the vision. There's something between us—something more than chemistry. It's magic, and I'm damn well going to find out what's causing it and stop it before it gets us into trouble."

"That is probably a good idea." Aradia turned and fled up the stairs. When he heard the door to her room close, he collapsed into a chair, dropping his head into his hands.

"What in God's name have I gotten myself into?"

Chapter Four

January 17, 2031

Greer rolled onto her side and reached out to trace the line of Damon's jaw with her index finger. He smiled and opened his eyes. "You do realize that Aradia will be up at dawn and that it's nearly midnight?"

"I know. She's actually what I want to talk about."

Damon rolled onto his back and tugged her against his side. "What about her?"

"Alaria and I have been working with her for two weeks. I know neither of us are witches, but we have some understanding of magic and spell work, especially Alaria, and this woman is more powerful than anything I have ever seen. I don't even think she's really letting loose yet. The more she practices, the more you can just feel the power coming off her. My fear is that it's going to be very difficult for her to control everything that she has."

"Has she been getting out of control?"

Greer shook her head. "No. As far as I can tell, she's got a lid on it, but it's pretty clear that she hasn't had the training she's needed. Her mother, the one that raised her, had less magic than I do, and she did her best, but Aradia needs more than that. I'm worried that none of us are going to be able to give her what she needs in terms of guidance and help, whether that's as an anchor or a partner or whatever."

Damon's eyebrows drew together. "What makes you think she's going to need anything from us?"

"She might not, but she's not used to this amount of power, and it's easy to get swept up in it. If she does, it's going to take more magic than any of us have to bring her back down."

"I think that's kinda the point, babe. There's never been a witch more powerful than her. There's no one out there that can defeat her if she's at full strength."

Greer shook her head again. "No, that's not true. She's the most powerful natural witch, meaning that the power she has within herself is unrivaled. However, we know that Garrick has ways of increasing what he has and that he's using black magic, which means he can access as much as he wants. Aradia is playing with white magic. I'm not sure it'll be enough."

Damon turned the light off. "Let me get this straight. You're worried that she's too powerful to control, but that she might not have the power needed to get this done? Greer, you need to relax a bit. I haven't seen anything from Aradia that makes me think she's losing control or that she doesn't have a handle on what's going on with her magic. She needs practice, which we can give her, and she needs someone to work with, which we can also give her. That's part of being a group. We have to be able to work together even when it's not our particular strength. I know that you're worried because she's coming into this so late, but I think she's been preparing for this all her life."

Greer sighed and snuggled into his arms. "I like her, Damon, and it worries me because there are so many things even she doesn't know about her power. I think it could get out of her control pretty easily until she learns both to access and manage everything that she has."

"She will. We have five months to prepare for the next fight. That's plenty of time." He pressed a kiss to her forehead. "When is Brax coming in?"

"I don't think he is. He's holding down the fort back in Scotland and working on some leads on Garrick and Javal. If anyone can find them, it's going to be Brax. I think he does better with that part than this anyway. Add in that this is January and the first anniversary of Griffin's death, and he's probably moping a bit, too. He's still having problems coming to terms with her death and it being for nothing."

Damon stared up at the ceiling. "It wasn't for nothing. If she hadn't

Chosen, there would be no stopping this because the gate would have been weaker. Instead of patching it, it would have been open permanently, and there wouldn't have been any way to keep our reality from being. She's the reason we have a chance of stopping this. I think he knows that."

"I don't think that makes it any easier. I know it wouldn't make it easier on me if I had to lose you just for the chance to stop something your death should have kept from ever happening." She smiled when his arms tightened around her. "He's getting better. Even in the few months I've known him, he's getting better." She yawned. "If only he could get his feelings about Alaria in check and figure that whole fucking situation out. She's the most emotionally unstable of us all."

He chuckled. "You just worry about everyone, don't you?"

Greer rolled back to meet his eyes. "They're our friends, Damon. I love them. I care about them, and I want them to be happy. Braxton's healing, but Alaria is getting worse. She's going to continue to get worse until she figures out what and who she wants."

"Is she still banging Gabriel?"

"I don't know. She hasn't come to me to talk about it, and it feels weird for me to always be the one trying to initiate the conversation with her. She's doing the best she can, but this is a lot for her to handle so soon after being made human. I think she's managing the guilt and the feelings she has about the things that she did as a Devil, but I still think she's having problems handling the feelings she has about other humans. She's not sure how to be friends with people, and she's not sure how to have a relationship. She thinks she loves Gabriel, and I think a part of her does, but I also think that part is getting smaller as she gets more familiar with being human."

Damon laughed softly, his breath warm on her ear. "For someone who started with the words 'I don't know,' you sure seem to know a lot."

"Most of it is just female intuition."

He pulled the blanket up around her shoulders. "When it comes to intuition, babe, I would lay down everything in my name on yours, but nothing is going to get figured out tonight, and I can barely keep my eyes open. Let's resume this conversation tomorrow night when we lay down, hmm?"

Greer giggled. "I've always been a fan of the late-night conversation." She brought his hand to her lips and pressed a kiss to his knuckles. "I love you, Damon."

He kissed the back of her head. "Love you, too. Get some sleep."

Aradia slammed the book shut in frustration. Dust billowed off the pages and hit her in the face, going up her nose and into the back of her throat. She coughed and wheezed, fumbling for the bottle of water that sat at her elbow. She gulped the cool liquid and wiped her mouth with the back of her hand. Behind her, Greer opened the door and leaned against the frame.

"Are you dying?"

Aradia turned in the chair. "The dust was taking revenge on me for disturbing it." She pulled her legs up into the chair and wrapped her arms around her knees. "I've been studying these books for two weeks now. The more I practice, the clearer it becomes that I do not need them. You have helped me access some of my abilities, and I'm getting stronger each day."

"You're doing really well. When you're going strong, the power just rolls off of you. I can feel you getting more powerful all the time." Greer sat down on the edge of the bed. "How are you handling everything else? I know being here has to be overwhelming."

Aradia rested her chin on her knees. "I miss my parents. I mourn their deaths. I miss my home as well, but I know that I'm needed here. I have to admit that I'm feeling restless. I want to leave this place. I haven't been outside Gage's home since the first night that I arrived here. I want to explore. At the very least, I don't understand why we can't go downstairs into the...what is it called?"

Alaria appeared at the door. "Casino. It's a place where people dress up, get drunk, and spend a lot of money." She rubbed her hands together. "No one has more money than Gage Windsor." She looked at Greer. "It couldn't hurt to go down for a few hours. We've all been working hard and making a lot of progress. Gage gets to go down to his glass castle every night to work, and we're all stuck here slaving away. I know the job is important and that we have a lot to do, but we have to have breaks sometimes."

"I think that sounds like a fine idea." Greer went to the closet and opened the doors. "Let's see what Gage's money bought as far as clothes." She rifled through the contents. "Damn, Aradia. There is some awesome shit in here." She wistfully ran her fingers over a red silk dress. "Stuff like this doesn't exist where I'm from."

Aradia stood and joined Greer at the closet. "Nor I. Would some of it fit you? You're welcome to whatever is here."

Greer studied the fabric with a suspicious look. "We're close to the same size, but you've got more than me in the chest and hip area. Damn you and your perfect curves." She held up the dress to her body. "It might fit."

Alaria joined Greer at the closet and yanked out several dresses in different fabrics and styles. "We're all close to the same size. We just have different builds." She held a green dress up to her own body. "I would be nearly popping out of this little number."

Greer giggled. "Try it!" She looked over her shoulder at Aradia. "Do you mind that we're raiding your closet?"

Aradia smiled. "Not at all! The woman at the store had these delivered. I don't feel like they even belong to me. None of this is what I would have chosen for myself. Women where I come from cover themselves more."

"It's a different time for both of us. Alaria has the advantage of being from here—at least as much as a Devil who has been alive since before there were people can be from any time."

Alaria stripped her t-shirt over her head and wiggled out of her jeans. "I vote that we all get dressed up and go downstairs to play. We can romp in here like three teenagers for an hour and then go spend too much of Gage's fortune, drink too much champagne, and flirt with strange men."

Greer obligingly zipped Alaria's dress when she held up her hair and turned. "I'll watch you two flirt. I plan to borrow one of Gage's suits for Damon and revel in all the evil looks I get from the single women down there."

Aradia eyed a smoky gray dress. "That one is a very nice color."

Alaria rolled her eyes. "Honey, from you, that's a rave review. Take your clothes off." She held up the dress and jutted it toward Aradia.

The redhead looked torn for several seconds before shimmying out of her sweater and pants. Feeling more at ease with the other women than she'd thought was possible, she slipped the fabric over her head and held her hair away from her neck while Greer tied the thin straps around her neck. Aradia smoothed the fabric over her thighs and stared at herself in the mirror.

"It's so short!"

Greer giggled as she unbuttoned her shirt. "It's not short from what I've seen. I've gotten the impression that hemlines got progressively shorter from your time to this one."

Alaria dug through the drawers of make-up on the vanity, moaning in delight. "Gage got you the good stuff." She smeared foundation on her cheeks and rubbed it in. "To answer you, Greer, you're right. Women have gotten progressively less modest. I think that's a good thing. We're taking control of our sexuality, making decisions about our bodies, and just being more assertive in general." She cast a look over her shoulder at Greer, who had shimmied into the red dress. "It looks like it fits."

Greer studied her reflection in the mirror. "Hell, if Aradia put this on, she'd give every man in that casino a fucking heart attack. I don't have much in the way of hips and it fits like a glove. There is no way this wouldn't burst at the seam with her hips in here."

Aradia wrinkled her nose. "I am not sure if that is a good thing or a bad one."

Alaria applied mascara with an expert hand. "It's a good thing." She swiped lipstick over her mouth with a practiced motion and stood. "Sit. There's no way I'm gonna trust you to do your own make-up without some instruction."

Greer leaned out the door and saw Damon engrossed with a game on the television set. She closed the door and perched on the end of the bed, crossing one leg over the other. "It's been a while since Gabriel came to see us."

Alaria's eye darkened briefly. "He's got other things to worry about. We're handling everything."

Greer knew she was pushing her luck but spoke anyway. "Have you talked to Braxton lately?"

"Not since we left. I think Gage checked in with him a few days ago." Alaria glanced up from putting eye shadow on Aradia. "If there's something you want to know, Greer, you need to spit it out and stop beating around the bush."

Aradia looked between the women. "Is there something going on that I don't know about?"

Greer chuckled. "Just a love triangle. Alaria's sleeping with Gabriel and jonesing for Braxton."

"I don't understand your terms."

Alaria fought to keep her face neutral. "'Sleeping with' is a less crude way of saying that I'm having sex with him. Well, I was. I haven't in a few months. 'Jonesing' means craving or wanting. I dispute that description. Braxton and I are friends, and there is a little confusion about the type of friendship we're going to have. I think I could very happily have sex with Brax and have it mean absolutely nothing other than that we'd both be a bit more relaxed."

"You have intimate relations outside of the confines of marriage?"

Greer snorted with good humor. "Oh my God, yes. We're not nearly as backward as women where you come from. We have sex when we want, with whom we want." She looked up from putting on blush. "Wait a second. You're a virgin?"

Aradia's face flooded with color. She jutted her chin up regally and glared at Greer. "Of course I am. I was a priestess in the temples. It was strictly forbidden. My people believed that our link to the Gods and Goddesses ran through our virtue. Were I to be deflowered, I would have been killed."

Alaria grinned. "We can fix that with no problem." She arranged Aradia's hair around her shoulders and stepped back. "Honey, looking like you do, there isn't gonna be a man down there that isn't going to want to put his hands on you."

Greer rubbed her hands together. "All we need are shoes."

"Mr. Windsor?"

Gage turned his head to acknowledge his assistant. "What is it, Katie?"

"It appears that your sister has brought your guests down."

Gage looked at the monitor and saw Alaria stepping off the elevator. When she'd regained her humanity, he'd arranged for her identity. It had been easiest to give her his name and use it to smooth the channels. "I can see that."

"Should I have security escort them back up to your penthouse?"

Gage shook his head. "No, thank you though. It's a quiet night, and I'm sure they could all use some fun. Send over a tray of champagne and an assortment of chips with instructions that they should have fun."

He watched Alaria, resplendent in a tight, short green dress, lead the others through the casino. Damon was sleek and smooth in a black tuxedo and Greer was on his arm, clad in red silk that showed off her athleticism and her legs. They were all gorgeous, but it was Aradia that drew his eye and kept it.

She wore a dress caught somewhere between gray and blue. It fit her body snugly, accentuating the flare of her hips and the curve of her breasts. It ended several inches above her knees with a strip of elastic that held it close to her thighs and was held up by a jeweled clasp around her neck, leaving her back nearly bare. Her legs were long and slim, and her feet were encased in black heels. He imagined she'd had to practice for hours before being able to walk in them. Her hair flowed over her shoulders in a red and gold sunburst. When she glanced up and he met her gaze through the security camera, he was struck by the intensity of the blue of her eyes. Even through the poor quality of the screen, they radiated magic and life.

He kept his eyes on them for the next ninety minutes. Damon and Greer were better than average at counting cards, and Alaria had a flare with the roulette wheel. Aradia generally hung just behind them, sipping champagne and clapping happily when they won. After an hour, he saw Greer drag her up to one of the tables. Aradia won five hands of blackjack in a row.

"Mr. Windsor, sir?"

Gage shifted his eyes from the camera. "Yes?"

"Camera eleven. I believe we have a problem."

He studied the craps table and sighed. "Get security down there to escort him out." He shook his head in disgust as he watched the man on the video feed. "That isn't even a good cheater. Collect his chips. Send him out with his original cash-in. He'll not make a cent from us tonight." He waited until Katie was done on the phone. "Nice catch, Katie."

He watched camera eleven until his security team had escorted the cheater out. It caused a minimum of fuss, and the situation was fully dealt with in no more than ten minutes. Assured that it was handled, he searched the monitors for his friends.

Damon and Greer were still at the blackjack table. Alaria was at the bar, arranging four drinks on a tray. He scanned the screens, looking for Aradia. There. He saw her push through the door and come out of the bathroom. A man walked up to her, and he watched the exchange suspiciously. When he saw the man reach out and use his arm to block Aradia from returning to the casino floor, he strode to the elevator and took it down. As soon as the doors slid open, his vampiric hearing picked up the exchange and had panic rising in his throat as he hurried to get to Aradia.

"How much for a night, honey?" The man stroked a finger down Aradia's cheek.

Confused and worried, Aradia shied away. "I don't think I know what you mean, sir."

"Sure you do." The man stepped closer. "I've been around these casinos for a long time, baby, and I know a fine piece of ass when I see one. I don't mind paying for it if it's nice enough." He slid his hand down her side and pinched her bottom hard enough that it brought tears to her eyes. "Name your price, baby. I'll pay whatever you want."

Aradia fought the urge to use her magic to deal with the situation. It would not do to bring unwanted attention to her abilities. "I'm not interested in lying with you, sir. Please, let me go or I'll scream."

"Oh, you'll scream all right, but it'll be while I'm fucking you, not here." He grabbed her wrist in his hand. "Come on. Now."

Aradia struggled against his grip. He outweighed her by over a hundred pounds, and he dragged her behind him easily. She planted her feet in the ground to make him tow her dead weight and let her magic whip up within her. As she prepared to level him, he went flying. Aradia whirled and found Gage, who was already striding to where the man lay on the ground. He bent over and lifted the man with one hand around his throat.

"I'm only going to say this once. This is my place, and the lady is a personal guest. I suggest you take this opportunity to get out of my casino before it becomes the last place you'll ever see." He bared his fangs, his eyes shifting from silver to red. "If I ever see you in here again, I will drain every drop of your disgusting blood." He cast the man aside carelessly, not even looking to see if he left. He saw Alaria grab Damon and Greer and rush toward them. He looked back to Aradia and stalked toward her.

She backed up a step for every one he took in her direction. She opened her mouth to speak but closed it with a snap when he shook his head. She opened it again and managed to force words to come out.

"You're angry with me."

"Not a fucking word." He smiled grimly when her back slammed into the wall and took another step forward, crushing her curves against his body. "I'm liable to bite you myself if you so much as say a word." He lowered his head to her neck and inhaled the scent of fear, blood, and, deep down, arousal from the close proximity of his body to hers. "I'm not angry with you. I was scared, and that's not an emotion I like, and it's not one I'm used to handling." He took in another gulp of her scent, reassuring himself that she was okay. "For future reference, the next time you come out looking like dessert, expect to get eaten."

He pressed hard against her, his desire clearly evident against the soft flesh of her belly. Her scent was intoxicating, drawing him in to her, drowning him in sensation. Helpless, he turned her head with one hand and fit his mouth over hers.

More prepared than the first time he'd kissed her, Aradia's mouth opened under his, timidly responding to the kiss, her hands sliding up his chest to hold onto his shoulders for balance. He streaked a hand down her side, drawing one leg up so that he could pin her more fully against the wall. When her tongue shyly brushed against his as he plundered her, he was shocked back to reality, releasing her abruptly and stepping back.

The vision enveloped them both almost instantly. Aradia saw herself writhing beneath him, her thighs wrapped tightly around his hips. She felt him pressed against her skin. His eyes bored into hers, passionate and intense. Around them, flames leaped and blood ran down the walls.

Light from the flames danced over his features and the heat of the fire scorched her naked body. The ceiling bled, and blood dripped onto her forehead and face, stinging her eyes and slipping between her lips.

As quickly as it began, it was over. Aradia sucked in a breath and clutched Gage's arm, overwhelmed with emotions. Desire flooded her from the kiss they had shared and fear knotted deep in her belly as a reaction to the vision. Gage looked at her, his eyes uncertain. She cleared her throat and spoke softly.

"That was different than the last vision we shared."

Gage laughed nervously and stepped back. "The last one was fucking sexy. This one was meant to scare us. I intend to find out why." He looked over her shoulder at Alaria, Damon, and Greer, who were watching the exchange slack-jawed. He bent to whisper in Aradia's ear. "I'd advise you not to dress like this again until you're more prepared for what it could sometimes make men think." He stroked one hand down her cheek. "You're in a different world now and you have to make sure you know what you're doing."

Trembling, Aradia nodded. "I thought this was appropriate. Alaria picked it, and most women look similar."

"Most women aren't so completely bewitching, Priestess." He cast a glance to Alaria. "Get her back upstairs. This little excursion is over."

Chapter Five

ALARIA SLIPPED down the stairs once everyone else was long in bed. She tiptoed across the living room and into the kitchen. Perusing Gage's very extensive wine selection, she selected a bottle randomly. She rifled through three drawers before finding a corkscrew and deftly popped the cork from the neck of the bottle.

Plucking a wine glass from a shelf, she poured the deep ruby-colored liquid into it. She opened the fridge to retrieve a slice of the chocolate cake Greer had ordered from the casino's kitchen the day before and snagged a fork from the dish rack. The first bite was almost to her mouth when she heard Gage's door open and close. Eating the bite quickly, she washed it down with a gulp of wine and rose to set out a mug for his blood. She was pouring the thick substance when he slid onto a stool next to her.

"Hell of a night." Alaria punched buttons on the microwave and set the blood warming. Gage frowned.

"You have no fucking idea."

She sat back down, looking at him appraisingly. "Is something going on with you and Aradia?"

"No." He pulled the mug from the microwave and sipped thoughtfully. "Someone—or thing—is trying to make sure something happens between her and I. It's not us. It started the night she got here. Every time we're close we see visions of the two of us in bed together. The first time was fucking hot. The second, well, it wasn't exactly a turn-on."

"What did you see?"

"Bleeding walls and blood raining down on us, and we just kept going at it. The whole room was on fire around us."

Alaria laughed wryly and took another gulp of her wine before speaking. "That'll kill the mood. What do you think it all means?"

"No clue, but I'm damn sure going to find out. I'm leaving to head to South America. I know a coven down there that has stayed out of the fight—at least up to this point. They've got some pretty good future seekers. I'm hoping that one of them might be able to tell me what the hell is going on."

"You could always ask Gabe."

"Well, that would require that he show his face, which he hasn't done often lately. He would also need to tell me the truth, which is another rarity, and he would need to tell me the whole story, which we both know he isn't going to do. He lives in a realm of half-truths and omissions. I'm not dealing with it. This is obviously going to be my task, and I'm not about to let myself be dictated to by an Angel."

"He means well. You know that." Alaria gulped the last half glass of wine and stared at the island. Gage reached out and covered her hand with his own.

"Alaria, Gabe is a good man. He takes his job very seriously, and he's doing what he thinks is the right thing. That doesn't make it the most convenient thing for us, but I have never doubted that he's doing it for the right reasons. There is nothing more important to him than pleasing God."

Alaria laughed bitterly. "That's exactly the fucking problem. I want to be more important than God. I want to be the one that he chooses."

"Then you need to tell him that. If you never ask, you'll never know, and the most important thing is knowing." He finished the mug of blood and stood. He leaned over the island and pressed a kiss to her hair. "You'll be fine either way. It's better to know than to wonder." He pulled on his suit jacket and hefted his duffle. "If you need me, you know the number."

She offered a small smile. "Be careful, Gage."

"Always am." Gage paused at the door. "I think it's best if you get them back to Scotland and to Brax. You're all safer there, and it would make me feel better to know you're all safe."

"I'll take care of it." She took a deep breath. "Is this about finding answers or running away from a pretty redhead?"

Gage grinned. "A bit of both, my dear. As long as I find some answers while I'm running, it's all worth it."

Alaria poured another glass. "Well, don't die."

He shut the door behind him, his words drifting back to her. "I've made it fourteen centuries. That isn't going to stop now."

Aradia blinked rapidly in the bright sunlight. Her mouth dropped open at the sight of the sleek silver jet on the runway. She grabbed Damon's hand tightly with both of hers and pulled him to a stop. "Is this safe? This is going to fly through the air? Like a bird?"

Damon squeezed her fingers. "We've been using these for a century or so. By the time I was born, there were only a few left and they were only used during battle. You're more likely to drop dead of a heart attack than you are to be in a plane crash."

Aradia wrinkled her nose. "If I were to suffer a heart attack, Greer would heal me. To my knowledge, the likelihood of surviving were this metal tube to strike the ground is very low and I would likely be incinerated before Greer could assist."

Greer walked up behind Aradia and rubbed her shoulders briskly. "That's a very good point, but we're not going to crash. I've been on Gage's jet a few times and there hasn't ever been a problem. I don't imagine that it would crash today. Besides, if anything goes wrong, Alaria will yell for Gabriel and he'll come whisk us all away."

Alaria sneered and brushed past them to ascend the stairs to the jet. "At this point, I don't think he'd answer me. We'd have better luck with Michael." She offered Aradia a tight smile. "We won't crash. This thing is like a palace on wings."

Aradia's eyes widened as she passed Alaria and entered the cabin of the jet. She took in the plush cream leather and the white carpet. There was a fully stocked bar against one wall, and a full-sized refrigerator and stove in the kitchen area. Two couches and four chairs made up the living area; a large television was tucked into an alcove, and she spotted a bed through a set of doors.

"This is a home. You could live here."

Alaria settled into one of the chairs. "On the other side of the kitchen is Gage's office and his bed. Beyond that is the cockpit, which is where the pilot is. That's the guy that flies the plane."

Damon deftly twisted the cork out of a bottle of wine and poured glasses, handing one to each of the three women. "Under different circumstance, I'd say this could be a guy's biggest dream come true. Alone with three gorgeous women." He dropped onto the couch next to Greer and lifted her hand to his lips. "Too bad the feisty blonde would kill me before I'd have any fun."

Alaria snorted. "That implies Aradia or I would have you." She winked at the witch. "Let's be honest. Greer's the only one that'll put up with you."

Greer lifted her glass and tipped it at Alaria. "Preach on, sister." She grinned at Damon. "Can't live with him, can't kill him."

Aradia jumped when the door to the plane slammed shut and dug her fingers into the armrest of the chair. "What's happening?"

Damon leaned forward and laid his hand on her knee. "The door has to close to get the pressure right inside. The captain is going to start the engines in a few minutes, and after they check all of the equipment, they'll take us out onto the runway. From there, the plane will build up speed until it's going fast enough to take off. At that point, we'll be in the air, and we'll stay there until we touch down in Glasgow."

Aradia gripped his hand tightly. "I imagine the fear will abate once I've done this. The first time is the hardest—is that true?"

Greer nodded. "Yup. First time is always the worst. You'll be fine. We all will be."

She giggled when Aradia jumped as the engines shuddered to life. The plane jerked and began to move. Aradia gripped Damon's hand so tightly that her knuckles turned white. The engines whined as the plane propelled down the runway. When it jumped and rocked as it took off, she squealed and jumped. After several moments, she eased her grip and relaxed back into the chair.

Damon patted her knee and leaned back, slinging his arm around Greer's shoulders. "How are you feeling about all of this? I know when we first got here we had a lot of adjusting to do. I think we're still getting used to some things."

Aradia lifted her shoulders in a shrug. "I'm concerned about the mission. I know that we have a hard fight ahead of us. Javal and Garrick are very powerful and the other Devils that are involved also have much power. We're six against an army. The creatures will come, and they will not stop until we're all dead. I'm not worried about adjusting. I'll be fine with the time period. I've been training for this for most of my life. I just want to concentrate on making sure that all six of us come out the other side of this alive and in one piece."

Damon crossed one leg over the other. "I understand how you feel. Believe me, I think we're all feeling it right now. What we have to do isn't going to be easy and it isn't going to be quick, but I still think that you need to give yourself time to adjust. You have to be able to understand this world before you can fight in it."

The flight to Glasgow was long and tiring. Alaria claimed Gage's bed and crashed before anyone else. After several halfhearted games of dominos, Greer and Damon retreated to the guest bed, leaving Aradia to toss and turn on the couch.

By the time the plane landed, she had black smudges under her eyes, and her hair, normally curly, was frizzy and wild. Her face was drawn and pale, and she clutched her bag tight to her lap as the sleek jet barreled down the runway and into the small airport. A sleek black car was there to meet them. Their bags were unloaded with a minimum of fuss and all four were ushered into the back.

The drive took an hour. Aradia spent most of it with her head on Damon's shoulder, finally sleeping. When the car jerked to a stop, she opened her eyes, blinking rapidly and looking out the window to take in the old estate and sprawling grounds. She whistled softly.

"Gage must be a very wealthy man."

Alaria slid out of the car. "That damn vampire is richer than some countries. Getting that way was his sole goal for several centuries." She slung her duffel bag over her shoulder and headed for the house. She tapped the security code into the door and strode inside. "Brax! We're home!"

When there was no answer, she wound her way into the kitchen and found dishes in the sink, coffee in the pot that had long ago gone cold and a piece of paper on the island. Swearing under her breath, she snatched it up and read the sparse note.

Guys,
Went to Philly. I needed to see her. Back as soon as I can. Don't worry.
Brax

Alaria crumpled the note in her fist and tugged at her hair angrily. Pulling out her phone, she dialed Braxton's number and scowled when it went straight to voicemail. When six more tries yielded the same results, she whirled and went back outside, brushing past Aradia as she headed to where the driver was preparing to leave. She stepped in front of the car.

"Hold it. I need you to call and get that jet ready to take off again."

The driver nodded. "Yes, ma'am. Mr. Windsor gave instructions that the plane is at your disposal. Where shall I tell the pilot that you're going?"

"Philadelphia. I'll just take a cab on that end. Get it ready as soon as is possible. Wait for me here. I'll be ready to go in half an hour."

"Yes, ma'am." With a sharp nod, the driver slid back into the car and picked up his cell phone to make the necessary calls.

Damon rubbed his hand over the stubble on his jaw. "What's going on?"

"Braxton took off. He's in Philadelphia. I'm going to go get him."

He looked at her skeptically. "Braxton can take care of himself. Why did he go to Philadelphia?"

Alaria pressed the heel of her hand to her eyes in an effort to stave off the headache. "He went to see Griffin. I have no clue how long he's been gone and no way to get ahold of him."

Greer picked up one of the bags. "Did you try his cell phone?"

Damon fished his out of his pocket and dialed. He pushed the button for speaker, and they all listened to it ring several times before it went to voicemail. Alaria reached out and ended the call before he could leave a message.

"He isn't going to answer. I knew better than to leave him alone this close to the anniversary of Griffin's death. I knew better, and I did it anyway. He could have drunk himself into a coma or he could be dead."

Damon chuckled. "We'd know if he was dead. You know that. He's probably just drinking too much scotch and banging too many women."

Greer glared at him. "Nice to know that's how you'll mourn me if I ever die."

He planted a kiss on her forehead. "Baby, I would drink myself to death if anything ever happened to you and would swear off women for the rest of my incredibly shortened life. Don't ever doubt that."

She shook her head wryly. "Thanks." She turned to Alaria. "If you feel like you need to go, then go. We'll hold it down here. I agree that it was pretty damn stupid of Braxton to run off without telling anyone before going. We don't know how long he's been gone or when he's coming back, and neither of those are good things. Just don't go off the grid, too. Call to let us know when you're there, and check in every day or two until you find him and drag him home."

Alaria nodded. "There won't be any finding him. I know exactly where he's going to be." She shrugged. "Well, the list is narrowed to about three possibilities."

Chapter Six

January 20, 2031 - Philadelphia

Braxton zipped his coat and trudged through the snow. His sunglasses reduced the glare of the sun off of the powdery fluff that came nearly halfway up his calves. Some of the headstones were completely covered, while others poked out of the white, starkly grey against the pristine snow.

He wound his way through the stones, his fingers chilling in his gloves and small shivers running through him. His leather jacket was not thick enough to handle January in Philadelphia. He stooped down when he reached Griffin's headstone and brushed the snow from it. He ran his fingers over the inscription and lowered his head to rest against the cold stone.

"I miss you, baby."

"I miss you, too."

Braxton toppled trying to whirl around, scooting back until his back collided with the headstone. Ten feet in front of him stood Griffin. Her blonde hair was loose around her shoulders. She wore a blue dress and her feet and shoulders were bare. He gaped at her, his mind and heart both racing.

"How? You're dead."

Griffin smiled softly. "Dead is just another state of being. I didn't stop existing. I just...changed locations."

Braxton ran his hands over his face. "How is this possible?"

"You're in pain. I hate seeing you in pain." She took a step forward, then stopped. "You haven't come to see me for a long time."

"It's been a few months. I'm sorry." He studied her intently. "You know when I come here?"

Griffin crouched next to him and reached out to wrap her hands around his. "I can watch sometimes. It's hard for me to be here all the time, but sometimes I get to see you."

Something wasn't right. Braxton struggled to put his finger on it. "I thought that once you died you didn't know people anymore?"

Griffin ran her fingers over his face. "The rules are different for the Chosen. I've seen how unhappy you are, Brax." She breathed on his face and he was struck by how cold it was.

"I miss you."

Griffin smiled. She reached out with both hands and wrapped them around his throat. "Then I think it's time you joined me."

Griffin changed as the demon dropped the visage and transformed into a man. He stood, lifting Braxton, his hands closing off the Warrior's windpipe. Braxton lashed out, kicking and striking with his fists, but the demon had the advantage at such close quarters. Black spots swarmed his vision and he struggled to suck air into his lungs.

"I never imagined it would be so pathetically easy to kill one of you. Who knew all I would need to do is take the form of a dead woman?"

Braxton's eyes moved quickly from side to side. He heard tires crunching on the snow and caught sight of a taxi. The demon holding him glanced to the side and quickly slammed Braxton into the ground to stay out of view of the passenger.

"Don't want anyone interrupting this. I can't tell you how good it feels to choke the life out of you with my hands. In thirty seconds, you'll be dead and your damned circle will be broken. Lucifer will shake off his binds and Hell will spill out onto Earth unchecked. We'll kill all the Angels and overthrow Heaven the way it should have been done the first time."

"Don't count on it." Alaria's voice was low and harsh as she strode forward. Her hands were steady on the gun she held and she planted her feet five feet from the two men. She leveled the weapon and squeezed the trigger before the demon could let Braxton go and dodge the bullet. The projectile slammed into his skull and burst through the back of his head before ricocheting off the granite of the headstone.

Braxton gasped when the demon's hands went limp and the body fell on top of him. Black and red fog poured from the mouth and disappeared as the demon left the body. Alaria grabbed the body by the coat and heaved him off of Braxton, standing over him with her hand extended.

"Pretty damn good thing I came hunting your sorry ass."

Braxton gaped up at her for a long moment. "How did you know I was here?"

She yanked him to his feet, but didn't drop his hand. "That's what you have to say? I just saved your ass, Winslow. Seems to me that you owe me a hell of a thank you."

Before he could talk himself out of it, Braxton pulled her close and hugged her tightly, burying his face in her hair and wrapping his arms around her waist. Her arms came around him so that her hands rested on his shoulder blades and she leaned into the embrace. A throat clearing behind them made them spring apart.

Gabriel smiled bitterly. "Far be it for me to interrupt such a—tender—embrace, but I have news."

Alaria wiped her palms on her jeans and smiled brightly. "Long time no see, Gabe." She stuffed her hands in her pockets and took a step to the side, putting distance between herself and Braxton. "What's going on?"

"Hell is getting worried. Now that the gate is blocked, no demons can get out and none can get in. Those being killed are forced to find new bodies instead of being returned to Hell. The good part of that is that there are some Devils trapped in Hell, which lessens your danger. Further good news is that the third task is carving the wings from the original Fallen Archangels. Lilith, Beelzebub, Azazel, Lucifer, Abalam, Abaddon, and Alaria. The four trapped outside of Hell are nervous to be involved. You've succeeded in blocking Hell from them. They would rather let you succeed in this task than risk you succeeding at the third. Their focus is now on finding a way back to Hell and a way to let Lucifer out. Their energies are not being spent on defeating you in this task. Your adversaries are Garrick and Javal."

"The three musketeers have gone AWOL?" Alaria lifted her eyebrows. "I don't know whether to do cartwheels or cry."

Gabriel blinked. "I do not know what that means."

Braxton rubbed his throat. "It means they're missing and she's not sure if we should be glad of that or not."

Gabriel refused to look at Braxton, instead focusing on Alaria. "I suggest that you use the reprieve from their involvement to focus on the task at hand. There is no need to look for danger where it does not have to be. It was necessary to complete the first task before the second and now it is necessary to complete the second before the third. Concentrate on the second and on closing that Gate by killing Garrick."

Alaria cleared her throat. "Aradia said something about expecting that we would need to go to Atlantis?"

"I do not yet know. That is not something that is required by my Father. However, it has come to my attention that Garrick and Javal are looking for a way to access the channels of time in order to end this before it begins. They intend to return to Atlantis and kill Aradia's mother before Aradia is born. If they manage to go there, I would take the rest of you back as well. This will be a battle unlike the one you last fought. It has the potential to affect all times and all realities. Lucifer is concerned only about the future. Garrick does not share that. He believes that the key is to stop it before it starts. He is looking for a way to bend time."

Gabriel shoved his hands in his own pockets, mirroring Alaria's stance and looking reluctant.

"You both know I don't like to reveal more than is necessary, but this I will tell you. Graciela, Aradia's mother, developed a portal. Along with being a very powerful witch, Graciela also controlled the Dream plane. No one was as strong there as she, not even Angels and Devils. She could take audience there with me, with other Angels, and some rumor that she even once spoke to God himself. She knew from one of these conversations, which was not with me, that there would come a time when her city would be lost. She also knew that it was imperative that her daughter, who had yet to be conceived, survive. She spent fifteen of your years weaving the magic that made the portal, which allowed her to enter the stream of time. When the city was attacked and it became clear that it would fall, she went through the portal and destroyed Atlantis. I believe that it was Garrick and Javal who sieged against the city and that they will find a way to go back and try to kill Aradia while she is still in the womb."

Alaria expelled a breath. "It must really make you hurt to tell us so much without us begging and making threats."

Gabriel's lips quirked in a ghost of a smile. "You have no idea. The point of this diatribe is that even though your foes are not Devils at this time, they are not to be underestimated. If I am right, it will not be one fight that you will have to triumph in. It will be a war."

Braxton planted his hands on his hips and mulled the information over. "We'll get ready. That's all we can do." He took a deep breath. "Who was the demon?"

Alaria looked at him darkly. "That was Javal. He's known for being able to take on other visages, even when he's possessing a body. He was a very powerful warlock before he died, and he retained some of those abilities once he was brought back after Abalam was done with him. He keeps increasing his power by eating witches."

"There are only so many witches out there to eat."

Gabriel brushed his hands together before smoothing one down the sleeve of his jacket. "He doesn't literally eat then. He devours a portion of their power. They are left to refuel, and then he does it again. Several witches, if he is careful, have the potential to be almost limitless sources of power for him." He shifted from foot to foot. "I will inform you if there is anything else that you need to know. Good luck."

Braxton laughed wryly. "He does love his entrances and exits." He hunched his shoulders against the biting wind. "Since I didn't get to ask before Gabe popped in, I'm guessing you're here to bring me back to Scotland, right?"

Alaria nodded. "Yeah, we need to get back. Aradia is here, which you know, but what you don't know is that Gage has taken off for parts unknown because he keeps having visions of himself in bed with the virgin witch."

"Gage needs to get laid, anyway. What's the big deal?"

She shrugged and headed for Braxton's car. "He's convinced there's something nefarious going on, and I'm inclined to agree. He sees himself fucking her, and then the world goes to Hell. He told me he sees the walls bleeding, fire everywhere. All sorts of nastiness you don't want when you're in bed with someone. I figure if he's burying his head in the sand and hiding out under the guise of looking for answers, we probably need the rest of us to be together."

Braxton unlocked the car door and slid inside. "You could have called."

"I did call." She snapped her seatbelt into place and leaned back against the seat. "Several times, both before I left and after I landed. Your phone goes straight to voicemail. I left seven of them, by the way."

He picked up the phone from the cup-holder and pushed the button on the side repetitively before throwing it back down. "It's either dead or broken."

"How long has it been since you charged it?"

He scratched his head thoughtfully. "No clue."

"Probably dead then." She plugged the phone into the charger sticking out of the car lighter. "There." She looked at him out of the corner of her eye. "How long have you been here, Brax?"

"I left a few days after you did. I've been here a week or so. It took me most of that to work up my courage to come here. I haven't been to see her since we buried her."

"She's not in that box, Brax. She doesn't know if you come to visit or not. That's for you, not for her."

Braxton turned the key to start the engine and put the car in gear. "Cold comfort."

"Is still comfort." Alaria pulled out her own phone and typed out a text message on the digital keyboard. "You could have called. I'd have gone with you. Gage would have gone with you."

"I wanted to go alone." He stared stonily at the road in front of him. "It's getting harder and harder to hold on to her, and the more she slips away, the more I want to dig in my fingers and hold tighter."

Her eyes conveying her sympathy, Alaria reached out and laid her hand on his knee. "You're healing. That's a good thing."

He shook his head swiftly. "She deserves to have someone mourn her for the rest of their life. She deserves more than a year."

"Her death was not a death sentence for you both, Brax." Her voice was quiet, but her words were firm. She patted his knee and withdrew her hand. "You'll realize that eventually."

"Don't lecture me about clinging to the past. You're the one still sleeping with it."

Her eyes flashed with hurt and anger. "Don't you dare judge me. You have no idea what I'm going through or how hard this is for me. I'm handling it the best way I know how."

Braxton held up his hand, palm out. "I'm not trying to pick a fight."

He waved his hand when she started to speak. "I know it came off that way." He squeezed her fingers. "Damn but we're a pair."

The air in the car contracted as it filled with what hadn't been said. Alaria leaned her head against the window and closed her eyes. "We'll figure it out sooner or later."

Braxton squeezed her hand one last time and withdrew his own. "I know. What I don't know is if that'll make things better or worse."

"Me either."

He took a deep breath and expelled it slowly. "I still have a few things I need to do here. Legitimate things. I have to meet with the lawyer on my parents' estate and the lawyer on Samantha. It'll take me a few days to wrap it up. I got a hotel room at the Seneca downtown. I'd be happy to get you one, too, if you want to stay. If you don't, I promise to come along back to Scotland as soon as I've finished with the lawyers."

Alaria shrugged. "I might pop in on Father Dooley and tug a few lines on some supplies. We're going to need to stock up on the magical wares for this fight. It's much less Heaven and Hell and much more magic versus magic. We can get a lot more here than we can in Scotland. I can keep myself busy for a few days."

"Will they be okay there for a few days?"

Alaria laughed. "A Hunter, a Healer and the most powerful witch of all time. I think they can probably fend for themselves for a few days."

Braxton turned onto the highway. "I'm sure they'll call if something goes down." He cast her a glance. "Hotel or food?"

Alaria grinned. "When have you ever known me to turn down food? It's one of the best parts of being human."

He glanced at her, his eyes dark and intense. "Honey, if you think food is the best part of being human, Gabe has a hell of a lot to learn." He smiled rakishly. "Red meat?"

Alaria nodded, her throat constricted by a maelstrom of unnamed emotions. "Sounds good."

Chapter Seven

Alaria tossed in the bed, her sleep restless and her skin damp and clammy. She mumbled incoherently, and tears leaked from her eyes. She struggled to emerge from the dream, trying valiantly to pry her eyes open. The curtain of black magic filling the room was too much for her to fight. It permeated her senses and filled her head until she was helpless to resist it.

Her eyes sprang open, blank and unblinking. Her body was rigid and jerky when it moved, as if she was being controlled by a puppeteer. She threw back the blankets and sat up. Her legs swung around, and she stood. Like a marionette, she marched to the balcony doors and knocked them open with a crash.

She struggled against the influence of the magic, throwing herself against the wall of the possession over and over, being thrown back each time. Desperate, she rebelled against herself when she started to climb onto the railing, jerking backward and forcing her body to tumble off the railing. She succeeded in making herself fall into the table and chairs when the force made her climb up a second time, but the magic took over again and she was forced to balance on the top rung. She looked down at the twelve-story fall and for a brief moment, felt fear. The voice filled her head, grainy and rough.

Jump.

Tears streamed down her face, and she fought to keep from jumping. The magic propelled her body forward and she lurched, caught in a vicious battle between her own free will and the power of the magic controlling her.

"Alaria?" Braxton's voice was sleep-filled as he opened the doors onto the balcony they shared through the adjoining room. "What the hell are you doing up there?"

The voice that came from her was not her own. "Alaria's not home right now. I never dreamed it would be so easy to get her. She's still so enmeshed in the dream plane she used as a Devil that it was child's play to lure her there and take over."

Braxton measured the distance to Alaria with his eyes. He shifted his body into a stance conducive to leaping. "What's the endgame here?"

"Are you really that stupid? Your friend is going to jump, and her brains are going to splatter on the ground. This is going to be good." Alaria's face split into a hysterical smile, and her eyes swam with terror. She jerked and wobbled on the railing and with a single shriek, she toppled over.

Braxton lunged across the narrow balcony and grabbed her hands. The force of her weight pulling down on him nearly took him over the tipping point, but he locked his feet into the railing and strained to pull back. After five terror-filled seconds, he regained his balance and looked down.

Alaria, her hair whipping around her face from the wind and clad in nothing more than a button-down flannel and underwear, dangled helplessly. She struggled to pull her hands free, the magic's hold on her still strong. Braxton tightened his grip and yanked on her.

"Alaria, dammit, I know you're in there! Wake the fuck up!" He heaved backward and groaned at the dead weight. "If you don't, I'm going to get pulled over and we're both going to die." His voice softened. "Come on, baby, open your eyes. Look at me! You can beat this bastard. He's not stronger than you. Concentrate on my voice and find your way back. You can do this! Don't you let him win. Don't you dare let him win. I need you, Alaria."

Her whole body shuddered, and her eyes cleared. She turned and saw the distance between her feet and the ground and screamed. She struggled, trying to climb up him, fear driving her movements. Braxton groaned under the weight and swore.

"Dammit, Alaria, work with me. I've got you. I'm not letting go. I need you to bring your feet up and find the ledge."

His voice washed over her, calm and sure. She stopped struggling and looked up. "Okay. I can do that. Okay. Don't drop me. God, Brax, please don't drop me."

"I'll never drop you. Lift your feet and find the ledge."

She wrapped her hands around his wrists and lifted her feet. In order to find the edge of the balcony with her toes, she had to lift her knees into her chest. After ten heart-stopping seconds of flailing, her toes brushed against the concrete, and she slid her foot, inch by inch, onto it.

"Got it."

Braxton loosened his grip on one of her hands. "I want you to let go with your left hand and reach out to grab the railing."

As soon as she pulled her left hand free, he grabbed her right with his own. She thrust her arm through the metal spindles and gripped it tightly. She stood up slowly, and Braxton released her other hand to wrap his arms around her and lift her over, cradling her body against his and pulling her back onto the balcony. Without putting her down, he carried her into her hotel room and deposited her on the bed, leaving her long enough to close the balcony doors.

"What the hell happened?"

Alaria rubbed her hands over her face. "I don't know. I went to bed and got sucked into the dreamplane. Garrick wiggled inside me. I don't know how the hell he did it, but it was almost like I was being possessed. I could see what was going on and feel what he was making me do, but I couldn't stop him. I struggled, but he was too strong. When I fell off and you grabbed me, it was like I woke up and I was dangling there. I think my brain was convinced that I was dreaming."

"I think you had to be. Garrick is a warlock. He can't possess humans." He looked around the room. "Didn't you put protections up?"

Sheepish, she shook her head. "No. I never expected an assault by a warlock. Gabe said the Devils were lying low, and I figured we were safe from that shit." She chuckled. "Good thing you're a light sleeper."

Braxton perched next to her on the bed. "Do you need me to stay with you, or are you okay?"

She leaned her head on his shoulder for a moment. "I'll be fine. I'm gonna put out some herbs and try to go back to sleep."

He reached out and let one finger drift down the line of her jaw. "If you need anything, I'll be right next door." He dropped his hand to his lap. "Try not to dive off the balcony again. I'm getting too old for this shit."

"I don't want to hear about you being old." She drew her legs up so that she sat cross-legged. "Thank you, Braxton. Without you, I'd be a pile of goo on the pavement." She laid her hand on his cheek and leaned forward until their foreheads met. "What the hell are we going to do about this?"

Braxton closed his eyes. "Ignore it and hope it goes away?"

"It's a completely human thing. We're both hurting and gravitating toward one another. Stressful situation, lots of hormones. It's a recipe for disaster. We're both in love with other people."

"Neither of whom are here or seem to have a fucking clue what we're going through." He sighed and leaned back. "I should get back to my bed before we do something we'll both regret."

Alaria stood and padded to the balcony doors. "You should probably go out this way, since I don't think you stuck your key in those boxers before running to my rescue."

He looked down at his black boxers and grinned. "You'd be very right about that." He brushed by her and went out the door before turning to glance back at her. "Goodnight, Alaria."

Alaria stared up at him, her heart pounding in her chest and her blood rushing through her veins. She reached out and laid her hand against his chest. "Kiss me."

He leaned down and brushed his lips over her forehead. "That's a supremely bad idea."

Breathless, she moved toward the heat rolling off of his body. "I don't care."

Braxton stared down at her, his eyes dark and tumultuous. "Fuck it. Me either."

He twined his hand in her hair and wrapped the other arm around her waist, lashing her to him. She had time to suck in a breath before his mouth clamped on hers, hot and hungry. She arched into the kiss, rising onto her toes and wrapping her arms around his neck.

He crushed her body to his, twisting his hand in her hair to turn her head, giving him greater access to her mouth. His tongue was velvety soft against hers and his hands were large and hot as they swept down her back, sliding beneath the shirt she wore and over the smooth skin found there. He wrapped his hands in the shirt and lifted it up, skimming it over her body and tugging it over her head. He cast it aside carelessly and slipped his hands around to cup her breasts.

They filled his hands, full and round. Her skin was deeply tanned and her nipples were a dark, dusky pink. He drew his thumbs over them gently, his nails biting into her skin to mix the pleasure with a hint of pain. He kneaded her flesh in his hands and trailed his mouth down the side of her neck and across her chest. He backed her across the balcony and into her room, pressing her to walk until the bed pushed into the back of her knees. She sank onto it, sliding back and bracing herself on her elbows as he covered her body with his own. Their breath meshed as they gasped for air between deep, seeking kisses.

Their legs rubbed together, the hair on his scratching against her smooth skin. She shivered at the contact and slid her legs up to wrap around his, enjoying the friction. He tugged her arms over her head and held them in one of his hands, slipping down her body to take one of her nipples into his mouth. He sucked strongly, rubbing the nub against the roof of his mouth. He swirled his tongue around it and scraped his teeth over it. She groaned and her hips bucked against his. His erection pushed against her belly, and she tugged her hands, desperate to touch him.

"Brax, please. I want you."

Braxton stretched up to kiss her again, warmly and deeply. "I know. I want you, too." He pressed his lips to her forehead. "We let that get away from us." He kissed her eyelids. "Never think I didn't want to do this tonight. I do, but we can't." He tugged her into his arms. "It isn't right, not for either of us. Not tonight."

She buried her face in his chest, embarrassed and hurt. "I've never experienced rejection before. This is a new feeling."

Braxton hugged her tighter. "This isn't rejection." He drew his finger down her face. "Until we can do this and not be thinking about other people, we shouldn't do it." He kissed her gently, lingering far longer than he should have. "You're my friend, Alaria. I don't take this lightly, and I don't want us to make each other worse. When we do this, and you'll notice I said when, not if, it's going to be just the two of us in this bed. No ghosts and no Angels. Just you and me."

Alaria rubbed her nose on his chest. "I hate being smart about things.

I'd so much rather be stupid and go on with this."

"Believe me, we're in the same boat there." He nuzzled her neck. "It's for the best. There's so much we need to figure out between now and then. Most of that being the fact that our hearts belong to other people."

She sat up and crossed her arms to shield her breasts from view. "Maybe this'll give us a reason to figure things out then."

Braxton stood and ran his hand over her hair. "Only time will tell. There will come a time when I'm not going to stop us from doing that, and I hope you won't, either. We both need to prepare for the ramifications that will have on everyone. Griffin is dead. Gabriel might just kill me if he finds out what almost happened in here."

Alaria's eyes clouded with pain and confusion. "I'm sorry. I'm just so mixed up!"

"You don't have to apologize. Gabriel was your first love, and this is hitting us out of left field. We'll just have to feel our way through it." He slipped out the balcony doors. "Goodnight."

Smiling softly, Alaria reluctantly returned the sentiment. "Night."

He pulled the doors shut behind him and went in his own. Gabriel stood in the middle of his room, his face arranged into an expression of neutrality and his hands on his hips. Braxton sighed and closed the doors.

"What do you want?"

Gabriel glared. "I came to help when I sensed what Garrick was doing. Imagine my surprise when I saw the embrace between you and Alaria."

"I'm not having some testosterone-fueled fight with you, Gabe. What happened is between me and her, just like anything that goes on between the two of you is between you and her. I don't owe you an explanation."

"I'm not here for an explanation." Gabriel smiled coldly. "Hear this well, boy. You may be the one she turns to in her tumult, but it is me that she will spend the night with. You'll be sleeping here alone, and I'll be with Alaria."

Braxton ignored the pang in his chest at the truth in the words. "Borrowed time."

"Be that as it may, you won't even have a real chance until my time runs out. If it runs out." He patted Braxton's shoulder as he brushed past the other man to go to the doors. "She loves me. Her human body desires you the same way it desires food. There is no emotion behind it."

Braxton shook his head. "This is ridiculous. It's not a competition for her. She'll make her choice, and whatever that choice is, we're both going to have to live with it. I'm not pining and secretly in love with her." He smiled sharply. "Make no mistake, Gabe. You're her first love. You'll always have a place in her heart. I'm going to be the last. Not because we're in love, not because this is some romance or we're meant to be. Because she and I are the same—we understand one another, we both do whatever is necessary, regardless of the cost, and there's no judgment. I don't expect her to be an Angel." He crossed his arms and grinned. "As a matter of fact, I like a little Devil in my women. It makes them more fun." He turned to stalk into the bathroom. "You can see yourself out."

Chapter Eight

ALARIA TIPPED her face up into the spray of water. She closed her eyes and let the water run over her body. Images of Braxton filled her head. They meshed with memories of Gabriel, of the last night they had spent together. A pool of desire formed in her stomach, and she groaned. Confusion permeated the want, and she was torn between grief and desire.

She hadn't ever truly believed that humans could have feelings for more than one person.

She loved Gabriel. She was as sure of that as she could be. The thought of losing him twisted her stomach until the desire faded and she was left with grief. Almost as soon as the thought formed, it was followed by the feeling of Braxton pillowing her head on his chest and his arms encircling her. That memory blended with that of with Gabriel burying his face between her thighs after asking how to make her feel good.

Cursing herself and both of them, she leaned her head against the wall and struggled to escape from the grasp of her emotions. The rustling of the shower curtain caught her off guard, and she jumped, whirling to see who was there.

Gabriel stepped into the shower. His suit was neatly folded on the sink, his shoes sitting on top of it. He didn't speak, merely drew her into his arms and took her mouth with his own. He pressed her into the tiles and anchored her body against his. He placed his hands at her hips and kissed her deeply.

She tugged her mouth free and stared up at him. "What is this?"

"You told me once that you were mine for as long as I wanted and whenever I asked. I'm here for the night, and I'm asking. Let me have you."

Tears flooded her eyes, and she struggled to fight her way through the myriad of feelings coursing through her. "Gabe." Her voice was a whisper. She dropped her head to his shoulder and closed her eyes. "I'm so confused."

"I can see that you are distressed. Let me ease it, Alaria. We will come through this together." He ran his hands up her back. "We will get through this."

She struggled not to feel the bolts of desire that pierced her as he stroked her flesh. "Please, don't."

"Why? Because you don't want to? Or because you are afraid?"

It was getting harder to focus. Gabriel trailed his hands around her body and slipped them up to stroke her nipples. They beaded in a blatant betrayal, and her body arched toward him. He pressed his mouth to the curve of her neck and nipped gently with his teeth.

Her head became fuzzy, and it was harder to remember why she shouldn't let him have her. He trailed his mouth down her chest and over her breasts, lapping at her nipple before continuing down her stomach. He nuzzled her thighs and slipped his hands over her ass.

"Would you like me to pleasure you here again? You seemed to enjoy it the last time."

Alaria groaned and spread her feet. She was struck with a memory of Braxton pinning her to the wall and telling her that he didn't need to ask how to make a woman feel good. She fisted her hands in Gabriel's hair and fought away the memory. Gritting her teeth, she forced herself to focus on the man before her.

His tongue probed her, and he used his hands to part her thighs to give him greater access. She tried to concentrate on his ministrations. Her hips jumped, and she inhaled sharply when he stabbed his tongue against her. She pulled his hair and lifted one leg to drape it over his shoulder. Her head fell back, and she closed her eyes, trying to lose herself in the moment.

Alaria stared at the ceiling, her mind racing and plagued. Her body responded to Gabriel's touch. Groans tore from her throat, and she felt an orgasm start to build. Guilt churned deep inside her as she let herself float away on pleasure. When he stood and lifted her in his arms, carrying her swiftly toward the bed, she let him.

Not bothering to dry either of them, he laid her on the sheets gently and covered her body with his own. She caught herself noticing how much heavier Braxton had been when he had pressed her into the same mattress. When Gabriel asked permission, she wrapped her legs around his hips and brought him into her body. She lifted her arms to hug him closely and closed her eyes.

He thrust into her rhythmically, planting himself deeply each time and driving her closer to the edge with each stroke. Her eyes snapped open, and she stared at the ceiling. Gabriel lowered his head and buried his face in her throat. Tears welled in her eyes and trickled down the sides of her face. She clung to him desperately, trying to find some remnant of the passion and heat they had shared the night before the Choosing. She yearned for that spark but felt nothing.

She nearly choked on the tears and focused on the love she felt for him. That was easier to find. She felt desperation and longing and want. Her heart swelled with the feelings, and she moved her hips beneath his. She dug her nails into his back and flung herself into the need she felt. The need to be loved. The need to be worthy. The need to be his.

She knew he loved her in the best way that he could. Angels felt things differently, but all of the love he had, he would give to her. The only thing he loved more was God. Alaria knew the only all-encompassing love an Angel could feel was for their Creator.

She also knew she would never be worthy. She bit her lip and nearly lost her train of thought as his thrusts increased in speed. She hitched her legs up higher and tightened them around him. He drove into her over and over, propelling them both toward release. The desire between them would eventually be what tore them apart. They had both known that the moment they had kissed in front of the fire, and they both knew every time they came together was one step toward parting. She would never be worthy.

Gabriel would have to choose, and she knew he would choose God. She squeezed her eyes shut and arched her back. She knew from his breath that he was close to orgasm, and she groaned, hoping it was convincing. She scratched her nails over his back and rolled her hips into his, clamping down on her internal muscles and groaning in what she hoped was an Oscar-worthy performance. He collapsed on top of her, and she ran her hands up and down his back soothingly.

Tears made her throat feel thick, and she blinked them back. She bit her lip in a futile effort to block the words threatening to come out. They burst from her and tumbled over her tongue and through her teeth before she could force them back.

"I want more than this, Gabe."

Gabriel rolled off of her and looked at her incredulously. "That is not the response I had anticipated. What more do you want, precisely?"

She turned onto her side to look at him. "I can't keep doing this. I thought I could. I begged you to keep doing this, and I swore it would just be sex. It's not—not for me anyway. I can't control these human emotions, and every time you come here, I feel emptier than the last time. It's like doing this and knowing that there will never be anything else is killing me, a piece at a time." She reached out and laid her hand against his face, stroking her fingers over his jaw. "I love you. I've loved you for millions of years, without fail. Even when I hated you, I loved you. I hope you know that. I know you love me, too, in the best way that you can. I don't want to continue to do this. If you want me, you need to choose me."

Gabriel blinked rapidly. "What is it that you want me to do? Ask to Fall? Carve off my wings and become human? Or perhaps I should take up arms against Heaven as you did and force my Father to cast me to Hell as a Devil?" He stood and stalked into the bathroom to pull on his clothes. "I am doing the best I can with the situation we are in. You were well aware that there would be no consistent contact between us. I am giving you the time I can. There is a war going on, Alaria! Angels are dying every day. My brothers and sisters are fighting yours, trying to stop the loss of human life. Lucifer is struggling against his bonds, and Garrick is raising witches and warlocks to weave magic to free him. In the midst of all of this, you want me to abandon my family? For you?"

Alaria tried not to cry. She valiantly sucked back the tears and yanked the sheet up to cover her nakedness. "I want to be more important than I am. I want you to prove you love me and that you want to be with me. I deserve more than sex whenever you can pencil me in."

Gabriel's eyes flashed. "You deserve more? You betrayed our Father, you slaughtered your brethren, you spent millennia torturing the beings that we were created to protect! You had a miraculous change of heart at the moment Griffin was at her weakest, and you stole her chance at life beyond the Choosing so that you could become what she was! Now, after taking that from her and doing all of the things you have, you demand of me to follow you into humanity? Do you sincerely believe I am as weak as you?" He tied his tie with jerky motions and snapped the cuffs of his jacket into place. "Why in God's name would you, even for a moment, believe that I would ever want to be some pathetic human?"

Before Alaria could open her mouth to respond, Gabriel was gone. Her fingers had flown to her throat at some point, and she rubbed at it, trying to force the lump that had formed to go down. She choked back sobs and reached for her shirt, dragging it on over her head. She grabbed sweats from the bag left open on the floor and stumbled out onto the balcony and into Braxton's room.

The click of the slide pulling back on a gun was the first noise that she heard. She froze. "Brax, it's me." She wiped tears from her face and waited while he reached for the lamp. When he saw her, he lowered the gun and dropped it onto the nightstand.

"What's wrong?"

She held out her hands helplessly. She opened her mouth to speak, closed it, then opened it again when tears streamed down her face un-checked. "Gabe."

Braxton sat up and swung his legs around to place his feet on the floor. "What did he do?"

She wiped her hands over her face. "He came to me. I asked him to choose me. He yelled and said awful things." She took a deep, trembling breath. "I don't know what to do."

Without a word, Braxton held out his hand and reached for her. He pulled back the blankets and tugged her down, adjusting their bodies until he was lying on his back with her head tucked against his shoulder. He reached out and turned off the light with his free arm, immersing them both in darkness.

"You don't have to figure it out tonight." He ran his hand over her hair. "Eventually, you'll have to, but not tonight. Gabriel isn't exactly my favorite person, so I'm not going to waste your time or mine talking bad about him, but I don't think he's doing right by you, and I think you're going to have to make some tough decisions." He pressed a kiss to the side of her head. "What do you need from me?"

She shook her head and sniffed. "I just didn't want to be alone."

"You never have to be alone unless you want to be." He shifted onto his side, wrapping his arm around her. "Get some sleep, Alaria. Everything will be right where you left it in the morning."

She took another deep breath and stared up at the ceiling. "I don't understand why things have to be so complicated. I always thought being human would make things easier. Instead, it's harder. Everything is magnified. Somehow, in all the years I dreamed about being human, I only ever imagined the good things would be magnified, not everything."

"You have to take the good with the bad. If it didn't feel so bad, the good wouldn't feel like it does." He joined her staring at the ceiling, remaining silent for several minutes. "We're both going to have to make some hard decisions sooner or later."

Alaria sniffled. "I'm hoping it's later rather than sooner." She turned her head to study the line of his jaw. "Aren't you going to ask about what happened?"

He shifted his eyes to meet hers. "I figured you would tell me if you wanted me to know. Do you want me to ask you what happened?"

She blushed, turning dark red. "I know it's silly, but it seems easier for you to ask than for me to offer up the information."

"What happened?"

"I asked him to choose me. He came to me after you left and asked me to be with him. I didn't want to, but he kept doing things, and I wanted to feel something other than confused, so I let him. I thought I'd feel better. Instead, I felt worse, and I couldn't keep myself from asking him. I thought it would make it easier. If he would make the decision for me, I wouldn't be forced to do it. He yelled at me and threw everything I've done in my face. He accused me of stealing Griffin's life, of taking advantage of her at her weakest moment and stealing her only chance at life. He called me pathetic and weak and asked why I ever thought he had any desire to be like me. It was awful."

Braxton chuckled. "We're a pair, aren't we? Doing what we did earlier, and now we're laying here with you telling me about the guilty sex you just had with your Angel boyfriend and instead of being pissed off, I feel bad for both of you." He pressed a kiss to the side of her head. "You and Gabe are the epic love story, Alaria, in the same way that Griffin and I were. You and I are practical. We make sense. We're not pining for one another and overcoming fierce odds to ride off into the sunset together. We're trying to figure out if we cling to that epic love story we both have or if we do what makes sense. We'll either figure it out or we won't, but as long as we keep trying, we'll both be just fine." He settled deeper into the pillows. "Get some sleep. We've both got a long day ahead of us tomorrow."

Gabriel appeared in the garden where Michael preferred to be, looking confused and unsure as to why he had been summoned. He strode down the stone path, barely noticing the lush bushes and colorful flowers. He followed the walk to a circle of stone benches. Michael stood in the center of it, his wings folded against his back and a serious look on his face.

"Why have you called me here?"

"He knows."

Those two words shook everything Gabriel was. His chest constricted with panic, and his eyes widened in fear. He cleared his throat, hoping he could speak. "How?"

"Your dalliance with Alaria is not a well-kept secret, brother. He has known since the beginning."

"I asked you if He knew, and you assured me that He did not."

Michael lifted his hands helplessly and started walking down the path. "I assure you, brother, I told you what I believed to be true. It was never my intention to mislead. I have only recently been made aware of what He does know."

"What is He going to do to me? Am I being called into His chamber?" Gabriel crossed his arms and glared at his brother. "What do you know, Michael?"

"You're not going to be punished." Michael turned and looked at him sympathetically. "Far from it. This relationship is meant to be. What you are going to be asked to do is more than He has asked of any Angel."

"What are you talking about?"

Michael dropped onto a bench and folded his hands in his lap. "They will fail the third task. Lucifer is taking steps to free himself from Hell. These are steps we cannot stop. God has deemed it necessary. If it does not happen now, it will happen later when the framework to defeat Lucifer is not already in place. I was summoned this morning to hear what

Father needs from you."

"Why has He not brought me to ask me Himself?"

Michael smiled softly. "I do not presume to know His mind. I only know what I have been told."

Gabriel sat across from Michael, crossing one leg over the other and placing his hands on top of them. "What have you been told?"

"That Lucifer will shake free of his chains. The demons escaping after the Choosing weakened them. The loss of Jesslyn redoubled his efforts to escape. Even as the humans succeeded in putting up the retaining wall, his chains began to crumble. The balance is tenuous at best, and each day that passes loosens them further."

"He's going to let them fail?"

Michael looked pained. "No. He is allowing things to unfold as they must because this is the best chance we have to put Lucifer back. If this happens years, or even centuries from now, we may not have the ability to put him back. With this group of humans, there is the best chance that will ever exist of fixing the problem."

"These six don't stand a chance against Lucifer. You know that."

"It is not these six who will battle him. Lucifer will walk the Earth for many human years. He will reign terror and destruction upon them. There is no way to avoid the future from which you plucked Damon and Greer."

Gabriel began pacing the clearing, his movements jerky and stiff. "God is going to destroy the Earth?"

Michael shook his head and held his hands out, palms up. "No. He gave you fifty years to correct this problem. The humans will seal the gate shut. They will succeed in what He asked them to do. He will not betray His word. The Earth will continue. They will earn that. None of this is why you are here. What I need to talk to you about is how we will defeat Lucifer and put him back."

"God is allowing us that information?"

"Everything I am telling you is sanctioned by God. There is only one way to defeat Lucifer without God's direct involvement. He is not willing to do that. He has made clear since the Choosing that He does not have the strength to wade into this war. He is going to allow this to unfold as it is meant to. However, He has asked me to make sure that steps are taken to ensure the humans can do what is being asked of them. You, brother, are one of those steps."

Gabriel looked confused. "What is it that Father needs from me?"

"The only way to defeat Lucifer is through the birth of a child. A child who will be half-Angel and half-Devil. A girl child, born for the sole purpose of defeating Satan. She will be the only one strong enough to wage war against him."

Gabriel's stomach dropped, and he felt slightly sick. "What does that require from me?"

"Alaria maintains some of her Devil properties. She is not a human as the rest of them are. You already have a relationship with her that is sexual in nature. God needs for you to plant your seed within her womb. A child will form from the union, and Alaria will carry and birth a daughter that will be Earth's only hope for survival."

Panic rose in Gabriel's throat, and he struggled to breathe. "You want me to father a child? Angels do not possess such an ability!"

Michael reached out and laid his hand on top of Gabriel's. "There have been times throughout human history when certain Angels have impregnated human women. The result is the Nephilim. They are not generally spoken of because God has always viewed them as an abomination to Him. This child would be different. A Nephil ordained by God to end the suffering of his most precious creatures."

Gabriel blinked rapidly, trying to understand what Michael was saying. "I don't comprehend what I must do."

"You must have sexual intercourse with Alaria for the purpose of creating a child. You have been made fertile, or will be made fertile, should you agree to do this great service for our Father."

Gabriel laughed bitterly and threw his head back. "Do I have a choice? Is this being asked of me, or is it being demanded of me?"

Michael's voice was soft and gentle. "It is being asked. You may refuse the request, and no harm will befall you. If you do refuse, God will begin requesting of other Angels that they do this task. You know our brethren well enough to know that he would find someone to do it. Someone who may not be as...tender...toward Alaria as she might deserve."

"Does she get a choice in this? Am I supposed to ask her to allow me to insert my penis and impregnate her? What happens if she says no? Am I to hold her down and rape her as one human does another? Will God do unto Alaria what He did unto Mary?"

Michael nodded slowly. "I know that this is upsetting. You care for her. No one doubts or denies that, and no one begrudges you an opportunity to be upset and to have whatever emotions you need to have. To answer your questions, God will not implant a child into Alaria. He is not taking an active role. If no Angel will do what is needed, He will initiate the Apocalypse. Alaria is not to be told. She would not agree to carry the child, and once she has conceived, there will be nothing other than an act of God that can undo what is done. You are to use your relationship to seduce her. It will only take once. If another Angel were to be tasked with this responsibility, it is likely that there would have to be some force used, yes."

Gabriel closed his eyes and leaned his head back. "Who does it if I say no? You?"

"No, I would not do that to her."

"Yet you want me to?"

Michael sighed deeply. "I don't envy you this choice, brother. I wish I did not have to relay this. It makes me feel ill to even think about plotting against Alaria in this manner, but I do not think we have a choice. It comes down to one or the other. You can have Alaria for a time, or you can ensure the survival of the human race. Unfortunately, this is not a situation where you can make the sacrifice. You have to take a choice away from someone you care deeply about and force upon her a fate that she does not want."

"This is forcing her to carry and birth a child she will get no input in creating. She will have to raise a child who will be half-Angel and half-Devil. What abilities would it possess? Would it be human?"

"The child will be precisely what it needs to be in order to do what God has determined is necessary."

Gabriel hung his head and closed his eyes tightly. "God or Alaria. That's what the choice comes down to, isn't it?"

Michael smiled slightly. "That was always the choice you were going to have to make. You just have to make it sooner than you had hoped. Father would never let you have her indefinitely. You have always known there was no future with Alaria unless you were willing to give up all you are. We both know that no matter how much you might care for her, your loyalty belongs with our Father, and it is He who you will always serve. You just need to decide how much you are willing to hurt Alaria in order to please our Father."

Gabriel looked ill. "Am I being given time to think about it, or does

He need a decision immediately?"

Michael patted his knee gently. "Take some time, brother. You will make your choice when the time is right."

Chapter Nine

February 2, 2013 - Rio de Janeiro, Brazil

"You'll bed her before this is over."

Gage whirled and faced the woman standing in the clearing. She was wearing a long, purple gown, and her hair was swirling down her back in blonde curls. He narrowed his eyes and glared at her suspiciously.

"Who are you? Where are we?"

The woman smiled brightly. "I am Graciela, Queen of Atlantis. I believe you know my daughter, Aradia."

"How did you bring me here? You're dead."

"I'm a Dreamweaver. My essence remained in the dream plane after my body died. It is remarkably easy for me to hail those I seek. This night, I need to speak with you, Gage Windsor."

His eyes still betraying his suspicions, he cleared his throat and crossed his arms. "What do you want?"

Graciela smiled again and held out her hand, waiting until he allowed her to slip it into the crook of his elbow before she spoke. "To talk with you about what you must do. You think you know the legend, Gage, but you know very little. There are things that will come to pass that you will retain no control over, things that must happen. One of those things involves my daughter."

Concerned, he turned his head to look at the woman. "What about her?"

"I can sense your attraction for my daughter. You know she returns it, though she's never felt desire before and has no idea how to react."

Gage shook his head in denial. "It's not real attraction between us. It's some trick. Javal—"

"No." Her denial was quick and adamant, leaving no room for arguing. "It is not Javal. He lies quiet yet, preparing and planning. He grows stronger, stronger than even you can imagine, Gage. He has not yet made his move. He awaits you in Scotland. He anticipated you would take them to your home there because of the magic that still lies in your mother's bones. The protections of a powerful witch are hard to break, and even though he knows where you are, he cannot yet reach you. You're smart to take them there to prepare. It will make it easier for Aradia to access her abilities."

"Alaria tells me she's been doing well. She's more powerful than anyone they've ever seen. She doesn't need the spells. She just needs focus and energy. If she can find the strength, I don't know if there's anything she won't be able to do."

Smiling with pride, Graciela withdrew her hand from his to clap with glee. "There isn't. I've known her whole life that she is something special. Unfortunately, without realizing who she is as a woman, as well as who she is as a witch, she'll never rise to her full potential."

Gage glared at the witch. "What are you getting at, Graciela?"

"You desire her. She desires you. In order to win, you must give in to your human urges. You must make her yours. You must take her as you have taken no one else." She looked at him intently. "You must bond with her."

"No." He shook his head. "I haven't done that with anyone in over a thousand years on this Earth. I'm not going to do it now."

"You will grow together if you do."

"Look, I already feel things for your daughter, things that any mother would hate for anyone to feel about their child. She twists me up in knots, and I lose my mind. That's why I've stayed away from her for weeks."

"Ahh, yes, weeks of a constant parade of women. Did you think you could take the edge off, Gage?" Graciela looked at him with a sharp glint in her eyes, as if she knew the answer before she asked the question. "Aradia is more to you than any of those women. She is more than any you have ever had. Your fates bring you together, Gage."

Gage looked sheepish for an instant. "I was hoping that it was just a lack of sex. It had been a while."

"Well, you are wrong. I would wager everything I have that as soon as you lay eyes on Aradia, those feelings, and more, will come rushing back. You won't be able to resist her, and more importantly, you must not try. It is fate, Gage. You and Aradia are meant to be. That is why I sent her to the temples. I've been saving her for you."

The thought turned his stomach. "I'm a monster. You've saved your only daughter to literally offer her up to a monster?" He growled at her. "You're dead. You had no control over it."

She ignored the last part. "You're not a monster. Not anymore. You haven't been for a long time. That's why you were chosen for this. Besides, just because you're immortal does not mean you have to stay that way."

He turned his head to stare at her intently, a vice closing around his chest. "What are you talking about?"

"As a gift for fighting this war, a war that does not belong to you, you will be given the opportunity to earn life. You must slay the demon and walk through fire, and you must feel a love like no other Immortal has ever felt. In that moment, your heart will beat again."

Gage didn't even think about what she had said before answering. "I don't want it. I'm not like Alaria or Jesslyn. I'm happy with what I am, and I have no desire to be anything else."

"You would turn down a chance at humanity?"

"In a heartbeat." His teeth flashed at the joke. "I enjoy my existence. I enjoy not having an expiration date. I'm not interested."

Graciela twisted her hands together out of worry. "Gage, listen to me. This is going to be hard, what you have to do. And the feelings you have for Aradia are not going to go away. Your souls were created for one another. The feelings are just going to get stronger. You're not going to have a choice but to give into them. She's going to need you to guide her. She knows nothing about how she feels or why she suddenly wants something she's never wanted before."

"I am not having sex with your daughter."

"Yes, you will." Graciela smiled serenely. "You just haven't come to terms with it yet."

"Look, do I have feelings for her? Yes, I do, but I don't like it, and

I'm not giving into them because they're not my feelings! They're some sort of magical fate thing that you, or Gabriel, or someone else has cooked up to help you get your way! I am not giving in to something that doesn't really exist."

With the patience normally reserved for a small child, she spoke slowly and calmly. "You cannot know it doesn't really exist if you don't give yourself permission to experience it and find out for yourself. Gage, I know what happened to you when you were turned—"

Instantly enraged, Gage growled low in his throat. "I would suggest that you don't say another word about that or I'll tear your throat out."

"You haven't harmed a human in hundreds of years. Don't make promises you have no intention of keeping. It's not attractive." Graciela led him to the edge of a cliff, where they could look down onto the waves crashing against the rocks. "Javal is very strong. Aradia is very young and very inexperienced, though she is very strong as well. He's going to go for her first and hardest. She is the greatest threat to his plan. If he can kill her before she comes into her own, then there is no chance the other five can defeat him. He knows that."

"Then both of you are seriously underestimating the rest of the group."

"No. Man to man, you are a match for him. Braxton is a great leader and will lead a great army into battle against Javal's forces. Alaria is powerful, of that there is no doubt, but Aradia is the only one who has a chance against the magical forces he is trying to tame. Greer and Damon are a force to be reckoned with and share a partnership unlike any other. Even with all of that, Aradia is the key. A body can only hold so much magic, and Aradia has already stretched the limits of hers. Javal has found a warlock that will stretch his just as far, perhaps even further. I believe members of your group have had interactions with Garrick already. In order to succeed, Aradia will need to find a way to tap into her power as a woman. I promise you, as a mother, I am not trying to do anything that will harm my child. I am trying to save her. You, and only you, can help me do that."

"By sleeping with her?"

Frustrated, Graciela threw up her hands. "It's not about sex, Gage! Listen to me! It's about connection, about love, about her soul! She is still a girl though her body is twenty-seven. Her heart is tender and soft, and her knowledge is that of a child's when it comes to things between women and men. She is becoming comfortable with who she is as a witch. She still has no idea who she is as a woman. In order to be effective, she needs to find out how to mesh those two sides of herself. You can help her with that. All I'm asking you to do is follow your instincts. Yes, that will include bedding her. Of that, I have no doubt. If you think you can do it without bonding with her, then be my guest. All I know is that if you don't do something, it will get you both killed."

"Have you told her about this?"

"No. Her mind is harder for me to access. It is too much like mine. I will talk to her, and soon, but you are the first I have come to. Your current alcohol consumption is making it very easy to slip into your head for a chat while you sleep." Graciela quirked an eyebrow. "Trying to drown her out, hmm?"

"It's not going to happen, and if you go to her and get it into her head that she needs to sleep with me in order to be a better witch, I swear I will find a way to come there and tear your throat out." He snarled dangerously. "You'll quickly learn that I don't make empty threats. She has enough to deal with without you getting things even more complicated by getting romance mucked up in it."

"Greer and Damon are already lovers. Alaria and Gabriel are as well."

"All of them are consenting adults who have more experience in these things than Aradia does."

"They will produce a child. She'll find herself heavy with pregnancy long before you march into battle."

Gage blinked in surprise. "Which one?"

"Perhaps both. New life holds much magic, and you need all the help you can get." She smiled softly. "This is not meant to be the end of any of you. There will be life afterward."

Gage scoffed. "Somehow I don't think Alaria or Greer is going to be picking out baby clothes any time in the near future."

Graciela lifted one shoulder in a graceful shrug. "Believe what you will, but when she grows large with child, you will see who is right." She turned and placed her hands on his cheeks. "It's time for you to wake up now, Gage, and to return to them. They need you to help train them. They need your confidence, your experience. Aradia needs you in general. To guide her and to show her how to navigate what she's feeling. Wake up, and go to them."

Gage opened his eyes, finding himself in a bed with a naked woman curled against his side, her leg wrapped around his waist. Bottles of liquor littered the floor, and clothes were strewn about the room. Without making a sound, Gage slipped from the bed and began gathering his things. He pulled on his clothes silently and left with nothing more than the soft whisper as the door swung shut. It was time to go to Scotland. It was time to go back and face Aradia and prove her mother wrong.

Greer laid her phone down on the table and turned to face Aradia and Damon. "Okay, so that was Gage. He's on his way back from South America, and Alaria and Braxton will be back the day after tomorrow. They're finishing up all of Braxton's stuff and leaving in the morning. Gage has ordered some shipments of supplies to hold us over for a while. A lot of it will be delivered, but I have to go pick up his supply of blood and a few other things. Do either of you want to go with me?"

Damon looked up from where he was laying on the couch watching television. "Roads are supposed to be nasty, babe. We're gonna get a storm tonight. I don't think you should be going into Glasgow alone. We should all go."

Aradia shook her head. "You guys go. I could honestly use some time by myself." She closed her book and laid it on the island. "Not that you aren't both great, but I haven't had even a second to breathe since I got here."

Greer studied her closely. "Are you sure you'll be okay? If it gets bad out, we might be gone for the night, and there's a good chance that if the weather delays us, it'll delay Gage, too. You might have to spend the night alone."

Aradia patted the book. "I have a whole library of these to keep myself occupied and a huge bathtub upstairs. I'll lay on the couch, read, soak, and go to bed." She sipped a cup of tea and sighed contentedly as the warmth seeped through her. "No offense, but the two of you work best together. If anyone should be alone, it's me."

Greer nodded slowly. "If something happens, you have our numbers. We'll be easy to get ahold of, and if you need us, we'll walk home if we have to. Hopefully, we'll be home later tonight, and Gage will get in before morning."

Aradia ignored the licks of excitement that rose in her at the prospect of seeing Gage again. She tapped her fingers on the island and stared at Greer as the other woman took stock of what was in the cabinets and made a list of things to buy at the grocery store. Damon had already ascended the stairs to pack an overnight bag in case the weather actually rolled in.

When the television newscaster turned the topic to a slaughter in France, Aradia's brow creased as she turned to Greer. "Is this how it started the first time?" Her voice was soft and unsure. "The reports on the screen about the strange attacks and sightings are getting more frequent, and I heard this morning that some societies are beginning to collapse."

Greer looked sad. "It's getting bad. I wasn't alive when it started, so I don't know exactly how bad it was. The stories I heard always said that within a decade after the Gate opened most countries were gone. This is just the very beginning, but we've already stopped the purge, so I don't think it will get as bad as it was in my time. There's a lot that's going to be different this time around."

"Do you miss your home?"

Greer shook her head. "No. There was nothing of my home left. It was destroyed in an attack the night before Gabe brought us here. We didn't have anything but one another. Regardless of the outcome of the next two trials, my time will be better off than they were had I not come back." She scribbled on the piece of paper in her hand. "What about you? Do you miss Greece?"

Aradia looked sad for a moment. "I miss it, but I always knew that it was little more than a place holder for me. I was raised to know that I was going to leave for a different time and place. I grieve for my parents, but other than that, it is nothing that I did not expect." Her eyes darkened. "I do wish that there had been a way for them to survive this. They died saving my life, and for that I will always be grateful."

Greer patted her hand reassuringly. "I know they had to know what was going on. They knew the risk when they agreed to raise you, and they made a decision to go with you that morning. You can't blame yourself for what happened. As much as it sucks, your survival is more important than theirs was."

Aradia nodded. "I know that. I think that's what makes it hurt the most. I had to leave them there and let them die because what I have to do is more important than their lives were. It hurts to think I am capable of making those decisions. I never thought I was, but put in the situation, I sacrificed them."

Damon came down the stairs with a small duffel bag. "We all have to make sacrifices. Greer and I ran from our city when it was overrun because we knew the people in it were going to die anyway and we could escape. I refuse to feel guilty about not sacrificing our lives to try to save theirs. Odds are, if you would have stayed, you'd be dead too and we wouldn't have a chance at succeeding." He ruffled her hair and slung his arm around her shoulders. "If you're going to sit and mope all day, go get dressed because you're coming with us. You have nothing to be sad over, and I'm not going to let you stay here and wallow in misery alone."

Aradia smiled and leaned her head on his shoulder briefly. "I'll be fine. Really, I just intend to read and nap and take a long bath. I'll not mope or wallow. I promise."

Greer grinned and shifted her eyes to Damon. "Did you pack my stuff, too?"

"Yup. We're good to go. If you're ready, I'll load this in the car and pull it around to the front. Do you need us to bring you anything back, Aradia?"

She shook her head. "I don't think so. I have everything I could possibly need." She patted Greer's back when the other woman hugged her and waved them toward the door. "The longer you stand here worrying over me, the more likely it is that you'll be forced to spend the night. Go on. I'll be fine. You two deserve to have a little bit of fun before the others arrive and the real work starts."

Aradia stood at the window and watched Damon pull the car out of the garage. Greer slid into it gracefully, and after one enthusiastic kiss, Damon aimed it down the long driveway and they were gone.

A smile on her face, Aradia plucked her book from the island and picked up her cup of tea before settling on the couch, the tea on the floor next to her and her head pillowed on the arm. The television was a low hum in the background, and Aradia quickly lost herself in the book she was reading. Her eyes grew heavy, drooped, and then closed, the book sliding down to her chest and her arm hanging over the edge of the couch.

Chapter Ten

GAGE WAS in disbelief as he disembarked the plane and stepped out into the brisk February air. For the first time in recent memory, his plane had gotten in early. The sun was still shining as he climbed into his car, even though he knew it would set within the hour. He took a moment to enjoy the cold air before closing the door and turning on the car. Sliding the transmission into gear, he pulled out onto the road and began the forty minute drive from the small, private airport to his estate. He'd tried to call Greer to let her know that he'd arrived ahead of schedule, but he'd gotten her voicemail and hadn't bothered to leave a message.

As he drove, he couldn't shake the feeling that something was wrong. Not with the other three, but something felt off. There was a presence he couldn't quite put his finger on, yet one that was so tangible it had him looking in the rearview mirror every few seconds to make sure he hadn't missed anything important. It was the time spent looking in the rearview mirror that made him miss the man in the road until it was too late to hit the brakes before he slammed into the stranger.

The car's frame bent, the hood crunched upward, and he skidded to a stop, turning almost two full circles before he managed to get the brakes to work and stop the car. The slash on his forehead from striking the steering wheel was already healing as blood dripped into his eyes.

He leaped from the seat as soon as the car stopped, wiping away the blood and looking around for the man he'd hit, knowing beyond a doubt that he was dead. The impact had been too great for any human to have survived.

"Then it's a good thing I'm not human."

Gage turned toward the voice and faced the man standing behind him. He took in the pitch black hair, the matching eyes, the long fingers, and the angelic features. "Javal. Different body than when I saw you last."

The demon smiled brightly. "Human bodies wear out so quickly. I found this one in medieval England. He was a great warrior before I killed him. Do you like it?"

"It suits you." Gage clenched his hands, concentrating on whipping up the bit of magic he had in a feeble effort to defend himself against the much more powerful demon. "What do you want?"

Javal tapped his finger against his lips. "Well, let's see. What do I want?" He clenched his fists. "I know. I want to find that fucking witch and tear her limb from limb. That work for you?"

"Sorry. You aren't going to get to her. You can't get in."

"I know. Your whore of a mother was a damn decent witch. I've been trying to get past those protections for years."

"You know I'm not taking you in. I'm not that stupid."

"Oh, I know. See, I figured if I can't get in to kill her, I'd just kill you and keep her from getting any stronger. That would break the circle, and with the circle broken, I win."

"We both know Aradia is strong enough to kill you."

"In order for her to stand a chance, she has to embrace her abilities. She hasn't done that. With you dead, my sources say she won't."

"Well, then, let's get this show on the road."

Before Gage could blink, the first wave of magic struck him, sending him flying. He caught himself and sprang to his feet, dodging the next wave and sending out one of his own. He followed through by flying across the road and colliding with Javal. His body slammed into the demon, and they both crashed into the ground in a tangle of arms and legs, both grappling for the upper hand.

Gage knew he didn't have a chance against the demon's magic. However, physically, he did. They fought viciously against one another, punching and kicking, the sound of breaking bone sharp in the air.

Gage managed to climb to his feet, grabbing Javal by the lapels and lifting him effortlessly, holding him several inches off the ground.

"You may be a demon. But I am the oldest vampire alive. You have no idea what I can do."

"Your magic is sadly lacking, boy."

"Demons aren't warlocks. We both know without feeding on witches, you wouldn't have any at all. If I did that, I'd be just as strong." Gage leaned forward and pressed his face deep into Javal's neck. "I should drink your blood and see if that makes me any stronger. I've beaten you this time, Javal."

Javal surged up, conjuring and driving a stake into Gage's chest in one motion, just missing his heart. "Be that as it may, you're the one with wood in your chest. Make one move and you're dust."

Gage didn't even hear him. He was already concentrating on sinking into his own mind, on finding the control over his body and using the magic he possessed to save himself. He focused on every atom making up his body, dissolving them one by one, until he disappeared with a loud crack, hurtling himself through space, aiming for his house. He fell a bit short, collapsing on the doorstep and unable to reach the knob to drag himself inside.

Aradia was dozing on the couch when she heard a thump outside. Instantly alert, she scrambled out from under her blanket and hurried to the door, her heart pounding in her chest as she crossed the room. She pressed her eye to the peephole and saw nothing. Unsure what to expect, she unlocked the door and opened it swiftly, ready to leap back if she had to. What she found was Gage, crumpled on the ground, bleeding profusely with a stake sticking out of his chest.

She dropped to her knees and seized him under the arms, dragging him into the house and slamming the door, turning the lock. She pushed him onto his back, her eyes going to the hole in his chest. He coughed and gasped, pain making his eyes hazy and his movements jerky.

"Gage. What happened?"

He managed to get his eyes open enough to look at her through the pain. "Javal. Fucker staked me. You've got to pull it out. Pull it out and get me some blood."

"I can't pull it out! It's too close to your heart! I could kill you!"

His fingers grasped her wrist tightly, and his voice was slightly panicked when he spoke. "If you don't, I'm dead." He led her hand to the
stake and folded her fingers around it. "Listen to me, Aradia. I'll try to
walk you through it. I can feel it brushing my heart, but as long as it
doesn't pierce it, it won't kill me. You're going to have to jerk hard and
fast, and straight up. If you move it to either side, I'm going to turn to
dust."

Aradia was crying by then and shaking her head out of both disbelief
and denial. "No. No, I can't. We'll wait for Greer. She'll know what to
do. She can just heal you. She'll be back soon. I'll call her, and they'll
turn around and come back."

Gage reached up and laid his fingers against her cheek. "Aradia,
there's no time. You have to do this. I can't see it like you can. Trust me.
You can do it. You have to."

Aradia locked eyes with him and she knew he was right. She didn't
have a choice. Nodding, she shifted to straddle his hips so that she was
pulling straight up instead of at an angle, letting the majority of her
weight rest on his thighs. She wrapped both hands around the stake,
and with one swift motion, yanked it out, her scream of terror echoing
his shout of pain.

When he didn't dissolve beneath her, Aradia forced her eyes open.
He'd pressed both hands to the wound, blood seeping from between
his fingers. She stared at him for a moment, amazed that he was still
solid and not a pile of dirt on the floor. It took several seconds for her
to notice the blood, and when she did, she paled.

"I can fix it." She stood and ran for the kitchen. "I can heal that. I
just need to clean it first."

She grabbed the teapot and was relieved when she found the water
in it was still hot. Snatching a rag from a drawer and the soap from the
sink, she raced back into the foyer. Her hands tore at his shirt, ripping
the shreds off and exposing his chest. She poured hot water onto his
skin and pumped soap into the wound. She used the cloth to scrub
away the debris and then rinsed it clean with the rest of the water, patting it dry with the cloth. Satisfied, she tipped her head back toward the
ceiling and laid her hands on his chest. Amazed, he watched her eyes
go white.

A wind picked up inside the house and whipped her hair around her
shoulders. Her face went blank, and her hands began to glow. Gage

writhed as he felt bone start to knit together, followed by muscle and finally skin. By the time it was over, he was praying he would pass out, so great was the pain.

Aradia collapsed to the floor next to him, the healing having drained her. It wasn't her natural ability, and forcing it took a lot out of her. Her chest heaved with each breath, and she struggled to stay conscious, knowing Gage wasn't out of the woods yet.

When he spoke, his words echoed her fear. "I need blood, and soon, or I'll die anyway."

"There isn't any. Greer and Damon went to get it today." Aradia forced herself to sit up and looked down at him with worry shining in her eyes. "They'll be back in a few hours."

Gage closed his eyes tightly. "I don't have a few hours. My body needs blood to continue functioning. Without it, I'll shut down. I'll be a pile of dirt by the time she gets back from Glasgow."

"Take some of mine."

"NO!" The denial was adamant and instant. Gage shook his head, rolling onto his side and trying to sit up. "I'm weak, Aradia. Even if I was at full strength, it's hard for a vampire to control feeding on a human. I could kill you before I even knew what I was doing."

She shook her head and squeezed his hands tightly. "You won't. I trust you, and you need it. I have enough. Just take as much as you need to get through until Greer gets here." She crawled into the kitchen and snagged a knife from the butcher block. Gritting her teeth against the pain, she dug the edge into the skin of her wrist, tearing through skin and opening some of the small capillaries just below the surface. Immediately, the smell of her blood intoxicated him.

Gage clamped his eyes shut and tried to ignore the smell of her blood. He pointed at her with one finger. "Stay over there. If you come over here, I'm not going to be able to stop it. I'm not feeding on you, Aradia. You're more important to this than I am."

Aradia dragged herself back over to him and lifted his head into her lap. "You're weak. I won't let you take too much. Please, take it." She pressed her wrist to his mouth, her blood dripping down his chin, crimson against the pale of his skin. "Gage, please."

It was too much to resist the taste and smell of her blood. As much as he wanted to, he couldn't make himself push her away. Damning them both, he wrapped one hand around her wrist and sank his teeth into her flesh. Immediately, her blood overpowered him. It was thick and rich and flowed through his mouth like a good wine.

He felt it soak into his veins, filling them and rushing to his heart and his organs. The power of her blood surrounded him, seeping into every pore. For a moment, he could have sworn he felt alive again, that he felt his heart beat once in his chest after so many centuries dead. He didn't know how long he drank from her and could barely find the strength to force himself to tear his fangs from her wrist. It was only then that he saw that she had slumped to the ground, her skin pale and clammy, her eyes barely open.

Horrified, he dragged her to him, still weak from blood loss and the wound to his chest. He managed to lift her in his arms, stumble the few feet into the living room and drop her onto the couch before collapsing next to it. She groaned once and reached for him, laying her hand on his face, blood still seeping from her wrist.

He bent his head to her ear and whispered, his voice ragged with guilt. "Why? Why didn't you stop me?"

Her voice was drifting and weak. "Because I knew you would stop. I knew you wouldn't hurt me. I knew you couldn't."

He placed his hand over hers and leaned forward to brace his forehead against hers. She lifted her eyes to meet his and offered a weak smile. "I could have killed you. I was so close to draining you dry."

"I knew you wouldn't. I trust you."

Gage watched until she slipped into unconsciousness, and only then did he give into the urge to join her, sitting up next to the couch, his head falling onto the cushion next to her, one of his hands wrapped tightly around her wrist to keep it from continuing to bleed. As he felt himself slip into the darkness, he knew Graciela was right. There was something about Aradia that had his blood boiling, and he thought he might explode if he didn't find out what it was.

Aradia regained consciousness slowly. The first thing she became aware of was the light streaming through the curtains. The second thing was how very full her bladder seemed to be. Squinting against the light, she threw aside the blankets and saw the thick white bandage on her wrist. In that moment, everything came rushing back.

She remembered finding Gage outside with a stake protruding from his chest. She remembered ripping it from him and healing him. She replayed the knife and blood and the feel of his teeth sinking into her flesh and him tearing his head away from her wrist, blood on his face, upset because she hadn't stopped him and worried that he'd taken too much. Vaguely, she recalled Gage half-carrying, half-dragging her to the couch and cinching the wound on her arm to keep it from bleeding more.

Suddenly worried, she struggled from bed, stumbling out into the hallway and starting toward the stairs leading to the room Damon had told her belonged to Gage. Before she was even halfway there, Damon bounded up the stairs and lifted her in his arms, carrying her back toward the bedroom.

"You have no business being up. You lost a lot of blood, and you're very weak." He deposited her in the bed, his mouth a thin line. "Do you feel up to telling us what happened with you and Gage?"

Confused, she looked around blankly. "Who? What?"

Damon perched on the edge of her bed. "Gage. Damn vampire nearly drained you dry. We came in this morning and found both of you passed out on the couch. Gage won't tell us what happened."

"He didn't hurt me! He was hurt! I made him!" She struggled out of the bed once again and darted for the door only to be stopped again by Damon. "Let me go! I need to see him!"

"He nearly killed you, Aradia. We need to figure out what happened."

Greer appeared at the top of the stairs at the commotion. "What the hell is going on?"

"Aradia is trying to get to Gage. She doesn't remember that he nearly killed her."

Aradia's eyes sought Greer's, met and held them. "He didn't hurt me! I made him take it! He would have died! Javal, and a stake, and so much blood, and I cut my wrist and forced my blood into his mouth until he fed on me because I couldn't sit there and let him die!"

Greer stepped forward, slipping her arm around Aradia. "It's okay. I tried to tell Damon it couldn't have been as simple as it seemed. Gage has been locked up in his room since we got back. You were out almost twenty-four hours." She smiled reassuringly. "Let's get you back to bed and fed, and then we'll see about coaxing Gage down." She glared at Damon. "I told you you were over-reacting about this. I had thought we'd moved past this mistrust of Gage."

Damon returned the glare. "I had moved past it until we came home and found her passed out and him with dried blood on his mouth."

Uncomfortable, Aradia squirmed. "Greer?"

Greer shifted her gaze to Aradia. "What's up, sweetie?"

"I really, really need to use the wash room! I was on my way there when Damon intercepted."

Greer helped her get out of bed, steering her toward the hall bath. "I think I can help you out with that."

"Thank God."

Damon shifted uncomfortably. "I'll just wait in your room."

Five minutes later, her bladder issue solved, teeth brushed, and hair detangled, Aradia came out of the bathroom, leaning heavily against Greer, already exhausted. Halfway across the hall, her legs gave out and she collapsed. Greer wrapped her arms around her and struggled to keep her upright. Before Greer could call out for help, Aradia was lifted in strong arms and cradled against a broad chest as one cradled a small child. She didn't need to look, the arms told her everything she needed to know.

"Gage."

Before he could answer, she had wrapped her arms around his neck and buried her face there, holding onto him with every bit of strength she had. Greer lifted one brow in curiosity, but Gage ignored her. Something deep inside him ached for Aradia, told him to hold her close and never let her go again.

He ignored Damon as he carried Aradia into her room and deposited her on the bed, taking a seat in the chair next to her. He didn't try to pull away when she grabbed his hands to keep from breaking the contact completely. Damon lifted his eyebrows and studied the situation from the corner of the room. He cleared his throat.

"Aradia cleared everything up, Gage. I owe you an apology for the way I reacted when we came in. It looked much different than it was."

Gage smiled wryly and waved his hand. "You reacted exactly as I expected you would." He glanced away from Aradia to stare at Damon and Greer. "Do you mind giving us a few minutes?"

Greer shook her head. "Not at all. I'll start some food. I'm sure Aradia needs to eat to rebuild her strength." She looked at Damon pointedly. "I could use your help in the kitchen."

Damon pushed off the wall and followed her out, pulling the door closed behind him. Gage waited until he heard them go down the stairs and start rustling around in the kitchen before he leaned forward and brought one of her hands to his lips, pressing a kiss to her knuckles.

"I am so sorry. I couldn't stop."

Aradia's free hand went to his face, her skin warm and soft against his. "Don't apologize to me." She shifted forward to lay her head on his shoulder. "I feel so different."

Gage looked sad. "It's called the bond. Best as I can figure, some of my blood ended up in you. The open wound and all the blood around, it's likely that's what happened. When a vampire feeds on a human, if the human is drained, and the vampire forces the human to drink their blood, the human will become a vampire. I didn't drain you, but I think you still ended up with some of my blood. You're a human, always will be, but it bonds us together."

"What does that mean?"

"I've never done it to anyone before. I don't exactly know, other than that it's taken very seriously by vampires. All those feelings you're having, I'm having them too, and I don't think there's a damn thing we can do about it."

"So this need to be near you, this sort of sixth sense about you is permanent?"

"I think so." He scrubbed his hands over his face. "I knew when you were weakening, it was like I didn't have a choice but to come to you. It'll get easier to deal with—at least I think it will." He sat straighter and rubbed his thumb over the soft flesh on her hand. "We have to resist it. We can't get tangled up in each other. It's not real. What we're feeling isn't real."

"I don't think knowing that is going to make it any easier." She smiled and shook her head. "I guess you're going to go back to avoiding me?"

"As much as I can." He sighed, despite his lack of need for air. "Aradia, you're human. You're beautiful and sweet and powerful, and your blood is like nectar. I could have drained you a hundred times and still wouldn't have had enough. I don't know what it is about you." He stood and paced the room. "I feel so goddamn guilty about what I did to you. What makes it even worse is that I could do it again. Easily, because it was so good."

Aradia stood, still a little wobbly on her feet, and crossed the room to him, laying her hands on his shoulders. "Gage, you stopped. You were weak, and you would have died, and you still managed to stop. As much as you would like me to believe you're a monster, when I look at you, when I touch you, when you kissed me, I don't see or feel a monster. I see and feel a man."

In less than a heartbeat, Aradia was pinned against the wall, her wrists being held securely above her head by one of Gage's hands. His body pressed into hers, her breasts straining the thin fabric of her white nightgown. "You can see whatever you want. I've lived for centuries. I've killed people, I've drained every drop of blood in their bodies, I've screwed more women than you can imagine, and I don't regret it. I will suck everything that is good and pure out of you and then demand more. I am a monster, whether or not you want to believe it."

Aradia shook her head slowly and met his gaze with a challenge in hers. "I don't think so. I think you're scared of what happened between us. I think you're scared of what could be. I think you're scared you won't be able to stop it, and I think you're scared because you think this isn't real." She jutted her chin up, her eyes flashing with a combination of desire and stubbornness. "Kiss me. Kiss me one more time, and prove me wrong. Prove to me this is just magic—that there is nothing more than chemicals and spells between us."

He kissed her before she could even take a breath. His tongue swept into her mouth and his taste clouded her senses. His hands released hers and streaked down her body, molding her body to his. Her knees went weak, and she clung to him desperately, her mouth soft and supple under his. Desire rose up and engulfed her, and she wrapped her arms around him tightly, pressing her body to him feverishly. He cinched one arm around her waist to anchor her to him, and the other hand went to her breast, gently kneading the soft flesh and rubbing his finger over the hardened point. She sucked in a gasping breath, and her knees gave out completely in the wake of a tumultuous storm of emotion.

Gage released her suddenly, stepping back toward the door. Aradia shivered, cold at his absence, though logically she knew he had no heat to offer her. He turned to look at her once before opening the door to leave.

"You're wrong. I'm scared because I think it might be real."

Chapter Eleven

February 5, 2031 - Scotland

Alaria leaned against the counter in Gage's kitchen, a cup of coffee in her hands and dark smudges under her eyes. Greer and Aradia sat across from her at the island and the three men were at the table. She lifted her cup and drank deeply, giving herself some time to think over what had been said.

"I think I should start by saying that I think it's a good idea. I'm all for giving us any advantage that we can get, and being able to make metal as fatal to vampires as the sun is certainly a big advantage. The problem I see is that none of us have any magic to help you with."

"I don't need magic, really. I just need someone to focus with." Aradia tapped her fingers on the granite. "You have more magic than the rest, Alaria. If you're amenable, I'd like to try it with you."

Alaria nodded. "No problem. Gage, did you find out anything in Brazil?"

Gage looked up from his mug of blood. "Not a damn thing. The coven down there is terrified of Garrick and so deep in hiding that they wouldn't even come meet with me. I managed to get one of them on the phone and they basically told me to go fuck myself." He took another sip. "The one thing that seems to be consistent is that no one wants to get close enough for Garrick or Javal to find them. That's good and bad for us. Good because it's limiting their food source, and bad because word has spread that we're the enemy, so no one wants to associate with us either for fear of getting on Garrick's radar."

Braxton chuckled. "Better than the trip we had. Garrick has learned how to control people through the dream plane a la Azazel. I had to keep Alaria from doing a header off a sixteenth story balcony in Philly."

Aradia's eyes widened slightly. "It is difficult to have power on the dream plane. Everything is dulled. It's like being in water. For him to have that ability is amazing. He was able to hurt Greer so badly because she did not believe he could not. The trick with the plane is to know deep within yourself that it is just a dream and that you can control certain elements of it. It would seem that since Alaria is obviously well versed in the plane, that Garrick has learned some new tricks. I'll weave some new protections on the grounds to help block him out some more. Gage, I'll need you to show me where your mother is buried so I can tap into the power of her bones to work on it as well."

Gage laughed. "She's buried under the foundation, dead center of the house. When I had it built, I consulted with a witch who told me that was the best way to maximize her powers."

Aradia smiled. "That witch was very wise." She stood and began rifling through the boxes of supplies Alaria and Braxton had brought back. "Alaria, please be ready in thirty minutes to work on the spell."

Alaria saluted Aradia with her coffee. "Sure thing, boss." She drained the contents. "I'm gonna grab a shower before the torture starts."

Thirty minutes later, Alaria was sitting cross-legged on the floor, her hands in Aradia's. Candles burned around them and a sword borrowed from Gage sat on the floor between their legs. Aradia closed her eyes and began chanting under her breath, feeling for the magic within her as she attempted to manipulate the steel.

They worked all day, stopping only to eat, with Greer switching in to give Alaria a break when she became too tired to continue. Several times, the blade glowed yellow and became too hot to touch, but before the spell took hold, they would lose their concentration and the sword would clatter to the ground, no different than it had been before.

After more than sixteen hours, Alaria groaned, trying to hold the spell, her hands held tight within Aradia's. Both had their eyes closed, concentrating on the magic pouring out from them. As it had countless other times the spell broke loose, and their hands separated. The sword that had been floating in the air between them clattered to the floor, and they both sank with it.

"Damn."

Aradia leaned against the wall, her chest heaving. "My thought exactly. We almost had it that time." She groaned. "This should not be that hard. All we're trying to do is-"

"Make metal as fatal to vampires as the sun. No, that's a pretty big spell." Greer grunted as she climbed to her feet and held out a hand for Aradia, who took it gratefully. "Let's call it a night. It's past midnight, and we all need sleep. With Braxton and Gage deciding you need to learn to fight, which you do, we've got a busy day ahead of us tomorrow. We have to continue to work on this spell, too."

Aradia brushed dirt off her jeans. "I'm amazed Gage is training me. He'll barely talk to me after what happened with the blood."

Suddenly serious, Alaria took hold of Aradia's arm. "I know Gage didn't do it on purpose and I know he tried to resist you. I've known Gage for centuries. There are very few people who could know him better than I do, and no one cares for him more than us here in this house. That having been said, vampires are notoriously more dangerous after they've tasted the blood of a human. I don't think you have anything to worry about, but Gage does. He doesn't trust himself not to give in to the temptation of your blood. If it were any other vampire, I'd be hiding you away somewhere because the hunger can overpower any of them. Gage is dangerous, whether you believe it or not. He keeps it pretty well leashed, but just don't tempt fate."

Aradia nodded, her eyes somber. "I don't think for a second that he is capable of hurting me, but if he wishes for me to stay away then that is what I will do." She offered a small smile and pulled her arm free, swiftly descending the stairs and locking herself in her bedroom.

Absentmindedly, she showered and pulled on a night shirt, brushing out her hair and using the strange contraption that dried it so very quickly. Then, exhausted from the physical training and the magic she and Alaria had been trying to weave, she slipped beneath the covers and almost immediately dropped into a deep sleep.

The dream started almost instantly. She was in a field, late at night, the stars bright against the black sky. The long grass had a silver cast to it, and the moon was full and luminescent. She looked around, knowing instantly that it wasn't a normal dream.

"Hello, Mother."

Graciela glimmered into sight, resplendent in a green gown. "Aradia. Walk with me, we have much to talk about."

Aradia automatically fell into step next to her mother. "Why did you bring me here?"

"I needed to speak with you, and this is the only way. We haven't much time. Javal is very strong on the dream plane, and it won't be long before he senses us here. I need to speak with you not about the mission upon which you have embarked, but about one of your companions."

"They're all great. They're a ton of help. Gage knows everything about demons and vampires. Braxton and Damon are great at fighting. Greer is a Healer with more talent than any I've ever even heard of and Alaria is a force on her own."

"Aradia, your powers are increasing almost exponentially. Even here I can feel the magic moving inside of you. You've embraced what you were born with, and your focus is incredibly strong. Unfortunately, you are not yet as good as you could become."

"Well then tell me what I need to do. I've been practicing as much as I can."

"Practicing spells and potions won't do a damn thing. You have embraced your power as a witch. It is time to embrace your power as a woman." Graciela stopped and tucked Aradia's hair behind her ear. "You have feelings for the vampire."

"He—we—bonded. He was hurt, and he fed on me, and somehow I got some of his blood. Gage thinks that's all it is."

"And you know differently."

"I think we both do. I've never felt like this. I don't know what to do, or say, or how to act."

"Aradia, you're a fully grown woman. I know I kept you sheltered, that I kept men from you. I couldn't allow anyone to touch your heart. You needed to be saved for Gage. Because he is the only one that can turn you into the type of woman you need to be in order to unlock your abilities fully."

Aradia stepped back, her eyes wide. "You did what?"

Graciela crossed her arms and looked stubborn. "It had to be done. I knew if you found someone and loved while you were in Greece that your duty would be jeopardized."

Incredulous, Aradia backed away. "You kept me from falling in love?

From having a family? You knew more than anything I wanted to be a wife, and a mother! And I listened to you because you told me becoming a priestess was the only way our family would survive."

"Aradia, this is your birthright. This is what you were born to do. I was only following the instructions of the Gods."

"You brought me here tonight to tell me to give myself to him."

"It must be done."

"Fuck you!" Aradia turned and stalked back through the field. "I'll be damned before I invite a man into my body just because you say it must be done! The only way I'll bed a man is if I love him, and he loves me, and no other reason! Not for magic, not for you, not even to save this whole world! I've given you everything, Mother. I've given you my life, but that is one thing you will not take away from me. I won't let you."

"Aradia, listen to me." Graciela grabbed her daughter's arms and gave her a brisk shake. "I do not like this. I do not like what I had to do. I had no choice, just like you have no choice now. This task is yours, for better or worse, love it or hate it. You are the one person in all the worlds that can defeat Javal and his army. The others are there to help you, but it is you who will take him down, or let him succeed. He brings with him more warlocks than you can comprehend, and more power than you have ever encountered. I do not want to send my only daughter to the bed of a vampire like a lamb to the slaughter, but I will do what I must, and so will you. You will go, because you feel for him what no woman has ever felt for a man, and he feels the same for you. You will go because it feels right, because you will open your heart to what you feel. And you will go because you know you have no choice."

Aradia quieted then and met her mother's gaze. "Answer me one question. If you lie, I swear on all that is holy you will never see me again."

"I won't lie to you."

"Is it real? Or is it magic?"

Graciela's face softened, and she stroked her hand over Aradia's hair. "Oh, baby. It's real. It's more real than anything that has ever existed. Your soul was made for his, and his was made for you. There will never be another that will complete you as he will. May the Gods strike me dead, I am not lying to you. There is no magic interference with your feelings. They're real."

Before Aradia could respond, Graciela was gone, and she was standing in the middle of a street, in a city she'd never before seen. Cars littered the street, blood coated the sidewalks, and there were bodies strewn carelessly about. Gunshots and screams filled the air, the sky was tinted red, and there was a gray haze hanging in the air that was so thick she could barely see through it to look at the horror.

Immediately terrified, she dashed behind a nearby car and crouched, trying to get her bearings. Glass bit into her sensitive feet, and she winced instinctively before remembering that she was still on the dream plane. Immediately, the pain dissipated. Things couldn't hurt you on the dream plane. At least, nothing without a lot more power than a piece of conjured glass.

The screaming was getting louder. Concerned, she shifted to the back of the car and stood slightly to watch a woman race down the street, being chased by a horrid monster, with scales and yellow eyes. As she watched in horror, the monster leaped onto the woman, lifting her off her feet and ripping her small body into two pieces. Aradia gagged at the sight of the blood and gore, then had to turn and retch when the monster proceeded to drink the blood.

"That makes you sick, and yet you let Gage feed upon you."

Aradia stood completely and found herself looking at a handsome man with shoulder length chestnut hair and sparkling green eyes. He was dressed in odd clothing—riding breeches and a ruffled shirt with long sleeves and a leather vest.

"Who are you?"

The man smiled invitingly. "I have many names. You know me as Javal."

Fear rose up in Aradia's chest and threatened to strangle her. "What do you want with me?"

"I want to kill you. But not tonight." He took her arm and tucked it through his. "Walk with me."

Feeling as if she didn't have a choice, Aradia followed him. "What is this place?"

"Home. This is what the Earth will become when I succeed. Has anyone told you what I'm trying to do?"

"No."

"There's a portal beneath your city. One that allows access to Hell. One that no one knows about and that your stupid fucking friends haven't sealed shut. Only Lucifer can come through it. I intend to open it. Once I do, demons will flood the Earth again and this is what it will become. My God will rule instead of yours."

"Hades."

"We prefer to call him Lucifer, but the jist is the same."

"I'm going to stop you."

"No you won't. You have no idea what it is that I can do. I feed on witches, taking their power and making myself stronger. I have warlocks who have lived thousands of years. Vampires, werewolves, an army of creatures. You have two witches, a Warrior, a Hunter, and a vampire. A traitor to his own kind."

Aradia glowered at him. "If you're trying to scare me, it won't work."

Javal patted her hand reassuringly. "I'm not trying to scare you. I'm going to give you one chance. One chance to leave them, to join me, and help me. If you refuse, I'll kill you."

Aradia pulled her arm loose. "Then come and kill me. I'll never work with a demon."

"You'd give your body to one though. You're living with a demon. What makes him better than me?"

"He's trying to save the world, not end it."

Javal laughed. "Oh, Priestess. By the end of this, I will dine on your flesh and bathe in your blood. Of course, I think I'll make the vampire watch me fuck you first." He leaned down and nuzzled her neck, his tongue darting out to taste her skin. "You'll be a delicious little meal I do think. I'll fuck you until you scream from pain. Then I'll rip your heart out of your chest and make you watch it beat in my hand while you die."

Aradia lifted her chin. "You're welcome to try, but you'll be the one who ends up dead. I promise you that."

Javal shrugged carelessly. "We shall see. I want to show you something before you go. I'm going to show you who Gage is. What he's capable of."

In a heartbeat, Aradia was standing on a cobblestone street, looking in the window of a large house. She saw Gage lying in bed, a bevy of women crawling around him. Some were naked, some halfway there, others were still fully dressed. Gage was naked as well, and he took the women, pleasuring them, pleasuring himself. They used their mouths and their hands on him—he entered them forcefully and quickly.

He took them one at a time, over and over until he was sated, burying himself deep within one woman as he climaxed, his hands gripping her hips and forcing her face into the mattress, her hands stretched forward to claw at the sheets, though Aradia couldn't tell whether it was from pleasure or pain.

His eyes changed from the light silver they normally were to clear red. He drew them in one at a time, burying his teeth in their flesh and drinking their blood until they each slumped to the bed, eyes staring lifelessly. Aradia tried to look away, but found she couldn't. Then, she found herself in the bed, covered in the blood of other women, Gage tearing open her gown.

She screamed and she struggled, but he stripped her, forced her legs apart, and buried himself in her. Tears streamed down her face and her body bucked on the bed as she tried to escape him. Then, he bared his fangs, drove them into her neck, and ripped. In the moment Aradia felt her own death, Gage turned into Javal, and she woke, screaming and sweat drenched, in her own bed in Gage's estate.

It took less than five seconds for the door to Aradia's room to burst open. Alaria charged in, Greer and Damon a heartbeat behind her. Within a split second, Gage appeared there too, having raced down from his third story retreat. Braxton was only a moment behind Gage, having come up from the basement.

Alaria sat down on the bed and grabbed Aradia's shoulders. "What's going on?"

Aradia gasped, trying to catch her breath, the blanket and sheet sticking to her sweaty skin. "Javal." She clutched at her neck, surprised when it came away red with blood. As soon as Gage saw the blood on her hand, he crossed the room and turned her head to the side to look at it.

"Just a scratch managed to get through the dream plane." He perched on the edge of the bed. "I didn't think he'd be able to get in here. It should be protected. How did it happen?"

"My mother pulled me in."

"So he's not strong enough to conjure it on his own." Alaria nodded. "Your mother was known as a powerful dreamweaver. If he was watching her, then he could sort of ride in on her coattails."

Braxton cleared his throat. "Graciela has been dead for almost thirty years. Or three thousand, depending on how you look at it."

Aradia smiled, amused. "It doesn't matter. If her spirit never moved on, she would have retained some of her abilities. If Javal knows that she's moving in and out of the dream plane, it's easy enough to find the opening and follow her through. Once he's there, his powers are multiplied." She threw back the blankets and rose to pad to the mirror to inspect her neck. A jagged scratch ran from the base of her neck down to her shoulder. Not even actually her neck. Javal's aim had been off. "I'm okay. I'm sorry I woke you all. The dream scream came out real."

Greer cleared her throat. "What did he show you?"

"His version of the world. I've never been able to master the dream plane, so I was helpless. He tried to kill me, but he's not nearly strong enough to force it through into reality."

Greer patted Damon's chest. "Well, we're going back to bed then. Put some herbs under your pillow from now on. It'll keep anyone from getting into your dreams. Demon or otherwise."

Damon paused at the door. "Do you want one of us to stay?"

Aradia shook her head. "No, no. I'm just going to change the sheets, wash this scratch and try to go back to bed."

Gage stood and watched the other four trickle out into the hallway. "I'll get you a fresh set and then be off myself."

Aradia was in the bathroom washing her neck when Gage returned with a set of clean white sheets. He quickly stripped the bed and disposed of the sweat and blood stained ones down the laundry chute, and then went to the closet to withdraw the extra quilt from the top shelf.

"I can do that."

Gage looked up at her voice from where he was tucking the bottom sheet around the corners of the mattress. "I've made a bed a time or two in my day. Are you going to be okay?"

Aradia slipped back into the bedroom from the bathroom. "Yeah, I'm fine. He just gave me a scare."

Gage crossed his arms and stared at her, his gaze unyielding. "Do you want to tell me what you really saw? You can lie to them, but I know you saw more than you said."

"I saw exactly what I said."

"And then some. What else was there?"

Aradia dropped into the chair next to the bed and nudged the door shut with her foot. "He told me what he's trying to do. There's a portal to hell under Atlantis. He's trying to open it to let all the demons out."

Gage finished spreading out the flat sheet. "Great. Not only is he trying to stop us from sealing the gate shut for good, he's trying to open up another one. That's not what had you waking up screaming at the top of your lungs though."

Sighing, she lowered her eyes to stare at her lap. "It was you."

"What was me?"

"That's what he showed me. He showed me you."

Gage exhaled, air he didn't need streaming from his lungs. "What did you see?"

"A house in a city. You in bed with a lot of women. I watched you lie with each of them. The things that you did, the way you treated them, it was as if they were nothing more than a sexual object."

Gage leaned forward and met her gaze steadily. "They weren't. I've been alive a long time, Aradia. I've done bad things. I told you that I'm a monster. If all you saw was me screwing a few women and handling them a little rough, then you're not as tough as I thought you were."

She averted her gaze yet again. "You killed them all. He put me there. In their blood, next to their bodies. I could feel their flesh brushing against mine. You wouldn't take no for an answer. You ripped my dress, and you forced yourself on me. It was horrifying and painful and I couldn't get loose. You killed me too. Just ripped out the side of my neck. I felt myself die." Her voice trembled at the end, and she was embarrassed to find that tears welled in her eyes at the memory. Gage crouched next to her, tipping her chin up with one hand so that her grey eyes met his silver ones.

When he spoke, his voice was low and steady. "I'm a monster. I've done bad things. But I've never raped a woman. I've killed them, and I've drained every drop of blood in their bodies, but I never got off on pain. I promise you none of them felt anything. And you have my word, I'll never put my hands on you by force. You've nothing to fear from me, Priestess."

"My mother told me that in order to succeed, I have to give myself to you. That we must become intimate."

"I'm not going to sleep with you because a dead witch tells us we have to. You deserve more than that."

"If it wasn't true, would Javal have tried to prey upon that? Would he have tried to make me fear what my mother wants me to desire?"

Caught off guard, Gage rose to pace. Damn but the girl had a good point. "Javal is going to do anything that he can in order to shake you, and to break us as a group. That includes making you scared of me."

He stopped and looked at her. "There's a lot going on right now. The dreams, your mother—and believe me, she's paid me a visit too—the bonding from the bite, and whatever this fucking magic is that's stirring us up. There is no way to know that it's real." He leaned against the dresser. "You're bright and full of life, and goodness, and you're pure. You're going to need all of that to defeat him. I am a monster whether you believe it or not. What you saw in your dream? That's a small taste. There were hundreds I killed the same way. I liked it, I would still like it."

Aradia stood and crossed the room to stand in front of him. She wore a simple white nightgown, held up by thin embroidered straps, and that fell to mid-calf, dipping low enough to show just a hint of her almost ample cleavage. Her red hair flowed down her back and around her shoulders, and it was all Gage could do to keep his hands fisted at his sides, so sweet did she look and so innocent.

"I'm a grown woman. I'm capable of making my own decisions."

"What you feel is not real, it's not coming from you. It's the Angels, or your mother, or Javal. They're trying to get us so wrapped up in each other that we falter in our task."

She reached out and laid her fingers against his chest hesitantly. "I don't believe that you would hurt me."

"I won't hurt you physically. Aradia, I would destroy you. Everything about you that drives me so crazy? I would take it all away, and when this is over, I would leave. I'm not going to be responsible for your heart."

"I'm responsible for my heart, and it's telling me that there's something here."

"Something that cannot be allowed to be."

Her voice was a whisper. "I'm not scared of you."

He laid his fingers over hers. "You should be."

"I feel like I want something, but I'm not sure what exactly it is." She lifted her other hand and ran it down his face, her skin warm against his. "I think you're afraid."

"Of what?"

"This. Me. That it might be real."

"I think I told you that once before."

"You kissed me before." She backed him against the wall. "I'm asking you to do it again."

"Aradia—"

"Don't. Don't tell me no. Don't tell me we can't. I know all that. I know it's wrong, and it's bad, and we shouldn't. Tell me the truth, just this once. Tell me whether or not you want me. Because I want you, in a way I didn't even know I could want someone. It's like I ache for you. I can't stop it, I can't fight it. Tell me, right now, and then you can pretend it didn't happen if that's what you want. For God's sake, Gage, tell me that I'm not the only one who feels this."

It had been nearly a week since he'd laid his mouth against hers, since he'd felt the soft curves of her body pressed against his. He was close enough to her that he could hear her heart beating, could hear her blood rushing through her veins. He could smell the scent of her skin. He bent, sliding his arms around her waist and pulling her in close to press his face against her neck. Almost immediately, her arms slid up to wrap around his neck.

"It's not just you. Magic, or trickery, whatever it is, I feel it too. The aching and the need."

Aradia pressed her body against his and felt his hands slide down her body to her hips. "I know it's wrong. I know it's playing with fire. That it'll likely make things worse rather than better, but I need you to kiss me."

"Aradia, please don't do this."

"I need you to take it away. I know it wasn't you, that it would never be you. But I can't stop the fear. Javal is good at his job. I know you wouldn't hurt me, but every time I close my eyes, I see what he made me feel. Just for a second, just this once, make me feel something good."

"It wouldn't make you feel good. The things I want to do to you wouldn't make you feel good. It doesn't make me feel good. If you could see inside my head, you'd run in the other direction."

"Tell me."

The challenge was hot in her eyes, and it was all he could do not to, but he shook his head and stepped away. "We can't start this, Aradia. I'm not going to let us get mixed up in something romantic when we have demons to kill."

With that, Gage left her room, leaving her standing alone, and feeling the worst she could ever remember feeling. Sighing, she gave up on going back to sleep and gathered her clothes for a shower. For someone who made her feel so many things when he was near, she certainly felt empty and alone when he wasn't. It wasn't a feeling she cared for.

Chapter Twelve

Braxton stared at the whiskey in his glass. There was a fire burning in the fireplace and the light from the flames danced off the glass and the amber liquid inside. Gage sat across from him, sprawled in a leather recliner, with an identical glass dangling from his fingers. Braxton stared at the cigarette in his hand and lifted it to his mouth for a long drag, the burn of the tobacco filling his lungs and stinging his throat.

Gage lifted his glass and took a long sip. "Who are you trying to fool with the cigarette? Me, or yourself?"

Braxton chuckled. "I don't smoke. That's no secret. Occasionally it makes me feel better. The last one I had was at my parent's funeral."

"What brought on this one?"

Braxton closed his eyes and inhaled deeply. "I fight demons, Gage. I fight vampires and werewolves, and other variations of hell spawn. Magic is outside my comfort zone. I've dealt with witches before, but not like this. The ones I've handled are warty and casting spells over a cauldron. This fucker can look at you and make your head explode. I'm out of my depth."

"We all are." Gage drained his glass and plunked it on the floor. "The question then becomes—what do we do about it?"

"The only thing we can do, I suppose. Trust Aradia to handle it." Braxton took another drag on the cigarette. "We had to trust Greer and

Damon to get us through the last task. It seems pretty clear that this one is meant for Aradia. Which I fucking hate, by the way. We aren't individuals or couples. We need to be doing this together."

"It isn't just Aradia involved in this. It's mine too."

Braxton sat up and stared at the vampire. "Something you aren't telling me, Gage?"

"In my defense, you took off for the States. I haven't had a chance."

"You took off for Brazil. What's your point?"

Gage laughed. "I'm surprised Alaria hasn't told you about it." He stood and crossed to his liquor cabinet. "Since the night she arrived, I've been having visions of the lovely Priestess and me in bed together."

Braxton lifted one eyebrow. "There are worse things to have visions of."

"It's not a wet dream, boy. Visions while I'm awake, of me fucking her. In one particular winner, the walls started bleeding and the whole room caught on fire. I don't have a clue why, but something is trying to push us together, and an equally powerful something is trying to make sure we stay apart. The result is that we're both so wound up we can't see straight, and there's no way to know if anything either of us feels is real or some illusion."

"Does it matter?" Braxton held out a hand when Gage started to speak. "Bear with me here. Obviously, both sides think it makes a difference whether or not the two of you sleep together. Why is that?"

"Graciela yanked me into the dream plane while I was in Brazil. She said it has something to do with Aradia accepting her power as a woman as well as a witch. That she has to have both in order to succeed and for some odd reason, I'm the one who has to deflower her."

Braxton laughed. "It doesn't sound like a horrible proposition. She's nice to look at."

Gage glared at the other man. "So is Alaria, and I don't see you jumping her."

"That situation is complicated."

"This one isn't? I'm a vampire, Brax. I'll see her grandchildren die. I'm never going to be what she needs. I don't even think I would want to be. I have not had a real relationship since I was turned, and I don't intend to start now. It's going to be hard enough to watch all of you grow old and die, but to let myself feel for someone like that?" He shook his head. "That wouldn't be good for me."

"No one said you have to marry her. They said you have to bang her." He stood and clapped Gage on the shoulder. "If what she needs is to experience sex and unlock her power as a woman, then for the love of all things holy, take one for the team and take the girl to bed." He paused at the door. "I don't think any of us want to take the chance that your oath of celibacy is going to end the whole fucking world, Gage. Grow a set and get it done."

Braxton stopped in the kitchen and snagged a bottle of beer from the fridge before heading outside. Damon was sitting on the steps leading off of the porch, a beer dangling from his fingers and a pensive look on his face. He glanced up when he saw Braxton approach and held up his beer in greeting. Braxton lifted the beer in greeting and sat down, fishing through his pockets for the pack of cigarettes that had only one missing.

"Please tell me you're not having drama, too." He held out the pack and offered one to Damon, who took it with a shrug.

"Not really drama. Damn I'll be sleeping on the fucking couch if Greer catches me smoking this thing."

Braxton passed over the lighter. "Gage has plenty of bedrooms. There's sure to be another mattress you can crash on." He inhaled deeply. "I hate these fucking things, but there's something about them that makes me feel better."

Damon exhaled a stream of smoke. "What's got your panties in a twist?"

"Gabriel."

"Ahh. Angel troubles. Anything I can do to help?"

"He tells me that we might have to time travel back to Atlantis to fight an actual, honest to God, battle. With armies."

Damon sighed. "I don't suppose you can fight an actual, honest to God battle without armies. Did the Angel have any details about the how, why and when?"

Braxton shook his head. "All he told us was that he thinks Garrick and Javal are going to figure out how to bend time to get to Atlantis before Aradia is born in order to stop us before we ever get started. If that happens, Gabriel is going to take us back to stop them. Given that Atlantis was sunk during a siege, it stands to reason that we're going to have to get involved in that. I don't think we could get lucky enough to not be in it."

Damon took a long pull on his beer and stared out into the darkness. "Nope. If we're going back, you'd better believe we'll be fighting a war." He sucked in a lungful of tobacco. "Do the rest of them know?"

"You make the third of us. Alaria knows since she was there when Gabriel showed up, but I don't think she's told anyone yet. It's been a rough few days. Javal figured out how to make himself look like my dead wife."

Damon winced. "Ouch. That's rough, man."

Braxton laughed. "You have no idea. The kicker is that later that night, Gabriel pops in on Alaria and I having a moment and decided that he just has to let me know that he's there to have sex with her."

"By moment you mean fooling around?"

"By moment I mean ten seconds away from beating Gabe to the punch."

"Double ouch." Damon crushed the butt of the cigarette under his heel. "You can't catch any breaks lately."

"Doesn't seem like it." Braxton exhaled and drained the beer. "If this shit goes on too much longer, I'll end up a fucking alcoholic."

"If anyone has a right to it, it's us." Damon groaned and stood as there was a shimmer in the yard and Michael appeared. "This thing can't even let us commiserate and bitch for a night." He clapped Braxton on the back. "Let's go see what the less annoying Angel wants."

Braxton stubbed out his own cigarette and stood. "At least Michael plays it straight. No riddles with this one."

Michael bit back a smile as they approached. "I haven't the time or inclination to speak in riddles. Where is the rest of your group?"

Damon glanced toward the house. "I think the girls are asleep and Gage is doing some work in his study. Do you need us to go wake them up?"

Michael shook his head. "I don't believe it's necessary for all of you to be present for this." He spread his wings once before tucking them tightly against his sides. "My brother is dealing with some very personal decisions at this moment. However, his inability to guide you does not lessen the need for the guidance. I am here to fill in the gaps created by his present circumstances."

Braxton nodded. "What do we need to know?"

"With the gate closed, it is causing a breakdown in communication between the demons on Earth and those in Hell. There are five Devils on Earth. Lilith, Azazel, Abalam, Beelzebub and Abaddon. They are currently hiding in order for the four former Archangels to avoid having the remnants of their wings carved from their backs. However, their absence has not gone unnoticed, and Javal is taking advantage of not having guidance from the upper echelons. With Lucifer unable to communicate with them from Hell, it is leading to dissent and to Javal mobilizing a great number of Hell's creatures."

Damon rubbed his hand over his face. "So what do we do about it?"

Michael smiled grimly. "There are not many options. I know that you are all preparing yourselves for battle, but I cannot encourage you enough to continue to prepare. As far as having specific information, I can tell, or will tell you, more than Gabriel has. You will return in time to Atlantis, and you will lead their forces against an army. That battle will occur on the summer Solstice and it will end with the sinking of Atlantis. The only thing that you are going there to accomplish is protecting Graciela and making sure that she survives to escape through the portal in order to birth the witch.

"Javal is the demon who sieged upon Atlantis in that time. He did not know the importance of Graciela or the child she carried at the time. Graciela was renowned as a powerful witch and a gracious Queen and he desired her city, so he laid siege to it with an army of vampires. In order to keep him from getting it, she sank it to the bottom of the ocean. He is now aware of the opportunity that he had and is concentrating all of his witches and warlocks on finding a way to return there or, failing that, to reach his past self and inform himself of the situation. Best case scenario is that he sends a message back. Given the recent developments and the way events have unfolded up to this point, we must assume that he will access the streams of time and that he will return to the past. That would require you to possibly battle two versions of Javal, likely in two different bodies."

Braxton decided that he was going to need another beer. "Is it just going to be one battle? Or is it going to be like the last two and there're going to be multiple skirmishes leading up to one big one?"

"I assume the latter." Michael tucked his hands in his pockets. "I will tell you as much as I can. Please know that details I do not divulge are because I am forbidden to do so, not because I do not desire to do so." He sighed. "There is much at play that is not going to be obvious and overt. What goes on behind the curtains is often as important as what you are doing. I believe that this place is safe for the moment. I encourage you to stay here and only leave when it is necessary. Your foes will remain silent until they decide upon a course of action. They will anticipate that you will follow them back in time. Because of that, I anticipate that they will attempt to kill you at least once more before they return in time to Atlantis. You are the most vulnerable when you venture away from this place. Do not leave unless it is necessary, and never leave here alone."

Damon kicked at the dirt with one toe. "Well, it seems like we're all going to get to know each other pretty damn well before the end of this." He clapped his hands once. "That's the trick of it, isn't it? Put six people together and make us stay together indefinitely and hope we kill each other before they have to try and kill us?"

Braxton laughed. "That might not be far from the truth."

Michael offered a tight smile. "I must leave you now. If you need assistance, you have only to call for me."

With a whisper, Michael disappeared and reappeared in a white room. There was a white armchair on one side and a white couch on the other, with a white marble coffee table between the two. To the side, a cheery fire blazed in the fireplace and a pitcher of tea sat on the coffee table, flanked by two crystal glasses. Gabriel, pristine in his white suit, sat on the chair. He gestured for Michael to sit and poured the tea into the glasses.

"I have made my decision, brother."

Michael closed his eyes briefly. "I wish that I did not have to ask you to make such a decision."

Gabriel smiled sadly. "As do I. Unfortunately, you were put in a position where you had to ask, and I am obligated to give you an answer." He sipped the tea. "I have considered the problem from all angles. I reached the conclusion that I do not have a choice. At least, not a meaningful one. It is my belief that our Father knew I would not feel I have a choice when he tasked you with presenting me with this dilemma."

Michael crossed his legs. "I suspect that you are right. What have you decided?"

"I will complete the task given to me." For an instant, grief passed over his face and he looked sad. "I will betray Alaria's trust and plant a seed in her womb."

Michael felt his chest constrict at hearing the words. His voice was soft. "I get no pleasure from this, brother. I wish I didn't have to be a part in this."

"As do I." He brushed his hands over the legs of his pants. "Nevertheless, here we are, and the decision has been made, like it or not. How is it that my task should be completed?"

"You must go to her before the second task is completed and copulate with her. Your seed will be planted in her and a child will be produced. The child is divined by God and will be in no danger. It will flourish and be born at the end of the ninth month after conception." He averted his eyes for a moment before lifting them to meet Gabriel's again. "Brother, you know that you will not raise this child. It will not know you as its father."

Gabriel carefully arranged his face into an expression of neutrality. "I am aware of that, yes." He gripped the arms of the chair tightly for a moment. "I suspect we both know who will take that task."

Michael nodded. "It is as it is meant to be. He will protect the child as if it was his own, along with the child of his sister."

Gabriel stared at his lap. "That is my greatest fear, brother."

Chapter Thirteen

April 5, 2031

Gage glanced at the numbers on the screen of his phone and scowled. Four a.m. He growled and kept walking, annoyed that he continually got the overnight patrols. He shined the beam of his flashlight over the shrubbery and shook his head when all that he saw was a surprised rabbit.

Nothing. Night after bloody night, there was absolutely nothing. He turned back toward the house and clicked off the light, letting his vampiric senses show him the way. Several steps later, he froze.

The hair on the back of his neck stood up and every nerve ending told him that there was something watching him. He dropped the flashlight to the grass and turned his head from side to side. He caught a flash of movement out of the corner of his eye and smiled, his fangs fully extended and gleaming in the moonlight.

Gage was being hunted; he knew that unequivocally. He crouched slightly and looked around again, trying to get a feel for how many foes he faced. He sniffed the air curiously. Vampires. Old vampires. They moved quickly and silently through the night, surrounding him and pinning him in.

He growled deeply and whirled when he caught another flash. He swiped with his claws and got nothing but air, though the scent of the vampire wrapped around him. He inhaled it deeply and held it in his lungs, extracting all the information it contained.

Six vampires, all of them old and all of them there to kill him. He spread his feet and squared his shoulders, preparing for the impact of the first attack. The air stilled and grew heavy around him.

"If you go peacefully, we'll spare your companions."

Gage bared his teeth and hissed. "If you leave now, you'll survive. Maybe."

A vampire emerged from the darkness and smiled. "Gage Windsor, as I live and breathe." He tipped his head. "Kind of."

Gage's eyes traveled over his face. "Penn Westbrooke. What rock have you been hiding under these last few centuries?"

Penn bared his teeth in a sneer. "I've been preparing for this day. Garrick is only interested in breaking the circle. Only one of you has to die. If you choose which and allow us entrance to the house, the rest of you will be free to go on and live what is left of your pathetic lives."

Gage chuckled. "We both know that only one of us is surviving this, Penn. There's way too much bad blood between us for there to be any other possible outcome."

"I didn't come alone."

"I never expected that you would." Gage glanced around. "You managed to find some relatively old muscle to bring with you."

Penn grinned fiercely. "You have no idea what Garrick has at his disposal. We will win, Gage. Earth as you know it will not survive."

Gage crossed his arms. "As much as you keep telling me some version of that, we always seem to banish the bad guys back to Hell and keep moving toward the third task. We won the Choosing, we put up the retaining wall, and we'll seal the Gate shut. We are going to kill your master, and we are going to rid the world of all demons."

Penn tossed his head back and chortled. "You're a demon, too. You'll burn with the rest of us if you help them succeed. There is no redemption for you, Gage. You've earned your spot in Hell and there's no getting around it. Your best shot at happiness is with us." He spread his arms wide. "Join us, brother. Come back with me and pledge your loyalty to our father."

Gage shook his head. "This is a waste of time." He rolled his shoulders and bared his teeth. "Let's get on with it."

Gage was ready when the first vampire rushed him. Penn held up one finger to initiate the attack, and a vampire lunged out of the darkness and barreled through the grass toward him. Gage braced himself and dipped his shoulder, slamming it into the vampire's stomach and flipping it over his shoulder. He followed it to the ground and wrenched the vampire's head, twisting it so far that it popped off.

He tossed the head in the air before it burst into ash, and then climbed to his feet slowly and deliberately. He brushed dust off his pants and turned in time to hold out his arms and clothesline the two vampires that charged him. He flipped one onto the ground and lashed out with a leg to send the other flying into a tree. Its head collided with the bark and it dropped to the ground, dazed.

Gage strode over to the second vampire and reached down, dragging it up by its collar. He held it up and slammed his free hand into the chest cavity, fisting it around the heart and yanking the organ from the vampire's chest. He dropped both of them, not looking to see both the heart and the body dissolve before they hit the ground.

Penn clapped his hands slowly. "Nicely done. I wondered if you were still the force that tore through Europe so many years ago. There's no need to continue this, Gage. Come with us and join us, and you will be a leader in Garrick's army."

Gage cocked an eyebrow. "I don't know how many times I need to tell you how uninterested I am in that." He looked at the other three vampires, then down to the one still lying on the ground. "Do the rest of you want to take a turn, or have you seen enough?"

"Get him."

Four vampires rushed at the same time, charging at Gage. He struck out with his fists, punching one in the face before using his claws to slash at another, digging deep rifts in the skin on its face. Yet another dared to get too close and allowed Gage to sink his teeth into its throat, ripping and tearing at the flesh until there was nothing left other than a gaping hole and gleaming blood where the throat had once been.

Penn stood back and watched as Gage battled his way through the vampires. By the time the fourth one dissipated, Gage was bleeding and struggling to stay on his feet. Penn shrugged off his suit jacket and dropped it to the ground gently.

"You can still walk away from this, Gage."

Gage spat blood. "Notice that I just killed your henchmen."

Penn shrugged carelessly. "Your mistake is in thinking that I ever cared about them. They're expendable and replaceable. Don't let it come to this. We can walk away from this together. All we have to do is kill one of them. I'll let you choose, and we'll do it together, so you don't have to be alone. We'll drain them dry and walk away from this. It can be like it used to be when we traveled the world with Laelia, learning at her feet and becoming what she molded us into being."

Gage shook his head. "I was never anything like Laelia, and I don't want to start being like her now." He straightened. "Let's get this over with and find out which one of us is living to fight another day."

Penn bared his teeth. "That's where you're wrong. You're exactly like her. You always have been. It's inside you, Gage. You have the most evil soul I've ever laid eyes on. You rampaged through Europe, terrorizing and killing with aplomb. It was an inspiration to the rest of us. For two hundred years, you were the worst vampire alive. Until one day, you disappeared. We thought you'd been killed, but you popped back up four centuries later in South America, impervious to sunlight and a bona fide gentleman." He shook his head. "You're a waste of potential."

Gage struck out and swiped his claws over Penn's chest. Blood welled and dripped out of the deep scratches and the other vampire stumbled back three steps. Gage clenched his fists and stood back, waiting to see what the next move would be.

"Your mistake, son, is thinking that living the way I do makes me any less powerful than I was back then. I didn't go off and develop a conscience, and I don't have a soul. I'm as capable of destruction and murder as you are. I just choose not to."

Penn pressed his hand to his chest and looked at the blood that covered it. "No one understands why you do this. Why do you fight for the other side? You're a vampire! It's demon blood that runs through your veins. You're the oldest alive. You could rule over the vampires if you chose to, and yet you lie low and make money. Why?"

Gage shrugged. "I like money. I need a lot of it to fund this little excursion. Without the money, I wouldn't be able to seal Hell shut again." He dodged a punch and followed it up with a roundhouse kick that sent Penn flying. "You want to know why? I'll tell you. Not having a soul doesn't mean I can't feel. I hate Laelia for what she made me do, and I hate myself for following along with her for so long. The one thing I felt when I came out of the blood lust was hate. For her, for myself, for every one of us. I've earned my ticket to Hell, and it's high time I punched it."

Penn laughed as he climbed to his feet. "You son of a bitch. This isn't about the humans. It's not even about God. This is a suicide mission for you. You want to die." He sneered. "All you had to do was ask."

The two vampires clashed violently. They used their fists, claws and teeth equally, rolling around on the grass and grappling for the upper hand. Penn was very nearly as old as Gage and just as strong. Each delivered crushing blows to the other, with neither gaining the upper hand. The sound of breaking bones filled the yard. They both heard the door of the house burst open and several pairs of feet racing across the yard.

Gage looked up long enough to see Greer with a rifle in her hands and both Damon and Braxton carrying pistols. Alaria had chosen a sword, and Aradia had only her magic. He growled and threw Penn off for long enough to speak.

"This is my fight. Don't get in it."

He dropped his shoulder and charged at Penn, taking them both back to the ground. Penn craned his head to look at the other five and pressed his face close to Gage's ear, whispering low enough that only he could hear what was said.

"Garrick and Javal told me that you've got a thing for the pretty redhead." He grunted when Gage's fist plunged into his ribs, cracking two of them. He returned the blow, grimly satisfied when he felt Gage's jaw fracture. "I think I'm going to drain her dry and turn her into my bitch. She'll be forever tied to me, and I'll take her to highs she hasn't ever imagined."

Gage roared and grabbed Penn by the shirt, tossing him away and staggering to his feet. He seized the other vampire by the throat and lifted him off the ground. He carried Penn across the yard and slammed him against a tree, thrusting his hand into the chest and wrapping his fingers around the heart. The organ was slimy and cold in his hand and he squeezed tightly.

He leaned down to whisper to Penn. "There's a part of me that wants to let you live long enough to go scrambling back to your bosses with your tail tucked between your legs. They'd kill you for coming back a failure, so maybe this is merciful. Did you really think you could kill me, Penn?" He snarled. "You don't get to come to my home, disrespect me and threaten the people I care about and walk away from it."

Gage sank his teeth into the side of Penn's neck and tore, the sound of shredding flesh unusually loud in the silence. He tore his hand from Penn's chest with a wet sucking sound and moonlight gleamed off of his blood covered arm for a heartbeat before the heart and the rest of Penn dissolved into dust.

He turned to face the other five, his jaw aching from the fracture. Greer shouldered her rifle and jogged to him, slipping under his arm to support part of his weight. She wrapped her arm around his waist and guided him back toward the house.

"Let's get you inside and stripped down so that I can heal you."

Gage didn't have a chance to answer before Aradia was on his other side, her hands warm and soft as she lifted his arm to drape over her shoulders and slipped her arm around him. He hadn't realized how weak he was until they were there to take some of the burden. He struggled to support his full weight but found that he couldn't and reluctantly allowed himself to let them help.

Aradia leaned her head against his shoulder and tightened her grip on his waist. "You're going to be fine. I think you're just—what is it you call it? Banged up?"

Gage laughed for a moment before the pain from his jaw told him it was a bad idea. He glared down at her. "Don't make me laugh. Yes, banged up is right."

Greer chuckled. "I can fix it with no problem." She turned to Damon. "Get the door, please."

Damon walked ahead and pulled open the heavy wooden doors. He met Gage's eyes as the women helped him through. "How did they get through the wards?"

Alaria answered as she followed them into the house. "Wards guard the house, not the property. There are traps along the property lines, which is why they sent in vampires. They could get right up to the doorstep."

Braxton entered the room with a bowl of water and a rag. "I figured you'd need to clean him off before you heal him, Greer."

"You would be right." Greer helped Aradia lower Gage onto one of the couches. She hastily unbuttoned his shirt and assessed the damage to his chest. "Damn, Gage. Four broken ribs and a punctured lung."

"Good thing I don't need to breathe. The ribs hurt some though." He moved his mouth. "My jaw is the worst."

Aradia brushed her fingers over his jaw and whispered, her words flowing over him. The pain in his face eased, and he leaned back against the couch. She stroked her fingers over his hair and perched next to him.

"Is that better?"

Gage gratefully took the snifter of brandy that Braxton held out. "How did you do that?"

Aradia smiled. "I'm not a Healer, but I do know how to numb the nerves so that you don't feel the pain from the injury as much. Healing it takes a lot of my strength. Given that Greer can make you whole again without weakening, I'll let her do the..." She trailed off as she searched for the right phrase. "Heavy lifting."

Alaria giggled. "You're really getting good at the vernacular." She laid her hand on Gage's shoulder and leaned one hip on the back of the couch. "Do you want to tell us what the hell that was all about?"

Gage shook his head and winced as Greer washed blood off of his face. "Not really."

Alaria sighed. "You don't really have a choice. Tell us what happened, Gage."

"His name was Penn. I've known him since about fifteen years after I was turned. He was sired by Laelia, the same as I was. We traveled together for almost two hundred years afterward. Laelia abandoned us about a decade after Penn was turned. I taught him what I knew about being a vampire. At first, we were both totally bonded to Laelia, and being around one another eased the pain of being away from her. Eventually, the bond went away and we were just traveling together because we always had. At some point, I got sick of what we were doing and we parted ways. That was when I dropped out of sight." He shifted on the couch and looked down at Greer. "Any chance you can heal my jaw before I continue with the story? It's fucking killing me, and talking just makes it worse." He glanced at Aradia. "The mojo you worked is apparently only effective if I'm not talking."

Greer smiled and laid her hands on his jaw. They glowed white for several seconds, and Gage rubbed it carefully, rotating his jaw to test the newly knitted bones. She leaned back and studied her work.

"Feel better?"

"Much, thanks." He grunted when she went back to cleaning his chest. "Apparently, to answer the question I think you were asking, Penn has been working with Garrick and Javal. If I had to guess, I'd say he's siring vampires for them now that Laelia is dead. Those of us Laelia sired, and especially the oldest ones, are going to produce the most powerful vampires possible." He shook his head. "I suppose it's possible that they're going to use demons to create more originals, but I doubt it. That only ever worked once, and believe me, they've tried. Anyway, they sent a squad to try and kill one of us. I don't doubt for a second that they knew all six were going to die. They're throwing everything they've got at the wall and hoping something sticks. As long as we're here, there's nothing they can do to kill us."

Alaria tapped her fingers against her legs. "That means they're going to do something to lure us out. Which also means that we can't leave this place unprotected. If we do, we'll likely come home to a pile of rubble."

Braxton nodded thoughtfully. "Two stay here at all times. If we do get lured out, and I think Alaria's right, four go. It's the safest way."

Greer laid her hands on Gage's chest. "I've never healed a vampire until tonight, so I don't know if this'll be more difficult or less difficult than healing a person, and I don't know if it'll take thirty seconds or thirty minutes. Bear with me. Your jaw felt pretty normal, but this is much more extensive. Try to relax, and no one talk for a few. At least let me get inside him before you start talking."

Everyone fell silent as Greer concentrated on healing Gage. She sank deep into him, seeking out and finding the broken ribs, then focusing on repairing them. Working methodically, she formed a patch over the ribs and knitted it into the bones before going deeper to find and repair the puncture in his left lung.

The tissue was black and old. It was rubbery when she prodded it, and black goo oozed out of the tear. It resisted when she tried to heal it, and she felt nauseous from the feel of the organ. It took several minutes before she was able to seal the slice and several more before she was convinced that it was truly healed.

She withdrew from his chest slowly and sat back, rubbing her head. "Damn. That was hard. Healing you is like trying to heal a dead body. I can repair the damage, but there's nothing in the tissue to work with. It all comes straight out of me."

Gage coughed and rubbed his chest. "That felt weird. It didn't take long, though. Only about five minutes." He drained his drink and held up his glass when Braxton extended out the bottle to pour him another one. "The show's over for tonight, guys. Tomorrow we'll try to put some more wards around the perimeter." He sat up and shrugged off his shirt. "I'm going to get a shower and try to get some sleep. I'd suggest you all do the same."

Damon exchanged a glance with Greer. "I'll take the watch shift."

Aradia laid her hand on Gage's arm. "I'll help you up to your chambers."

Gage stood. "That's not necessary." He started for the stairs. "Thanks, guys."

Aradia stared at her lap for several seconds before standing and going to the other set of stairs. "Good night."

Chapter Fourteen

April 7, 2031

Father Brad Dooley sat in his office long after the parish staff went home. The television in the corner blared a basketball game, and he alternated between reading a trashy romance hidden inside a scholarly looking book jacket and watching the game. Next to the sagging, well-worn couch, he had placed a cold beer and a bowl of potato chips.

The door separating his office from the sanctuary was closed and the sounds of a ball striking the floor, and shoes squeaking filled the room. His ears perked up when he heard a scraping noise outside the door, but when it wasn't repeated, he shook his head and picked up a fistful of chips.

Crunching happily, he picked up the beer and looked around furtively, as if expecting one of the sisters to be hiding in a corner to chide him for drinking on church property. Sighing contentedly, he took a long drink. The beer was tipped completely up and the amber liquid ran into his mouth and down his throat. He closed his eyes in bliss and swallowed.

The sound of breaking glass filled the air and his eyes snapped open, the view distorted by the thick glass on the bottom of his bottle. He lowered it, carefully placing it on the floor and wiping his mouth with the back of his hand. He stood slowly and shuffled to the desk, opening the bottom drawer and carefully pulling it all the way out before reaching inside to remove the panel below.

Inside the hidden compartment, was a semi-automatic handgun and two clips. He tucked one in the pocket of his slacks and slid the other into the butt of the gun as silently as he could. He slipped out the door on the far side of the wall and into the confessional booth. He closed the door behind himself and opened the hatch to crawl into the other side of the booth. He stood and carefully unlatched the door, stepping out into the hallway that led to the side entrance.

He looked over his shoulder nervously, judging the distance both to the door and then on to his car before he took a deep breath and ran for the door. He reached it undetected and slammed his shoulder into the heavy wood, pushing it open and darting through it. He made it four steps before an arm shot out and smacked him across the chest. He yelped and fell backward, striking his head on the cement. Black dots swarmed his field of vision and he struggled to stay conscious.

When his sight cleared, there was a man standing over him. The man was handsome, with long hair and classic features. He smiled brightly. "Good evening, Father. My name is Javal. I'm going to need you to come with me."

Dooley looked up at him. "Get behind me, Satan. You have no power here. In the name of Jesus Christ, my Lord and Savior, you shall not enter this place."

Javal sighed and picked Dooley up. "That would work if you were still inside the church. However, since you stepped through that door, you're fair game." He patted the priest's head. "Don't worry. I'm not going to kill you. Even I don't want to invite God's wrath by killing a man of the cloth. I need you to accompany me somewhere safe, and when the time is right, I'll need you to make some phone calls and play a part. If you do as you're told, I promise you that no harm will come to you."

Dooley glared at him. "I don't see as I have much of a choice."

Javal smiled. "Good man."

Aradia woke up when the door to her room opened. Rubbing sleep from her eyes, she sat up, hugging the blanket to her chest. Greer and Alaria stood in the doorway, still in their pajamas. Greer held a tray with coffee and cups on it, and Alaria carried a plate stacked with muffins.

"Is everything all right?"

Greer grinned and closed the door. "Everything's fine. Damon just came in from his shift at watch and is asleep. Braxton and Gage have their heads together over maps and symbols to spray paint on the grass. We thought we'd have a little relaxation time this morning before we have to jump right back into the real work."

Aradia pushed herself up further in the bed and leaned against the headboard. "Neither of you seem the type to want to gather and gossip." She crossed her arms. "What is it that you seek to discuss with me?"

Alaria laughed. "She's good, Greer." She looked at Aradia. "We couldn't help but notice the little exchange between you and Gage last night. We were both up early this morning checking on things, and got talking about it. We wondered what's going on with the two of you."

Aradia shook her head. "You didn't have to bring me breakfast to soften me up first. I'd have told you what you want to know if you had just asked me for the information." She drew her legs up and patted the bed. "Nevertheless, I welcome the company."

Greer grinned and plopped on the bed, coffee nearly sloshing over the sides of the mugs. She handed Aradia one, then Alaria, taking the third for herself and dropping the tray onto the floor. Alaria crossed to the other side of the bed and perched on it.

"For the record, I'm as much an unwilling part of this as you are." She took a bite of a blueberry muffin. "I typically find gossip and conversations like this one is going to be uncomfortable and miserable for everyone involved, but Greer insists that you need some time with the rest of us possessing a vagina in order to make you feel better."

Aradia nearly choked on her coffee. "I don't think I've ever met someone as brash as you are."

Greer rolled her eyes. "She's one of a kind, that's for damn sure." She chewed thoughtfully and studied Aradia. "Here's what we know." She giggled when Alaria snorted. "Yeah, yeah, we've already put our heads together to combine information."

Alaria wrinkled her nose and glared at Greer. "That means that she pounced on me at seven in the fucking morning with the first pot of coffee and basket of carbs to pick my brain about what I know. Which isn't all that much, actually."

Greer waved her hand. "Shush. What we know is that you and Gage had a moment in the casino that was intense enough to make him disappear for weeks. We also know that you shared a vision of the two of you having sex but that it was all fire and brimstone. We know of another moment after he drank your blood, though we're fuzzy on the details there, and whatever the hell happened last night was obviously due to Gage not wanting to be alone with you. What we want to know is why he doesn't want to be alone with you and any important details that we've missed."

Aradia sighed deeply. "He kissed me the first night after I arrived through the portal. That was when we first shared a vision of us in bed together. There were no flames that time. We both suspected that it was magic of some sort. The casino was the second vision. I have had no further ones since then, though I do not know whether Gage has."

Greer bounced on the bed. "Wait. The first night? Damn boy works fast!"

Alaria glared. "Let her finish telling the story."

Aradia smiled. "When he came back from Brazil, he fed on my blood after I cut my wrist open to force him to do so. During the course of this, Gage believes that a portion of his blood got into my body, causing a bond."

Greer interrupted again. "Wait a second. He fed me his blood when I was hurt. I didn't get bonded to him."

Alaria swallowed her bite of muffin and washed it down with a gulp of coffee. "The bond is something that can only be done when there are emotions shared between the vampire and human. It's their version of scent marking a mate. Gage bonded you?"

Aradia blushed bright red. "He didn't intend to."

"No, I imagine not. It's very rarely done and taken very seriously. It's cemented when you have sex and he feeds off of you. That's taking the mark, and it's giving yourself to the vampire. At that point, you would be his for the rest of your life. It's very strong magic." She leveled her gaze at Aradia. "Have you fucked him?"

Aradia got even redder. "No, I have not."

"Good." Alaria took another drink of coffee. "What else is there?"

"The night that Javal pulled me into his version of the world, he forced me to live through being killed by Gage. He put my consciousness into the body of a whore and forced me to experience being violated and murdered." Aradia lowered her gaze to her lap. "I don't know what to think. It feels as if Javal and Garrick are trying to keep Gage and me apart, and my mother is attempting to push us together."

Greer looked confused. "What does Graciela have to do with any-thing?"

"She has pulled me on to the dream plane to talk to me about the importance of lying with Gage. She told me that she has saved me for him, and that it is my fate to be with him. She said something to me about accessing my power both as a witch and a woman and that until I do, I won't be able to succeed in the fight against Garrick."

Greer expelled a deep breath. "Well, that's certainly some extreme pressure."

Alaria whistled softly. "What do you intend to do about it?"

"Gage thinks that we have to ignore it. That's why he's trying so hard to stay away from me as much as he can. He thinks if we give in to the desire, it'll be giving them what they want."

Greer nodded. "What do you think?"

Aradia blushed and looked down at her hands. "I think I've never felt anything remotely like what I feel around him. I'm drawn to him in ways that I can't explain. I don't know whether the cause is merely the bond or if it is something more than that. What I do know is that I desire to explore the feelings, and Gage will not allow it."

Alaria leaned against the headboard and stared pensively at the wall. When she spoke, she didn't look at either of them. "The problem with this whole thing is that Gage will live forever. He's not going to die. He's going to have to watch you find love again, marry someone, and have a bunch of babies because he can't offer you a future and won't want to hold you back. He'll watch your great-grandchildren grow old and die." She paused for a moment, and Aradia thought she saw tears shine in Alaria's eyes. "You need to think about what a relationship would do to Gage. I'm concerned that the two of you would destroy each other."

Aradia's brows drew together. "How could we destroy one another?"

"Gage is a vampire. He doesn't have a soul like you do or even like I do. He's not human. He will use you. I'm not saying he can't love, be-cause he can, and if I had to guess, it's the fact that he thinks he could fall in love with you that makes him hold back so hard. If he loves you, it's going to destroy you both when it ends, and it will end. Romances like that never last. They can't. It's not because you don't want them to or because you don't care for each other, but it's because you aren't meant to be together. You'll have to let go and be able to move on and be happy. If you don't think you can do that, you have no business getting involved with him."

Greer's voice was soft. "Are we still talking about Aradia and Gage?"

Alaria shook her head and bit her lip in a futile effort to control the tears. "I don't know."

Greer climbed to her knees and wrapped her arms around Alaria, who pressed her face into the blonde's neck. She struggled against the tears for several seconds before giving into them and collapsing into Greer's arms, clinging and sobbing. Aradia slipped her arm around Alaria's shoulders and patted her back awkwardly. Greer stroked her hair and murmured softly.

"It's okay. We're here. You're going to be just fine."

Chapter Fifteen

April 15, 2031

Aradia gritted her teeth out of concentration and held tight to Greer's hands. She tried to find Greer's energy, to use it to heal the deep cut on her thigh. She felt the thin cord and fumbled to grab it. It slipped through her fingers, cool and slick, and ascended out of her reach. Frustrated, she dropped Greer's hands and slapped her own against the floor on either side of her.

"I think we just have to accept that I am not ever going to be able to heal people the way that you do. It's not my gift."

Greer leaned back onto her hands and studied the other woman. "You healed Gage, though. That's what made me think this was worth a try in the first place."

"I also knocked myself out doing it. I have magic, and a lot of it, but it's not suited for healing. I can force it, and it'll get the job done, but not time and again like you. I'm good for an emergency. I use outside forces to manipulate flesh. You use their own energy. It's totally different approaches."

Greer nodded thoughtfully. "You're probably right about that." She climbed to her feet. "Are Braxton and Alaria back from Glasgow?"

Aradia closed her eyes in bliss as Greer leaned down to press a hand to the wound, sealing it shut. "Thanks. I don't know if they are or not.

Braxton told me that it would take all day. They had to rent a truck to go replenish our food stores, and I know they had to go a few places." She gratefully took the hand Greer held out and let the other woman heave her to her feet. "What're Damon and Gage doing?"

Greer looked out the window and rolled her eyes. "Sparring." She crossed her arms. "I swear to God, it's been over a month since Damon and I had sex. One of us is always on watch, and we're flailing trying to maintain a relationship and deal with all of this." She looked at Aradia out of the corner of her eye. "This is one of the biggest reasons I didn't want to start something with him."

Aradia slid her feet into her delicate leather sandals and plaited her red hair into a loose braid. "Have you spoken to him of your desires?"

"A time or two. It's not entirely his fault. We're dealing with a lot lately, and we just haven't had time."

Her eyes glimmering with humor, Aradia looked out the window. "What if I convince Gage to go for a walk and get you two the house to yourselves for an hour or so?"

Greer grinned. "Could you manage that?"

"I'll try my best." She grabbed Greer's hand. "Let's give it a try anyway."

Gage and Damon were in the yard practicing with bows and arrows when Greer and Aradia strode across the yard. Gage was immediately caught by the way the warm Spring wind blew her sundress around her legs. The sage green garment tied around her neck and left most of her back bare, and tendrils of rich red hair had escaped from her braid to blow around her face.

Damon elbowed Gage in the ribs. "You're staring, dude."

Gage shook his head ruefully. "I've kinda given up on pretending not to." He offered a grim smile at the women as they approached. "How are the healing lessons going?"

Greer lifted one shoulder in a shrug. "They aren't really." She idly picked up one of the bows and toyed with the strings. "We've come to the conclusion that Aradia isn't going to be able to heal people. She doesn't have the right kind of energy for it."

Aradia stood next to Gage and laid her hand on his arm to draw his attention. She rose onto her tiptoes to place her mouth close to his ear. "Would you come with me? I think I'd like to take a walk."

Gage almost agreed. The thought of walking with her in the cool spring air was appealing. The sun was little more than an annoying tingle and she looked perfectly suited to the Scottish countryside. He shook his head. "I don't think so."

Greer and Aradia exchanged a long look. Damon looked between the women, his eyes showing his suspicion. "You're up to something. What are you two planning?"

Greer placed her hands on her hips and glared at Damon before turning her gaze to Aradia. She offered a smile that was equal parts wicked and clever. "My period is late."

Gage cleared his throat and extended his elbow to Aradia. "A walk sounds great. Shall we?"

Greer waited until Gage and Aradia had disappeared from sight before wrapping her arms around Damon's neck and nipping his earlobe. "I lied. We now have the house to ourselves for at least an hour. What d'ya say we take advantage of it?"

Damon's face slowly split into a grin. "You scared me there for a second." He stooped and swept her up into his arms. "Lucky for you, I'm in a forgiving mood."

Aradia walked slowly, her arm tucked through Gage's. The sun was bright, but a brisk breeze kept it from being hot. They walked across the sprawling yard and into the woods that surrounded Gage's estate. They were quiet until they were far out of sight and hearing range. After several minutes of companionable silence, Gage spoke.

"Please tell me Greer isn't pregnant. I don't think we could handle that with everything else."

Aradia laughed. "Greer is not carrying a child. She and Damon are having some relationship difficulties, and she thought it would be beneficial if they could have some time alone to sort things out."

He looked down at her, surprise in his eyes. "You and Greer plotted to get us out of the house so she could get laid?"

Aradia considered that for a moment. "I suppose so. I didn't know she would announce that about her menstrual cycle, though. That was of her devise."

"How long should we stay away?"

She looked up at him, her eyes showing innocence belied with a hint of a challenge. "I don't know. How long do you take to make love with a woman?"

Gage nearly choked on air he didn't need and he turned his head to avoid her gaze. "We'll give them a couple hours."

Aradia looked around the forest and smiled. "You have a beautiful property, Gage. It reminds me so much of home."

He tugged on her arm gently and led her down a path. Neither paid attention to the traps painted in the grass that they walked over as they changed direction. "Let me show you something." He led her off the path and through thick underbrush. Within a few yards, she heard running water, and as they pushed through the brush into a clearing, she found herself looking at a wide stream which ran into a deep, crystal clear pool before flowing out the other side in a waterfall.

Her face lit up with wonder and she lifted her fingers to her mouth. "Oh." She took a few steps toward it. "It's beautiful."

Gage smiled and watched her walk to the edge of the water. "The pool is heated by an underground hot spring, so it's warm. Not hot, because the water flowing in is cold. It's quite nice. I remember swimming in it when I was a child."

"There's a place like this, well, sort of, in Greece. It's a grotto, just a few hundred yards before it flows into the sea. There's a waterfall and a rock ledge behind it. The water is a hundred feet deep and you can see all the way to the bottom."

Caught up in the moment and in her wistful look, he smiled "It sounds beautiful. Maybe you can show it to me someday."

She looked over her shoulder and met his gaze. "I'd like to do that." She eased closer to the bank and kicked off one sandal before reaching out to touch the water with one foot. "Is it safe to swim?"

Gage waved one arm in the direction of the water. "Be my guest. Unless you're scared of fish and turtles, there's nothing in there that could hurt you."

Shy, Aradia stepped behind a bush to pull her dress over her head, unsure if her plain cotton bra and panties were modest enough for him to see her in. She looked over her shoulder quickly and found that he had turned around so that he couldn't see her. Sighing in relief, she darted into the water, quickly sinking up to her shoulders, her feet buried in the smooth pebbles at the bottom.

"You can turn around now."

Though he didn't particularly want to, Gage knew he couldn't stand with his back to her for two hours. He turned and perched on a fallen tree near the bank. "How is it?"

"Perfect." She slipped beneath the water, her body long and fluid as she sliced through the pool. She surfaced near the ledge, her hair slicked back from her face and water droplets clinging to her skin. "How close to the edge can I get?" She gestured to the waterfall questioningly.

"There's a pretty good current, but it shouldn't be strong enough to take you over."

She pushed off the bottom, swimming strongly toward the edge. She braced herself on the small rock ledge that bordered the pool from the waterfall and lifted herself out of the water to look over the edge. Gage was immediately captivated by the line of her back, the delicate bones of her spine, and the soft curve of her backside. Her underwear clung to her body and had become transparent, giving him an unencumbered view of her bottom.

"It's beautiful."

His voice was raspy. "It certainly is."

Aradia turned slowly, her eyes seeking his out. A breeze picked up in the clearing, swirling leaves and dirt around them. She inhaled, smelling lavender and magic. The air grew heavy and hot and snapped with electricity. She turned in the water, looking around for an intruder out of habit but feeling no danger.

Gage looked from side to side, his expression suspicious. "What is that?"

She smiled reassuringly. "Magic."

"Yours?"

Aradia turned back and held out a hand, her eyes steady and her demeanor calm. "Ours. Come swim with me, Gage."

"I don't swim."

"Yes, you do."

She walked toward him, rising out of the water. Droplets ran down her skin as she moved and he tried to force himself to look away, but found himself unable to stop staring. Her red hair was even more intensely colored when it was wet, streaming down her back almost to her waist. He took in the sight of her body hungrily, devouring the look of her strong shoulders and a narrow waist that led to flaring hips. His eyes raked over the line of her legs, and the cooler air outside the water hardened her nipples inside the fabric of her bra until he could see them clearly through the delicate white lace. She smiled beguilingly and stretched out her hand again.

"It won't kill you to have a little fun. Come play."

Even though her smile was bright and playful, he knew she was much more serious than that. His gut knotting, he slowly unbuttoned his shirt and slipped out of his shoes. She waited in the shallow water until he was stripped down to his boxers then dove back in, surfacing in the middle, where her feet barely touched the bottom.

He slipped beneath the water, staying under much longer than a human would have been able to, enjoying the warm water on his cool skin and trying to delay what he knew was inevitable. Finally, he surfaced several feet away from her. The wind had gone still and not even a bird stirred in the trees above their heads. The air was heavy with a perfume and smelled like magic.

"What is going on?"

Aradia smiled softly and drifted nearer, letting her legs brush against his. "A taste. This is a taste of what we could make. Don't you feel it all around us? The magic is palpable. It's inevitable, Gage. This is our destiny."

He stared at her intensely, his eyes hot and his expression serious. "If you do this, there is no turning back. I'll ruin you."

"Or maybe I'll make you better." She braced her hands on his shoulders and stared into his eyes. "I don't know what's going to happen. All I know is what the magic tells me. Right now, it tells me that it's time. Our time."

He swallowed the lump that formed in his throat and held in a lungful of air he didn't need before expelling it with a whoosh. "Your move, Priestess. I'm not taking responsibility for this."

Aradia studied his face for a long moment then slowly shifted forward, her face less than an inch from his. He could hear her heart pounding and could almost taste the fear and the desire. She wanted something, but had no idea what. She knew that what was about to happen would change her forever. There would be no turning back, no changing her mind. She would give him everything she was, everything she had, and when he demanded more, she would dig deeper and find it. For the first time in her life, she felt a purpose. Regardless of what they had to do, in that moment, she knew why she had been born. She had been born for him.

She took a deep breath and leaned forward. Her breath caressed his face and her hands tightened on his shoulders. He kept his eyes open, and they burned into hers. Slowly, hesitantly, she looped her arms around his neck and kissed him.

The second she touched her mouth to his, he took possession of her. His hands streaked down her body, lifting her up to wrap her legs around his waist. He pressed himself against her and crushed her small body tightly against his much larger one. Her hands timidly wound through his hair and her mouth was fearful but avid on his, accepting the invasion of his tongue, shyly lifting hers to tangle with it.

Her small body molded to his, her curves flush against him, every inch of her touching him. He felt her warmth seeping into him, boiling the blood he had left in his veins. The smell of it was pungent and made him groan deep in his throat from want. He ripped his mouth from hers to trail searing kisses down her neck and throat, walking toward the bank several steps so that the water was waist deep. Gently, he unfolded her legs and placed her on her feet, meeting her hazy gaze with his hot one. In one motion, he gripped the front of her bra and ripped, the fabric giving easily, baring her breasts for his gaze and his hands.

Aradia's head fell back as he took possession of her flesh with his hands. He kneaded her gently, almost reverently, his fingers stroking the skin and his thumbs rubbing over the tightly beaded tips. Her knees went weak and she grabbed his shoulders for balance. He dipped his head, his tongue darting out to stroke her, and she sagged against him as foreign sensations shot through her body. Fascinated by her body, he licked, sucked, and nipped lightly with his teeth until her skin was flushed red and her breath was coming in short, shallow gasps. Just as she thought she might collapse from the pleasure, he bent and lifted her into his arms, cradling her against his chest as he walked toward the shore.

His voice was demanding and ragged. "Tell me what you want."

Her hands went to his face, framing it, and she pulled him down, kissing him deeply and softly. "I want to be with you. I want to know you in the way a woman knows a man. I want to feel you inside of me. I want to be yours."

Unreasonably touched, he stared into her eyes. "Then that is what you shall have."

"Unfortunately, I think this little lovers' rendezvous is going to have to wait."

As soon as the unfamiliar voice penetrated the lust-fueled haze, Gage put Aradia down and pushed her behind him, his eyes focusing on Javal, who stood several yards back from the bank. She, too, recognized him and stepped out from behind Gage, unconcernedly walking to the shore and picking up her dress. She drew it over her head to cover herself and turned to face the demon. When she spoke, there was no trace of fear in her voice.

"You're here for me."

Gage reached out for her. "Aradia, get behind me."

Aradia shook her head, all her focus on Javal. "He's been feeding on some very powerful warlocks. This is my test. Don't you feel the power rolling off him?" She chuckled. "Didn't like that I escaped your dreamscape intact, did you?"

Javal bared his teeth in a snarl. "I won't make that mistake again."

Enraged, Gage started to stride toward her when Aradia's voice shocked him by sounding in his head *"Let me do this. A demon's body can only hold so much magic. He isn't a warlock, and he's stretched his boundaries. I can handle him. This is my part in this, Gage. I'm the witch. Don't distract me by having to protect you, too."*

Grudgingly, Gage held out his hands. "You don't know what you're dealing with, Javal. You should run while you have the chance."

Without warning, Javal threw out his hands and sent a bolt of black energy at Aradia. With one flick of her wrist, she sent it back at him. It veered slightly off course, striking a tree and felling it as he leaped out of the way. She spread her arms, and the wind picked up, blowing her hair behind her. Her eyes began to change color, first turning thunderstorm grey, then black, and then to pure white.

Javal climbed to his feet and brushed himself off, his eyes glowing yellow. Fire whipped up around Aradia, licking the edges of her dress and slashing at her skin. With a sideways look, she extinguished it, then lifted her hand and concentrated on forming a ball of fire in her palm. It came to life in her hand, glowing white hot. With a casual look, she launched it at him, striking his hip as he dodged the projectile. The skin where the fire touched melted and sizzled from the heat.

He pressed his hand to the wound for a moment and smiled wickedly. "You're a powerful little witch. I'll give you that.

Aradia lifted her eyebrows and cocked one hip, her stance confident and sure. "This all you got?"

In a heartbeat, he sent out a stream of energy so hot and strong that it was all Aradia could do to match it with one of her own before it slammed into her. Thunder rumbled and the sky opened, rain pelting them all, even the weather disturbed by the show of magic. Gage could hear Greer yelling back at the house and could feel the Healer reaching out, trying desperately to find Aradia with her mind.

Aradia was too focused on Javal to notice. Her body was tense; the energy pouring out of her was an electric blue that sizzled where it clashed with the black that came from Javal. Her mouth was closed tight and her eyes open wide, crackling with power. A trickle of blood started from her nose, and he could see a change in her as she shifted from offense to defense.

Javal was making progress against her. She stumbled back a few steps until she was up to her thighs in the water. She closed her eyes, chanting under her breath, tapping in to all the power she possessed. She threw her head back, her eyes flying open and the stream of energy intensifying. When she lowered her head, her eyes were glowing red. The stream changed color, darkening until it was as black as Javal's. She forced him backward, still muttering under her breath, managing to get almost to the bank.

The trail of blood coming from her nose thickened, and Gage saw a trickle come out of her ears as well. Whatever she was channeling, it was taking its payment in blood. He looked around hurriedly and found a heavy branch with a sharp point. Dipping his head, he charged Javal, driving the branch all the way through the demon. In a split second, his energy stream sputtered, and Aradia's hit him full in the chest. He screamed as his skin boiled and disintegrated. In the next moment, it was over. Javal opened his mouth, his essence flowing out of the body he had been possessing, which fell to the ground, limp and lifeless.

Aradia wavered on her feet for several seconds, trying to get her balance. Unable to steady herself, her eyes rolled back in her head and she fell into the water. Gage leaped to her, scooping her out and lifting her in his arms, her hair streaming over his arm halfway to the ground. He lowered her to the ground once to pull on his pants and shoes, then struck out toward the house. Before he was halfway there, Greer and Damon came barreling through the woods. He brushed off their hurried questions with a glare and continued toward the house, his only thoughts those of the unconscious woman in his arms.

Chapter Sixteen

"WHAT THE hell did you do?" Alaria plopped down on the couch next to Aradia, her eyes dark with fury.

Aradia sighed into her tea. It had taken her several hours to fight off the pounding headache the magic had left her with and another forty minutes to shower, dress in sweat pants and an oversized T shirt, and curl up on the couch. By then, Alaria and Braxton had returned from Glasgow and been filled in on what had happened. Alaria and Greer had immediately pounced, the men close behind them.

Feeling stubborn, Aradia scowled into her tea. "I did what I had to do."

Greer shook her head. "Gage said your eyes went red. You channeled black magic."

"Just a little. I had to. The fight would have drained me dry if I'd kept trying to fight him that way. He was about to explode he'd eaten so many witches and warlocks. His power was extremely unstable. He couldn't hold anymore."

Damon held up a hand, looking confused. "Black magic?"

Greer inhaled deeply and spoke. "Magic comes in degrees, the same as people. Most witches channel white magic. Kitchen magic, healing magic, whatever its form. That's what Aradia and I tap into. It comes from nature and from charms and crystals. It's natural. We can only access as much as we're meant to. Which is why most witches can only do a few tricks. Black magic is different. It's evil—from Hell—for lack of a better term. It's what demons and vampires—sorry Gage—and were-wolves have. It's inhuman, it's harsh and unpredictable, and hypothetically, you can access as much of it as you want to pay for."

Gage perched on the arm of the couch near Aradia's shoulder. "Pay for?"

Alaria spoke softly. "White magic has limits. You can't take more than your share. Black magic is almost limitless, but it costs you. To some—like evil witches and warlocks or sorcerers and sorceresses—it takes a part of your soul, until eventually it consumes you and starts to use you instead of you using it. For someone like Greer or Aradia, it takes it out of your hide. Blood and pain. Take too much, and it can kill you. By accessing it, not only did Aradia risk her soul, she risked her life."

Aradia closed her eyes in meager defense against the headache that had already returned. "I got nowhere close to the threshold. I used it to augment my power. I wouldn't have done it if I could have destroyed him on my own. He won't be able to take much more. Demons have an essence that they drive into human bodies with when they escape from the underworld. Even they have their limits, and he's pressing his. If he goes much further, he'll explode."

Braxton grinned. "Well, let's hope for that then."

"He has a warlock. He has to. A powerful one who is helping him. I could sense a trail of the other magic in his. Javal knows he took too much. He was shaky with it, unstable. But he thought he could kill me. He didn't think I'd do it. He'll be nursing his wounds for a long time, and he'll never be able to take so much again. He's burned himself out." Aradia groaned. "We'd been operating under the assumption that Garrick was just helping Javal, but I think Javal might be feeding on him, too."

Gage stood, his eyes hot with anger. "I don't give a flying fuck about Javal. What I care about is the fact that you nearly turned your brains to mush to prove a point." He grabbed her by the upper arms, jerked her off of the couch, and shook her harshly. "Don't you have any clue how important you are to this? You die, we all die. We're here to help you to succeed, but if he takes you out before June, we're done and he's won. Is that what you want?"

Aradia swallowed back anger and looked at him calmly. "I don't think you even have to ask me that."

"Obviously I do." He dropped her abruptly. "From now on, you don't leave the property. If you do, I'll knock you out and lock you in the basement." He glared at Greer when she started to speak and stalked from the room. With a dark look at all of them, Aradia darted after him.

"Gage—"

"Go away, Aradia."

"No."

He whirled, his eyes red and his fangs bared. He pinned her against the wall in an instant and punched it hard enough that his fist went through the drywall. "You do not want to mess with me right now. That was an unacceptable risk and you damn well know it!"

"Your definition of unacceptable and mine are obviously different." She pushed at his chest half-heartedly. "I'm not scared of you."

Gage crushed her against the wall, using the small bit of magic he had to push memories into her head. He gave her memories of him feeding on people, murdering them and enjoying the bloodshed. He showed her visions of himself with all of the women in Brazil months earlier. He let her see him in bed with them, writhing and groaning. He showed her images of him doing horrible, bloody things—things that had her shaking and looking at him with eyes full of fear.

"You should be. Everything you see, I could do to you. I could do it to you and not regret it. I could drink every drop of your blood and throw you aside like a rag doll. Fuck the magic, fuck what you think you feel, and fuck what you made me think I felt. This is the reality, Aradia. I am as much a monster as Javal. Stopping the end of the world is my priority. Anything else with you is nothing but a good roll in the hay. The sooner you stop pretending there's anything more here and realize that I'm in charge the better things will be." He snarled at her, and nearly winced when he saw her tremble. "Remember this—the next time you ask me to fuck you, this is what you get. I'm not a man. I'm not for you. I'm a vampire. A heartless, cold-blooded demon. I'm as likely to eat your soul as that magic you channeled. Do us both a favor, and leave me the hell alone. If you can't, or if you won't, just remember what Javal showed you. Because that's what I am. That's what I'll do to you."

When Gage stormed off that time, she didn't follow. Her knees gave out and she sank to the floor, caught somewhere between hurt and fear. Ten seconds later, Damon stepped into the hallway, lifting an eyebrow at the dent in the wall. He stared at her for several moments, trying to decide what to do and finally sat down on the floor next to her.

"Want to talk about it?"

"I don't need someone else telling me what to do or how to feel today."

He drew his knees up and turned his head to look at her. "Did he hurt you?"

She shook her head and stared stonily ahead. "No."

"If he laid a hand on you..."

She didn't let him finish the sentence. "He didn't."

Damon grimaced. "I can't believe I'm going to ask you this. Are you and Gage sleeping together?"

"No."

"You can tell me if you have. You'll get no judgment."

"We haven't." She took a breath, and her chest trembled with tears. "There's so much happening that I don't understand. So much that confuses me. It makes me question everything I thought I knew about these things."

"Is there anything I can do to help?"

Aradia smiled softly and turned her head so that she could meet his gaze. "With just my power, I would have lost today. I had to channel the black magic. Alaria is right, the price is high. I don't regret it. I would do it again. I'm going to need more power than I have if I'm going to defeat him."

"You'll have Greer and Alaria to help."

She shook her head. "We all have our roles. Greer is to Heal the wounded. You and Braxton will lead the army. Alaria is going to be the key to the final task. My part is to kill the warlock and make Javal weak enough for Gage to kill him."

Damon looked confused. "What does this have to do with Gage?"

"My mother came to me in a dream. She told me that to win, I have to access not only my magic as a witch, but my magic as a woman as well. That I have to know both sides of myself to access my full potential." Aradia cast her gaze downward. "She told me to give myself to him. That there is some sort of connection between us two that will make us stronger. Something about the six needing to act as one, and until Gage and I give in to our urges, we won't be able to fight together."

"Is all of this between you just magic?"

"Mother swears it's not. After today, I agree with her. There was this moment, this feeling in the clearing today that was just filled with magic. If there's magic, it's not outside, it's created by him and me. The feelings aren't false. I think he knows that, and I think it scares him."

"How does it make you feel?"

"Terrified. I felt as if that were the purpose for which I was born. To love him. In some way, this is as important as the battle."

"If it's an integral part, it may very well be. And why else would Javal be working so hard to keep it from happening?"

"That is my thought. Greer and Alaria spoke to me about it. Alaria thinks Gage feels the same as we do, only he has forced himself not to show it. She told me that if I don't avoid him to spare my heart, I should avoid him to spare his. Because he would have to watch me grow old and die, possibly love another and have children. He has nothing but eternity."

Damon slipped an arm around her shoulders. "If you want my advice, the choice you're facing is pretty simple. I know it feels complicated, but the way I see it, you have two choices. Do you spare yourself a lifetime of heartbreak? Or do you take a chance at love for the moment?"

Tears escaped her overly filled eyes, and she leaned on him. "I don't know what to do, Damon. I feel so much. I'm terrified that I'm wrong, and I'm terrified that I'm right. I'm scared we'll all die. I'm scared Javal will win and the world will end. I'm scared I won't be able to access enough power."

"Are you scared to be with him?"

Aradia buried her face in his neck. "And just as much, I'm scared not to be."

"Aradia, if you look inside your heart and you can say honestly that you think being with him would increase your chances of winning, and you can honestly say that you think you could, or do, love him, you owe it to yourself to do the most you can to have your happiness now. I know what he is. I know what he's done. He's not a monster. If you're this mixed up, I imagine he's just as bad. Only, he can't talk to people the way you do. Don't believe what he says when he's hurting. I know it was horrible, but anyone with eyes can tell he was scared he'd lost you. He feels. What, exactly, I don't know. I don't believe he would hurt you." He kissed the side of her head. "So what do you do?"

Aradia shook her head. "I wish I knew. I know what I want, and I know what I feel that I need, but I don't know how to get it."

"Is that him?"

Tearing up again, she nodded. "More than anything else."

"I think he shares your feelings, so go to him. When the time is right. Give him your heart. I don't think he'll treat it so callously as he treated your head today."

"You're a brash soul speaking to my daughter the way you did."

Gage glared at Graciela. "I'm not interested in another conversation with you about why I should take ruthless advantage of Aradia."

Graciela glared back at him and began walking along the stone path that trailed through the lush gardens she'd brought him to. "It's not for that reason that I am here, vampire, though it is something we will speak of. I refuse to let it go unsaid how completely disappointed I am in you for your handling of the situation. Aradia does not have the power that she needs. Can you not see that?" She threw out her arms in frustration. "Without embracing every aspect of herself, she cannot defeat Javal's warlock. She will die trying, and as she goes, so will the rest of you. You have a decision to make, Gage Windsor. She will come to you, her heart in her hands, and ask you to love her. If you turn her away, she will lose herself to the black side of magic, and you will win, but the price will be her life. If you accept her, and all she seeks to give you, if you allow her to explore her sexuality and her femininity with the one person in all the worlds that her soul aches for, then she will find a way to access enough of the power she was born with to defeat Javal without using an amount of black magic that will kill her."

Gage sighed deeply. "You're saying either way she's going to have to tap into the bad magic."

The Queen huffed as regally as one could possibly huff. "There is no such thing as bad magic. Magic, in and of itself, is neutral. It is what it is used for that makes the difference. Black magic has been manipulated over millennia until it wears a coat of evil, but at its core, it is still magic, and Aradia can manipulate it for a good purpose. It takes a lot of power and a lot of concentration to do that, and it will be one of the most difficult things she has ever done, but it must be done. Without full access to the power she needs, she won't be able to control the magic and it will take her over. It will kill her. Being with you will hurt her. It will break her heart and send her flying at the same time." She drew to a stop and placed a hand on his arm, her eyes swimming with emotion. "I know you'll leave at the end, and so does she, but this is a choice that both of you have to make. It's a cruel twist of fate, Gage, and I know it as such. Whether you like it or not, your souls were made to be together. Across time and space, you'll always feel a small part of her. For you, she'll never be completely gone. The choice you have to make is knowing what her choice will cost you. Her heart or her life. It's not as simple as wanting to do the right thing."

Frustrated and confused, Gage whirled to face her. "If this isn't why you're here, let's get to it then, shall we? I'm not interested in more reasons why I should bang her. It's not going to happen, so drop it already."

"If that's what you want. There are times throughout this that you will need to be instructed on what you will have to do. I have been charged with that task in addition to Gabriel and Michael. Your mind is the most open to me."

"You said that one other time. Why is that?"

"Because it is always easier to access the mind of an Immortal or another witch. After what happened with Aradia the last time, I felt it was the safest choice to come to you."

"What is this instruction?"

"You know Javal is working with a warlock named Garrick. What you do not know is that he is the oldest warlock alive. He was a wizened immortal by the time you were born. He feeds on human energy much in the way you feed on blood to stay alive. He's raising an army. Many vampires have joined with him, along with werewolves and other witches. All who wish to free Lucifer are falling in line. I know that you were aware you would face an army, but they have changed the playing field. They have already found a way to cross back in time. Javal went with them and found himself at the time of Atlantis."

"Michael warned us that might happen, but we didn't know they'd already found a way. There are two of him, then. One then and one now."

Graciela smiled. "Time is not a straight line, especially not when you're dealing with immortals. There are infinite versions of yourself throughout time. You can meet them and talk with them as much as you and I can talk. The biggest issue that this creates is that they are already preparing in two times. Here, to kill you before you return, and there, to kill you if you succeed here. There is no way to alter the path for you to return before you're called. You have to meld as a team first, and God won't allow the return to Atlantis until you're ready to succeed. There are more trials ahead of you. Javal will challenge Aradia again. I do not know how, and I do not know when. I do know that it will not be him, personally. He is sending his warlock after Aradia. Warlock against sorceress. It will pit her against the strongest warlock that I know of. It will not be easy, and it will not be won without a cost."

Gage sat down on a boulder. "We know some of that already. We know we're going back in time, we know that we're likely looking at Javal squared, and we know that there's going to be a lot more shit to wade through before we get there. What we don't know is how we can get to the point that we're ready to go back. There's only two months until the Solstice."

"You need to work together as a team. Use your contacts, Gage. They're trying to find the portal and destroy it to stop you from getting to Atlantis. I know if they manage to keep you in this time, they win. Atlantis will fall, and it will touch all the worlds." She sighed, her eyes clouded with worry. "I know I have made you angry with the way that I do things, with the way that I push, but I never want you to doubt that I love my daughter. I gave my life to bring her into this world, and I would do it again a thousand times. I do not do things to hurt Aradia. I do them knowing that her hurting is the foregone conclusion, and not because I enjoy her pain, but because of what will come from it. Children have to fall, they have to make mistakes and they eventually have to hurt. Aradia's task in life is much greater than that of most people. Her pain, by necessity, must also be greater. If I could spare her any of this, I would let them carve it out of my flesh. But there are no alternatives. She has to make difficult choices because she was born with the power to stop this. It is her gift and her curse. Without fulfilling her destiny here, she will die. The only choice is win or lose. It's not her heart I'm worried about, Gage. Her heart will heal. I'm worried about her life."

With that, Gage woke in his bed, heaving for breath he didn't need and covered in a cold sweat, Graciela's words echoing in his head. The weight of his decisions bearing down on him fiercely, he rose to dress. After pulling on slacks and a button down, he started down the stairs. He'd made it halfway down when his cell phone began to ring. He glanced at the number and swiped it to answer.

"Brad, how are you?"

The voice on the other end was terrified. "Gage, the demon fucker snatched me from the church. They've had me holed up for a couple of weeks. They're making me look at old scrolls and books, trying to find some reference to a portal. I don't have any clue what they want."

Gage was immediately serious. He dashed down the stairs and to his office, tapping keys on the computer as fast as he could. "Where are you? Which demon fucker?"

"I don't know where. We were in a car for a few hours. Had to be going south or west. The demon's name is Javal. There's some warlock here, too, and a whole bunch of underlings. They left one demon in here with me. I was able to exorcise him and got my phone back from him. I don't know what the hell to do."

"What you do is hold tight and do whatever they want. You don't put a toe out of line. You tell them whatever they want to know, and you do it as fast as you can. We're coming for you. Don't do anything heroic or anything that could possibly make them kill you. Don't worry about us. You give them everything you have, do you understand me?"

Dooley's voice was harried. "I understand."

"Delete the call log and put the phone back where you found it. Don't risk calling again. We'll be there soon."

Gage hung up without another word and looked at the results on his computer screen. A map spread across the screen with a red dot and a blinking address. He hovered the mouse over it and grunted softly. Miami.

Chapter Seventeen

"It's OBVIOUSLY a trap." Braxton bit off a piece of bacon and chewed thoughtfully. "Dooley could be possessed, he could be dead, or he could be working with them."

Alaria snorted. "He's not working with them. Regardless, we know it's a trap, and we're going to go anyway."

Gage cast a look around the room. "It's probably a trap. Unless they're really that stupid, which is possible. If Dooley was left alone with just one demon, it's possible he could have exorcised him. He's smart, and he's well-trained. He could have blessed any water they gave him, and the rest would have been relatively simple. The trick is that we can't all go. We know that they need to kill Aradia in order to remove the retaining wall and let Lucifer out. If it is a ploy, it's to lure her there."

Greer swirled her coffee around her cup as she mulled over the situation. "Why would they use someone Aradia doesn't even know to lure her out?"

Braxton nodded. "Good point. Regardless, we're not going to give them what we think they want. Aradia will stay here."

Aradia scowled. "Do I get a say in this?"

"No." Gage's voice left no room for an argument. "I know we can't be sure of what we're walking into. Brad Dooley is a good man, and if there's even a chance he's still alive, we have to go get him. Garrick and

Javal need to get their hands on Aradia. She's their key to the Gate. Another possibility is that they're trying to lure us away from here. We're safe as long as we're within the traps, and they can't get to us. If we have to leave, we're easier to take. We're going to have to split up."

Damon swallowed a gulp of coffee. "Greer and I are going. We're soldiers. That training will be valuable walking into what's going to be an ambush."

Alaria reached across the island and snagged a bite of Braxton's toast. "Brax and I need to go, too. We know Dooley better than the rest of you." She looked at Gage. "Why the hell did he call you, anyway? He barely knows you."

Gage shrugged. "That's another question we're going to need an answer to. It could have been part of the trick, or it could be that he called the landline, which I know he had, and it came through to my cell." He sipped his blood. "Aradia can't stay here alone. She doesn't know how to use half the technology, and the worst thing to do is leave the one they need the most with the least protection."

Greer cocked one eyebrow. "Four go, two stay. You stay here with her, Gage. Get some of your fancy private security to patrol the grounds, and you two stay in the house until we get back."

Gage struggled to think of another option before he assented. "That's the only way to work it. I'll get the jet ready for you. Get packed."

Two hours later, Damon, Greer, Alaria, and Braxton were securely buckled into seats on Gage's private jet and taking off toward Florida. Greer waited until the plane was safely in the air before she unsnapped her belt and unrolled the plans of the building Gage had determined Father Dooley was being held in.

"Okay, from what I can tell, this is a warehouse near the docks, which is perfect as far as what they need it for. I don't think for a second that Javal and Garrick are still there. I'm sure they have plenty of man power there, and I'm sure they were there, but my read of the situation is that it isn't a trap. I think Brad Dooley is one of the only Biblical mythology scholars alive, and they're looking for something that they think he can help them find. Simple as that." She glanced up when no one responded. "I know you don't agree with me, but that's my take."

Braxton lifted his shoulder. "We know that they're looking for another Hell Gate. One we don't think the Angels know about. If that's what this is about, then there's a good chance that you're right and it has nothing to do with us. Why they have him doesn't change what we're doing."

She pointed to an area on the plans. "Here is the main entrance, which is at the end of the warehouse area here by the coast. It's isolated, and there's only one road in. I think we're going to have to have multiple escape routes, which is going to mean planting a car close, but out of their detection range, and coming at it by boat. We can dock a couple slips up and swim over. I'm sure Gage has enough money to get us everything we need to do that." She slid her finger along the plans and jabbed it at another area. "From these renderings, we can see that the back portion of the warehouse is divided up into several rooms. Gage's contacts report that there were permits issued for some construction there recently. We think that means they were reinforcing an area to hold Dooley, but we can't be sure."

Alaria's brow creased. "Why would they apply for construction permits?"

Braxton chuckled. "You'd be surprised how many politicians are actually demons. With something like this, the last thing they would want is interference from the authorities. Better to have some minion wade through red tape and do it on the up and up. It takes less time than disposing of bodies, and the risk of exposing the operation is less. It's smart." He gestured to Greer. "Go on."

She smiled and moved her finger to another area. "My suggestion is that we each go in different entrances. It's a huge warehouse, and there are more than forty rows and thirty rooms. It's tens of thousands of square feet. It's riskier, yes, but sticking together, or even being in pairs, poses its own set of risks, and this way, we'll be quicker. We can stay in touch via headsets. If we cover all four entrances, we can spread out and cover the warehouse quicker." She pointed to a cluster of rooms. "I think it's the most likely Dooley is going to be back here, so Braxton, you head straight there. He knows you better and trusts you." She pointed to another area. "It looks like these are the offices, which is where we're the most likely to get information. Alaria, I think you should head there and see if you can find out what they're up to and what they know."

Alaria shook her head. "This is a rescue mission only. We don't have time to go on an information search, and the odds that they've left anything there for us to find are slim to none."

"Only if it's a trap, which I don't think it is." Greer pointed again. "I think these are minions on a mission for Javal and Garrick. This might be a good chance to get ahead of them and find out what they're up to. It's a risk, but I think the reward is worth it."

Braxton made a noise in his throat as he considered the situation. "I agree. We'll play it that way." He bent over the plans. "That covers the West and North entrances. I assume the two of you will take South and East?"

Greer nodded. "I'm going to take East. There's a ladder that looks like it goes up to a catwalk and some beams. I can keep an eye on everyone from up there, move quicker than I could on the ground, and it'll give me the high ground to pick off demons. With a good rifle and a silencer, I could do some real damage from up there."

Damon placed his index finger on the South side of the plans. "This is the dock entrance. I'll sweep inward and make sure the retreat is clear. If I get into trouble, I'll make as much noise as I can and draw them out after me. The boat'll be close, and I can be gone before they could catch me."

Braxton sat back and folded his hands. "It's a solid plan. I'll call Gage and let him know what we need. By the time we get in, it'll be mid-morning in Miami. That'll give us enough time to plant the getaway car and load up on supplies. With any luck, we'll be on our way home with Father Dooley in thirty-six hours."

Alaria stood and went to the kitchenette for a can of soda. "We'll have to have the plane fueled and waiting on the runway. Once we do this we have to get back as soon as we can. We'll also need to have someplace safe to take Dooley to. We can't very well leave him at the chapel in Philly and expect that he'll be fine. They'll go back for him, and this time, they'll kill him."

"You're right. I'll call in some favors with some Hunters in South America. They have a compound down there, and they're doing pretty well against the demons right now. Having a priest like Dooley on site might give them a boost, and it'll keep him safe." Braxton stood and opened the fridge. "We've got a sixteen hour flight, boys and girls. We've got a damn good plan, and I'm going to make arrangements for some supplies, a hotel to stay at tomorrow while we wait, and flights for Dooley." He gestured to the television anchored to one wall of the plane. "I suggest you all enjoy the time off. We'll be plenty busy when we land."

Greer looked at Alaria. "What do you want to bet Gage and Aradia do it before we get back?"

Alaria dropped down onto the couch. "God, I hope so. Aradia apparently has to have sex to finish off Garrick, no pun intended, and Gage has been trying not to fuck her since the second he laid eyes on her. It would do them both some good."

Damon looked confused. "Why in the world would it make a difference if the two of them bang?"

Greer chuckled. "Apparently, Aradia can only defeat Javal and Garrick if she unlocks her abilities as a woman as well as a witch. It's basically saying that she's got two sides and she has to use them both to win."

"Why Gage though? Can't we just take her out to a bar and teach her how to pick up guys?" He wiggled his eyebrows. "Or rent her a porn and buy a vibrator?"

Alaria giggled. "I don't think it works like that. According to Graciela, they're made for each other. At this point, I don't think that we should question it. We're just going to have to let them figure it out for themselves."

Damon flipped though TV channels and settled on a movie as Braxton slipped back into the office. "Sounds like it might be good that we're leaving them alone again."

Greer curled up against his side and laid her head on his shoulder. "I hope it works out. I'd like to see us all get some happiness."

Alaria snorted. "The only thing we're going to get is a temporary reprieve from death. I still don't think we're all going to survive this third task, and the life the rest of us get after it's done isn't likely to be worth living. I don't believe for a second that the third job is going to rid the Earth of demons forever. The Choosing was supposed to do that, and it obviously didn't work. It's another stopgap measure. The only end for this is going to be the Apocalypse. Lucifer is always going to find a way out. He is always going to find a way around the rules, and there is nothing that we can do about it."

Braxton scoffed from the desk. "You're certainly pessimistic. If that's the way you feel, why didn't you ask for your wings back?"

She glared at him. "At least this way I get a choice in things. That's what I wanted. Besides, I didn't know what Lucifer was up to. I had no idea about the back-up plan. If I'd known, I'd have done something to sabotage it before I became human."

Greer cleared her throat. "Let's just focus on today. We need to get Father Dooley back and we need to finish this task. It's a fucking warlock and a demon. We can handle that. After we're done with this one, then we'll worry about the next. Don't borrow trouble."

Conversation was sparse for most of the day. They touched down in London to refuel and break before the long flight over the Atlantic. There would be another layover in Maine before the last leg to Florida. They watched several movies, went over the plan multiple times, and chatted briefly for most of the day. Once the sky blackened, Damon rose from his seat and glanced toward the first bedroom.

"I think I'm going to call it a night." He looked at Greer. "Are you staying up or coming with me?"

Greer yawned and stretched. "It's only seven hours until we hit Maine. Might as well log a few hours of sleep before we get there. God knows the next opportunity will probably be on the flight back."

She held out her hand and let Damon pull her to her feet. She tossed a careless "goodnight" back to Braxton and Alaria before following Damon into the bedroom and closing the door. They changed into pajamas silently and slipped beneath the covers. Neither spoke until they heard the television change stations to another movie. Whoever was in control of the remote increased the volume. Damon rolled onto his side and reached out to touch Greer's face.

"What do you want to do once all of this is over?"

She laid her hand over his. "If Alaria is right, it's never going to be over."

"I have to believe we'll get through everything. We're going to get to live a good life, Greer. That's the whole point of coming back and doing this. We're going to make it work."

Greer leaned forward to press her mouth to his gently. "I hope so. We've got a lot to get through before the end of this task, let alone the third. We'll manage. That's what we do. When this is all over, we'll do whatever we need to do to make sure that it stays over. Whatever comes of it, we'll do it together."

Damon smiled in the dark. "That's how we've done everything else."

She rolled onto her other side and shimmied over to press her body against his. "I love you. No matter what, we're in this together."

He slipped his arms around her and settled his chin into the curve of her neck. "What do you want to do when this is over? If you could have anything in the world, what would you want to do?"

She sighed deeply and smiled. "I want to see the world. I want to lay on a beach and drink fruity drinks and not worry about getting attacked by werewolves. I want to get married and have babies and not worry about whether or not I'll live long enough to raise them."

Damon was silent for several seconds. "I want to marry you and watch you grow our babies." He kissed her shoulder. "We have to believe that we'll get there, Greer. If we don't, there's no reason to keep fighting."

"It's hard to imagine a world where we won't have to keep doing this over and over."

"We'll make it one." He squeezed her fingers tightly. "Marry me. If we get through this tomorrow, marry me. We'll go to Glasgow. We'll spend a night in a fancy hotel and have crazy sex all night. We can't stop living just because this is going on. We have to make a world worth living in, Greer. We can start by not letting them take away our happiness. What d'ya say? Will you marry me?"

Greer spent ten seconds fighting through the flood of emotions that swept over her. Her eyes filled with tears and she struggled against the urge to pretend she hadn't heard him. "I want to. More than anything else, I want to." She pressed her face into his arm. "Okay, let's do it." She rolled over to face him. "You're right. We have to keep living." She kissed him. "Let's get married."

Damon wrapped his arms around her and crushed her to him. "I will make sure we get through this, Greer. We'll have the life we want. We're going to get through this, and we're going to make sure we have a world worth living in." He kissed her deeply. "I promise I'll buy you a ring someday." He laughed. "I fully believe that when this is all over, we'll have jobs and a house and kids just like everybody else. That's the life I want."

She slid her arms around his neck. "I don't need it. I don't even really want one. I've only ever wanted you."

Damon slipped his hands under her shirt and worked it over her head. "You've got me." He kissed her collarbone and lowered her pajama bottoms. "Think you can be quiet?"

Greer giggled and tugged his shirt over his head. "I'll give it a try." Her hands wiggled into his boxers and wrapped around him. "You're normally the noisy one."

He rolled her beneath him and pinned her hands over her head. "With what I'm about to do to you, you're the one who's going to want to make noise."

She grinned and relaxed into the pillows. "Oh yeah?"

"Yeah."

She lifted her hips to allow him to remove her panties. She left her hands over her head, even though he was no longer holding them. "Then you'd better get started, Casanova."

Chapter Eighteen

Braxton was the only one who had been out on a boat, which some-how made him qualified to drive it. He shook his head and gritted his teeth as he turned the wheel on the speedboat and turned it toward the docks. Getting the damn thing out into the ocean had been the easy part. It was getting it close enough to the slip to moor without hitting it that was going to be the trick.

He throttled down and let the boat slow to a drift. When it floated close to the dock, he held up a hand and gestured to Damon, who jumped out and tethered the boat to the wooden pole sticking out of the shallow water. He wrapped the rope several times and tied a knot to secure it. Greer tossed out his pack and rifle before climbing out her-self. She waited until Alaria and Braxton were on the dock before she spoke, her voice muffled.

"From what I can tell, there are only a few guards. I want the three of you to hang back here, near the dock. I'm going to circle the building and pick them off." She held up her hand when Braxton started to speak. "Don't even bother trying to talk me out of it. You can ask Da-mon, this is my specialty."

"She's the one we sent in when we needed something done quickly and quietly. With our link, I'll know if she's in trouble before she could radio us. Believe me, I wouldn't be letting her go in if I had a doubt that she was the best person for the job." Damon grinned. "I know you're a Warrior, Brax, and that you're a kickass Devil, Alaria, but this is what we did. We were soldiers—mercenaries. We'll get you in and out."

Alaria nodded slowly. "Let's just get it done. If she's the quickest and will kill all the fucking demons, then I say we let her go. The building is within my teleportation range if she gets into trouble."

Greer checked her scope and made sure there was a bullet in the chamber of her gun. She handed it to Damon to stoop and check her pistol before doing another inventory of her pack. Satisfied, she slipped her arms through the straps and buckled it across her chest. She grinned at Damon as she took her weapon back.

"Once I've taken care of the outside, I'll radio back. You each take your assigned entrance. Once we're in, we need to be out in fifteen minutes. If we have to scramble, we rendezvous at the hotel."

Greer took off at a brisk jog, fading into the blackness, her black fatigues blending into the night. She reached the chain link fence surrounding the warehouse and dropped to her stomach. She unzipped her pack and withdrew a second clip, tucking it into the pocket of her vest before pulling out a pair of bolt cutters.

She worked from the bottom up, cutting through only as much fence as necessary to allow her to shimmy underneath it. She pressed her body tight to the metal and peered at the roof. She lifted her rifle to her shoulder and pressed her eye to the scope, scanning the building for guards.

She counted four and looked between them half a dozen times before deciding which to kill first. She leveled the barrel and gripped the stock with her right hand, her left index finger lightly touching the trigger. She judged the distance at eighty yards and held her breath to steady her aim before she squeezed the trigger.

The gunshot sounded like little more than a door closing, and at the distance the demons were, she wondered if any of them even heard the whisper of it. The demon at which she aimed dropped to the floor with a noise she could not hear. She efficiently discharged the shell and loaded another, the sound of the receiver and slide louder than the one the gunshot had produced. She aimed again, took a breath and fired, the second demon dropping the same way the first had.

Once four shots had been fired, she shouldered her weapon and reached for the radio on her shoulder. "West entrance is clear. I'm moving to the South."

She turned off the radio before a response could come through and skittered along the fence line until she rounded the corner of the building and again counted demons. Seven shots later, she was racing for the third side. Sweat ran down her back and her stomach jumped with nerves. There were only three on the East side and she dispensed of them quickly. She spoke into the radio tersely before racing along the fence to the final side.

No demons. She scanned the roofline several times before reaching for the radio. "We're all clear. Move in. I'm going in now. I'll take the high ground and provide cover fire."

Greer lowered the volume on the radio and darted across the grass to the door. She used her bolt cutters to break the padlock and slipped inside. She eased the door shut behind herself and pressed against it for a moment, her eyes darting from side to side. She could hear voices in the distance, but there was no one within sight. She knew that as soon as she had to fire, she would draw the attention of every demon in the building. She didn't have the advantage of distance inside the building. The gunshots would echo.

She skirted the rows of shelving units and found the ladder leading up to the catwalk. She slung her rifle over her shoulder and ascended the steps. Once she was up top, she had a view of almost the entire warehouse and the advantage of being shielded by the great black beams.

Alaria came in first. Greer watched the other woman slip in through the big double doors and slide them shut almost noiselessly. Alaria looked both directions before striding into the office and closing the door. There was a muffled shout and the scraping of a chair moving back before a brief struggle and a thump.

Greer lifted her rifle and anchored it tightly to her shoulder. She heard footsteps rapidly approaching and she leveled the barrel of the gun, focusing it on the door to the office. Three demons rounded the corner at full speed. Greer fired rapidly, her bullets striking the demons before they reached the door.

In the warehouse, even the silencer couldn't muffle the sound of the shots completely. They rang through the air, leaving no doubt as to their origin. Shouts sounded from inside some of the rooms, and demons flooded the main floor of the warehouse. Out of the corner of her eye, she saw Braxton slide in through the side door and disappear down the hall leading to the rooms where they thought Dooley was being held.

Greer fired rapidly. She calmly exchanged her empty clip for a full one and resumed pulling the trigger. Damon raced from the other side of the building and joined Alaria in the fight. He hacked through the crowd viciously, and Alaria used her whip to beat them back. Greer continued to fire, one bullet after another finding its mark. Blood coated the walls and the floor.

Damon slammed his back against Alaria's and glanced over his shoulder as the demons pressed in against them. "You okay?"

Alaria nodded. "Let's get these fuckers."

Together, they worked their way through the throng. Alaria flicked her wrist and wrapped her whip around the throat of one demon and dragged it close to her so that she could slash its throat with her knife.

She stepped forward to go after another, and slipped in a pool of blood, hitting the ground hard. Before she could even take a breath, four demons were on top of her. She hacked at them with her dagger, grunting when an elbow rammed into her gut and swearing when one of them managed to punch her in the face.

Damon heaved one off of the pile, pressing his gun to its head and pulling the trigger. He slammed his elbow back, cramming it into the face of the demon coming over his shoulder. Both knew Greer was methodically working her way through the crowd, but they were overwhelmed with demons.

Alaria drove her knife into the eye of another demon and managed to force herself to her knees. A female demon fell on top of her, forcing her down onto her stomach. She struggled and kicked, but was unable to free herself. She heard Damon swear and the female was yanked off of her.

Damon extended his hand and heaved her to her feet, dragging her close to him as he fired. The gun clicked twice, signaling that it was out of ammo. Tossing it aside, he drew his buck knife from his belt and began slashing.

Greer saw Braxton drag a man wearing a white collar from one of the back rooms and out the door. She reached out with her mind and swam along the tether that connected her to Damon, slipping inside his head with ease.

"Brax has Dooley. Let's get out of here."

"Little busy here, babe. I can't exactly just walk away."

Greer fired four more times, dropping three more demons. She dropped out the second clip and bent to withdraw a third from her bag before snapping it into place and continuing her assault on the demons. She shot what she hoped was the last three, and descended the ladder quickly.

Damon jogged over to the ladder and lifted her down off of the last few steps. Alaria offered a tight smile, and they all ran toward the back door that Braxton had exited through. Greer led them to the hole in the fence and held it back while the other two slipped underneath. They didn't stop to look back at the warehouse before running in the direction of the dock.

Ten minutes later, Damon pushed the boat away from the dock and jumped onto it as Braxton turned the key to start the engine. He jammed the throttle into position and cranked the wheel away from the piers. No one said a word until the coast was completely out of sight and the GPS was directing them back toward the dock near their hotel.

Braxton whistled under his breath. "I don't think any of us were expecting there to be a fucking army of demons inside that building. I think I killed ten on my way down that hall."

Damon laughed. "Ten? Dude, there were probably fifty in there. Not to mention the ones Greer picked off before we even went in. How many did you kill, babe?"

Greer opened the cooler under the seat and tossed the Priest a bottle of water. "I don't keep track. A hell of a lot more than any of the rest of you is all I know." She twisted the cap off a second bottle and drank deeply before leaning forward and offering Dooley her hand. "I'm Greer Dawson. This is Damon Mackenzie. Are you hurt?"

Dooley shook his head. "They didn't hurt me."

Alaria crossed her legs. "What the hell did they have you looking for?"

"A second Hell Gate. The one that was used to put Lucifer down there. It's the only Gate through which he can be freed."

Braxton looked over his shoulder. "We knew they were looking for another Gate. We were operating under the assumption that it was located in Atlantis."

Dooley nodded. "They mentioned that. Blew my mind to find out Atlantis is actually a real place. The wizard thinks that the Gate always has to exist and that since Atlantis is no more, it has to be somewhere. He wanted me to find it, thinking there has to be some reference to it somewhere."

Braxton eased the throttle back and checked the GPS to make sure of their course. "What did you find out?"

"That there are a lot of references to a Hell Gate and not a lot of references to one through which only Lucifer can come. I didn't give them the answers they were looking for because I couldn't find them."

Greer polished off the bottle of water and dragged her hand across her mouth. "Couldn't find it at all, or didn't find it yet?"

"I couldn't find it based on what they had given me up until the point that you burst in to rescue me." Dooley took another drink. "If they gave me something with the right information, I'd be able to tell."

Alaria nudged her backpack toward Dooley with her foot. "I emptied out their files before we took off. Every paper they had, we now have."

Dooley unzipped the bag, looked at the mass of loose paper, and sighed. "I suppose it's entirely too much to hope that it's in any sort of order."

Alaria chuckled. "I crammed it in as fast as I could. There might be some pages that're in order, but probably not many." She patted his arm. "It'll give you something to do while you're in hiding."

Braxton angled the boat in toward the dock. "End of the line, kids. Father, your ride is waiting at the dock. You're heading to South America and some friends of mine. You'll be safe there. Gage's private jet is waiting for you at the airport now. It'll go straight there. From there, you'll be guarded by Warriors until this is over. If you come up with anything useful, call me and we'll go from there."

Dooley clutched the bag to his chest. "If I find anything at all, I'll call." He accepted Damon's hand to help him climb out of the boat. "Thank you all for coming to get me." He brushed crusted salt from his robe. "I don't even hold all the anti-demon tests against you." He shook hands with each of them.

Braxton led the Priest to the car and spoke briefly with the driver, who was a dark man in a black suit. There was a shotgun lying on the seat next to him, and a huge handgun in a holster on his hip. Dooley was ushered into the back, and the driver sped out of the parking lot. Braxton put his hands on his hips and watched until the car was out of sight before turning to the other three.

"Our car is almost a mile inland from here. I stashed us clothes in those bathrooms." He pointed to a building. "We'll change out of the army gear, dump it a few blocks over, then reverse course and get to the hotel." He shot a pointed look at Alaria. "Given that hotels aren't as safe as Gage's estate, we're still going to be in the one big suite we spent the day in. The jet will be back tomorrow night, and we'll leave in about thirty hours." He fished out his phone and swiped the screen to open up the dial pad. "I'll call Gage and let him and Aradia know we'll be on our way back home soon."

Chapter Nineteen

GAGE CLICKED off the phone and stepped into the kitchen. Aradia stood at the stove cooking. She wore a light blue camisole and jeans, her feet were bare, and she had her hair hanging down her back in damp ropes. He caught himself studying the delicate lines of her back and shook his head, his good mood already darkening.

"Braxton just called."

Aradia jumped when he spoke, her hand flying to her throat. She whirled and pressed herself against the stove. "Were they successful in their rescue of the priest?"

He stretched to retrieve a mug from the cabinet. "They got him. He's on my jet, headed to South America. They raided the files of the demons there and Dooley is taking all of that with him to continue the work the demons had him doing, only for us instead of them." He gestured to the cutting board and vegetables on the counter. "What're you making?"

Aradia glanced back at the pan and squealed when she saw black smoke rising from it. She grabbed the skillet from the burner and rushed to the sink, tripping on the rug and stumbling. Her grip on the handle slipped, and she dropped the pan on her foot, sending eggs everywhere. She bent to retrieve it, burning her fingers on the scalding metal as she did so.

Calmly, Gage stepped around her and took the skillet, tossing it carelessly into the sink. He took her hand in his and turned it over, examining her fingers, which were red and singed. Before he could talk himself out of it, he lifted her hand to his mouth and pressed his lips to each one. Aradia sucked in a breath and held it.

"Is your foot hurt?"

Though it burned from the contact with the egg, Aradia shook her head. "No."

Gage wrapped his hand around hers and took half a step closer to her. "There's some ointment in the medicine cabinet upstairs. Would you like me to put some on your fingers?"

Aradia smiled. "I can heal that much, Gage. A scalded finger takes only the magic of the weakest kitchen witch." She looked down at her hands and closed her eyes. Her fingertips glowed for a moment, and the skin faded back to pink, the blisters disappearing. She shifted her eyes back to his, allowing her gaze to trail over the planes and curves of his face before settling on the carved line of his mouth.

She lifted her other hand and smoothed a lock of raven hair away from his forehead. His skin was cool, and she shivered at the jolt she got from touching him. When he didn't pull away, she rose onto her tiptoes and pressed her mouth to his in a gentle kiss.

The vision swept them away. Aradia saw herself naked. She walked to Gage, going willingly into his arms. She watched him lower her to the mattress and press her into it with his body. She felt him probe and slide into her. She saw her body respond, watched herself wrap her legs around him.

Blood poured from the ceiling and ran down the walls. It coated the floor and rained down on them. Candles flickered on the dressers innocuously before leaping out of their glass prisons and igniting the entire room. She saw them reflected in Gage's eyes as he hammered into her, the pleasure turning to pain.

She thrashed and struggled on the bed, but he was too big and he held her down. His face twisted from the handsome visage she knew into one of a monster. His fangs descended and his eyes turned red. He gripped her chin with his hand and yanked her neck to the side, exposing it to his bite.

Pain shot through her as his fangs pierced her skin and he hungrily sucked blood from her body. She screamed and pushed at his shoulders. He lapped her skin with his tongue and ripped flesh from her, chewing hungrily. When he lifted his head, it was no longer Gage, but the twisted features of Javal.

Aradia was shaken from the vision when her bottom collided with the hard tile floor. Her hands flew to her neck and she ran them over her skin, feeling for wounds. Gage was flattened against the fridge, his expression belying the shock and horror he felt at what they had experienced. She gaped at him, her eyes showing her fear. He shook his head and wiped his hand over his mouth.

"It wasn't real. It wasn't a dream. Nothing came through into reality."

She ran her fingertips over her face. "I know. That was worse than any of the others." She accepted the hand he held out to help her up and climbed to her feet. "Even though it was not real, it has taken my appetite from me."

He stepped back from her and put the island between them. "I don't blame you. I don't think I would be very hungry after having my throat torn out, either."

She lifted her gaze to his. "It wasn't you that did that, and it was not I who experienced it. I don't know if it was a true vision or a memory from some other woman pushed upon me, but I know without question that you are not capable of inflicting such pain upon me."

Gage reached for his cup of blood. "I'm going to go work for a while. The others will be back the day after tomorrow."

Aradia was again left alone.

Aradia sat on the edge of the bathtub, rubbing lotion into her legs. The water from her bath was still draining, and she had a towel wrapped both around her body and her hair. She stood to unfasten the towel around her body and began to massage lotion into her torso and arms. She pressed her fingers to her neck where she'd felt Javal rip and sighed in relief when it was still intact.

Gage hadn't come back out of his office since leaving her in the kitchen. He had spent the whole day in there, not coming out until after she'd retired to her own room to bathe before bed. Aradia had spent the entire day downstairs and had not seen him even once. She'd cooked dinner, eaten alone, and then gone up to her room for bed. It was once she'd been laying on top of her blankets that she'd begun thinking about Gage, and the situation they'd found themselves in.

The one thing she knew for certain was that there was something between them, and until they explored it, they weren't going to be able to defeat Javal and Garrick. It had also become glaringly obvious that Gage was not going to make the first move, which left it up to her. While her experience in romantic things was negligible, she'd come to realize that there was no other choice. If she wanted Gage, she was going to have to go get him.

She absently rubbed her hair with the towel while mulling over the contents of her underwear drawer and all of the scraps of lace the woman from the shop in Las Vegas had filled it with. Her hair flowed over her shoulders in wet cords and she picked up the blow dryer to dry it. She hadn't intended on bathing twice in one day, but seduction seemed to require it.

She finished her hair and padded into her room, sitting on the bed and staring at the dresser, an internal battle raging as she struggled against her fears. Sighing, she stood up, went to the dresser, and combed through the drawers, looking for something appropriate. Finding nothing, she reached for her robe—an emerald green satin garment that flowed to her ankles and tied at her waist. Nerves making her stomach flutter but her mind made up, she squared her shoulders and headed up to Gage's private quarters on the third floor.

She took the stairs slowly and paced in front of the door for five minutes before working up the courage to knock on it. She knew that Gage could hear every step she took from inside, but even that knowledge hadn't been enough to make her knock sooner. When she finally managed to knock on the door, he opened it within a heartbeat, assuring her that he had been aware of her presence and had been waiting for her to strike the door with her hand.

He leaned against the door, blocking her entry. He lifted his eyebrows and studied her carefully before speaking. "Need something?"

Aradia pushed past him into the room and went straight to the decanter and set of glasses he kept on top of the dresser. She poured a generous three fingers of whiskey into the glass, swallowed it in one gulp, and set the glass down with a sharp clink. Amused, Gage turned around and continued to lean against the doorway.

"Well hello, Aradia, come on in. Can I offer you a drink?"

Instantly humiliated, Aradia flushed bright red. "I'm sorry. I—well, um." She took a deep breath. "Close the door, Gage. There's something

I need to talk to you about."

Gage heard the fear in her voice and knew that it was important. He closed the door softly and leaned against it, unwilling to get too close to her. "What's wrong?"

"Can you come over here?" She waited until he'd crossed the room and stood a foot from her. She took a deep breath. "I can't do this anymore. I can't tiptoe around you, never knowing what's happening or what you're feeling, or what I'm feeling. I know that blood bond thing is coloring it, but it was happening before that, and there's not one thing that either of us can do about it. I don't know why it's happening, or if it will last, or if it's us, or Javal, or my mother, or some combination of all of those things. What I do know is that I can't stop thinking about you. Every time we're in the same room, I can barely breathe for feeling all these things I'm feeling, and I can't go one more day without knowing." She took a gulping breath. "I know the visions are scary. They terrify me. I'm not sure if this will make things better or worse, or make no difference at all, but I know what I want, and I'm pretty sure I know what you want, and I'm sick of neither of us being able to have it." Hands shaking, she untied her robe and let it float to the floor, leaving her body completely bare and exposed to his gaze. "Here I am. I want you, Gage. I want to know what it's like. I want you to show me how to be a woman. I want to feel you. I want to be yours. If you want it to, I am standing here, and I am asking you to take me to your bed and make love with me."

His stomach clenched in a tight knot, Gage held himself rigid. He forced himself to take three deliberate steps backward. "Aradia, you have about ten seconds to put that robe on and get out of here. If you don't, I won't be held responsible for what I do."

Her heart pounding in her chest, Aradia shook her head. "I'm not leaving." She extended her hand toward him. "You're going to have to ask me to leave. If you want me to go, tell me." She took a quivering breath. "If you want me to stay, I'm here, and I'm yours."

Gage closed his eyes tightly and tried to force the vision of her naked body from his mind. He opened them slowly, not sure if he hoped she was still naked or had covered herself. When he saw that she was still bare, he cursed under his breath and strode across the room until he was so close to her that her breath caressed his face.

"Sweet Mary Mother of Jesus, forgive me for the things I am about to do."

He laid his hands on her hips and inhaled the scent of her skin. He slid one hand down her body until he wrapped one arm around her waist and the other behind her knees and lifted her into his arms. He carried her across the room to the expanse of his bed, bending his knees and lowering her onto the mattress.

"There's not a thing in the world that's going to stop me this time. You had best make sure that you are ready for this."

Aradia reached up and laid her palm against his cheek. "I think I was born for this."

Unreasonably emotional, Gage lowered his mouth to hers, taking it in a gentle kiss. When she came alive under him, all remnants of logic left him. All that was left was Aradia, and he was helpless to do anything except love her.

Where he had been frenzied and desperate for her in the grotto, he was determined now to take his time. He wanted to explore every inch of her body with both his hands and his mouth. He slipped his tongue into her mouth, hers lifting to tangle with it.

Aradia hesitantly lifted her hands to lay on his face as she returned his kiss. She slid her arms around his neck and feverishly pressed her body against his. Unfamiliar feelings pooled deep within her and she dug her fingers into his back. Gage lifted his head and gently kissed her nose before shifting slightly to lay his mouth against her neck.

His tongue and teeth sent bolts of electricity straight to her center and she gasped, desperate for breath as he kissed her. He slipped further down, trailing his mouth over her skin. He scraped his teeth over the rise of her breast and rose to his knees, taking the mounds of flesh in his hands.

Aradia's eyes were clouded with desire, and her skin flushed red when he dragged his fingers over her nipples. He kneaded her gently, the points of her nipples pressing into his palms. He leaned down and touched the tip of his tongue to her nipple, the cool appendage a delicious contrast to the heat being produced by her body.

He sucked it into his mouth, rolling the bead between his teeth and rubbing it with his tongue. He released it and blew cool air over her warm skin, watching chill bumps rise on her skin before licking her nipple again, all the while massaging her other breast with his hand and fingers.

Slowly and carefully so he didn't hurt her, he slipped one long finger between the folds of her body, and she gasped at the intrusion. Her fingers fisted in the sheets, and her hips lifted against his hand, acting of their own volition. He stroked her nipple with his tongue, stroking her at the same time. He pressed his thumb against her clitoris and rubbed it gently. Her breath caught in her chest and whooshed out in a gasp before she sucked in another lungful.

Gage kissed the underside of her breast and nuzzled her nipple with his nose, tickling her before he slid down his body. He gripped her hips with his hands and nosed her legs apart. He inhaled deeply, taking in the scent of her. It flooded his nostrils, earthy and sweet. He closed his eyes, allowing himself to revel in it for a moment.

He parted her with his fingers and stroked her with his tongue. Her body leaped, jerking off the bed. Her hips writhed from unfamiliar sensation, and she groaned softly. He dipped his tongue inside, stabbing into her with it. The softness of it, along with the pressure from his thumb against her was too much to handle. Aradia's skin dampened with sweat and she squeezed her eyes closed. Something built within her, unfamiliar and overwhelming. She grabbed at Gage's hair, alternating between begging him to stop and to keep going.

He held her hips snugly and continued his assault upon her. Her moans became breathy and loud and her hips came off the bed. He shifted upward an inch and rubbed his tongue over the nub of her clit. She gripped the sheets in her hands, pulling at them and crying out as an orgasm rolled through her body. Her toes curled under and her back arched, thrusting her breasts up at him in an offering.

Grinning, Gage spared a moment to wipe his mouth before sliding up her body and taking her mouth again. She curled into him, seeking contact and comfort in the aftermath of climax, and he wrapped his arms around her, giving her both. When she lifted her face and touched her mouth to his in a deep, searching kiss, he rolled her onto her back once again and rose above her.

Satisfied that she was as ready for the act of penetration as he could make her, Gage stood long enough to remove his clothes before sliding back into the bed, laying on his side next to her. Her eyes were still clouded by desire and pleasure, and she rolled to face him, pressing her chest to his, her fingers timidly reaching out to explore his body. They trailed over the muscles in his chest, over his abdomen. She wrapped her arms around him and ran her palms down his back, brave enough to skim them over his ass. When they curled around him, stroking him gently, it was all he could do to hold still. He was hard and thick, and his erection quivered beneath her touch. Gaining courage, she slid her hand up and back down, her other hand sliding around his head to pull him down for a kiss.

Unable to take it, Gage folded his fingers over hers, easing them up his body to lay on his chest. Confused, she drew back. "Did I do something wrong?"

Gage gathered her close, kissing her deeply. "God, no, baby. You could never do anything wrong." He nudged her onto her back. "The problem is that it felt too good. Everything about you is too good." Gently, he slid between her thighs, using one hand to lift her hips, the other one stroking her cheek. "This is probably going to hurt. If you let me, I can take away the pain, but I won't do it without you knowing."

Gage hoped that she would allow him to use the Thrall. It was a talent most old vampires possessed that allowed them to hypnotize humans for enough time to feed. It took away pain and made the process of feeding more pleasant for all involved. In sex, he would use it to take away the discomfort of first penetration if she allowed it.

Aradia shook her head. "No. I want to feel this. I want to feel you."

She bent her knees, lifting her hips to press against his, the head of his penis pressing against the soft folds of her body. Gage nodded, and in one smooth stroke, buried himself inside her, absorbing her cry of shock and pain with his mouth. In that instant, they both saw the same scene: them, standing on the stairs in Gage's Las Vegas penthouse, reeling from the vision of them in bed. Gage buried his face in her neck, straining to hold himself still.

After several beats, he lifted his head and gazed down at her, his eyes bright with emotion. "It was always going to end up this way, wasn't it?" He nuzzled her neck. "We were always going to do this."

Aradia stroked his back. "There's no other way it could have ended up." She groaned as she shifted. "Make love to me, Gage. Just like we saw the first time we met. Make me yours."

Gage slid almost completely out of her before pushing back in fully, stretching her body to accommodate him and making them both groan. "As you wish."

He stroked into her over and over, his body cooler than hers, the contrast creating delicious friction on her skin. Her legs lifted to wrap around his hips, her fingernails bit into his back, and she tossed her head back, her eyes closed from ecstasy. He kept the pace slow and easy, his hands caressing her hips as he held them. Her fingers again clenched at the sheets and her chest flushed with color. She was wet and tight around him, squeezing his erection like a fist.

His penis gleamed with moisture when he withdrew from her, and she gasped when he slid only the thick head inside, rubbing the entrance to her body for a different sensation. Pleasure speared through her, and she dug her heels further into the mattress, pushing her hips higher, silently begging for more.

He gave it to her. Gage sank into her inch by inch, rocking his hips to continue giving her friction. When he was again fully seated within her, he leaned over, bracing his arms on either side of her head and thrusting deeply, burying himself deeper with the new angle. Her eyes sprang open and her whole body jumped. He was smiling when he buried his face in her neck and thrust harder.

Her legs came back up, sliding over his hips and anchoring their bodies together. Her hands spread on his back and her nails dug into his muscles. She moved her hips against his, her muscles clenching around him, driving them both ever closer to the edge of orgasm and the release they both craved. He lifted his head enough to press his mouth to her ear.

"Let go, Aradia. Let go and fly with me."

When he drove her over the edge, he went with her, collapsing on top of her and dragging her as close to him as he could. Her breath was coming in heaving gasps, and he could hear both her heart racing and her blood pounding in her veins. He rolled quickly to get his weight off her and draped her across his chest, wrapping one arm around her snugly while using the other hand to stroke her hair gently. When he spoke, his voice was worried.

"Are you okay? Did I hurt you?"

Aradia lifted herself onto her elbows to look at him, locking her stormy blue eyes onto his clear gold ones. "You could never hurt me, Gage." She settled back down on his chest and listened to the silence of his chest. "I never dreamed that I could feel such things."

Gage rubbed her back with one hand and pulled the blanket over them with the other. "I don't want you to get cold. I can't exactly keep you very warm."

She lifted her eyes to his hesitantly. "Gage?"

Sleepy and sated, he cracked open his eyes and looked down at her. "Hmm?"

"May I stay here tonight? Or would you prefer I go back to my room?"

He stare at her intently, trying to decide on an appropriate answer. She looked nervous and scared. Gage ran his finger over her face. "Do you want to stay with me?"

She nodded slowly. "I'm not sure how to do this. I don't know what I can and cannot say or how it is appropriate to act."

He laughed, his chest rumbling with the sound. "There are no right answers. I think we both know that this isn't a one-time thing." He gripped her elbows and hiked her up to kiss her. "I like the idea of you in my bed."

Aradia smiled. "I'd like to stay." She rolled off of him. "May I get a drink?"

Gage chuckled. "I'll get it." He kissed her again and rose from the bed, unabashedly nude, and crossed the room to a wine rack. He selected a bottle and opened it deftly, pouring two glasses before returning to the bed. Aradia sat up and pulled the sheet around her body to cover it. She took the glass he held out and sipped, the sweet red wine quenching her thirst and sliding down her throat, cool and smooth.

She looked up at him through heavy-lidded eyes. "Will you teach me how a woman pleases a man?"

Gage looked at her, his eyes hot with need. His penis lengthened and hardened at her words. He reached out and snagged her glass, placing them both on the ground. He yanked the sheet away from her, leaving her body bare. He raked his eyes over her soft curves and the alabaster skin.

"There is nothing you can do that's wrong." He gripped her thighs and dragged her down the bed until she laid flat. "Just looking at you pleases me. Being inside you—" He parted her thighs and climbed onto the bed, positioning himself between her legs. "—well, that's as close to Heaven as I'll ever get." He plunged inside her and lowered himself onto her. "This is just the beginning, Aradia. I hope you're ready for this." He thrust methodically, smiling when her eyes rolled back in her head and she moaned softly. "I hope to hell we both are."

Chapter Twenty

May 4, 2031

Alaria stood at the stove, stirring a pot of spaghetti sauce. "We have seven weeks before the battle with Garrick and Javal. We still don't know how we're going to get back to Atlantis, and we don't know how big of an army we'll have or how big an army they'll have."

Damon looked up from chopping cucumbers. "No offense, but I think that's a good thing. The longer it's quiet, the better off we are. If there're a lot of skirmishes between now and then, each one increases the odds of us dying before we get to the big one. We know they aren't prying open another Gate because they don't know where it is, and we know they haven't succeeded in knocking down the retaining wall because killing Aradia is the only way to do that."

Aradia smiled. "I'm still alive."

Alaria snorted. "Quiet is never good. Quiet means they're scheming and plotting."

Gage entered the kitchen and leaned his hip against the island. Aradia blushed and looked down, staring at her lap. He fought the urge to laugh and addressed the others. "I'm almost done making arrangements for us to go into Glasgow this weekend. I'm planning to go ahead a couple days to put protections and wards on the hotel. I've hired some Warriors to guard the house while we're gone." He looked between Damon and Greer. "I don't want to hear any objections. The two of you came back in time, you left everything you've ever known, and you've risked your lives to save this world. I am throwing you a wedding."

Greer shook her head. "Gage, you're doing too much. We just planned to go to city hall or something."

Gage reached out and patted her hand. "Greer, love, I have more money than you can imagine. I enjoy spending it. We've said since the beginning that we can't forget to live during this. If we stop living, we let them win. It's two nights. I'm making sure that we'll be protected, and we'll be back here quickly."

Damon picked up a tomato and began dicing it. "Gage, you're too generous." He looked at Greer. "We never expected you to pay for anything. You've been incredible to all of us. Letting us live in your house for going on a year, feeding us, providing transportation and weapons—dude, it's way above and beyond the call. I'd say we'll pay you back for all of it, but I don't know if we'll ever make enough to pay for the jet. I don't know if we can let you pick up the tab for our wedding, too."

Gage crossed to the cabinet and took down a mug for blood. "We each have our own part in this. We were all chosen for different reasons. The difference with me is that I've had centuries to accumulate money. I have more than I could spend in a hundred lifetimes. We're all giving up our lives for years to do this. It's the least I can do to spend a bit of what I have to make this more palatable. I want to do this, and it will hurt my feelings if you don't let me."

Greer squeezed his hand and smiled. "Keep it small."

Gage nodded. "I'll take care of everything." He drank deeply and placed the mug in the sink. "I'll be leaving on Tuesday to make sure of the arrangements. Since we won't all be sharing one room, it's important to take precautions to make the hotel safe. We'll be there for three nights." He checked his watch. "There's no way I can arrange time for a honeymoon now, but as soon as this is over, I'll send you both someplace tropical."

Damon grumbled under his breath as Gage left the room. "I wanted to be able to do this on our own, Greer."

Alaria laughed. "Don't sweat it. It's just going to be the six of us. Not like he can possibly throw a shindig for two hundred. We don't know two hundred people." She turned on the faucet and filled a pot of water. "I think it's a great idea. Aradia and I can wear slutty dresses and pick up hot single guys at the hotel bar while the two of you have wild newlywed sex."

Aradia flushed bright red. "It didn't go so well the last time I allowed you to dress me. I think something more conservative is called for." She smiled when Damon placed a salad in front of her, then Braxton, and finally, Greer. "I don't want to repeat that experience again."

"I'll keep a better eye on you this time. Don't worry. We're all going to have fun." Alaria opened the freezer and withdrew a loaf of frozen garlic bread. "It'll be good to get out of the house for something other than a rescue mission."

Braxton speared a tomato and popped it into his mouth. "We could all use a break, truthfully. It's been four months since Aradia got here, and we've been working on this task since she arrived. I've been dealing with this whole crock of shit for a year and a half now." He chewed slowly and swallowed. "We haven't seen much of Gabriel lately. That makes me nervous."

Alaria's eyes darkened and she tightened her grip on the spoon in her hand. "I'm sure Gabe has plenty of things to do. He'll pop up when it's the most inconvenient." She poked at the cooking noodles with the spoon. "Don't tempt fate, guys. We need to take this time to prepare and to rest. Once we go back to Atlantis, not only are we going to be living in super primitive conditions, we're going to be trying to train an army."

Greer cleared her throat. "Not to be a pessimist, but why even bother? Those people are dead anyway. Atlantis is going to sink. Other than Graciela, and us, of course, no one is making it out that we know of. Obviously Javal and Garrick made it out the first time somehow. Point being, why don't we let the battle play out and go straight for the two we have to kill? Or even just go for Garrick. He's the one holding the Gate open. All we have to do is kill him."

The kitchen fell silent as they all processed what had been said. Alaria drained the pasta and dumped it in a bowl. Damon finished his salad and rose to fill glasses and set out plates. He counted forks and knives and poured them each a glass of wine. Alaria put the bowls of noodles and sauce on the table and sat down. She folded her hands and sighed.

"There was a time, until about a year ago actually, that I would have gladly stood aside and let them all die. The problem with having a soul is that we *think* no one made it off that island. We don't know for sure. I don't know if any of us could live with ourselves knowing that we didn't give them the best shot possible."

Damon nodded. "I agree. We know Atlantis sinks, and we know we shouldn't mess with that. There's a lot of crap associated with screwing with time, and I don't think we should go there. Atlantis is also an island, which means some people might have escaped in boats. I have to believe that we're only going to be able to change what we're meant to change, and if the Angels are right, and time is fluid, it isn't going to make much of a difference." He shrugged. "It would be easier if we could do it that way, and there's a part of me that wants to go that route, but I don't think any of us can."

Greer averted her eyes and looked at her plate of pasta. "I didn't mean to suggest it would be easy. Only that we're going to have to make hard decisions and it might require knowingly leaving people to die there. We aren't going to be able to save them, and I'm not sure we should try."

Braxton laid his fork on his plate. "I think we all know that the people are going to die. They've been dead for thousands of years. We aren't there to change things. We're there to keep Javal and Garrick from changing things. They're going back to kill Aradia before she's born. We have to kill Garrick, and make sure that doesn't happen. If we save anyone, or allow anyone to get off the island, whatever happens to them is what's supposed to happen, nothing more and nothing less."

Aradia finished her pasta. "I think we'll know what to do when the time comes." She sipped her wine. "We have several weeks to consider the ramifications, but I think the more pressing issue is the upcoming wedding. I think we'd all benefit from a break. It's been a long few months and we've all experienced unfortunate things. A few days off isn't going to make us less ready, and it will likely help our mental fortitude." She stood and placed her plate in the sink. "I think I'm going to retire early. I'm going to take a long bath and get some sleep."

Alaria didn't say anything until Aradia had disappeared up the stairs. She exchanged a curious look with Greer. "Has anyone else noticed that Aradia is going to bed early every night and that Gage is suddenly always locked up in his room?"

Greer giggled. "Gage needed to get laid. I kinda hope they are going at it." She drained her glass of wine and took another bite of pasta. "If they are, it's their business and none of ours unless they decide to tell us. I imagine it's difficult for Aradia to accept a sexual relationship, given how she was raised."

Damon held up his hand. "If the two of you want to gossip about whether or not they're banging each other, go somewhere else. I don't want to hear the conversation."

Braxton lifted his wineglass in a toast. "Amen, brother."

Gage laid in the dark, Aradia curled against his side, her chest rising and falling rhythmically. He stroked his hand over the bare expanse of her back and stared at the ceiling. He heard Alaria climbing the stairs before she reached the top and rose, pulling on slacks and a shirt and opening the door before she could knock.

"Is everything okay?"

Alaria offered a smile. "Can I come in?"

Gage looked over his shoulder and saw that Aradia still slept soundly. "I assume you knew before you came up here?"

"I've known since we came back, or suspected anyway." She sank into one of the chairs near his fireplace. "We've known each other for a long time, Gage. We weren't really friends until recently, but I've known of you since you were turned."

Gage poured two snifters of bourbon. "Yeah. What's going on, Alaria?"

"I know about how you were turned."

Gage froze. He stared into the flames for several moments before speaking. "What do you know?"

"Everything. Laelia bragged about it for a hundred years afterward."

"What does that have to do with anything?"

"What do you know about Aradia's father?"

He shook his head. "Nothing. Why?"

"King Liam was killed during the siege on Atlantis. He rose as a vampire and made it through the portal."

"How do you know that?"

Alaria laughed softly. "I was around for it, Gage. I existed when all of this happened. My point is this, Liam came through the portal into eighth century Ireland. He joined with Laelia, and he was the other vampire there when you were turned."

"Are you sure?"

She nodded. "I'm sure. I haven't ever told you because we weren't sure we would have to go back, and then I didn't know what good it would do to tell you something that you would be worried about. Conversations tonight made me think that you needed to know. You can't change it, Gage. You have to let it happen. If you don't, you might not be turned, and that's not a good thing."

Gage felt his chest constrict and he ran his hands over his face. "My God. Will what we're asked to endure never end?" He swallowed the liquor in one gulp. "I don't know if I can, Alaria. What they made me do..."

Alaria reached out and took his hand. "I know. I can't imagine how hard this is going to be for you, but you're going to have to come through it. You can't mess with it. You're so imperative to this, Gage. We wouldn't be able to do it without you." She glanced over her shoulder at Aradia, still asleep. "You have her now, too."

"Mina was my wife." He looked sad and stared into the empty glass. "Dammit. Why can nothing be easy?"

"You need to tell her."

Gage's head snapped up. "Tell Aradia? Are you crazy?"

Alaria squeezed his hand. "It's her father, Gage. She's going to want to know him, at least as much as she can. She deserves to know what he becomes. She deserves to know how connected the two of you are."

"This isn't as serious as you're making it out to be." He gestured to the bed. "It's sex, Alaria. We both wanted it, and we're having it. Once this is over, we'll go our separate ways."

Alaria shook her head and stood. "Keep telling yourself that. From what I know, you've never let a woman in your bed in centuries. You always keep them in hotels." She went to the door. "She needs to know, Gage."

Gage sighed deeply when Alaria left. He stood and turned to stare at Aradia, his gaze intense and confused. He sat the glass down on the dresser and left the room, closing the door behind him. There was no way he was going to be able to sleep until he'd sorted through the conversation with Alaria. He headed down to his office to get some work done.

In the dark, Aradia rolled and sat up, tears running down her face. She reached for her clothes and pulled them on quickly.

Barely restraining her sobs, she fled Gage's room and raced down the stairs to her own, closing and locking the door behind her. In her own bed, alone in the blackness, she clutched her pillow close to her chest and sobbed.

Chapter Twenty-One

May 6, 2031

Gage glanced at the clock on his mantle. Eleven-thirty. He'd heard Greer and Damon go to bed thirty minutes earlier and knew Alaria and Braxton were in the basement inventorying the supplies he was taking to Glasgow in order to protect the hotel. Aradia had gone up to her room by ten, and he'd expected her to wait only long enough for everyone else to be securely elsewhere before she came to his room, the same as she had every night since the first time. In nearly two weeks, she'd not spent a night away from him until the night Alaria had come to see him. In the two nights since, she'd remained in her own bedroom.

They hadn't spoken much since then, either. He glanced at the clock again and swore under his breath. He struggled to remember how sure he had been that she was asleep. Her heartbeat had been slow and steady. Her breathing had been deep and even. He was sure she had been sleeping, at least at first.

Dammit. Gage plunked down his glass of whiskey and strode to the door. She'd been awake. He opened the door and descended the stairs, his pace clipped and steps staccato. He strode down the hall purposefully and went to Aradia's door. He gripped the knob and turned, mildly surprised when he found it locked. Irritated, he rapped his knuckles on the wood.

"Aradia, open the door. I need to talk to you."

There were several beats of silence before her footsteps moved across the door. He heard the lock slide out and she opened the door a few inches. Her hair was mussed, and her eyes looked sleepy. She wore a pair of shorts and a tank top. Her feet were bare. Gage swallowed. God help him, her toenails were painted pink.

She reached behind the door and grabbed her robe, pulling it on over her pajamas to cover herself. Gage felt his dead heart constrict at the movement. She looked up at him with a gaze equal parts hope and hurt.

"What is it?"

He forced himself to stop staring at her toes and thinking about how somehow being painted pink turned them into something sexy, and reached out to touch her face. Blinking in surprise when she took a step back to avoid the contact, he cleared his throat. "I thought you would come up."

Aradia crossed her arms and stared at him. He noticed then how tired she looked. She gripped the door, prepared to slam it in his face. "What's the point? We obviously want very different things. I'm not interested in being one of your whores, Gage."

Anger flared at her words, and he stepped into her room. "I have made you no promises. I'm not wooing you with wine and flowers. I am not your suitor."

Aradia's eyes flashed, too. "I never claimed that you were and never expected you to be. What I expected was to be more important than a random roll in the hay. I have feelings, Gage. Big, all-encompassing, confusing feelings that I don't know what to do with or how to handle. The entire time, I took comfort in knowing that you were going through the same thing. Even if I couldn't handle it alone, I knew you were feeling what I felt. To find out in such a cruel way that the only purpose for which you wanted me was to sate your libido is worse than being alone with my emotions."

Gage sucked in air he couldn't use and held it until well past the point human lungs would have burned. "You really think that? You think I told you no so many times because I was playing a game? You truly believe that I have kept you in my bed for the last two weeks because I'm horny?"

Aradia took a step back. "You're the one who said what is between us is only sex."

Gage moved faster than she'd thought was possible. He grabbed her and swung her up into his arms, clamping his mouth over hers in a searing, angry kiss. He held her tight when she struggled and walked back out into the hallway and up his private stairs to his room, Aradia thrashing in his arms in a desperate attempt to get free the entire way.

He kicked the door shut, sat her down, and dead bolted the door. She tried to step around him, but he grabbed her arms and held her still. She glared up at him and her hands clenched. Her eyes snapped with anger and magic and she took deep, heaving breaths in an effort to calm down.

"You're lucky I don't turn you into a toad."

Gage glared at her. "That's both trite and a threat unworthy of you." He faltered when she pulled her robe tighter. "Dammit, Aradia, I don't want you to be scared of me."

She crossed her arms to cover her chest. "I'm not scared of you, but neither am I your plaything."

"I never said you were." He gripped her upper arms and jerked her toward him, wrapping his arms around her in a hug. "I was waiting for you. I waited last night, and you never came. Instead of talking to me about something you heard that you know nothing about, you hid out like a child." He breathed in her scent, enjoying the smell. "How much did you hear?"

She refused to meet his gaze, instead looking stubbornly away. "Just the tail end, I believe. I heard Alaria whisper something I couldn't make out, and then I heard what you said about what is between us only being sex."

"You know we cannot be together after this is all over."

"I am aware of our limitations, Gage." Angry again, she yanked her arms free and stalked across the room to put some space between them. "I don't expect to get married and spend the rest of my life with you. I know what this is, and I accept it. I pursued it. But to call it just sex cheapens and vulgarizes it. What is between us, I thought, is emotion and magic and power. It felt like more than I could have ever imagined."

"You heard a snippet, Aradia. I'm a private man, and I don't want to discuss this with the others. It seemed most prudent to make it seem less serious. They would worry if they knew how wrapped up in each other we are." He threw up his hands in frustration. "For Christ sake, I carried you up here caveman style to make you listen to my side of it all." He reached for her. "I like having you sleeping here. I like waking up with you beside me, and I like knowing that I can reach out and touch you through the night."

Touched, but unwilling to completely let go of her hurt feelings, she ignored his confession and lifted her eyes to meet his. "I don't know what horny means."

Gage's eyes darkened with desire. "It's a word used to describe sexual desire. It means you want someone." He drew her into his arms and kissed her deeply. "I want to show you exactly how I feel about you if you'll let me, but this is your decision." He brushed his fingers over her jawline and down her neck. "Aradia, I've never lied to you. I feel everything you do. The bond makes us closer than we should be, and this magic shit intensifies the feelings, but everything you're going through, I'm going through, too."

Aradia took a step closer, pressing her body firmly against his, and wrapped her arms around his neck. "I want to believe you. I want to forget I heard it." She looked up at him through her eyelashes. "I want you to take me to bed, Gage, like you have before, but unless you're sure that we're in this together, I'm going to ask you not to."

He stepped back and reached for the ties on her robe, pulling them loose and sliding the fabric off her shoulders. "I hate when you cover up with me. I like looking at you, and I don't want you to be uncomfortable with me seeing you."

Gage gripped the hem of her shirt and lifted it over her head. He cast it aside and knelt, drawing her shorts down her legs. She stepped out of them and he followed the motion with an identical one to remove her plain cotton underwear. He stood and laid his hands on her hips, kneading the soft skin and muscle beneath his fingers.

"I don't want to be gentle with you, Aradia. I want to bury myself inside you and forget."

She fit her body against his. "Take whatever you need." She unbuttoned his shirt slowly. "I'll give you all I have."

His mouth was hungry. He took possession of her with both his mouth and his hands. He backed her up until she dropped onto the bed. He stripped off his clothes with ruthless efficiency and fell onto the mattress with her, the thick comforter soft beneath them.

Aradia lifted he face to press against his, fearlessly answering his demand that she give more. She slid her hands down his body and gripped his ass, pulling his hips into hers. One hand slipped between their bodies, and she cupped his erection, her fingers soft and warm against the steely hardness.

She wrapped her hand around him and rubbed gently, moving her fist up and down slowly. She felt a drop of moisture at the tip and jumped, afraid she'd done something wrong. Gage pulled her hands away, placing them above her head and holding them lightly with one of his.

"You're gorgeous." He dipped his head and sucked her nipple into his mouth, scraping the sensitive tip with his teeth and soothing the slight sting with his tongue. He pressed his palm against her, feeling the heat of her body.

Gage parted her thighs and slid into her with one thrust. He allowed her a moment to adjust to his girth before he was thrusting into her, driving his penis in and out with long, heavy strokes. He hitched her legs up so they wrapped around his waist and he held her hands loosely. She surrounded him with wet heat and hugged his body tightly.

He sought and found her mouth, allowing his tongue to explore it leisurely. His thrusts increased in speed and her breathing became raspy as she neared climax. He freed her hands and rose onto his knees, holding her hips in his hands and pounding into her. Her head thrashed on the pillow and her hips jumped in his hands as she tried to meet his strokes. He felt the wave of pleasure rising and knew he was close.

Aradia came apart, her body undulating around him and her wetness increasing until she was slippery with it. Her chest darkened with color and she groaned, the sound loud and raw, her eyes squeezing closed as she rode out the orgasm. He rode her through it, driving her back up the crest before she'd come all the way down. She whimpered and gasped. Her body felt as if every nerve ending was exposed, and she felt every sensation magnified.

Gage felt her clench around him and he recognized it as a telltale sign that another orgasm was getting closer. He yanked her down on him, anchoring himself deeply within her. He rocked his hips against hers to give them both friction and followed her over the edge into climax.

He collapsed to the bed next to her and dragged her against his side. Her chest heaved as she tried to catch her breath and he stroked her hair gently with one hand, the other holding one of hers. She laid her head on his chest and pressed a soft kiss to his skin.

They laid in silence for several minutes, content to just be together. Gage ran his hand up and down her arm and stared at the ceiling. When he spoke, his voice was distant and faraway.

"When I was a human, I was a farmer. I raised cattle and horses and grew some corn. I married a woman from my village named Mina when I was nineteen. My first son was born when I was twenty-five. We'd tried for years, but we didn't have luck. After Jonathon was born, the children came quickly. He was two when Mina had Elizabeth, four when Christopher was born, and seven when Rachel joined us."

Aradia remained silent, sensing that Gage needed to tell his story. His eyes were clouded with grief and guilt, and his face was twisted with emotion. His hand still laid on her arm, though he'd stopped stroking her skin. She laid hers over his in an effort to comfort him.

"We were happy. Four beautiful children, a house of our own, and a few acres of farmland. We were poor, but we never went hungry. One night, I heard the horses in the barn crying. We had a problem with wolves, especially in the winter when it was cold, and if the horses died, I wouldn't be able to feed my family. I went out with a lantern and my bow. I expected it would be wolves, but instead, I found a couple."

Gage fell silent for several moments, lost in memories. Tears welled in his eyes and he pulled away from her, sitting up and pulling on his clothes. He moved to the chair in front of the fireplace. Aradia wrapped the blanket around herself and followed him, dropping into the other chair.

"You don't have to tell me this if you don't want to."

He didn't look at her, choosing to stare into the fire instead. "They were nearly frozen and were huddled in the hay. They told me they were travelers and that their carriage had wrecked miles up the road. Their horse had broken its leg in the crash and they'd had to kill it. They were hungry and needed a place to stay for the night. I made up a pallet and invited them into the house."

He rose again, went to the array of bottles on top of the dresser, and poured whiskey into a glass. He drank it in one gulp and poured another. Aradia reached out to touch his hand as he returned to the chair with the bottle and glass.

"They were vampires, weren't they?"

Gage laughed bitterly. "My wife made them soup to help with the chill. The man ate it. I think he was trying to keep up appearances, or maybe he was still new enough to think that he could stave off the bloodlust with real food. The woman laughed and laughed when Mina put the soup in front of her. We thought she was mentally unstable, and I remember wondering if I should call for the priest. Before I could say anything, the woman attacked Mina. She grabbed her and buried her teeth in Mina's neck. I'd never seen anything like it. The thing's teeth grew and her eyes turned red. Mina screamed and screamed." He choked back tears and ran his hands over his face. "God, I haven't ever told this story."

Aradia twined her fingers with his and held his hand tightly. "If it's too much, you don't have to tell me." She offered a smile. "I don't like seeing you in pain."

"You need to hear this." He squeezed her fingers and tugged gently. She stood and curled up on his lap, tucking the blanket around them both. "I tried to save her. I could hear the kids waking up, and I knew they'd be scared. The man got to me before I got to Mina. He bit me and drank. It burned and hurt. I could hear the woman yelling at him to stop, that I was hers. She bit herself and shoved her wrist in my mouth. Her blood was bitter and thick, and I'm still not quite sure if it was the man drinking my blood or choking on hers that killed me."

He took a moment to sip whiskey. It burned his throat as it went down and he remembered the feel of fangs in his neck and blood running down his throat. He shuddered at the memory. Aradia mistook the motion for a chill and cuddled closer, wrapping the blanket tighter around him.

"When I woke up, I tried to breathe. I've learned how to do that without trying to use the air now, but that first time, it hurt. I think it was the worst pain I'd ever felt. Everything looked different, and I was struggling to see. I saw my kids tied up, and my wife was lying on the floor. She was unconscious. The vampires were sitting at our table drinking beer. When they saw that I was awake, they were excited.

"The woman clapped her hands like a little girl. She told me they'd been waiting for me and that I was going to be theirs. I don't remember what else they said because it was about then that I realized I was hungry. I remember racing around the kitchen and shoving everything I could find into my mouth. Nothing helped. Food tasted like paper. Liquid was better, but it didn't even start to fill the hole in my gut. After half an hour of watching me, Laelia, the woman, came to me and put her arm around me."

Gage ran his hand through his hair and threw back the rest of the liquor. His eyes filled with tears again and he shook his head to clear it. If the first part had been hard to tell, the last was going to gut him. He spoke again, his voice trembling and thick with tears.

"She told me that no amount of food would quell the hunger. She told me I'm a vampire and that the only thing that would keep me alive was human blood. I was the first she'd made, she said. Her companion had been bitten long in the past by another original vampire. The longer they talked, the hungrier I got."

Aradia felt tears well in her own eyes. She had a horrible feeling she knew what had happened. She tightened her grip on him and nuzzled her nose into his chest. He took several seconds to beat down the grief that threatened to overwhelm him.

"Gage, you don't have to do this. It's too much for you to talk about."

He spoke quickly, trying to get the whole confession out before he lost the ability to speak. "I ate them. One after the other. The human part of me was sickened. It screamed and struggled to break through, but the hunger and the demon was too much." Tears streamed down his face and his voice cracked. "I bit my babies, and I drained them dry. When I was done, I threw them aside and moved to the next. They made Mina watch. Rachel was only two. She looked so innocent and tiny in her white nightgown. When she landed on the floor, her skin was so pale, and it looked like she was sleeping."

Gage choked on sobs, tears dripping off his chin and soaking into the blanket. The grief in his eyes was deeper than any Aradia had ever seen. She held him tightly and murmured words of comfort, rocking back and forth as she would a child. He took a shuddering gulp of air and expelled it slowly, using the time to gather himself. His eyes were red and his face swollen. He forced himself to speak, his voice rough and thick.

"Mina was last. She reached out to me and told me she didn't blame me. She knew what they'd done to me, and she told me it was the demon inside me that was making me do the things I'd done. She put her hand on my cheek when I grabbed her to bite her, and she looked into my eyes. My wife, who had just watched me murder our children, touched my face, looked me in the eyes, and told me she forgave me." He wiped his hands over his face. "That was enough to break through the bloodlust. After that, I was a monster. I killed the man. When she saw her mate die, Laelia ran. She waited for me in the woods for weeks before the hunger drove me out again, and that's when she got her claws in me, but for that moment, I was able to stay in control.

"I tried to save Mina, but Laelia had bitten her, and the wound was infected. I sat by her bed for four days before she died. I buried our babies and carried her out to see the graves. I learned quick not to go out during the day." He hastily dragged his hand across his eyes. "When she died, I fed her my blood, thinking that I could do to her what Laelia had done to me. She woke up three days later and was so crazed from the hunger that she butchered our entire village. I had to rip her head off to stop her from killing anyone else." He sighed, the sound wobbly. "After that, I think my mind couldn't take what I'd done, and I buried it. I became a monster."

Aradia laid her hands on his face and pressed her mouth to his. "You have done all you can to make up for it. Gage, I'm not going to hold something against you that you did more than a thousand years ago." She sat back. "Why tell me this now? This is so painful for you to talk about, so I can't imagine you just felt like discussing it."

Gage hugged her close. "When Alaria came to see me the other day, she wanted to talk to me about your father. Do you know much about him?"

Confused, Aradia shook her head. "No. Only that he was the king and that he died in the battle. What does that have to do with anything?"

"Alaria told me the vampire who was with Laelia that night, whose name was Liam, was your father. He was turned early in the battle and rose before the city sank. He made it through the portal and found Laelia. They were two of the first vampires. It took Laelia a few hundred years to figure out how to turn people, and she'd only tried it a handful of times before me. Alaria thought I needed to know so that we could make sure not to change things. She was scared that if I knew, I would kill him myself or stop him from being turned in hopes that it would change things for my family."

Aradia leaned back and studied his face carefully. "I couldn't blame you if you intended to do that." She laid her hands on his chest. "It could give you a chance to live out your life with your wife and children."

Gage laid his head against hers. "They've been dead for thirteen hundred years. They're buried here on this land. I don't know if I could bring myself to sacrifice our mission for them." He stared at her, looking deep into her eyes. "I loved them, Aradia. I love them still. It's a hard thing to face the feelings I have for you and remember how I loved my wife. When she died, I swore to myself that I would never love another woman. Eventually, the grief and the love faded to a memory. The pain I feel when I remember what I did is still bright and fresh, and I don't know if I'll recover as long as I live. I don't still pine for Mina. I'm immortal. I've held myself back from loving because unless I find another vampire, whomever I love, I'll see die." He pressed his mouth to hers. "Until you. I'm not going to try to change it, because changing it might take you away from me. Maybe that just cements me as a monster, that I'm not doing everything I can to get them back, but I came through that grief. I want to spend whatever time we have to be together with you."

The blanket slid down as Aradia wrapped her arms around him, leaving her naked to the waist. The fire gleamed off her skin, giving her a rosy glow, and the flames intensified the color of her hair. She shyly lifted her eyes to meet his. Her hair flowed over her shoulders, covering her breasts so that only her nipples poked out between the curls. Gage caught himself looking down and averted his eyes back to the fire.

"It doesn't make you a bad person, Gage." Aradia stood, the blanket falling to the floor. She straddled him, pressing her chest against his. "Thank you for telling me your story. I wish I could take the pain away, but that's beyond even my magic." She slid his shirt off. "What I can do is make you forget for a while."

Gage felt himself harden, his body reacting without his permission. "Aradia—"

She lifted up long enough to remove his pants. "Let me make you forget, Gage. Let me take the pain for a few moments, anyway."

She lowered herself onto him, taking him into her body and making them both groan. She sprawled her hands on his chest and ran her nails over his skin. He shivered from the sensation and lowered his hands to grip her hips. She rode him hard and fast, giving in to their desires and the demands of her body.

As climax threatened, she threw her head back, her hair streaming down over her shoulder blades, nearly touching her waist. When she looked back at him, her eyes were full of desire and need. When she spoke, her voice was breathy and feral.

"Do you feel what I do?"

Gage nodded, his mind muddled from the sensations rocketing through him. "Yes."

She met his gaze. "Then tell me. If it's only once for as long as I live, give me the words, Gage."

"I love you."

She rose over him, driving them both over the edge of release. "And I you."

Chapter Twenty-Two

May 9, 2031 – Glasgow, Scotland

Greer looked around the bridal shop in awe. Aradia wore an identical expression, and Alaria looked only mildly interested. Gage stood at the desk, talking to the sales clerk. He grinned and gestured for them when he caught sight of the women.

"Good, the hotel gave you my message." He held out a hand and took Greer's. "I know you want small, and it is. I've only reserved the hotel chapel, and there are no guests. However, I know women, and I know the dress is the most important thing about a wedding. I've arranged for the three of you to get any dress in here, on me." He winked at her. "Don't say no. I want to. It'll hurt my feelings if you don't let me." He wiggled his eyebrows at the other two. "Besides, I get something out of it, too. I get to see those two all dressed up and gorgeous."

Greer found herself smiling. "Does any girl ever manage to tell you no?"

Gage kissed her forehead. "Not any straight ones." He patted the saleswoman on the shoulder. "Lucy is going to take great care of you." He smiled at the petite brunette. "Spare no expense."

Lucy shooed him toward the door. "You may regret saying that, Mr. Windsor." She turned to the three women. "Do you have any idea what style you might want?"

Greer turned in a circle, staring in awe at all the dresses. "Umm..."

Lucy smiled sympathetically. "What kind of ceremony is it? I know Mr. Windsor said small."

"Simple." Greer looked around again. "I don't want anything big and puffy. There's a lot of big and puffy in here."

"Big and puffy is what sells dresses to a lot of brides." Lucy led the three down a row of white dresses in clear plastic bags. "Do you want long or short?"

Greer looked at Alaria and Aradia helplessly. Alaria smiled and spoke. "I think long for her. Something that fits close to the body. Greer isn't much for fancy stuff, so I think something lacy, not blingy."

Lucy looked at Greer closely. "Are you an eight?"

Greer shook her head. "Closer to a ten." She patted her hips. "It's the hips that nudge me up a size."

The sales clerk pulled out three bags and led them back to the curtained off areas. "I think these are a good place to start. This is a cut called fit and flare, which means it'll hug those fabulous hips. The first one has cap sleeves and a sweetheart neckline. It'll give you some great cleavage without being strapless. The back is open to give you some sex appeal, and it buttons up with the little silk-covered buttons for a little bit of old world elegance."

Greer felt like her mind would melt. She nodded at what the clerk was saying and followed the other woman into the dressing room. She never wore anything fancier than nice jeans and a button down. The woman chattered about veils and shoes and jewelry while Greer shimmied into the dress. She heard Alaria and Aradia talking outside the curtain and smiled. As much as she worried about taking time off close to the second task, she knew they would all be better for it.

The dress was ivory and hugged her curves. There was a gemstone buckle at her waist, and it swept behind her in a short train. The sleeves barely covered her shoulders with delicate lace, and it dipped low across her breasts. It fastened in the back across her shoulder blades, and the buttons ran from her waist all the way down the train. Greer stared at herself in the mirror, her hand at her throat. Lucy stood back, hands on her hips, with a satisfied look on her face.

"You're gorgeous."

Alaria huffed from outside the curtain. "Let us see." She stepped back when the curtain opened. "Oh, Greer."

Aradia's eyes filled. "It's spectacular, Greer. I think that's it."

Her hands shaking, Greer ran them over the bodice of the dress. "I think so, too." She looked over her shoulder. "I don't need to see anymore."

Lucy tugged on the fabric. "I'll need to take it in a little bit here and pull the hem up an inch. The ceremony is tomorrow, right?"

"Yeah, tomorrow at seven."

"I can have it ready by then. Now for you two." She glanced at Aradia and Alaria. "Let's find you some dresses to make you almost as pretty as the bride."

Aradia adjusted the clip in Greer's hair and stood back to survey her work. Greer wore the dress she'd chosen. Her hair was loose in waves around her face, and she'd done her makeup in subdued shades with bold red lips. A bouquet of light pink and white roses lay on the table near the door.

Alaria came out of the bathroom wearing a strapless red dress that appeared painted on. She smiled when she saw Greer and paused to put on her earrings. "Greer, you look beautiful. Damon won't be able to look away." She reached out and took Greer's hands. "This is much happier than the last wedding I went to."

Greer sobered. "Griffin?"

Alaria nodded. "I remember walking into that room to talk her out of it. I thought it was a waste of time and resources when there was so little time left. She was in the bathroom in her damn underwear and so bony I could've knocked her over with a feather. Instead of convincing her to call it off, I conjured her a wedding dress and veil." She smiled at the memory. "I'm glad I get to be here."

Greer rushed forward and hugged Alaria tightly. "You convince yourself you're not, but you're a good person, Alaria. I can't think of many people I'd rather have in my corner other than you." She stepped back and grinned. "I say that as someone who has seen the inside of your brain."

Aradia gathered her hair into a ponytail low to the side of her neck, laying it so that it curled over one shoulder. Her dress fell to the floor in an emerald green cascade. It tied around her neck, leaving her back completely bare, and a thin jeweled belt nipped in her waist. She'd foregone makeup and jewelry and had slipped on a pair of silver sandals.

She glanced over her shoulder to look at the other two women.

"Shall I go tell Damon that you're ready?"

Greer grinned. "Yes. I'm ready."

Aradia slipped from the room and went down the hall to the suite where the three men were. She knocked softly and stepped back when Braxton opened the door. He waved her inside, and she looked around at the three men, all of whom wore tuxedos.

"You all look very handsome." She looked to Damon. "Greer is ready."

Damon bounced on his heels nervously. "Guess it's show-time then." He looked at Braxton and Gage. "I suppose we'd better get on downstairs and wait for my bride." He laughed. "God, I never thought I'd ever say that."

Braxton clapped Damon on the shoulder. "This is a happy weekend. We're all going to enjoy it."

The three men shuffled from the room and into the elevator with little fuss. Aradia returned to the other hotel room long enough to get Alaria and Greer before they went down as well. They each kissed Greer on the cheek before entering the chapel and taking seats between Gage and Braxton.

Damon stood at the end of the aisle, a pastor in a dark suit standing next to him. The pastor gestured to a woman sitting near the back and she pushed a button on the stereo. Music flooded the room, and Greer appeared at the back of the aisle. She looked from side to side before focusing on Damon and striding up the aisle.

The pastor waited until Damon had taken Greer's hand in his and turned to face him. "Dearly beloved, we are gathered here today to witness the joining in Holy Matrimony of Greer Dawson and Damon Mackenzie. The bride and groom have elected to write their own vows. Damon, we'll start with you."

Damon coughed. "This seemed like much less pressure a week ago when you suggested it." He laughed nervously. "Seriously, who knew that marrying a woman you've known since you were a kid could be so nerve wracking?" He squeezed her hands. "When we first got tangled up, I swore to you that nothing between us would change. Well, I lied. Everything has changed. Before, we were friends. We were partners." He took a breath. "I have loved you for fifteen years, Greer Dawson. I fell in love with you the night I nearly lost you, and I'll love you until the day I die. The difference between then and now is that now I get to wake up to you every morning, and I get to hold you in my arms each night. You're it for me, babe, and I wouldn't change it for anything in the world. I love you, and you're making me the luckiest man alive by agreeing to be not only my friend and partner but my wife."

Greer cleared her throat and blinked back a sheen of tears. "I wish they'd've let me go first so I didn't have to be all choked up." She pulled one hand free to dab at her eyes. "I have struggled against this from the start. I dragged my feet, I pretended it wasn't happening, and I tried to make us both believe we couldn't have it all. You've made me see how wrong I was. We're stronger together. We always have been. You have been my rock, Damon. You've always been there for me, through every step of every single thing we've ever come up against. There is no one that I trust more, and there is no one that I would ever dream of standing here with other than you. I love you. I'm honored to be your wife, and I'm proud to have you as my husband."

The pastor smiled. "Very nice. Are there rings?"

Damon shook his head, but Gage stood and swiftly handed the pastor two ring boxes. The man opened them swiftly and handed Damon a gold band. Damon spared a glare over his shoulder for Gage, who grinned brightly.

"Damon, please place the ring on the third finger of her left hand and repeat after me. I, Damon Mackenzie, take thee Greer to be my wife."

"I, Damon Mackenzie, take thee Greer to be my wife."

"I give you this ring as a token of my love and devotion."

"I give you this ring as a token of my love and devotion." Damon stumbled over the words slightly.

"With this ring, I commit myself to you wholly, until death do us part."

"With this ring, I commit myself to you wholly, until death do us part."

The pastor repeated the process with Greer, leading her through the vows. She placed the ring on Damon's finger carefully, her hands shaking as she did so. Once the vows were complete, the pastor addressed them both.

"By the power vested in me by God and the city of Glasgow, I now pronounce you to be husband and wife. You may kiss your bride."

Damon wrapped one arm around Greer's waist and pulled her tight to him. He dipped her backward and kissed her deeply, the other four cheering behind them. He righted her and tucked her arm through his own, leading her down the aisle toward the door. Greer grinned jubilantly next to him. As they passed, she tossed her bouquet to the side and laughed when it landed in Alaria's lap.

They pushed through the doors at the back of the chapel and out in to the hotel. Gage caught up to them several steps outside and hugged them both. "Congratulations. I reserved us a table at the restaurant. We'll eat, or you'll eat, I'll drink, and then you two can do whatever you want for the night."

Greer grinned. "Thank you for everything, Gage. I don't think we'll ever be able to thank you enough for this." She kissed his cheek gently, then wiped the smudge of lipstick away. "You're a wonderful man, Gage."

They heard a slight pop behind them as Gabriel appeared in the lobby. He immediately turned to Greer and Damon. "I would like to offer my congratulations. I regret that I was unable to attend the ceremony, but there were other things requiring my attention."

Alaria came through the door, her arm tucked though Braxton's. She froze when she saw Gabriel and dropped Braxton's arm, taking a step to the side. She smiled nervously. "Gabe. Long time no see." She hugged him quickly and pressed a kiss to his cheek. "I wish you'd have come for the wedding."

Gabriel smiled tersely. "I came for the celebration. It was the soonest I could get away." He turned back to Damon and Greer. "Shall we eat?"

Damon nodded. "Sure thing." He leaned in close to Greer as they walked. "Do Angels eat?"

Gabriel chuckled. "I can hear you, Damon. Yes, we can eat if we choose to." He laid his hand on Alaria's back possessively. "I can do anything a human can do."

Alaria had never been truly drunk. As a Devil, she'd never been able to reach that state, regardless of how much she drank, and as a human, she'd never drunk enough to get her to the point that she was unable to think at all, though as she downed the dregs of the third bottle of wine she had consumed on her own, she wondered why she didn't do precisely that more often.

The other six people were talking around her. She sat between Gabriel and Aradia, with Braxton across the table from her. He'd tried twice to tell her she'd had enough, but she did nothing more than smack his hand and pour more than she'd originally intended to. She needed it to deal with sitting at a table with both the men she was tangled up with.

She sipped another glass of wine and studied Gabriel. He sat stiffly, with his hand on her knee. He didn't laugh when one of the others told a joke, and he participated in the conversation only when someone addressed him directly, which they did every few minutes in an effort to include him.

Braxton, on the other hand, laughed and teased Greer. He toasted her and Damon, and he got into a rousing debate with Gage over some political thing. He glanced to Alaria several times, and his expression became worried when he saw her reach for the bottle again. She tried to smile to reassure him, but he just looked more worried.

It was more than she could take. Gabriel was possessive and jealous, and Braxton was worried. She stood abruptly and shoved her way around the table. The others fell silent when she rose, waiting for her to say something. When she did, her voice was slurred and wobbly.

"I'm going to bed. I'll see you all tomorrow."

She stumbled from the dining room, tripping on the rug and pitching forward, grabbing onto the door frame to keep her balance. All four men at the table jumped to their feet to help, but Gabriel was faster than all of them. He wrapped his arm around her and held her steady. When she bent over and removed her heels, he looked over his shoulder darkly.

"I'm taking her to bed. She'll be fine. Do not worry."

Gabriel half-carried Alaria to the elevators and pushed the button for her floor. She tried to ask how he knew which button to push but couldn't make the words come out. He took her purse and rifled through it until he found the key card. When she stumbled stepping into the elevator car, he picked her up and draped her over his shoulder, carrying her down the hall. Carefully balancing her with one arm, he used the other to stick the card into the lock and pushed the handle when the light turned green.

He deposited her on the couch in the sitting room and fetched a glass of water from the bathroom. She took it and drank greedily. Her hair was mussed and frizzy around her face, and her mascara darkened the skin around her eyes. He went to the door, touched the handle, then dropped it and turned.

"Is there anything you need before I go?"

Alaria laughed. She leaned to the side until she was lying on the couch, and tears streamed down her face from laughing so hard. Unsteady, she climbed to her feet and stalked over to him. She jammed one finger into his chest.

"Now you care? Now you want to know if I need anything?" She jabbed him again and weaved from side to side, trying to stay steady. "You didn't give a fuck when you were here last time! I begged you to choose me. I begged you not to make me want you, and you did it anyway. Here you are, in your perfect fucking white suit..." She trailed off when he started to brush his shoulder. She grabbed his hand. "God dammit, Gabriel! There is no fucking lint on your goddamned, mother-fucking suit!"

Gabriel pulled his hand from hers and stared down at her. "There are things I have to do that will make you hate me." He ran his hand down the side of her face. "I only ever wanted to make you happy."

She looked up at him with a blank expression. "What the hell are you dithering on about?"

He looked at her sadly. "Alaria, my love, you're not going to remember a bit of this tomorrow, but I want you to know how truly sorry I am for the things that I have done and will yet do. When the time comes that you find out about all of these things, I hope you can believe that I am only trying to protect you from a fate much worse than the one I am about to impose upon you."

Alaria blinked rapidly. She giggled drunkenly and batted her eyes. "I don't know what any of that means."

She twisted her arms behind her back and unzipped her dress. She lowered the straps and shimmied out of it. The dress hadn't allowed for a bra, and she wore nothing other than a black thong. Gabriel averted his eyes and she laughed hysterically, reaching up to grab his chin and yanking it to the front.

"Nothing you haven't seen." She wrinkled her nose. "Hell, it's nothing you haven't licked, sucked and fucked."

Gabriel closed his eyes briefly against the pain he felt at knowing what he had to do. He reached out and ran one finger from her collarbone over her breast to the nipple. He rubbed it gently and drew her close with his other arm. She came willingly, if not steadily.

"Don't cheapen what we've had, Alaria. Neither of us deserve that."

"I'm not cheapening it." She leaned up and sank her teeth into his lower lip. "I almost fuck Braxton, then I do fuck you. I sit at that damn table, looking between the two of you, wanting you both and knowing I've got no business having either of you."

Gabriel gripped her shoulders and forced her to look at him. "You're human, Alaria. You're allowed to have confusing emotions. You're allowed to be mixed up, and you're allowed to want more than one thing or person." He kissed her eyelids. "All I need to know is this. Do you, at this moment, want me?"

"Wanting you is not the problem, Gabe." She wrapped her arms around him and lifted up onto her tiptoes. "I've always wanted you. I think part of me always will." In a moment of clarity through the drunken stupor, she met his gaze. "This is different. It's the last time, isn't it?"

He smiled sadly. "Yes. This will be the last time. All we'll do is continue to hurt one another."

She smiled sadly. "I wish things were different."

"Yet, they are as we see them." Gabriel swept her up in his arms and carried her to the bed. "We knew from the very first time that this was not something we could continue to do indefinitely. You love me, and I love you, but I can never leave the service of our Father. Not even for you."

Alaria tugged his shirt out from his slacks. "Shut up. We both know the score. Give us what we both want."

They tumbled to the bed in a tangle of limbs. Gabriel shed his clothes efficiently and pressed her into the mattress. He gave in to her urging and entered her quickly, foregoing any preparation for the dark slide into her body. Tears stung his eyes, and he strained to continue making love to her.

He was creating a child whose mother did not know about it and was unlikely to want it. He was taking choice away from Alaria in an effort to keep someone else from taking it in a more forceful manner. He had interfered with her ability to choose her own path, and he was forcing upon her a destiny not of her making.

He was forcing her to conceive a child he would never know, one that would be raised by another man. One that would call someone else Father and know him only as a guardian, if it knew him at all. That thought was almost enough to make him stop what he did. Only the thought that someone else would take his spot spurred him on.

Alaria clamped around him in climax, her body arching and pressing against his feverishly. He emptied himself within her, a loud groan erupting from his chest. She flung her arm out, gasping for breath and covered in sweat.

Unbeknownst to her, deep within her, a second joining occurred. As she drifted to sleep—the deep sleep of the very drunk—the tiny spark of a potential life flickered into flame.

Gabriel watched her fall asleep, tears running down his face. He felt more grief and regret in that moment than he had ever felt before. He placed his hand on her hair and leaned down to press his lips to her ear.

"In every way I could, I loved you. I'm sorry for all the pain I have caused and will yet cause. I hope you know, beyond everything I've done to the contrary, that my only intention was to protect you from as much as I could. Even in this horrible betrayal, I do it to protect you from a fate much worse." He slid his hand down to her abdomen. "You'll be a wonderful mother, Alaria. I can only pray that you'll let me know our child in some way."

He watched her sleep for several minutes before rising and pulling on his clothes. He tucked his shirt into his slacks, fastened his belt and pulled on his jacket. He started to brush his hand over the sleeve in a habit long ago developed and paused, smiling. He lowered his hand and tucked it into his pocket. He spared one more glance toward the woman asleep on the bed and disappeared.

Chapter Twenty-Three

GREER FOUND herself standing in an abandoned city. She knew immediately that she was in the dream plane and looked around for a weapon. Spotting a dead police officer ten yards down the road, she looked around to make sure she was alone and dashed for the cop.

She wrenched the gun from its holster and darted back out of sight. Crouching behind a car, she checked the clip to make sure there was ammo and was looking for shoes to cover her feet when she heard whistling. She crawled to the end of the car, staunchly ignoring the glass and gravel biting into her skin.

"Come out, come out, wherever you are."

Greer pressed herself against a building and tried to wiggle behind the dumpster that sat there. She held her breath to avoid the sound, and concentrated on calming her heart. She closed her eyes for a brief moment, willing herself to become invisible.

When she opened her eyes, Javal's face was less than an inch from hers. She shrieked and struck out, hitting him in the face. She dashed down the street, trying to put some distance between them.

"There's no use running, Greer. This is my world." He spread his arms and the sky darkened until it was pitch black. Walls erupted from the ground all around until Greer was boxed in and there was no more room to run. "I can make it into whatever I want to."

Heart pounding in her chest, Greer turned to face him. "What do you want?"

"What I've always wanted. I want to kill one of your little group. I need to kill the witch to truly win, but I'll settle for killing you now and her later. That'll be enough to stop you from succeeding."

"You've tried to kill me in here before."

Javal grinned. "I didn't have all the knowledge I have now. See, before, I didn't know that you have that pesky mental link to the Hunter that allowed you to borrow his energy to heal yourself. I know that now. You'd have never been able to heal yourself without him. Now that I know that, I've taken steps to ensure that it won't be a problem."

"You're not that powerful."

"It's not me you should be worried about. It's Garrick. We've got more friends than you can imagine. I knew the moment you all left that wretched house to come here. Those fucking bones and the magic under that house prevent me from getting to you all there. Once you left, however, you were free for the picking. The wards Gage put on the hotel are only effective if someone doesn't remove them, and I have a lot of humans in my employ. I brought them down before you even got here. Gage's biggest downfall is that he's cocky. He never thought to check to make sure they hadn't been tampered with."

"You're not going to kill me." Greer tightened her grip on the gun. "I'm not a wilting flower, y'know. I handled you once before."

"If I remember correctly, I ripped your heart from your chest while it still beat. I'm not sure how you claim that as a victory."

"I survived, which means you failed. That's all I have to do this time."

She leapt to the side when he tossed out a ball of flame. Concrete bit into her shoulder and she winced at the contact. The pebbles scraped her skin and the scent of blood filled her nostrils. She climbed to her feet and glared at Javal.

"That wasn't very nice." She gasped when Javal struck her in the face. The back of his knuckles split the skin above her cheekbone and blood dripped out of the wound.

"I'm not sure what makes you think I'm at all nice." He blocked her punch and grabbed her wrist, yanking her toward him. "You're a human, Greer. You have no power in the dream plane. Aradia can barely come against me here, and she's a very powerful witch bitch." He ran his nails down her throat, tearing the skin and allowing blood to flow.

Greer struggled against him. She kicked, punched, and bit. As soon as she landed a blow, Javal healed and landed one of his own. He kicked her across the box he'd created, and the cracking sound told her he'd broken her ribs even before the pain swept over her. She managed to rise to her hands and knees before the next blow landed.

She flew ten feet and crashed into the cement barrier. Her head struck it, and black spots swarmed in front of her eyes. Blood ran into them, stinging and thick. She wiped at the blood and coughed. Her knees gave out when she tried to rise, and she landed on her stomach, flat on the ground.

Javal strode to her, standing over her and staring down at her with a look of jubilant satisfaction. He lifted his boot and slammed it into her head. When she gasped for air and tried to roll over, he did it again, and a third time, then a fourth, until she no longer moved. In her bed, back in the hotel room, her nearly lifeless body rolled from the bed and onto the floor.

Damon woke when he heard a thump. He leaned over and turned on the light, illuminating the dark hotel room. He blinked sleep from his eyes and turned to check for Greer. The bed where she'd been was cold, the sheets rumpled. He saw two drops of blood on the pillow, and his heart sank.

He leaned further and found Greer on the floor, blood seeping from her eyes, nose, mouth and ears. Part of her skull looked deformed, and she was barely breathing. He felt for the link between them and blanched when it was absent.

He pressed two fingers to her throat and shook his head when he couldn't feel a pulse. He pressed his ear to her chest and heard her heart moving weakly. He ran to the door, wrenched it open and fled down the hall.

Aradia laid on her stomach, her skin glowing. Gage climbed into the bed beside her, running his hand over her bottom and up her back as he did so. She rolled onto her side and propped herself up on her elbow.

"I missed you these past couple days."

Gage smiled and kissed her shoulder. "I missed you, too." He cocked his head to the side, his vampiric ears picking up something she couldn't hear. He rose and pulled on his pants, walking toward the door. "I hear Damon."

He opened the door and stuck his head out into the hallway. Damon stood two doors down, wearing only his boxers and pounding on Aradia's door, looking hysterical. Gage looked over his shoulder at Aradia.

"Put a shirt on." He turned back. "Damon. What's wrong?"

Damon continued pounding. "It's Greer! Fucker got to her! She's barely breathing. Dammit, Aradia, open the fucking door! She's unconscious and I can't wake her up!"

Aradia shoved past Gage and raced down the hall in nothing but Gage's shirt. She burst into Damon and Greer's room and fell to her knees next to the unconscious woman. Before the men entered the room, she pressed her hands to Greer's head and tossed her head back, her eyes turning white. She spared one glance toward the door and saw Alaria and Braxton run in before her vision went dark.

Aradia was not a Healer. She could use her magic and energy to heal, but it was not her natural ability, and it took more out of her than almost any other spell. She murmured under her breath, spinning magic and forcing it into Greer's body. She cried out from pain when she connected to Greer's mind and felt what the other woman felt.

She pushed hard, delving deep within Greer and seeking out injuries. Seven broken ribs. Both lungs were punctured. Her skull was fractured, and there was brain damage, which was the reason the link between Greer and Damon had been severed.

Aradia knew she didn't have enough magic to heal Greer completely. She tapped in to everything she had, channeling it out through her hands and into the other woman. Her murmurs became more desperate and louder as she forced more magic from her body. It wasn't enough. Aradia could taste death.

Healers couldn't bring people back from the dead, but witches could. Aradia opened her eyes and chanted in Latin. Her eyes turned from white to red and blood trickled from her nose. Bones cracked as they shifted back into place, and Greer began whimpering as her brain regained function.

Aradia forced herself to maintain the link. She cried out, and blood dripped from her ears. She had taken too much black magic. She struggled to stem the flow and to stop the thick tar of the black that surged through her. She slammed the door that allowed her to access it and collapsed to the ground, her whole body shaking in a violent seizure and blood pouring from her eyes as the magic seeped out.

Gage snatched her up and deposited her on the bed, cradling her head in his lap until the shaking subsided. She took several gulping breaths and then passed out, her breathing slow and even. He looked up in time to see Damon helping Greer climb to her feet.

"What the hell happened?"

Greer looked grim. "They've been watching us. They knew when we left your house, and Garrick sent humans to tamper with the protections on the hotel." She gestured to Aradia. "Is she okay?"

Gage looked down. "I think she'll be okay. Fucking black magic again." He sighed. "I don't know how much more she can handle."

Alaria crossed her arms. "She'll handle whatever she has to. If she doesn't open up to it, we're all fucked anyway." She rubbed her forehead. "I have the worst fucking hangover of all time." Her head snapped to the side. "Did you hear that?"

Gage climbed off the bed. "I did."

Damon lifted his eyebrows. "Hear what?"

Gage opened the door and stuck his head out. "I smell blood." He crossed the room and leaned over the balcony to peer down.

Damon sighed and repeated himself. "Hear what?"

Alaria stood still for a moment. "Fuck. This was only an appetizer." She gestured to Geer and Aradia. "They knew you could help her. If they killed her, all the better, but you've been the real target from the beginning."

Braxton held up a hand. "Does one of you want to tell the rest of us what the fuck is going on?"

Gage closed the balcony doors. "The hotel is inside a magic shield. I think we can pass through if we can get out, but it's keeping people on the street from hearing what's going on in here. I smell blood, and I can hear some muffled screams down on what I think is the first floor. I can't tell yet if they're moving up or down, which means they're either getting started or finishing."

Alaria shook her head. "Not enough blood for finishing. They're getting started. I hear squads on the roof, I think the tenth floor, and the ground floor. Vampires, all of them. There are wolves outside the building, but not a lot because that would be drawing too much attention. The vamps are new. They can't help it."

Greer shook her head. "What the hell are you talking about?"

Gage answered. "The attack against you was a diversion to distract us to the point we wouldn't notice the vampires coming into the hotel. They're killing people. A lot of people." He listened again. "They're coming down from the roof and up from the lobby, and Aradia is the target."

"What do we do?" Greer tossed Alaria a pair of yoga pants, which the other woman pulled on. "We can't leave all of these people to be slaughtered."

Damon cast a glance around the room. "That's what they're banking on. We absolutely should just leave these people to be slaughtered. If they get to Aradia and kill her, we lose, and the whole world dies."

Alaria hopped on one foot to pull on one of Greer's shoes. "Greer's right. It may be a trap, but we'd still have to fight our way through the crowd. We're best off keeping Aradia here, where she's protected by one of us, and the rest of us clear out the vamps." She glanced between them. "I'll stay here with her. Damon and Braxton go up, Gage and Greer go down. Greer and Damon keep in contact with the brain mojo."

Gage looked at Aradia, still unconscious, and nodded sharply. "I need two minutes to put on a shirt and some shoes and get us a few guns."

Greer pulled on shoes. "I'll come with you. We can head downstairs from there." She stopped briefly to kiss Damon. "Don't die."

Ninety seconds later, they were in the stairwell, descending eighteen flights to the ground floor. Gage led the way with Greer close behind him. Both had guns loaded with wooden bullets and stakes stuck in waistbands in case they ran out of ammo. Gage held up a hand to signal silence, and he carefully opened the door leading into the lobby.

The lights were on and music still played. Everything looked exactly as it should, save for the smears of blood on the tile floor. By silent agreement, they headed behind the front desk. Greer stepped over the bodies of the desk clerks and bent to study them.

"How can I tell if they've been turned?"

Gage shook his head. "You can't. If the body is messed up badly, assume it's not. Any missing limbs, throat torn out, partial decapitation—anything like that, and you're not gonna turn them. I'd be willing to bet they turned loose a fucking herd of just risen vampires that can't control the bloodlust." He tapped the keyboard on the computer behind the desk. "Where are you, you mother fuckers?" He went through the different cameras, searching for the vampires. "There. Third floor, heading up. We'll get up to four and head them off."

Greer looked at the cameras. "We need to get this done as soon as we can. They're up to something more than just shedding blood."

Gage looked at her with a dark expression. "I know exactly what they're after. They're here to kill Aradia, and we're playing into their hands by trying to get rid of the fucking newborns in time to save people who are probably already dead." He led her back to the stairs. "The sooner we get this done, the sooner we can go home."

Greer started climbing, her voice bitter. "So much for my wedding night."

Aradia regained consciousness slowly. She blinked against the bright light above her and groaned, gripping her head with both hands to alleviate the pounding. She rolled onto her side and gagged, trying not to throw up. She closed her eyes and took deep breaths until her stomach settled.

Alaria appeared in her field of vision, holding a gun in one hand and a wet cloth in the other. She offered the cloth and crouched next to the bed, her expression serious. Aradia forced herself to sit up and pressed the cool rag to her forehead.

"What happened? Is Greer okay?"

"Greer's fine. The problem is that she was a diversion. The hotel is under attack. There are vampires inside, and they're killing, well, everyone." Alaria rifled through Greer's clothes and tossed a pair of jeans to Aradia. "Put those on." She tossed over a pair of shoes. "You're the target. If they kill you, they pry open that retaining wall we put up and the gates stay open forever. I'm your bodyguard, and the others went to hunt vampires."

Aradia pulled on the jeans and slipped her feet into the sandals. "How long ago did they leave?"

"About fifteen minutes." She led Aradia to the balcony and pointed to a shimmer near the ground. "Garrick has the hotel wrapped in some magic bubble."

"It keeps sound and calls from getting out. No one will be able to help." Aradia gathered her hair back into a ponytail. "If they're after me, why aren't they pounding on the door?"

Alaria shrugged. "Best I can gather is that they know we're here, but they don't know the precise room. There are some coming down from the roof and others coming up from the lobby. They'll get here sooner or later unless the boys and Greer kill them all first."

Aradia rubbed her temples. "They're smarter than that. Garrick would have read the magic that I used to help Greer." She went to the window and looked out. "It was never about killing her. It wasn't a diversion, it was part of the plan."

Alaria paled. "What do you mean?"

"It took a lot of magic for me to do that. When I did it, it was like a giant torch lit up and told Garrick exactly where I am. The vampires are to draw out the others. They have a better chance of taking me if I'm not with five other people."

Alaria dug through Damon and Greer's belongings. She turned up two extra clips for the gun Damon had handed her and a pair of stakes. "Well, since neither of us are psychic, we're going to have to figure this one out on our own. Is your magic working?"

Aradia bit her lip anxiously. "I'll make it work. I'm not dying here. Not tonight." She paced the length of the room. "Are they coming?"

Alaria pressed her eye to the peephole and surveyed the hallway. "I don't see anything yet, but I can hear them on the stairs." She listened intently. "I think Damon and Brax are a few floors above us, and Greer and Gage are on what I think is the sixth floor. It's hard to tell without all my demonic senses, but they're at least a hundred feet below us."

Aradia splashed water on her face and scrubbed the dried blood from her skin. "I'm weak, Alaria. It zapped me healing her."

Alaria glanced over her shoulder before going back to the peephole. "No offense, but how are you going to defeat Garrick if one spell zaps your energy?"

"It's not spells that zap me. It's healing. It's a totally different type of magic, and one I don't have a lot of." She returned to the sitting room. "Just because I'm tired doesn't mean I can't defend us. I'm not going up against Garrick and Javal. They don't want to get close enough to me because they know I could kill them. They're sending vampires because they have an almost unlimited number of them and because they were hoping I'd be a sitting duck after saving Greer. The fact that I'm not means their plan isn't going to work."

Alaria tensed. "I hope you're right. Here they come." She pressed her eye to the door. "I see about thirty vampires." She looked around. "Help me push the dresser against the door."

Aradia chuckled. "Give me a break. Move back."

Alaria took a step back and held out her hands. "Be my guest."

Aradia stared at the dresser. It shook and banged against the wall before flying across the room and slamming against the door. The women backed into the bedroom and Aradia closed the door with a flick of her wrist, sending the armoire flying across the room to barricade the entry.

Alaria loaded a round into the chamber and backed Aradia into a corner of the room. She planted her feet and squared her shoulders. The first crash on the outer door made them both jump. Aradia laid her hand on Alaria's back.

"If they come through that door, then you shoot. Until then, this is mine to handle. I'm not going to be able to talk to you for a few minutes."

Aradia closed her eyes and retreated within herself. She opened her eyes, which had turned black. She reached out, straining to see beyond the door. Slowly, her consciousness moved past the barrier and she flew to the door. Vampires crowded the hallway and pounded on it.

She drifted over their heads and focused on the last one. She reached into the creature and formed a ball of energy within him. He clutched his chest and stumbled backward, clawing at the skin. Aradia increased the heat and energy until it burst and the vampire disintegrated into dust. One down.

Each became harder than the last. Her energy waned from the exertion of healing Greer, and the energy expended to incinerate the vampires was significant. She opened herself again to the black, taking it inside her body and battling it, forcing it to transform into pure magic that she could manipulate and use.

The vampires began to notice what was going on. They scrambled down the hall, fleeing from the inferno. Aradia tried to reign in the power, but couldn't. She went after them, stretching out with the magic and driving it into them, one after the other. Within moments, the hall was covered in dust.

She couldn't stop. She flung herself further, sinking through the floor and dropping down to where Greer and Gage were locked in a losing battle with two dozen monsters. She screeched with anger and let the power wash over her. Flames burst into existence and surrounded the creatures, turning them into a mob of begging, dying things.

Gage was bleeding and sank to the floor. Greer was immediately beside him, her hands going to the wound. Convinced that she would care for Gage, Aradia reached upward, seeking Damon and Braxton, who had not yet found the vampires they sought.

She found them first. She reached into each of them, seized their hearts, and ripped. Blood sprayed the walls and ceiling as the vampires exploded into dust, looks of shock on their faces. She searched the rest of the hotel for more threats and, finding none, she retreated into her own body.

She reached herself easily and tried to sink back in, but found she couldn't. There was too much power coursing through her and she had expended too much energy. She was locked out of herself.

Chapter Twenty-Four

GAGE PACED the room. "How long has she been like this?"

Alaria perched on the bed and stared at Aradia, who was sitting on the floor, staring blankly ahead. "Fifteen minutes maybe. I don't know what she did."

Michael appeared with a rustle. "I'm sorry. I've only just found out about the attack here tonight."

Alaria laughed. "If I hadn't experienced the delays in Angels getting notified of things for myself, I'd be very suspicious of how you and Gabe always arrive after the action."

Michael touched Alaria's shoulder and looked at Aradia. "Her consciousness is trapped outside of her body."

Gage stopped pacing. "How the fuck did that happen?"

Michael turned to him. "When Aradia used her abilities to kill the vampires, she detached her mind from her body in order to be able to stretch herself far enough to kill the ones attacking the rest of you. She went too far into black magic and has not yet found her way back into her body."

Greer leaned against the dresser. "I don't think I can fix that."

"It's not an injury, so no, you cannot fix it." Michael crouched in front of Aradia. "However, I can bring her back."

He reached out and touched Aradia's forehead. His hand glowed softly, and Aradia began blinking. She looked around blankly and fell to the side, hitting the floor with a soft thud. Michael smiled grimly and climbed to his feet, addressing everyone in the room.

"She'll be fine. She is learning to control it, but not fast enough. I believe the time has come that it will be necessary for you to return to Atlantis. The only one I know of that can help her access more of the black without allowing it to consume her is Graciela." He glanced around. "It will not be long before Javal and Garrick know they failed. I suggest you gather your things and leave as soon as is possible. If you wish, I'll wait so that I can transport you back."

Greer pushed off the dresser. "I'll go pack Aradia's stuff. Gage, do you want me to get yours together, too?"

"Please." He bent and scooped Aradia into his arms. "You're sure she'll be okay?"

Michael smiled reassuringly. "There is no damage to her. She'll wake up within the hour and will be fine. She did very well against the vampires. You should be proud of what she accomplished here this night." He looked at Gage pointedly. "She is only doing what is necessary to ensure success."

Gage chuckled. "I can't help it. I worry about her."

Michael smiled. "May I speak to you alone, Gage?"

Gage exchanged a look with Damon and Braxton. Damon nodded. "Go on. I'll watch her."

Gage followed the Angel out into the hall. "What's going on?"

Michael looked from side to side. "Graciela did not lie. As reward for your participation in this, which so clearly goes against your very nature, I have been authorized to make you human once more."

"Why is it that you think now is the time to talk about this? I told Graciela that I wasn't interested."

"Now is the time because I am aware of the situation and we are in the same location with nothing more pressing to do other than wait for the others to pack their things." He glared at the vampire. "You are not in possession of a soul, and yet you grieve for your family and you love Aradia like two humans love one another. How is it that you are not interested in being what they are? In being what you once were?"

"I lived my life as a human once, and it didn't go so well. I'm not going to get into another position where I'm vulnerable. I've lived long enough to know I don't care to grow old."

Michael held out his hands. "The option is there. I will tell you this, there is a prophecy in some of the human scrolls about a vampire whose heart began to beat once more. In it, to succeed, you must love as no other creature has loved and be purified in fire. Once those two things are done, an organ long dead will come to life." He paused briefly. "God has brought the dead back before, when it serves His purposes. You are not out of His reach, Gage. If He thinks you should be mortal, then mortal you shall be."

Gage crossed his arms. "Are you telling me I might not have a choice?"

"If your humanity is gained through the fulfillment of some ancient human prophecy, then no, you may not have a choice. If you do not succeed in the task, then no, you will not have a choice. If you succeed and it is offered, you may turn it down. However, before you stress to me again how uninterested you are in being human, allow me to ask you this. How would Aradia feel if she knew you had the chance to be with her for a lifetime and turned it down because you were afraid?"

"Why are you pushing this, Michael?"

Michael took several breaths while he thought about a response. "I've known you for a long time, Gage. Even at your worst, you were more tortured than you were evil. For the last eight hundred years or so, you've been an ally for us. I guess I just don't quite understand why you wouldn't jump all over an offer to get back what you lost and have a second chance at life."

Gage considered Michael's words carefully. "I like you, and more than that, I trust you. You've always been straight with me, and I always know where I stand with you. That's a rare trait amongst the angels. The long and short of it is that I don't deserve another shot at it. I killed my children. I murdered them. I drank their blood and drained them dry, Michael."

"I'm aware of what you did." Michael's voice was soft. "What I don't know is how much you plan to punish yourself before allowing yourself to move on."

"I'm never going to move on."

"What about Aradia?"

Gage looked pained. "I tried to avoid it. I love her. I've got no fucking clue how that's possible given that I have no soul, but I damn well remember the emotion enough to know when I'm experiencing it. All I can hope for her is that she's able to move on and find someone else that will make her happy."

"What of the bond?"

"I'll go far enough away that she won't be able to feel it."

"If you change your mind, I'll do whatever I can to help you." Michael glanced back at the door toward the others. "It would be nice to see someone get a happy ending."

"That would be Greer and Damon." He looked down the hall to where Greer came out of his room with a bag on each arm. "They deserve it."

Michael opened the door and motioned for Gage to precede him into the room. "You all do."

Damon looked up when they walked back in. "Everything okay?"

"Everything's fine." Gage offered a tight smile to Alaria as she came back in with her bag. "We need to get out of here, though."

Braxton and Greer came through the door at the same time. Braxton spoke to Michael. "Let's get this done."

Gage picked up Aradia in his arms and cradled her against his chest. Michael reached out and touched each of them on the forehead. Within the span of a heartbeat, the hotel room faded and the kitchen of Gage's home appeared. Michael smiled and looked around.

"I believe you'll all be safe here. Is there anything you need before I go?" When he was answered with shaking heads and a chorus of voices thanking him, he nodded. "If you need assistance in the future, you need only call."

Gage looked down at Aradia, who was beginning to stir. "I'm going to get her upstairs and taken care of." He looked at the clock. "It's four in the morning, so I'm going to try to sleep for a couple hours. I'll see you all in the morning."

He ascended the stairs with Aradia held securely in his arms. He bypassed her room on the second floor and went directly to his own on the third. He deposited her gently on the bed and returned to the door long enough to turn the lock. Aradia made a sound and stirred on the bed, and he laid one hand on her head.

"Come on out of it. You're back where you should be, Priestess."

Aradia blinked and squinted against the light. "Gage? What happened?"

"You got trapped outside your body. Too much too fast according to Michael. He put you back. Do you remember anything?"

She sat up and rubbed her hands over her face. "I remember projecting out and killing the vampires. It was like I couldn't stop. I had to destroy them all. When I finished and came back, I couldn't get into my body. I was trapped, and no matter how much I tried, I was stuck outside. I didn't think I was ever going to be okay."

Gage sat next to her. "How much did you use?"

Aradia looked down. "More than I intended to use." She toed off her borrowed sandals and drew her legs up. "Are you angry with me?"

He reached out and laid his hand on her leg. "I'm not angry. I was worried about you." He rubbed her knee. "Was it easier? Or was it still hard for you to get to the black magic?"

"It was easier. It was waiting for me right underneath what I have. I could control it, Gage. I could make it do what I wanted it to do, and I made it bend the direction I told it to. It was an incredible high. It was like there was nothing I couldn't do, but when I let it sweep me away, I couldn't come back."

"What can I do to help?" He ran his hand over her hair. "It seems like you don't really have much of a choice in using the black magic, so I'm just going to have to accept that as a reality. What I need to know now is if there is anything that I can do to make sure that you can come back from it."

Aradia leaned her head on his shoulder. "I wish I knew. I think I need to practice. As scary as that is, I have to be able to maneuver in and out of it."

"Michael thinks that going back to Atlantis will help with that. He believes that if anyone can help you figure it out, it will be your mother."

"He's probably right." She closed her eyes. "I'm exhausted. Do you mind if we sleep?"

"Not at all, love."

He stood and opened his closet, withdrawing a shirt for her to change in to. She donned it without a fuss, sliding between the sheets. Gage stripped to his boxers and slipped into bed beside her, reaching out to turn off the lamp before drawing her close and aligning her body to his.

"Gage?"

He yawned. "Yeah?"

"Thank you for not being mad."

Gage kissed her shoulder. "You're welcome."

Gabriel was waiting in the garden when Michael appeared. He rose from the bench and greeted his brother with a nod before gesturing for Michael to sit. Michael looked at him suspiciously before dropping to one of the stone benches.

"It is unusual for you to be here without me having hailed you."

"I have done what has been asked of me."

Michael's face fell. "Oh." He shook his head. "I don't know whether I was hoping you would or hoping you would not. I take it you did not discuss this predicament with Alaria?"

"She knows nothing."

"She will shortly." Michael crossed one leg over the other. "Human women often know within merely a few weeks that they are with child."

"Will her gestation be the same as a human woman?"

Michael smiled reassuringly. "This is a child ordained by God. She will not give birth to a monster, Gabriel. She will deliver a healthy daughter with a destiny more important than any human ever born, including Griffin. This child will have the ability to kill Satan."

Gabriel blinked. "You told me the child would chain Lucifer to Hell so that he could never break free."

"No, I told you the child would be born for the purpose of waging a war against Lucifer." Michael sighed and folded his hands on his knee. "Are you at peace with your decision?"

Gabriel laughed bitterly. "It's done, isn't it? I've betrayed her in the worst possible way. I've taken away her choice and her ability to control her own destiny. I sacrificed the only woman I will ever love in order to please our Father. I gave her up. Isn't doing all of that good enough? Now I'm supposed to be at peace with it, too?"

Michael reached out and laid his hand over Gabriel's. "I want to help you, brother. I know how difficult this has been for you and how difficult it will be yet. What can I do to make this easier?"

Gabriel pulled his hand away and plowed it through his hair, displacing it. "There's nothing that can make this easier on me, Michael." He pinched the bridge of his nose between two fingers. "How long will it be until she discovers the existence of the child?"

Michael lifted his shoulder in a shrug. "I am not a fortune-teller, Gabriel. She'll alert you when she knows, of that I am absolutely sure. Have you given thought to what you will tell her?"

"Do I have a choice?"

"You could lie."

Gabriel shook his head. "No. I'll tell her the truth. This could be the one thing that will free her from me enough to find happiness elsewhere. She deserves to know that I am little more than a rapist who seduced her into a pregnancy she has not consented to and likely does not want."

Michael looked stern. "For all the grief that you are entitled to over this, and I'm the first to admit that it is substantial, you must not doubt that this was necessary and that the choice you made will spare Alaria pain in the future."

Gabriel's last words echoed through the clearing as he disappeared. "Somehow I doubt very much that she'll see it that way."

Chapter Twenty-Five

May 31, 2031

"The time has come to join me in Atlantis."

Aradia looked around the clearing and smiled when she saw her mother. "We can't come until the Angels take us."

"You will come when you're needed, regardless of Gabriel and Michael. Once you come back, you will be outside of their reach." Graciela took Aradia's arm and linked it through her own. "It is time."

"What do we need to do?"

"You'll know when the time is right." She patted Aradia's hand. "How are you, darling?"

"Did you bring me here for gossip?"

"I brought you here for a few reasons." She smiled brightly. "One of which is to check on your mental status after what has arisen between you and the vampire. Which brings me back to my question. How are you?"

"Better than expected. Gage is amazing. I don't know what will happen after all of this is over, but I know that I'll have no regrets."

"Good." Graciela shifted topics seamlessly. "When you come back to Atlantis, you cannot allow me to know what happens. You were not there the first time around, and I worry about how I would react to knowing about the future. There will be some things you must make known, but I must impress upon you the importance of making sure that you do not reveal more than is necessary."

"How will we deal with the fact that I am named the same name you will give to me when I'm born?"

Graciela smiled softly. "There are so many conundrums when it comes to time travel. You'll know the right thing to do when the time comes. I have no doubt about that."

Aradia shook her head. "I wish there were more concrete answers to these questions."

"There are no absolutes other than that you must succeed. As long as you emerge through this successfully, you have made all the right decisions and have done whatever is necessary." She patted Aradia's hand gently. "This is complicated. I know that, and I'll be here whenever you need me to be. If push comes to shove, I'll handle telling myself about what is going on."

"Is it safe for us to be here? With Javal and Garrick attacking us as they have, do you think it's the best thing for us to be here?"

Graciela shook her head. "No, I don't. I needed to talk to you, and this is the only way to do it. You have to be prepared for the things that will come." She led Aradia down a dirt path. "Atlantis is a beautiful place. The things that are going to happen are bigger than even I ever dreamed."

"Like what?"

"You'll find out when it's time. These tasks are just the beginning, Aradia. I know your companions look at this as a way to bring the world back to where it should have been, and in a way, that's true. However, out of this tragedy and trial will come something better than any of you imagined. Lives will change. New life will be born from these things, and you will bear witness to the most important birth in human history. Well, other than Jesus, of course."

Aradia looked at her mother in confusion. "What's going on, Mother?"

"I can't give you all the details. I would if I was allowed, but I'm not. These are exciting times, Aradia. There is the potential to change this world into what it was always supposed to be. God never intended for there to be Hell. He never intended for Earth to become what it is. These next years will give the opportunity to restore everything to the way God intended."

Aradia stopped walking. "What do you mean?"

Graciela shook her head. "You'll find out in due time. There are still things that need to happen. I shouldn't have said as much as I have. I'm excited about the prospects that are coming into focus. You must remember, Aradia, that change takes time. You and the others are beginning what will be finished by others. This will take more than your generation."

"You're telling me that we're just going to pass this burden on to other people?"

"No. You are going to finish your part of it. You will accomplish what you were meant to do. This is not all for you, child."

Aradia sighed. "I don't want anyone else to be stuck with this the way we are."

Graciela squeezed Aradia's hand. "Trust me. Trust God and Gabriel and Michael. We will not lead you wrong. The Choosing was intended to definitively change the way the world is. Lucifer circumventing that is what has caused what you are now going through. In response to that, God is, what is the phrase people use in your time? One-upping?"

Aradia giggled. "I think so."

"God is one-upping him. If this goes as planned, Lucifer will not survive, and Hell may cease to exist."

Aradia turned and gaped at her mother. "Are you serious?"

"I am. You must not doubt yourself, Aradia. Do what you feel is right, and it will not lead you astray. I promise you that." Graciela embraced Aradia briefly. "I need for you to listen very carefully. It is time to return to Atlantis. Get the vampire to ready his flying device. You all must make your way to Greece. The house where you are will not be safe indefinitely, and you must leave as soon as possible. Once you arrive, the Angels will give you further instruction."

Aradia nodded, her expression serious. "I'll do the best I can."

"This is not going to be easy. If you remember any one thing I have told you, remember this—you must do nothing that will change the present. Do not change the past. No matter how painful it is, or how much you might wish to change something, you must not. Everything happens for a reason, and there will be healing with time."

"What does that mean?"

Graciela leaned forward and pressed a kiss to Aradia's cheek. "You'll know when you need to know. Go now, and relay my message to the rest."

In Gage's bed, Aradia sat up blinking. She looked beside her and found Gage sleeping deeply. Moonlight streamed through the curtains and the sky was an inky black, telling her that dawn was still several hours away.

She climbed out of bed and went to the window, wrapping a throw blanket around her shoulders and leaning against the window pane. She peered out and smiled at the silver cast the moon gave to everything. The hair on the back of her neck stood up, and she looked around carefully, trying to find the source of the anxiety.

There.

Across from her window, at the far end of the property, just over the line of traps and wards. An old man stood in the shadows, barely visible. His eyes glowed green in the dark, and he had long, gray hair that nearly reached the ground. In one hand, he held a staff, and in the other, he had a ball of fire spinning slowly.

Aradia jumped when Gage appeared beside her. He looked out, his eyes finding the same thing hers had. He laid a hand on the small of her back and glared out.

"Garrick?"

"I think so. I've never seen him before, so I couldn't tell you for sure, but it feels like him. I can sense the magic he's got, and it's the same as what was coming off of that shield at the hotel."

Gage bent to pull on his slacks. "Can he get in?"

"I don't think he's even trying to. He's just standing there, knowing I can see him. It's a show. He wants us to know he's here, and he wants us to know he could get in if he wanted to."

"He could get in if he tried, then?"

"He's always been able to get in, I think. I don't know him, Gage, but I feel like I can tell everything about him that I need to. He's hands off. He sends Javal to do his bidding because he doesn't want to get his hands dirty. He much prefers to be at the back issuing orders than in the trenches fighting the war. I think he's annoyed Javal hasn't been able to kill me, and he's come to lure me out."

"You're not going. We'll go get Greer and send her up to the roof with a sniper rifle. She'll end him before he knows what's happening."

Aradia chuckled. "You can't kill him with a bullet any more than you could kill me with one. He'd bat it away like a bug. He's not here to fight. He just wants me to know the time has come. He's done sending other people to do the work for him. He's ready to fight me."

Gage jerked the curtains closed. "What can we do to keep the house safe from him?"

Aradia sat on the edge of the bed. "There isn't anything we can do. I was going to wait until morning to tell you. My mother took me to the dream plane tonight. She told me it's time to leave here. She wants us to head for Greece. From there, we'll apparently know how to get back to Atlantis."

Gage nodded. "Is Garrick going to start a fight before then?"

Aradia shook her head. "No. He and I have always been meant to face off in the battle, and I think we've both known it the whole time. All of these skirmishes have been his way of testing me. In a way, I think he wanted to make sure I was worthy of him."

"You know an awful lot about a warlock you've never met."

"I don't know how to explain it. You can learn a lot about a witch or warlock through their magic. Each one has a different signature, and it tells you a lot about who they are and what they're doing. He's making no effort to filter it, either. His magic feels cocky and sure. He isn't scared of me, and he doesn't care if I know what he's thinking because he doesn't believe it will make a difference. He thinks he can beat me anyway."

"Are you filtering?"

"Yeah. I'm not letting him get anything." She stood and pulled on her clothes. "I think we need to leave as soon as we can."

Gage opened the door and led her down the stairs to the first floor. "I'll make flight arrangements as soon as the airport staff is back on duty. It'll be ten or twelve hours before we can take off." He glanced back toward the stairs they had just descended. "Is it important enough that we need to be waking everyone else up?"

Aradia's face split into a grin. "She'll never hit him, but a few shots might piss him off."

Gage couldn't stop the smile that spread across his mouth. "Let's wake them up."

Alaria raced to the bathroom. Her eyes had sprung open thirty seconds before, and she'd spent those seconds trying to convince her stomach not to rebel. Nausea was a new sensation and one she did not care for.

She hit the floor on her knees, and wrenched the lid of the toilet up before leaning over it and retching. The smell of the water and porcelain made her stomach clench and she gagged again. Remnants of her dinner and splashes of stomach acid sprayed the porcelain bowl, turning the water a brownish yellow.

The sight of it made her sicker and she fumbled for the handle, flushing the toilet. Water sprayed her face as it flooded the bowl, and she swiped at it in annoyance. She coughed and heaved for several more seconds. After heaving four times and producing nothing other than acid that burned the back of her throat and stomach, she collapsed to the floor in a shivering, sweaty heap.

Alaria closed her eyes tightly and took deep breaths. Her stomach roiled and churned, but nothing else made its way up her esophagus. Unsteady, she climbed to her feet and smeared toothpaste on her toothbrush, cramming it into her mouth and scrubbing viciously.

She spat out blue foam and rinsed her mouth with water before rubbing a bar of soap between her hands and slathering it on her face. Holding her breath, she scrubbed her face vigorously for several seconds before shoving her whole face under the faucet and washing off every trace of toilet water and vomit. She patted her face dry with a towel and leaned against the doorway until she completely regained her balance.

Steadier, she changed from her pajamas into jeans and a t-shirt and headed downstairs. Greer was in the kitchen cleaning a rifle, and Aradia was pacing around the island. The three men sat at the island looking concerned. The light coming in the window was the pale lavender and orange associated with sunrise.

She looked between them, her brows drawing together in confusion. "What's going on?"

Braxton stood to pour her a cup of coffee. "Garrick made an appearance."

"Why didn't someone wake me up?" Alaria took the coffee and glared at him. "You just let me sleep through a fight?"

Greer chuckled. "There was no fight. He was gone before I got the gun and got up to the roof. The boys did a sweep of the property, and there was no other signs of anyone, or anything, else. We think he was just trying to rile Aradia."

Alaria looked toward the redhead. "Did it work?"

Aradia shook her head and smiled tightly. "Not one damn bit." She drank deeply from her cup. "It was, what do you call it when men face off against one another?"

Alaria chuckled. "A pissing contest?"

"Yes, that's the phrase!" Aradia snapped her fingers. "It was a pissing contest."

Gage took a drink of blood. "We'll be packing up and leaving for Greece as soon as we can. The jet is on standby."

Alaria pushed the plate Damon sat in front of her away and got pale, her stomach roiling. "No, thanks. Why are we leaving for Greece?"

Aradia looked at Alaria strangely but answered the question. "It's time to go back to Atlantis. My mother came to see me last night, and she told me that we need to go to Greece, and from there, we'll know what we need to do."

Alaria stood to put as much distance between herself and the food as she could. "Let's get packed and out of here then. Can I assume we won't be coming back here in the three weeks we have left?"

"I think that's a safe bet. Pack as much as you think you'll need. I don't know how much we can take back with us, but we'll at least take it to Greece with us."

Alaria drained her coffee cup and sat it in the sink. "I'm going to go pack then. Leave in an hour?"

Aradia stood. "Fine with me. I'll walk up with you."

Alaria made a beeline for her bedroom. She tried to close the door, but Aradia was quicker and darted into the room before she could get it shut. Ten seconds later, Greer shoved her way in and closed the door behind her. She looked between Aradia and Alaria curiously.

"What's going on?"

Aradia stared at Alaria. "How long have you been sick?"

"Just this morning. It's a stomach bug, I'm sure." Alaria pulled a duffel bag from her closet and began rifling through her drawers. "You two oughta pack so we can leave."

"I've never once seen you turn down breakfast. Not even when you were hungover."

Greer wrinkled her nose. "Are you okay?"

Alaria dumped a stack of jeans into the bag. "I'm fine. Jesus, a girl can't even puke without an intervention in this house." She piled in shirts. "Go on, get outta here."

Aradia crossed her arms. "Are you pregnant?"

Alaria scoffed. "In order to get pregnant, I'd have to be having sex with a human."

Greer sat on the edge of the bed. "Can Angels not get women pregnant?"

"It's not done. If it does happen, which is extraordinarily rare, the child rarely survives pregnancy, and there hasn't ever been one survive to adulthood."

"Is it rare, though? I mean, how many Angels have sex with women?" Greer crossed one leg over the other. "I got the feeling it's pretty unheard of for an Angel to bang a human, which might make a resulting pregnancy rather common."

Alaria glared at them. "I was a Devil for millions of years, and before that, I was an Angel. The odds are that I don't even have a uterus."

"Do you have periods?"

Alaria gaped at Greer. "What the hell kind of question is that?"

"If you have periods, you have a uterus and ovaries." Greer yawned. "Just get a test. It's an easy way to settle the argument."

Aradia looked between the other two women. "A test?"

Greer nodded. "It's a stick that you pee on, and it measures your urine to tell if there are any pregnancy hormones present."

Alaria sighed. "How the fuck do you even know that? Did they still have pregnancy tests where you come from?"

"They were expensive but available." Greer stood. "Come on. We'll announce we need tampons for the trip and make a quick trip to the market in the village. It's ten minutes each way." She went to the door. "Hell, I'll go get it myself if you'll take it."

Alaria crossed her arms. "I'm not going."

Aradia jumped up. "I'll go with you."

Alaria watched the other two leave, her heart pounding in her chest. She staunchly ignored the nerves and forced herself to focus on the task at hand. She finished packing and moved into Aradia's room, packing the other woman's clothes quickly and efficiently. One look into Greer and Damon's room told her that Damon was taking care of Greer's stuff, and she returned to her room to wait.

Within thirty minutes, Greer and Aradia had returned. Greer had a box of tampons tucked under her arm and a small bag in one hand. She dropped the former into a drawer in the bathroom and handed the latter to Alaria with a stern look.

"Go pee."

Alaria snatched the box from Greer's hand. "When this is negative, I get to slap you for the trouble."

She moved into the bathroom and closed the door. Greer and Aradia exchanged a long look, their faces identical expressions of concern. They waited silently until Alaria flushed the toilet and emerged from the bathroom.

"Three minutes."

Aradia stuck her head in the bathroom and stared at the white stick on the counter. "What does it do?"

Greer chuckled. "If it's negative, there's only one line. If it's positive, there are two."

Aradia peered down at the results window. She studied it for a moment before exiting the bathroom, a somber look on her face. "The magic pee stick informs us that you are with child."

Black spots swarmed Alaria's vision and the floor rushed up to meet her.

Chapter Twenty-Six

Damon heaved the last of the bags into the storage compartment of Gage's jet and dusted his hands off. He pushed the button to close the hatch and pulled off his sunglasses. Braxton stood behind him, hands on his hips and his own sunglasses perched on his nose. Damon quirked one eyebrow.

"What's up?"

"Something's going on with the girls." Braxton glanced toward the steps leading up into the place where the three women and Gage waited. "They're hiding something."

Damon shrugged. "No clue, dude. They're women. They only tell us what they want us to know." He checked the latches to the compartment. "What do you want me to do about it?"

"Greer is the one most likely to talk. I thought maybe she'd said something."

Damon snickered. "The three of them are getting tighter by the day. At this point, I'd have more luck trying to infiltrate Hell than that circle."

Braxton sighed. "That's what I was afraid of. I don't care if they're gossiping or doing whatever women do, but I've got a feeling something is wrong. The fact that Alaria was so damn gung-ho to get going this morning and then spent the whole day locked in her room with the two of them doesn't make me feel any better about the situation." He glanced up at the setting sun. "I had figured we'd be there by now."

"If something was really wrong, they'd tell us. They all know this is too important for us to not all be in it together. They're probably just fretting over Alaria. It's odd seeing her sick, but it happens to the best of us. Even I get a stomach bug on occasion."

Braxton headed for the stairs. "True enough. I suppose we've all been pretty lucky that we haven't seen more sickness since we've all been here. Other than getting hurt, we've all been pretty healthy." He glanced back. "But if Greer does mention something..."

Damon nodded in solidarity. "You'll be the first to know."

They entered the plane together. Alaria was laying on the couch, a pillow clutched to her stomach and a glass of ginger ale at her elbow. Greer and Aradia sat in chairs close to her, and Gage was at his desk with his laptop open. He exchanged a look with Damon and Braxton as they entered and swiveled to call out to the pilot.

"We're ready to take off." He looked back to the rest. "It's about a six hour flight to Athens. There's a storm headed our way, and we've got a small plane, so there's a pretty good chance we'll be diverted. If we have to land, we'll stay on the plane if it's just going to be a few hours, mainly because it's safer than a hotel. I'm having a rental property prepared in Athens to hold us over until we can travel to Atlantis." He glanced at his watch. "It's almost nine now, so we won't get in until three-thirty in the morning. I'll suggest just spending the night on the plane."

Damon shrugged. "Fine with me." He yawned. "I could go to sleep now if I'm honest about it. We've been up since three this morning."

"It's been a long day, that's for sure. Greer, you and Damon can have the bed. Alaria and Braxton can take the couches, and Aradia can have my bed. I'm going to work since this is probably going to be the last chance I have to work on anything." Gage looked around again. "If no one cares, I'm going to pull the door closed so I can get this done." When no one objected, he stood. "I'll see you all in Greece."

Alaria groaned and forced herself to sit up long enough to take a drink of the ginger ale. Greer stood and lowered herself to the floor in front of the other woman, patting her hand gently. Alaria closed her eyes and tightened her grip on the pillow.

"I think I can help."

Alaria opened one eye. "How can you help?"

"I'm a Healer. I can at least try to take away the nausea."

"There's no taking it away." She turned her face into the couch. "Just leave me alone, Greer. I just want to sleep."

Greer nodded. "If you change your mind and want me to try, the worst that can happen is that it doesn't work."

Braxton cleared his throat. "Why won't you let her try? There's no point in you being sick if you don't have to be."

Alaria looked up and glared at him. "Mind your own damn business."

Braxton leaned back in his chair and crossed his legs. "Fine. I won't offer advice."

Greer laid her hand on Alaria's arm. "Alaria, please let me help you."

Alaria shifted her gaze to Greer. "Can you make everything go away?"

Greer shook her head. "No, sweetie. I can't."

Damon and Braxton exchanged a look. Damon cleared his throat. "Is there something going on that we should know about?"

Alaria laughed. "Nothing other than the misery that is my love life."

Damon stood. "I don't need to hear this. I'm going to bed. Come in when you're done, Greer."

"I will." She turned back to Alaria. "I can help if you'll let me."

"Fine. If letting you make me feel better will make you leave me alone, just do it." She sat up. "Come on, then. Make me feel better."

Greer reached out and laid her hands on Alaria's stomach. Within moments, Alaria felt the nausea ease and the burning of stomach acid subsided. Greer stepped back and smiled softly. Alaria reached out and squeezed her hand.

"I'm sorry I'm being bitchy."

"No apologies necessary. I understand." She exchanged a look with Aradia and rocked back on her heels several times. "I guess I'll go lay down with Damon. I imagine tomorrow will start early."

Braxton stood and grabbed blankets and another pillow out of a closet. He draped one of the blankets over Alaria and stretched out on the other couch. Aradia looked between them and stood.

"I'll retreat as well. Good night."

Aradia slipped through the sliding door and closed it behind her. Gage sat at the slender table, typing on his laptop. He glanced up when she came in and swiveled to face her. She slid past him and reached for a glass from the cabinet above his head. She turned on the water and filled it.

"Everyone else is getting some sleep."

Gage nodded. "What's going on with Alaria that you know about and those of us with penises do not?"

Aradia blushed. "I can't tell you. She's asked us not to."

"If it's something that's going to interfere with her ability to help us get through this, we need to know, Aradia."

"She'll be fine. It's a personal thing."

"What kind of a personal thing?"

"Gage." Aradia smiled and leaned against the counter. "I cannot tell you. Alaria confided in me, and I will keep her troubles to myself. It's a woman thing."

Gage reached out, drawing her into his lap. "Very well." He nuzzled his nose into her neck. "Do you want to go to bed?"

"Don't you have work to do?"

He kissed the curve of her jaw. "You're more important than work."

She looked at the computer screen. "What are you working on?"

Gage reached out and closed the laptop. "I was just updating my will."

"Your what?" Aradia looked confused. "I don't know what that is."

"It's a document that tells my lawyers what I want done with the things that I own if I die."

She leaned back and stared at him. "That's morbid."

"It's normal in this time. I'm dividing up my belongings among the five of you. There are some things that I know none of you would want or know what to do with, so those are going to charity. My businesses have trusts so they'll keep running without me. I want to make sure you're taken care of if I die."

"In my time, the elderly make it known what their wishes are, and their children, or others in the village, make sure that those desires are carried out. There is no need for written instructions."

Gage smiled. "Times have changed, Priestess."

Aradia finished her water and rose to refill the glass. As she stood, the plane lurched and she pitched forward. The glass tumbled from her fingers and struck the floor, exploding into small pieces of glass. She struck her forehead on the counter and cried out from the pain. Gage surged out of his chair and lifted her into his arms, carrying her to the bedroom so that she didn't step on shards of glass.

He left her long enough to go to the fridge for ice, which he wrapped in a towel and pressed to the purpling bruise on her head. He swept the pieces into the trash bin and returned to the bedroom, sitting next to her and taking the towel to look at the damage.

Aradia touched the knot on her head and winced. "What was that?"

"It's called turbulence. It's basically when the air outside the plane gets blowing too quickly and it rocks the plane around a bit. It's not dangerous. The pilot will try to get us above it if he can, but if not, we might have to just go through. If it starts to get too rough, we'd land."

"I don't think I like flying." She touched the knot again. "Greer can fix this in the morning. It's not worth waking her up over."

Gage kicked the door shut to the small bedroom. He nudged Aradia to lay back and stretched out next to her. "I think they know about us."

"No one has said anything to me." She giggled when he kissed her neck. "Is it really so big of a secret that we don't want the others to know?"

"No. I thought you preferred it this way."

Aradia struggled to keep a clear head through the sensations his mouth was causing. "I wanted to avoid judgment from the others. Where I'm from, this would have gotten me hanged."

"Good thing you came forward in time instead of going backward then, isn't it?" Gage efficiently removed her t-shirt and took possession of her bra-clad breasts with his hands. "I don't care if people know. We're not doing anything wrong, and no one on this plane is going to judge us for it. We aren't exactly a passel of blushing virgins, Aradia. You were the only one with that title."

Aradia flushed red and turned her head to the side. "That's not been an issue for some time now."

Gage buried his face in her neck. "I'll never forgive myself for what we're doing. I know we're both walking into it with our eyes wide open, but I will always wish I'd had the strength to turn you away. I hope you know that I don't want to hurt you, even though I know I will."

Aradia hugged him close. "The time isn't upon us yet. We should enjoy the time we have and not borrow trouble." She lifted her face and pressed her mouth to his in a kiss. "I love you, Gage. We may hurt one another, but I will never regret the time we spend together, no matter how brief it may be."

Gage shook off the somber tone and rolled on top of her. "In this time, we have something called the 'Mile High Club.' Do you know what that is?"

Aradia shook her head. "No."

"It's a term for people who have had sex in an airplane." He brushed his lips over her chest. "How do you feel about getting a membership?"

"I think I like the idea."

Gage slipped into the cockpit and sat in the empty copilot chair. His pilot, Hank, looked over in greeting. He adjusted one of the instruments and checked the radar. Rain pelted the windshield, and the clouds churned with energy.

"Evenin', boss." Hank pointed to the radar. "We've got a hell of a front coming at us. It didn't look nearly this big when we took off. I think we're going to have to shoot for Italy. I've radioed into Pamplona for permission to land. We're over the Adriatic Sea right now, and as long as we're on a seaward path, it's going to get rougher. We'll spend the night in Italy and take off as soon as the storm breaks."

"Sounds like a good plan to me. Once we get to Greece, I want you to fly back to Scotland and take some time off. We'll be there for a few weeks. I'll call for you when we need to fly home."

Hank reached out to touch the controls. Lightning struck the nose of the plane and lit the control panel up. Hank's hands clenched the handles and his entire body jerked. Gage grabbed the other man and wrenched him from the metal, laying him on the floor gently. He pressed his fingers to Hank's neck and swore when there was no pulse.

He sprang to his feet and tried to work the controls, but found that they were fried. He tried the radio and got nothing but static. Panic rose in his throat and he ran to the back of the plane. Braxton was sitting up and rubbing his eyes, though Alaria still slept soundly.

"Get up! Everyone wake up!"

Braxton pulled on his shoes. "What's going on?"

"The plane's been struck by lightning. The pilot's dead. We have to jump."

Alaria groaned and rolled over, blinking rapidly against the light Gage turned on. "Really? Fucking hell, can we not get a break ever?"

Damon and Greer came out of the bedroom, and Aradia stumbled in from the other room. Gage pointed to Damon. "Up above your bed is a cabinet that has parachutes in them. Get them." He looked at the women. "Get everything you absolutely cannot do without. You have ninety seconds."

Braxton began shoving weapons into a large duffel bag. Gage returned to the controls for one final try at keeping them from crashing. He tried the radio again and then slammed it down in frustration. He went to his laptop and with a few keystrokes backed up everything to his sky drive. He grabbed his phone, put it in a plastic bag, and stuffed it in his pocket.

Greer had taken charge of strapping Aradia and Alaria into the parachutes. She moved with brutal efficiency, her fingers flying over the latches and cords. She pelted them with instructions on which cords to pull and how to position their bodies on the way down. Damon, who was already strapped in, was lashing the duffel of weapons to his chest, out of the way of the cords.

Braxton tossed Gage a parachute. "There's no telling what's going to be waiting for us." He tucked a knife into his waistband. "We have to assume that this is not just a storm."

Aradia looked between them, fear in her eyes. "I don't understand what's happening."

Gage framed her face with his hands. "The pilot is dead. When the lightning hit the plane, it sent electricity through the controls that make it fly. Without them, the plane falls. We're over the Adriatic Sea, which is a narrow canal that runs along Italy. We'll be fine." He pressed a kiss to her forehead.

Damon grabbed the handle on the emergency exit and pried it open. He kicked the door and sent it flying. Outside, the air was thick and heavy from the storm, and lightning split the sky. Thunder rolled, so powerful they felt it before they heard it. Damon looked down and whistled.

"We're falling faster than I thought." He looked at the others. "When you get clear of the plane, pull the red cord. If it doesn't work, pull the green. When you hit the water, the first thing you have to do is get the chute off. It will fill with water and drag you down. To get it off, push the clip in the middle." He reached over to show Aradia where it was. "If you can't get out of it, there's a knife in the pocket on the right side. Hack it to pieces as quickly as you can. Once you're in the water, locate the North Star and swim directly toward it. That will both get you out from under the plane when it hits the water and put us all swimming in the same direction. Questions?"

Pale and clammy, Aradia shook her head. Her hands trembled, and she gripped the straps of her parachute to steady herself. Greer leaned out the door and measured the distance between them and the water. She grabbed both sides of the door for balance and looked over her shoulder at the others.

"We have to do this quickly to make sure we're not too high or too low when we go out. As soon as I jump, one after the other."

Greer looked out the door of the plane again. She exchanged a long look with Damon, and with a grin and a shout, Greer launched herself out of the jet and plummeted through the air. Braxton took a deep breath and followed, Alaria a heartbeat behind him. Gage pushed Aradia toward the exit. He grabbed her chin and kissed her hard.

"Don't worry. I will find you. I don't need to breathe, so I don't want you to worry about me or wait for me. You hit the water, you get out of the chute, and you swim. Do you understand?"

Tears gleaming in her eyes, Aradia inched forward, her steps hesitant and jerky. Damon and Gage exchanged a look. Gage nodded slowly and Damon lurched forward, grabbing Aradia around the waist and taking her out the door with him. Her scream echoed through the air and Gage watched until he saw the chute open. He spent twenty seconds strapping a parachute to the dead pilot's body and shoving it out the door, pulling the cord as it fell before he took one last look around the jet and jumped.

Chapter Twenty-Seven

The water was cold and heavy. The nylon of the parachute filled with water quicker than Aradia had imagined it would. Damon was a strong swimmer, and he had an arm banded around her waist, his grip like a steel rod. He slashed through the cords of his parachute with brutal efficiency and within thirty seconds, the weight dragging them to the bottom of the sea dropped off and they bobbed to the surface.

"Can you swim?" Damon shouted to be heard over the storm.

Rain pelted Aradia's face and her hair stuck to her skin. She fumbled to release the clasp on her own, never opened parachute and let it fall off her and sink. She kicked her legs, struggling not to let the choppy waves take her under. She gasped for breath and wiped her eyes.

"I can swim."

"Stay close and yell if you need help. We need to get out of the danger zone and find the others." He shifted the bag of weapons from his chest to his back. "If it gets too hard to stay above the surface, start losing clothes. They weigh a lot when they're wet, and it'll drag you down. Start with shoes."

Aradia laughed, the sound only slightly hysterical. "I didn't take time to put on shoes."

"Just as well." He glanced at her, unable to make out anything other than her shape in the dark. "Let's go!"

They paddled through the water, making very little progress. Within seconds, Damon felt Greer prodding his mind and smiled. He opened the door and let her in, immediately speaking to her.

"Where are you?"

"Headed North. Probably a hundred yards in front of you. I've got Alaria and Braxton with me. Do you have Aradia and Gage?"

"I've got Aradia. Gage was right behind us. I had to take her down with me. She was scared to jump."

"I don't blame her. I would've been, too, in her shoes. We'll tread water here until you catch up."

"I'm going to bring her up to you guys and come back to look for Gage."

"No!" Greer's insistence was immediate and strong. *"That wreckage is going to be hitting within the next two minutes. We have to wait until it's had time to go down to avoid the suction from it."*

Damon knew she was right, and he hated it. He led Aradia safely away from the area where they'd landed and to the others. There was a moment of elation as the women exchanged wet hugs and then panic began to set it as they waited both for Gage and for the plane to hit the water. After five minutes of treading water with nothing happening, Damon cleared his throat.

"I think it's a safe bet to say we're not in Kansas anymore, folks."

Aradia wrinkled her nose. "Where's Kansas? Were we ever there?"

Greer laughed despite the fear clenched around her gut. "It's a movie reference. He means he thinks we're not where we were when we jumped out of the plane." She looked between them. "Or when we were when we jumped out of the plane."

Alaria cackled. "Of course we would time travel in the middle of a storm by having to jump out of a jet and into the water with no idea where—or when—we are and no clue how to find the fucking beach."

Braxton fished through the pack strapped to his back and came up with a flashlight. He pushed the button to activate the beam of light and shined it around. He swore under his breath.

"Mother fucker." He pointed to his right. "Do you see the shape there in the water about five hundred yards out? You can barely make it out against the horizon."

Damon kicked his legs and turned. "I'll be damned. Shore."

Aradia looked between the other four people. "Where's Gage?"

Greer looked pained. "He might've come down in a different spot.

We should head to the beach and wait until morning. He'll find us. He's a vampire, it's not like he could've drowned." She managed a half smile. "It's dark and we came through a time tunnel. He might've gotten disoriented or something, or gotten dragged down by wreckage and popped up somewhere else."

"Or he could be waiting for us on shore already." Alaria looked up at the sky. "It's starting to get light, guys, and dawn is when sharks feed the most. I vote we're all on dry land before things big enough to eat us want to have breakfast." She looked around once more before starting to swim. "Fucking Angels and their 'call if you need us.' We needed them more than maybe ever when the fucking goddamned plane was crashing, and where are they? Probably off playing poker."

Braxton chuckled. "Let's focus on the task at hand." He kicked harder and stroked toward shore.

Within ten minutes, the water was shallow enough that their feet touched bottom. After that, it took another three to plod toward the water and up onto the beach. They collapsed onto the sand, chests heaving from the swim and eyes burning from the salt. The rain had subsided, and the sun rose over the horizon.

Aradia sat up and looked around, her eyes widening as she took in the surroundings. They were on a narrow strip of beach that led to a thick, lush forest. To the right were mountains, and to the left was a giant city surrounded by thick stone walls. In front were two wooden gates. She climbed to her feet and studied it.

"We're in Atlantis." She turned in a circle. "I can feel the magic here. My God, I've never felt a place with so much power."

Alaria cracked open one eye. "At least we made it where we were supposed to go, then." She forced herself to sit. "What the hell do we do now?"

Aradia put her hand up to shield her eyes from the sun. "Well, I imagine we should talk to the men on horses that just came through that gate and are headed our way."

Braxton lunged to his feet and grabbed the bag of weapons. He unzipped it, finding nothing other than stakes and knives inside. He swore and tossed a wicked looking buck knife to Damon before tucking a bowie knife in the waist band of his pants. Greer pulled her knife from its sheath and held it close against the side of her leg. Aradia looked over her shoulder and shook her head.

"We're supposed to be here, remember?" She brushed sand off her pants. "My parents are the King and Queen here. They aren't going to hurt us."

Damon exhaled slowly and looked at Greer. "I wish I'd have remembered about the weapons not coming back through time before I packed that bag." He looked at the six men on horses suspiciously.

The leader of the group dismounted and approached them slowly, one hand up to stop his men from doing the same and the other on his short sword. He stopped ten feet in front of them and surveyed them.

"It seems you've been shipwrecked. Where were you trying to go?"

Aradia stepped forward. "We were sailing for Greece, sir, and were caught in the storm."

"Quite a storm it was, lady. We lost a dozen and half fishing boats to the wind and waves. You're nowhere near Greece, though. It's a week's sail from here." He smiled at her. "The storms have been going for days. It's little wonder you were blown from your course. You've landed in Atlantis."

"We had another companion, a man. Have you found him?"

The man shook his head. "You are the first to reach our shores. Are you sure he survived the wreck?"

"We're as sure as we can be." Greer smiled brightly. "What's your name?"

"Ronan, lady. If you would like, I can arrange for you to stay within the city until a ship sets sail for Greece. It would likely be several weeks. The Solstice is nearly upon us, and all of our citizens are working the fields and the nets."

Aradia cleared her throat. "I would ask that you take us to see Queen Graciela and King Liam. I understand that the Queen is a great witch. I have abilities that may be of great use to her. Truthfully, Greece was but a stop along our journey to get here."

Ronan looked at them with curiosity. "Are the King and Queen expecting you?"

Aradia shook her head. "No, but they'll want to see me. I might just be the only witch on Earth more powerful than Graciela."

Ronan drew his sword, the motion prompting all of his men to follow suit. He levelled the tip of the blade at Aradia's throat and stared at her, his eyes boring into her. "If you know of Graciela, then you know that there is none more powerful. Tell me, witch, do you mean my Queen harm?"

Aradia reached out and touched the blade, pushing it away from her throat. "I mean no harm. I come only to assist the Queen and King."

Ronan looked at his men. "Let's both of us hope you speak the truth. Bind them all, hand and foot. We'll take them to the castle, but I want none of them able to flee."

Greer looked around the chamber they'd been taken to. She plucked at the green gown and sighed deeply. Alaria looked miserable in a dress, and the men both looked out of place in riding breeches and rough chambray shirts. Aradia was the only one comfortable in the attire, and she was radiant in a blue gown with her hair running down her back in curls.

"I thought they'd take us right in to see your parents." Greer picked at the cotton and plopped down in one of the chairs. "Where the hell are we even?"

Aradia looked over her shoulder. "We're in a holding room. It's where guests are stored until the Queen or King decides whether or not they're going to entertain them. The fact that they gave us clothes bodes well. If I know anything about my mother, she won't be able to pass up the opportunity to see us." She crossed to the window and looked out. "I wonder if they've found Gage yet."

"Ronan said they would keep looking." Damon laid a hand on her shoulder reassuringly. "I'm sure Gage is fine."

Braxton crossed one leg over the other, resting his ankle on his knee. "What are you going to tell your mom?"

Aradia sighed. "I'm honestly not sure yet. Before we came here, my mother told me to keep what I tell her to a minimum to lower the risk of changing things. She's afraid that if she knew what was going to happen, she'd do things differently trying to stop it."

"Don't you think it's going to make her suspicious that a stranger shows up with the same name as her unborn child?" Alaria stood to pace the room. "That seems like something that would strike me as very odd."

Aradia tossed out her hands. "What do you want me to do? Disclose everything? Walk in there and announce that I'm her daughter? And oh, by the way, that they're both going to be dead within weeks and that I'm here to make sure we kill some demons and that they both die exactly on schedule?"

Alaria shook her head. "Sorry. I know it's a difficult situation."

Greer slid her arm around Aradia's shoulder. "We'll figure it out together. I think some version of the truth is best. If your mother is as powerful as we think she is, she likely has some sense that something big is coming. I'd be willing to bet she might figure out the rest on her own. A powerful sorceress will know the importance of maintaining the time line, and I'd bet she'll work with us."

Before Aradia could answer, the door opened and a maid entered. She dipped into a curtsy and addressed Aradia. "My lady, the Queen Graciela, has requested that you present yourselves before the thrones. Please, follow me."

Aradia led the rest down the hall, trailing closely behind the maid. The woman led them through several hallways and one large ballroom before they were ushered through double doors leading into the throne room. Graciela sat on one of the thrones, gorgeous and swollen with pregnancy, her hand resting protectively on the mound beneath her gown. Liam sat next to her, a handsome man with red hair, a full beard, and an easy smile.

Graciela stood when the five entered the room. "Who speaks for you?"

Aradia stepped forward. "I do, my Queen."

"What is your name?"

"Aradia."

"And from whence do you hail, Aradia?"

"My companions and I hail from a time far in the future. We've been sent here by Gabriel to aid you in the coming battle."

Graciela's hand stilled on her belly. "What do you know of what plagues my city?"

Aradia looked up and met her mother's eyes. "I know that there are beasts who take the form of men. They have red eyes that glow and fangs like an animal's. They drink blood and feast on flesh and can only come out at night. I know that your magic is strong but not strong enough to hold them off forever. I know the prophecy, Queen."

Graciela jutted her chin up and spoke loudly and clearly. "Speak it."

"I know that in less than three weeks' time, this city will be under siege. King Liam will be counted amongst the dead, and you will flee this place through a portal you have been working on in secret."

The two royals exchanged a long, worried look. Liam sat up straight and leaned forward. "How do you know all of this?"

Aradia shifted her gaze to meet his. "I am a witch. More powerful than even your wife. I have been sent here because there are forces from my time that are joining with the ones you face here. We have been tasked with defeating them, and the battle has hailed us back to here. The demons are stronger than they were before, and the stakes much greater than you can know. Things have changed since you consorted with the Angels."

Graciela stepped off of the platform and crossed the room gracefully until she stood toe to toe with Aradia. "Show me. If you're so powerful a witch, surely you wouldn't mind a demonstration of your abilities."

Aradia recognized the challenge and lifted her chin. "What would my Queen have me do?"

"There are many varieties of witches. Some have merely parlor tricks and projections. The most powerful magic lies deep within the mind. The mind is the hardest thing for another witch to break into. I want you to read my mind, Aradia."

Aradia reached out and slammed herself against Graciela's mind before the words were out of her mouth. Her mother was quick and threw up protections as soon as she felt the foreign presence. Aradia felt her way along the walls, picturing a large door with a lock. She worked her way to the lock and felt it, searching for a weak spot that would allow her in.

She found it a heartbeat before Graciela did and slipped in the door, accessing the other woman's mind. Graciela sensed the intrusion the moment it happened and threw Aradia out with little effort. The demonstration was over; Aradia had won.

Graciela nodded. "Very nicely done. You're certainly powerful. What is it that you're here to do?"

"We are here to make things happen as they should. The enemy we fight knows how important the child within you is and seeks to end her life before it begins. If they succeed, the world in our time will cease to be. We wish to work with you to protect your child and make sure that you escape from here alive."

Graciela placed both hands on her stomach very deliberately. "My child must be born. It is ordained by God and handed down to me by the Angels. It is His will."

"There are those who seek to stop His will." Aradia took a step forward. "If I can see into your mind, so must you get a glimpse at mine. You know now as surely as I do that we are not here to do you, or your people, any harm. We are here to help."

"You've made your point well." Graciela returned to the throne and sat down. "The battle has been ordained to occur as the Solstice does. That is eighteen days from now. I understand from my servants that you are missing one of your companions?"

"That's right."

"I'll have the beaches patrolled for the next several days. If he washes up on our shores, he will be found. I've made arrangements to spend the next week in the temples in prayer and meditation. Upon my return, we will prepare for the battle together."

For the first time since entering the room, someone other than Aradia and Graciela spoke. Alaria stepped forward and addressed the Queen. "With all due respect, you're going to need more than eleven days to prepare for this. We need to train together and prepare your citizens."

Graciela smiled softly. "Liam is in charge of the army. There is nothing to stop you from preparing the citizens for battle while I am gone. Believe me, eleven days is enough for what Aradia and I will do." She gestured to one of the servants. "You'll be given quarters here in the castle and a chambermaid to see to your needs. Clothing will be provided, and a seamstress will be along tomorrow to measure you all. Please, let her know what it is that you would like to wear when she comes. I understand enough to know that our dress here may not be the kind you are accustomed to, and we want you to be comfortable."

Aradia dipped her head and lowered her eyes in a gesture of respect. "Thank you, Queen, for hearing us. We look forward to working with you."

No one spoke until they had been placed into bedrooms. Once the maid had left, they all gathered in Aradia's room. Braxton broke the silence.

"Well, that was an interesting experience. I'm glad we don't live in a time with kings and queen."

Damon rolled his eyes. "Seriously. That was incredibly formal. To be honest, I had a hard time not laughing during most of it."

Aradia smiled. "It's a good thing this was the way of it where I grew up as well. I'm familiar with the manner in which things are done." She looked out the window at the ocean. "I'm worried about Gage."

Greer and Alaria exchanged a look. Alaria shook her head. "We might have to face the possibility that he's stuck in our time. If we believe that we fell into a wormhole of some sort, there's a chance it could've closed before he dove out of the plane." She looked at Damon. "Do you know if he was right behind you or was there a lag?"

Damon shook his head. "I don't know. I thought he was coming out right behind us, but he could've gone back for something or gotten scared for a second or any other of a hundred things. If he is stuck back there, though, we have to believe that Gabriel or Michael, or hell, even God, will make sure he gets to us by the time we really need him. What we know for sure is that this only works if the six of us are together, so Gage has to be here before the battle." He shrugged helplessly. "That means all we can do is wait."

Chapter Twenty-Eight

GAGE WOKE up with the sun shining on his face. He swiped at his skin in a sleepy, half-conscious effort to stop the annoying sting from being in direct sunlight and opened his eyes. An inch above his chest was the point of a sword. Attached to the sword was a burly blond man with a serious expression. Gage looked around nervously, seeing that he was surrounded and was quite obviously not in Greece.

"Who are you and what business have you in Atlantis?"

Atlantis. Gage closed his eyes for a moment and swallowed a bubble of laughter. Of course he was in Atlantis. Everything fell into place. The storm made sense, the lightning made sense, even the death of the pilot. He remembered feeling as if he'd been falling for days before he'd hit the water, and then he'd floated until he'd passed out from either lack of sleep, blood, or both.

He forced himself to open his eyes and looked up at the man with the sword. "My name is Gage Windsor, and I was travelling with five companions. We were sailing for Greece and were caught in the storm. I'm not sure how long ago it was."

The man stepped back and held out a hand to help Gage to his feet. "We'd almost given up hope, son. Your group has been here for almost a week. The King has had patrols walking the beach for the last five days hoping that you'd turn up." He grinned and shook Gage's hand. "I'm

Ronan. Nice to meet you, Gage Windsor. Can you walk, or do you need a ride?"

Gage rolled his shoulders. "We'll find out, I suppose. Where are my friends?"

"At the castle. The King and Queen have put them in quarters there. We've got a big battle coming apparently, and the two men, and even two of the women, are helping train everyone to get ready to fight. Mighty good thing they got here when they did. Rumor is that the pretty redhead is more powerful a witch than even the Queen. She's been locked in the Queen's tower since she arrived, working magic, I suppose."

"What's the date?"

"The eighth of June, sir." Ronan offered Gage a skin filled with water. "I have some bread and cheese if you'd like some food."

Gage drank half the water and passed it back. "I think I'd just like to get back and see my friends." He gestured to the setting sun. "If the evil coming is nearly as bad as what we're expecting, we'd best get inside before dark."

Ronan nodded. "You would be right about that. Let's get to the castle. It'll be dark in an hour, and we've got almost a three hour trek to the castle."

Gage groaned. "Suddenly, the offer of a ride doesn't seem all that bad."

Ronan gestured to the wagon strapped to two donkeys. "Hop in."

Aradia laid in bed staring at the ceiling. She had worked until dark and would rise again at dawn to continue. She'd seen the other four at dinner, all of whom had been so exhausted from the physical training that they'd filed up to bed almost immediately after scarfing down as much food as possible.

There had been no sign of Gage. Liam had apologetically informed them that he was calling off the search if Gage had not been found by the one week mark. Aradia turned her head into the downy pillow and fought the urge to cry. Damon was staunchly convinced that if Gage was dead, they would know somehow. She wanted to believe that.

She sniffed and sat up when she heard footsteps coming down the hall. She threw back the quilt and rose, her white nightgown falling to her feet. Hurrying to the door, she reached for the handle just as the first knock sounded. She wrenched it open to find her chambermaid on the other side, with Gage directly behind her.

Aradia's hand flew to her throat and she choked back tears. "You're alive!"

The chambermaid, Breanna, dipped low in a curtsy. "Please excuse the intrusion, miss, but the gentleman insisted upon seeing you before I showed him to his quarters. I informed him how inappropriate it was to visit a lady in her bed chamber, but he would not be discouraged."

"It's all right, Breanna. Come in, please."

She held the door for both Breanna and Gage. Gage's cheeks were hollow and his eyes were sunken in his head. She grabbed her robe from the back of the chair and pulled it on, drawing it tight to make the maid more comfortable. Breanna looked between them, concern in her eyes.

"I'll show you to your room now, sir, if you'll allow me."

Gage leaned against the wall. "Breanna, if you don't mind, I desperately need something to eat."

Aradia sucked in a breath. He hadn't had blood in almost a week. "Gage."

"It's okay, Aradia."

Gage reached out and laid his hands on Breanna's shoulders. "I'm not going to hurt you." He looked deeply into her eyes, his own turning red. Breanna froze as if she was in a trance, looking up at him and repeating obediently.

"You're not going to hurt me."

"You'll feel no pain when I bite you, and I will only take enough to sustain me until I can find a butcher tomorrow for some animal blood." He ran his thumb over the maid's neck. "Hold still and do not move."

"I'll feel no pain. I won't move."

Gage lowered his head to Breanna's neck, his fangs extending. He slowly broke through the skin and drank deeply. Aradia pressed her hands against her stomach and watched, horrified and mesmerized in equal shares. Gage met her eyes over Breanna and held them while he fed. Aradia's body reacted, desire pooling deep within her as she watched the intimate act of his feeding.

Gage released the girl and wiped blood from his mouth. He leaned down and licked the two puncture wounds. Aradia watched in awe as they closed and disappeared. He gripped Breanna by the shoulders again and turned her chin so that her eyes met his.

"You're going to go to your chambers now. You'll go straight to bed and sleep through the night. When you wake up tomorrow, you'll be a bit tired but will remember nothing of this. You took me to my room and then went to bed. Do you understand?"

Breanna nodded, her expression blank. "I understand, sir." She went to the door and left, closing it softly behind her.

Gage turned to Aradia and looked pained when he saw that she was flushed and panting, her eyes wide and her hand laid at the base of her throat. He took a step forward and shifted his eyes down when she took one back.

"I'm sorry you had to see that. I didn't think I could make it until morning without some blood, and it's too late to find the butcher. I swear she'll be fine. I didn't hurt her." He stuffed his hands in the pockets of his borrowed beeches. "I don't blame you for feeling disgusted."

Aradia slowly met his gaze and took an unsteady breath. She opened her mouth to speak, thought better of it and turned toward the fire place. She laid her robe over the chair deliberately and swiveled to face him. Her chest was heaving as she breathed, her breasts straining the fabric of the thin, white nightgown she wore. A line of tiny buttons ran from the top of the garment all the way to the hem.

Gage caught the scent of the change a split second before Aradia launched herself at him. She drove him back until his back slammed into the wall. She grabbed his shirt and ripped it open, sending buttons flying and bouncing across the stone floor. She fused her mouth to his and splayed her hands on his chest, raking her nails over her skin.

Gage groaned deeply and returned the kiss, tasting her desire and need. He shucked the ruined remains of his shirt off of his arms and tossed it onto the floor. He laughed when she fumbled at the clasp to his pants and shoved them down his legs rather than let her continue to struggle. Naked and hard, he stooped to lift her, gathering her in his arms and crushing her to his body.

He rotated them so that it was her back against the wall and pinned her there with his hips to free his hands. He hiked up her nightgown and found her bare underneath. Groaning, he parted her legs and drew them around his hips. She wrapped them around him tightly and threw her head back, the back of her skull grinding against the wall. Gage tore at the bodice of her night dress, sending a dozen of the little buttons to join the ones from his shirt as he tore the delicate fabric.

She tightened her legs and jerked her hips into his, desperate for the joining. He gave her what she wanted, plunging into her with one long stroke. He wrapped his arms around her ass to balance her better and dipped his head to nuzzle her breasts, sucking one nipple into his mouth to suck deeply as he thrust into her.

Aradia's head ground against the wall and her breathing came in shallow gasps. Her body clenched around his, wet and hot, and her flesh was sweet and warm in his mouth. Gage drove into her faster—harder—and brought one hand up to cover her other breast, kneading the mound with his fingers He tweaked her nipple with one finger, rubbing the nub to bring her more pleasure.

She exploded around him, orgasm tearing through her and wrenching a ragged cry from her. She clenched him like a clamp, undulating and tight. With a roar, Gage followed her into climax, emptying himself in her and quivering from both the effort of holding her against the wall and the sensation of the orgasm he had just experienced.

It took him thirty seconds to be sure his legs were sturdy enough to hold them both before Gage pushed off the wall and carried her to the bed. He collapsed with her onto the feather-filled mattress and drew her close against him. Aradia snuggled into his arms, resting her head on his chest and draping one arm over his stomach.

"I wasn't disgusted by what you did. I knew you wouldn't hurt her." She pressed a kiss to his chest and ran her fingers up and down. "To borrow a phrase from Alaria, I actually found it hot." She blushed red. "I felt like I was witnessing something between you and Breanna that was completely intimate but that you intended for me to see."

Gage chuckled. "I never wanted you to see that. I may be a monster, Aradia, but I don't relish the thought of you witnessing my darker side."

Aradia lifted herself onto her elbows. "You may be a monster, but you're the monster that I love." She looked down into his face. "I thought you were dead. I've lain awake every night praying that you'd be found and having less hope each night. It made me realize that I don't want to lose you. Not when this is over, not when I grow old and die, never." She bent and kissed him gently. "When this is done, I want you to do something for me."

Gage closed his eyes, dreading her next words. "I'll give you anything I can, Aradia."

"I want you to turn me into a vampire."

Gage shook his head before she finished talking. "I can't." He sat up and swung his legs around to place his feet on the floor. "I don't want to lose you, either, but if I turned you, if I made you into what I am, I'd be taking away all the things I love about you the most. You are the embodiment of goodness and life. I won't be responsible for killing you." He ran his hands through his hair. "Some vampires never escape the bloodlust. Mina never did. I had to kill her. I don't know if I could bring myself to kill you twice, Priestess."

Aradia rose to her knees and pressed herself against his back. "I'd prefer it to a life without you."

Gage knew he had to be the strong one—the one to make the hard choices. "I've been honest with you from the start. I've never led you to believe that we have a future after this is over. I love you more than I've ever loved anyone, but I'm not going to change my mind. It might very nearly kill us both, but I am leaving once this is done, and you'll not see me again."

Tears stung Aradia's eyes and she wrapped her arms around him. "I was afraid you'd say that." She smiled sadly. "I had to try."

"I know you did. Just like I have to say no."

She kissed his back. "I know that, too." She pulled him back down beside her. "Will you make me a promise?"

Gage pulled her closer and kissed her forehead. "As long as it doesn't require me killing you, then yes."

"If I'm dying, will you turn me?"

Gage was silent for a long moment as he struggled to fight his way through the maelstrom of emotions he felt at her request. He felt grief at the thought of her dying and at the thought of her as a vampire. Finally, after nearly a full minute, he answered.

"I promise."

Aradia kissed the line of his jaw and pressed her face into the side of his neck. "I'm glad you're here. What happened when you fell out of the plane?"

Gage yawned. "I think that whatever it is that brought us here had started to close before I jumped. I went back to get the pilot's body, so maybe it was only set up for six and the pilot dropped through and whatever it was got confused. I really have no clue. All I know is that I floated for what felt like forever. When I finally came to, I was in the ocean, but I was miles from shore. I swam and floated and swam and floated, and I didn't think I'd ever make it anywhere. I think I was in the water for nearly two days before I saw the coast. By the time I got here, I washed up on the sand and just laid there until Ronan found me today."

Aradia reached down and grabbed the blanket, dragging it up onto them. "You're here now, and that's all that matters. My mother will be back in two days, and that's when my training will start in earnest."

"I want to make one thing clear to you and to everyone else. Javal is mine. Garrick is your part in this, and I won't interfere with that, no matter how badly I want to. Javal is for me."

"I understand why you feel that way. I'll honor the request unless your life is in danger." She shook her head when he started to object. "No, Gage. You can't tell me you would let Garrick kill me just so I could prove a point, and I'm not going to agree to do the same to you. That's what makes us so strong as a group of six. We would all die for the others."

Gage nodded. "Okay. I can respect that." He drew her up for another kiss. "I really missed you, Aradia."

Aradia giggled and looped her arms around his neck. "I really missed you, too, Gage."

He slipped the nightdress off her shoulder and nipped the tender skin there. "I think I should show you just how much I missed you."

She groaned and closed her eyes when he slipped one finger inside of her. "When do I get to show you?"

"Next time." He tore the rest of the buttons off. "It's my turn."

Chapter Twenty-Nine

June 18

"How are you feeling?"

Alaria glared at Aradia as they climbed the stairs to Graciela's quarters. "Physically, I'm fine, but I still don't want to talk about it."

"Have you spoken to Gabriel?"

Alaria tried to glare harder. "What part of 'I don't want to talk about it' is escaping you?"

Aradia laughed. "The part where you don't tell me what I want to know. We're friends, Alaria. Friends talk."

Greer spoke from behind them. "I agree with the redhead. We're friends, whether you like it or not."

"I don't like it, actually." Alaria took a gasping breath. "Jesus Christ, how many stairs are there?"

Greer looked up. "A lot more." She gritted her teeth and kept climbing. "So have you spoken to Gabriel?" She snapped her fingers. "Hey! Have you fucked Braxton? Could it be his?"

"No, no, and no." Alaria sighed deeply. "I've called for Gabe, but he's either not answering me or can't hear me. Since they said they wouldn't be coming back with us, it could really be either. I don't know what I'd even say to him. I don't know how it's possible or why it happened or what I'm going to do about it."

"If you don't want it, you could always terminate. You have to be pretty early into the pregnancy."

Aradia looked horrified. "You can't kill your child!"

Alaria stopped and turned around to level a fierce look at Aradia. "I could, and I would feel no regret if that's the decision I made. I just haven't decided yet what I want to do. There are bigger things to think about right now. Like getting to the top of these fucking stairs." She took another breath. "In all seriousness, I haven't talked to him. I might not. It's not like we're going to get married and settle down and raise kids. I asked him to choose me, and he told me no. Gabriel and I are over."

Aradia squeezed Alaria's hand. "A child could change his feelings."

"I don't care. I don't want him because he feels obligated. If he didn't want me enough to choose me when I wasn't pregnant, he doesn't deserve me now."

Greer chortled. "Good for you. You're exactly right." She heaved herself onto the landing at the top of the steps. "Have you told Braxton?"

Alaria shook her head. "No. I don't know how to."

"Do you want to?" Aradia held the door open for the other two.

"He'll find out one way or the other. It's not like you can hide a pregnancy indefinitely. I'll start to get bigger eventually. It's inevitable."

Greer smiled sympathetically. "That's not what she asked. Do you want to tell him?"

Alaria's eyes shimmered with unshed tears. "No, I don't want to fucking tell him. I've been so tangled up with the two that I can't even see straight. There's something between Brax and me, and a part of me was glad when it was over with Gabe because that meant I was one step closer to being ready to explore that. This changes everything."

Aradia looked at Alaria sternly. "If he wanted you non-pregnant and doesn't pregnant, he's not worthy of you, either."

Graciela stood in the middle of a round room, her hands folded on her stomach. "I agree." She extended her hands to the three women. "Thank you for coming. I know the stairs are numerous."

Aradia took Graciela's hand and curtsied. "I thought we weren't training today, my Queen."

"We're not. There are only three days until the battle. We've been working hard. My mind is weary, as I know yours must be, but I wanted to do one exercise with you, Aradia." She looked at Alaria and Greer.

"You and your men have done a tremendous job training the army. I believe we're as ready as we can be. I've called for a party tonight at the palace. Everyone in Atlantis is invited. It will last all night and will be good for morale. My people need to know that we are confident that we will win."

Aradia exchanged a look with the other two. "I don't think that's a good idea. We know the battle is coming, but I'm sure you can feel it the same as I can. Our enemies are numerous, and they are here. If we let our guard down and celebrate, they may exploit that weakness and attack sooner."

Graciela shook her head. "I didn't bring you here for a debate. My mind is made up, and there is nothing that will change it. I brought you here to help me." She picked up two chunks of crystal and handed them to Aradia. "You've been doing well, and your control of black magic is getting much better. Between the two of us, I'm not sure there is an enemy in existence that has a chance. However, I've been thinking of ways to make you more comfortable with what you believe you must do."

Aradia looked at the crystals in her hands. "I've never needed crystals and potions."

"Needed, no. You're very powerful without them. I think if you use them, you may be able to channel the innate energy of the crystals into a magnifying glass to concentrate your power."

Greer cleared her throat. "That sounds incredible, but why did you call for Alaria and me?"

"To act as anchors while we try this. Aradia is familiar with you, and she trusts you. If she were to start to get out of control, you are here to pull her back."

Alaria crossed her arms. "That's fine and dandy, but no offense meant, Queen, we're not going to be able to hold her hand when this battle comes. Greer and I both have our roles."

"If she cannot handle the power, she won't be trying this in the heat of battle." Graciela looked at Aradia. "Are you ready to try?"

Aradia turned the crystals in her hands. "There are many types of crystal. It'll take a while to determine which I connect with best."

Graciela smiled. "I think you'll find that I have all you could need." She gestured to two chairs. "Please, have a seat, ladies. We could be here for a long time."

Aradia moved through the crystals slowly and methodically. She tested quartz, amethyst, topaz, emerald and peridot before picking up a chunk of citrine. Even before she worked it, the stone felt warm in her hand. She rolled it on her palm and sought out the energy of the gem. When she found it, it was bright and hot. Mirrors sprang up around her, magnifying her power and reflecting it back in on itself.

Curious, Aradia tried to arrange the mirrors into an array that would allow her to control where the streams of magic went. She shifted them, testing the refraction and making adjustments where she needed to.

Color surrounded her, bouncing off the mirrors and lighting up everything around her. She formed a circle with the mirrors, placing them so that the stream of energy was mirrored into six streams. She placed the gem in the center of the mirrors, turning it into a prism and using it to focus the magic into one singular rivulet.

Aradia's vision cleared and she jumped back, the citrine dropping to the table, still glowing with a rainbow of colors. Graciela reached forward and picked it up, turning it over in her hand.

"Not what I use, but a very effective gem nonetheless." Graciela laid the stone down. "Citrine is the only stone that does not require cleansing before it is used as a mirror. It's naturally pure. When worn, it also guards the wearer from the dream plane and gives you psychic strength."

Alaria leaned forward. "Is that it? That's all she had to do?"

Graciela laughed warmly. "That was the simple part. Now that she's calibrated the stone to where she can use it to magnify her magic, she's going to open the door to the black and let it in. If she can filter it through her prism, she stands a chance at purifying it and joining it with her magic to increase her power."

Aradia looked at the citrine. "I've never used crystals. Even with having it prepared for my magic, I'm not sure I have the concentration to control the flow of dark magic."

"There's only one way to find out, Aradia." Graciela extended the stone. "If you can do this, the amount of black magic you can access would be unlimited."

Greer crossed her legs. "If you're not comfortable trying, then don't. Black magic is nothing to play with, and it'll know if you don't have a clue what you're doing."

Aradia looked between them. "I think I need to try." She lifted her shoulder in a shrug. "What's the worst that could happen?"

Alaria snorted. "Well, your brain could melt and leak out your ears, for one."

Aradia reached out and grabbed the crystal. She wrapped her hand around it and concentrated on forming the room with the mirrors. It took much less time to direct the stream into the prism than it had the first time. That task accomplished, she opened the door and let in the black.

It rushed in like a tidal wave, rolling over her and barreling into the mirrored room. She struggled to control it, to shut the door or to stem the flow somehow. She threw herself against the door, using her whole body to move it closed inch by excruciating inch. Once it was closed, she turned to deal with the torrent of black magic in the room.

She first worked on corralling it into one corner. The dark magic was a living thing, strong and hot. It rebelled against her, trying to escape from her influence. She pushed and tugged, forcing it to bend the way she wanted. Once she directed the black through the first mirror, it poured through them, winding its way through the mirrors until it reached the prism in the middle.

The clear yellow of the citrine turned into a swirling mass of black and purple. For several heart-stopping moments, Aradia thought the black was going to overwhelm her magic. She held her breath, watching the two streams meld together until they merged into one thick red cord that Aradia could mold and manipulate into whatever she wanted it to be.

She closed down the prism and looked down at the crystal in her hand. It had changed color from a light lemon yellow to a rich amber. Graciela reached out and took it from her, studying the gem for several seconds before looking at Aradia.

"You did it, Aradia. You bent the black to your will." She smiled jubilantly. "It took you a quarter of an hour to do it, but the first time will take the longest. You know how to do it now. I want you to continue to practice. If you're to use this in battle, you need to be able to do it almost instantly."

Aradia dropped into a chair. "That was exhausting."

Alaria looked at Aradia pointedly. "I'd worry more if it was easy for you. Working with black magic should always be hard. If it gets easy, it's starting to work you more than you're working it."

Aradia nodded. "I'll keep working on it. If this is how I win, then I need to get better at it."

Graciela clapped her hands. "Wonderful. Greer and Alaria will keep you company. I need to check on things for the ball tonight. I'll have gowns taken to your rooms."

Alaria was silent until they could no longer hear Graciela's footsteps. "What the fuck is that woman thinking, throwing a party three days before her city is going to sink?"

Greer chuckled. "She doesn't know her city is going to sink, and Graciela is right. People need to have good morale or they won't fight as hard." She closed her eyes and took a deep breath. "I wish there was a way to save them."

"There's not. We're doing what we came here to do, which is to stop them from killing Graciela and to kill Garrick and Javal. Those are the three goals. Once that's done, we run like hell to the portal and stuff Graciela through it before we go through ourselves." Alaria looked pointedly at Aradia. "Get back to work. You have a lot of practicing to do before we go to this stupid fucking party."

Alaria held the post of her bed as her chambermaid tightened the corset to the dress she was donning. The gown hung in the corner, a deep red Grecian style that had thin straps with strips of fabric that fluttered over her arms and a high slit that went well above her knees. Alaria lifted her eyebrows and looked down at the girl.

"I thought people were supposed to be modest."

"We're not nearly so backward as you seem to think us, miss. Women of Atlantis do not hide their bodies. Instead, we teach our sons to respect them."

Alaria smiled. "That's a concept the future hasn't managed to grasp yet." She stepped into the dress and let the girl slide it up to her shoulders. "This is a beautiful gown."

"We have very talented seamstresses." The girl stepped back. "You're ready. Shall I take you down to the ballroom?"

Alaria shook her head. "I can hear the music from here. It won't be hard to find it. Thank you, though."

She exited the room and descended the stairs to the castle entrance. Turning right, she followed an ornately decorated corridor in the direction of the music. Entering the room, her eyes widened as she saw the crowd in the huge room.

There were hundreds of people. The women wore fancy dresses and the men wore tuxedos that looked straight out of a Jane Austen novel. There was a long buffet with dozens of dishes of food, and a bar on the opposite end held kegs of beer and wine. Alaria already saw Greer and Damon on the dance floor. Aradia was standing near her mother and nibbling on some chicken, and Gage was circling the room.

"It's incredible, isn't it?"

Alaria whirled when Braxton spoke near her ear. He'd slipped up behind her and leaned against the doorframe, bending down to brush his lips against her ear as he spoke. She crossed her arms over her chest and glared up at him.

"It's not nice to sneak up on people." She turned back to the party. "If by incredible you mean stupid and dangerous, then yes, it's incredible."

"Gage spent half an hour trying to talk Liam out of letting Graciela host this, but he was determined to make her happy. She wants a ball, so she's getting it." He sighed. "I just hope this doesn't get people killed."

"We tried with Graciela, too, and obviously had no luck."

Braxton laid his hands on her shoulders. "Do you want to dance?"

Alaria looked out at the dancing couples, who were engaged in something that looked like a waltz. "I don't remember the last time I danced. Probably sometime in the nineteen twenties."

"Well, no time like the present. Or past, as the case may be." He held out a hand to her. "What do you say?"

Alaria laughed and placed her hand in his. "Why the hell not?"

Braxton led her onto the dance floor and spun her around before drawing her close. He placed one hand on her waist and took her hand with his other. She laid her hand at his shoulder. They moved slowly, getting a feel for both the music and one another. After several moments, Alaria spoke, her voice low and unsure.

"Gabriel and I are over."

Braxton's steps faltered slightly, and he looked down at her. "How over?"

"As over as it gets. He'll be lucky if I don't murder him the next time I see him over."

"Why tell me this?"

Alaria looked up, unsure. "Because for better or for worse, you and I have been careening into something for months now. It felt like something you would want to know."

Braxton's fingers tightened on her hip, and he laid his cheek on her head. "I know we have. I'm not sure we're ready to go headfirst, though. I still have unresolved issues, and even though the thing with Gabe is over, that doesn't mean the feelings are gone." He let go of her hand to tip her face up. "What do you want to do?"

She shook her head. "I don't know, Brax. I feel like I'm being pulled in different directions. I won't lie to you. I have feelings for Gabriel. I loved him. Part of me will always love him. But it is over. After what he's done to me, I could never trust him enough to be with him again."

"There's something I don't know, isn't there?"

She nodded slowly. "I didn't tell you about Gabe and me so that we would fall into bed together and never look back. I'm talking to you about this because I had every intention of telling you what I'm going to tell you."

Braxton cut her off by pressing his mouth to hers in a short, heated kiss. "Just spit it out, Alaria."

"I don't know how. I haven't wrapped my own head around it enough to know how I feel, let alone how to tell you about it. I never thought Gabe would do this. I'm not even sure how he did."

"What did he do?

Alaria's eyes filled with tears and she dipped her head to blink them back. She took a deep breath, her chest quivering. "The night of Greer and Damon's wedding, after I got up to my room, Gabe started blabbering about hoping I could forgive him for what he was going to do. He was saying some nonsense about protecting me from a worse fate. I don't remember the specifics. What I do remember is him doing a one-eighty from chattering about that to asking me to have sex with him. I did. When I woke up, he was gone."

Braxton's brow furrowed. "What does that have to do with anything?"

"I'm pregnant, Braxton. I don't know how, but what I am sure of is that Gabriel knew he would get me pregnant, and he convinced me to go to bed with him for that purpose."

Braxton took several deep breaths. "What are you going to do?"

"I thought about an abortion, but if Gabe knew, then I have to believe he was acting under orders, and if God ordered it, I could probably subject myself to a hundred abortions and I'd still be pregnant."

He spoke slowly. "I'm not sure what to say."

Alaria looked at him with a sheepish expression. "I passed out. Aradia was the one who figured it out. Greer made me take a test."

"It was morning sickness on the plane." He did some quick math in his head. "You're about six or seven weeks, then."

"About that." She looked around at the crowd and then at the door. "Can we maybe stop pretending to dance and go somewhere?"

"I think that's a good idea." He took her hand and led her from the room.

They wound their way up the stairs and back down the hall toward the rooms where they were staying. Braxton opened the door to his room and ushered her inside. A fire crackled in the hearth, and a pitcher of water sat on the dresser with two goblets next to it. He gestured to one of the two chairs in front of the fire and poured them each a glass of water before perching in the other.

"I'm not mad at you, if that's what you're thinking."

Alaria looked sideways at Braxton and smiled. "I don't know what I'm thinking. I know this further complicates an already complicated situation." She ran her hands through her hair. "I'm sorry, Brax."

Braxton laughed. "Sorry for what? For getting used as a pawn in this game of cosmic chess God is playing with Lucifer?" He reached out and squeezed her hand. "None of us have had a choice about much in this whole damn thing. This is just the latest way in which God is informing us that we only exist for his amusement."

Alaria giggled through the tears tracking down her face. "When Gabriel and I ended things, I thought it would give us a chance. I knew I needed time to get over him, well, as over him as possible, and that you still needed time to work through the Griffin stuff, but I still had hope that the proverbial window would open."

"I want to tell you it'll be okay." Braxton looked at her sadly. "I want to tell you that it doesn't matter and that I'm in the same place you are, but it wouldn't be the truth. At least not the whole truth. I don't know how I feel about it. I don't know if it changes anything or what it changes or how much it changes things." He left his chair to crouch in front of her. "What I do know is that I'm here for you. Aside from all the muddled up feelings, you and I are friends. We've been stuck with each other for almost two years now. Whatever you need, whether it's a hand to hold or a shoulder to snot on or someone to vent to, I'm your guy."

Alaria went into his arms willingly, her head finding a place on his shoulder. He hugged her to him firmly, one hand on her back and the other stroking her hair. She relaxed against him incrementally until he was supporting all of her weight. He shifted so he was the one sitting in the chair, her curled up in his lap.

"I know he knows what he did to me. Part of me wants to yell and scream and confront him about it, and another part of me wants to pretend he never existed. I'm mad and hurt and a thousand other things I don't understand and don't want to feel." She sniffed. "I wanted to be human so I could make my own choices and so I could have a life. Not so I could play surrogate to some Nephil. There's no telling what this child is going to be, Brax. There's never been one to survive past toddlerhood. God considers them an abomination and has them killed."

"I think it's a safe bet that God wants this one born." He rubbed her back gently. "You're not in this alone. You've got five people who care about you and who will help you with whatever you need."

"I think I wanted to be a mother. I wasn't sure yet. I've only been human a year and a half. I don't want to be a single mother raising a Nephil baby. That I'm positive of."

Braxton tucked her head against his chest. "You don't have to do anything alone that you don't want to. Whatever role you want, Alaria, I'm here. I don't say things I don't mean. You've known me long enough to know that. I'll help you with whatever you need, regardless of what things are between us."

Alaria smiled softly, her eyes heavy with sleep. "You're a good man, Braxton Winslow."

Braxton chuckled. "Shh. Don't blow my cover."

Chapter Thirty

June 19

Aradia triumphantly released the door to the black magic and let it pour into her mind. She directed it into the mirrors and propelled it through them and into the prism of citrine at the center. It melded with her own magic and lit up into a red stream. She withdrew from the room and looked at Graciela, her eyes glowing white with power.

"How long did that take?"

Graciela smiled and rubbed her belly. "A three count. Very, very good." She stood and walked to the window. "You're ready, Aradia. There's nothing left for me to teach you."

Aradia dropped into one of the chairs in the circular room. "We still have two days to practice. I should get better at it."

"You should take those two days to rest your mind and prepare yourself for what is coming. Take time to meditate and pray." Graciela put her hands on her hips. "Your man Gage, he is a vampire, is he not?"

Aradia froze. "How did you know?"

"Don't insult me. I'm a very powerful witch, Aradia. I know when there is something not human in my home. I've known since he was brought here. He's a good man, as far as I can tell, despite his nature. The two of you are lovers, yes?"

Aradia nodded. "Yes."

"Has he bonded you?"

"Yes."

Graciela smiled softly. "Love is a fickle creature, my dear. It's a magic more powerful than either you or I. It strikes where it is not wanted and holds on long after it should leave. The only thing to do is try not to be hurt by it. Has he marked you?"

Aradia turned her head to the side, her face quizzical. "Marked me? What does that mean?"

Graciela sat next to Aradia. "When a vampire takes a mate, he can bond them, which is a mental and magical link between the two. It makes the relationship stronger and allows the pair to be more keenly in touch with one another. It's a highly personal thing. Marking is a physical symbol of it. It is when the vampire, in the throes of passion, bites his or her mate for the purpose of leaving a mark. It is a scar that announces to other creatures that the human has been claimed as the mate of a vampire. It's only done when the vampire intends to spend a lot of time with the human, whether that is all of their life or just a number of years."

"Gage has never bitten me."

"Do you think he will?"

Aradia shook her head. "Gage would never do something like that. He's leaving once our tasks are complete. He and I aren't going to be together. This is only for now. We both know that."

Graciela made a noise in her throat. "Do you love him?"

She smiled softly, her eyes shining. "Yes, I do."

"Does he love you?"

Another nod. "He does."

"Then if it is meant to be, you will find a way to be together." She stood. "I want you to take the rest of the day and spend it with your man. There are horses in the stables just south of the castle. Tell the boy there that you need two mounts. Once you leave the castle grounds, head directly west. About a mile out, you'll find the forest line. If you head straight in along the path, it will take you to a creek. Tie the horses there and follow the creek downstream a quarter of a mile. It deepens into a pool that is crystal clear and a hundred foot deep. There's a waterfall spilling both into and out of it and it has some of the best views of the countryside that can be had. Take him there. I think the two of you would enjoy it."

#

Gage stood watching the soldiers spar. He offered corrections where they were needed, and praise when it was earned. He, Damon and Greer watched the group carefully. Alaria was teaching another group rudimentary self-defense, and Braxton was consulting with several sword-smiths.

Gage saw Aradia coming toward him when she came out of the stable, wearing a long white dress and holding the reins for two horses. She talked to the animals softly, murmuring to them as she covered the distance between the stables and the practice field. He made his way over to her, stooping to press a kiss to her forehead.

"I thought you'd be working with Graciela."

"She declared me done. Said there's nothing left to teach me and ordered me to take the rest of the day off." She looked around. "Can Damon and Greer handle this for a couple hours?"

Gage looked over his shoulder. "Probably. Why?"

"I was hoping you'd come out for a ride with me."

"It's two days until the battle, Aradia. I don't think I should be leaving to go on a pony ride."

Aradia looked up at him darkly. "No offense, Gage, but I don't think the entire mission is going to be lost if we go for a ride for a couple hours."

Gage glanced around again, meeting Damon's eyes. Damon made a shooing motion with his hands and turned to Greer. He said something too low for even Gage to hear, and Greer grinned. Gage looked back at Aradia and shook his head.

"I feel like I'm being ganged up on." He took the reins for one of the horses and swung into the saddle. "Where are we going?"

Aradia mounted her own horse and nudged it into a walk. "You'll see."

They rode in silence for close to an hour. Aradia smiled when she found the creek and swung down. She tied her horse to a tree and waited while Gage did the same. Both animals had enough room to get to the creek for a drink, and Aradia spent several minutes gathering foliage for them to eat before turning to Gage.

"I might not ever get to show you the place in Greece with the waterfall, but my mother told me about this place, and I think it's going to be just as beautiful." She hopped on one foot to pull off her sandals. "Are you going to try to resist swimming with me this time?"

Gage unbuttoned his shirt, laughing as he did so. "I think my days of resisting you are long past, Priestess." His eyes lit with good humor. "Or should I call you Princess?"

Aradia untied the straps holding up her dress and let it fall to the ground. She wore only a thin slip that did very little to cover her body and that turned translucent in the sunlight. She folded her dress and sat it on a low branch of the same tree they'd tied the horses to, hanging her sandals near it.

"You may call me whatever you like." She stepped into the cool water and shivered from pleasure at the sensation of the current running over her feet and legs. "Come on, Gage." She held out her hand. "It won't kill you to relax for an afternoon and have some fun with me."

Gage shucked his pants and waded in wearing boxers. The water deepened quickly, and within forty feet of stepping into the brook, they were up past their waists. Aradia rolled over and laid on her back, floating along with the current. She stared up at the sprinkling of sunlight that managed to penetrate the lush canopy of greenery. Gage walked next to her, one hand lightly placed on her abdomen to guide her around a bend in the path of the water.

The creek emptied into a pool. At one end was an opening that flowed over the edge and down into an inlet leading out to the sea. At the other end was a waterfall feeding into the pool from a small river up above. Gage turned in a circle and whistled softly.

"This is impressive."

Aradia righted herself and looked around, her eyes widening. "This is beautiful." She turned and caught sight of the waterfall. "Wow."

"Atlantis is a spectacular place." Gage paddled through the pool to the end, lifting himself up to perch on a rock. He leaned over and peered down at the inlet and the bright blue ocean beyond. "It's a shame there's nothing we can do to save it."

Aradia hauled herself out of the water to sit next to him. "We were never supposed to. I wish it was different, but the dangers of changing the past outweigh the good we could do."

Gage turned to look at her, and the words on his tongue slid back down his throat. Her slip had turned completely see-through in the water and clung to every inch of her body. He could clearly see the curve of her breasts, the darker skin of her areolas, and the hardened dusky points of her nipples. He raked his eyes over the soft curve of her belly and the flare of her hips, down to the juncture of her thighs.

Aradia leaned forward, bracing her elbows on her knees. Her hair fell over her shoulders in wet curls the color of a sunset. "I almost feel guilty enjoying myself with what we have to do here."

Gage cleared his throat. "If this make you feel guilty, you'll be impossible to be around after what comes next."

She cocked her head to one side and stared at him with curiosity. "What are you talking about?"

He dropped back into the water and held out his hand to her. "Because you look downright edible in that slip, and I've never been good at turning down sweets."

Aradia's heart skipped a beat and her breath caught in her throat. She placed her hand in his and climbed down off the rocks and into the pool. Gage drew her into his arm and took her mouth with his. Her arms twined around his neck, and she returned his kiss.

The cool water was a direct contrast to the heat of her body. Her nipples tightened and beaded almost painfully in the water and she shifted against Gage's body, trying to create enough friction to allay the discomfort. Gage backed her through the waterfall, laughing when she gasped and squealed as the water pelted their heads.

Behind the waterfall was a shallow carved-out place in the rock wall. There was a ledge there that was several feet wide and covered in a sheen of water. Gage lifted her onto it before climbing up himself. He dragged her against him and yanked the slip over her head, tossing the garment aside and pressing her naked curves against him.

He took one breast in each hand, reveling at the feel of their weight in his hands. He drew his thumbs over her nipples, using his nails to gently scrape at the tender flesh. Her head fell back and her hair streamed down her body, almost reaching her waist. Gage bent and took one nipple into his mouth, sucking deeply and rubbing the nub with his tongue.

He gently lowered her to the stone and parted her legs with his hand. He stroked her clit with his fingers, humming in satisfaction when her body grew damp and hot from his touch. He slipped one finger inside while maintaining pressure on her clitoris. Her chest flushed and her hips jumped against his hand as he curled his finger and stroked into her firmly.

Gage used his teeth to scrape over her nipple, then soothed the sting with his tongue. Aradia sucked in a gasping breath and her eyes rolled back in her head. He released her nipple and blew cool air across it, watching chill bumps rise on her skin. He pressed a kiss to her ribcage, then to her stomach before nestling his face between her legs and inhaling. Her scent was earthy and sweet, much the same as her taste. He lapped at her center with his tongue, tasting the wetness there.

Gently, he penetrated her with his tongue, using both his mouth and fingers to bring her pleasure. Her breathing became shallow and moans rumbled in her chest, music to his ears. He drove her up the crest of orgasm ruthlessly. He stabbed his tongue against her clit and rubbed firmly with his thumb. Aradia writhed on the stone floor, unable to form a coherent sentence and content not to even try.

A shallow cry wrested its way from her throat as she came. Her hips lurched and bucked and her whole body trembled from the force of the orgasm. Her hands fisted at her sides and her toes curled. Gage pressed one final kiss to her before lifting his head and surveying his work with a look of satisfaction.

Aradia spent several moments allowing her breathing to return to normal before she rose to her knees and reached for him. She hooked her fingers in the waist band of his boxers and lowered them down his legs, tossing them to join her slip. She ran her hands over his chest and down to his hips.

"Lie down."

Gage did as he was told, stretching out on his back, his erection jutting out from between his legs, long and thick. Aradia straddled his legs and cupped his penis in her hands, stroking her fingers over his staff and rubbing gently.

She looped her fingers around him and ran them up and down. Hesitantly, she lowered her mouth and extended her tongue to touch the tip. His skin was smooth and silky and she ran her tongue over the length, curling it around the head and sucking it into her mouth.

Gage reached down and tangled one hand in her hair. Aradia slid her mouth down, taking him in and sliding back up. She surrounded him with heat and wet, using her teeth to gently scrape his skin and her tongue to drive him crazy. She was hesitant and careful, her movements slow and deliberate. When she sucked deeply, rubbing her tongue on the sensitive head of his dick, he thought he was going to die.

"God, baby, stop." He reached down and touched her head, trying to tell her to move.

Aradia sat up, her mouth swollen and red and her hair hanging over her shoulders. "What's wrong?"

Gage shook his head. "Nothing's wrong other than that felt amazing. Much more and I'd be done for." He sat up and reached for her, pulling her into his lap and kissing her deeply. "You're amazing, Aradia." He lowered his head and nipped at her neck.

Aradia lifted herself, placing one knee on either side of Gage's thighs. She reached between their bodies and wrapped her hand around the base of his penis, holding him still as she lowered herself onto him, taking him into her body.

She slid back and forth in his lap, wet and easy, with her hands on his shoulders for balance, and his on her hips. She rocketed them both toward climax quickly, squeezing him tightly with her body and leaning back to create delicious friction that rubbed just the right spot to send her flying.

Gage reached between their bodies and pressed his thumb against her clit, sending her over the edge and into orgasm. Before she could come back down, he flipped her on her back and rose over her, plunging deep within her. He lifted her legs to wrap around his hips and drove himself into her deeply. Aradia wrapped herself around him, her nails biting into his shoulders.

Gage pressed his face into her neck. He could smell her blood through her skin; rich, thick, and sweet. It pumped through her veins. Her pulse beat just below her skin, quick and powerful. He remembered the taste of it running over his tongue and down his throat. The urge to bite, to mark her as his own was almost more than he could resist.

"Do it." Aradia's voice was husky and passion filled. She reached up with one hand and pulled her hair away from her neck, baring her creamy skin for him. She held her head to the side and pressed it toward him. "I want you to. Do what you've never done to anyone else. Make me yours, Gage."

He was helpless to tell her no. Gage reared back, his eyes reddening and his fangs extending. He bared his teeth and sank them into her skin, drinking in the sweet nectar of her blood. He ripped his fangs from her, dripping with blood, and roared as a powerful orgasm ripped through him. Surprising them both, Aradia exploded around him, shuddering and jerking from her own climax.

"Are you okay?"

Aradia tied her dress around her neck and looked at Gage, who was already dressed and staring at her. She put her hands on her hips and glared. "You've asked me that half a dozen times already. I'm fine, Gage."

Gage untied their horses and returned the dark look. "Excuse me for being worried about you when I bit you and drank your blood like a monster."

Aradia reached out and jabbed her finger into his chest. "You listen to me. You didn't do a damn thing that I didn't both let and encourage you to do. You might think you're a monster, but you're a vampire, and along with being a vampire come certain behaviors. I wanted you to see that I accept all of you." She jerked her head back to reveal the jagged, already-healing bite. "I want it all, Gage. Not just the pretty stuff that isn't too bad for poor little Priestess to see. I want it all. The good and the bad. No secrets, no shame. This is a part of you, and dammit, I accept it!"

Gage tried not to be moved by her words. He held out his hands and helped her mount her horse before swinging into the saddle himself. "I don't want you to accept it, Aradia. I wish to hell you'd never met me."

Aradia looked sideways at him. "I love you."

"I know you do. I love you, too. Doesn't change the fact that I wish I could have spared you all this hurt." He patted his horse and directed the beast back toward the castle. "That bite will announce to the world that I claimed you. It might make you a target for other vampires."

Aradia snorted. "More likely, other vampires will be too scared of you to come after me and..." She trailed off as the wind picked up. She looked around and tipped her head back to see the sky.

Clouds moved into view quickly. The sky darkened until it was almost black, and it was nearly impossible to see in the woods. Rain fell from the clouds in sheets. Aradia swiped it away from her face and looked down at her hand in shock. It wasn't rain that fell from the sky. It was blood.

Gage gagged when a drop of the rancid blood splashed into his mouth. "What the fuck is going on?"

Aradia kicked her horse in the sides, urging the animal into a canter.

"It's Garrick. He's here. The battle is starting."

"It's too early!"

She shook her head. "I should have realized before. It was never supposed to start on the Solstice. It was supposed to end then."

Chapter Thirty-One

Gage and Aradia had nearly made it to the castle when a lone rider galloped toward them. Gage recognized the man immediately as King Liam and felt his heart sink into his chest. He looked at Aradia and saw an identical expression of dread on her face.

"Graciela sent me to find you. The Dark Ones are flooding the city. Our gates are holding them out for now, but we are sending troops out to fight them."

Aradia drew her horse to a stop. "We're on our way now. The rest of our group?"

"They fight like monsters." Liam smiled grimly. "You're a well trained—"

Liam stopped speaking and gasped for breath, both hands going to his throat. A red stain appeared on his chest, spreading outward. From behind him, a man, to that point unseen, chortled. Javal materialized, his hand deep inside Liam's back. He ripped it from the king, bloody and wet. Liam slid off the saddle and onto the ground. Javal looked at Gage, his eyes alight with glee.

"Your choice vampire. He has to have blood in his system before he dies. You can either ensure you become a vampire, or take a chance that Laelia on her own won't find you."

Aradia extended her hand and formed a ball of fire. Her eyes darkened until they were nearly black. Her horse moved nervously beneath her. "I'm stronger than I was, Javal. I'll incinerate you."

Javal crossed his arms and looked at her appraisingly. "Seems to me that you made a promise to vamp-boy here. You could break that promise and kill me. Gage has a choice. He can either kill me, or turn dear King Liam. He can't do both." When no one moved, Javal tapped his wrist. "Time's ticking, boy. The longer you wait, the more likely it is that you disappear and go back to your wife and those four glorious children."

Gage stared at Liam, who was very quickly bleeding to death. His heart was barely beating and he was no longer breathing. He struggled with the decision, feeling grief at either one. He looked at Aradia, fierce and beautiful, covered in blood and ready to wage battle. He thought about his wife, delicate and kind, and of their children, who had died far too young.

He fought an intense internal battle. With a strangled cry, he launched himself off of the horse and ripped his wrist open with his fangs, forcing his blood into Liam's mouth. Aradia closed her eyes for a moment, both grief and relief coursing through her. Javal put his hands on his hips and grinned.

"Looks like he loves you more than his wife and children, witch. That'll make it all the more satisfying when I rip your heart out and make him watch while I eat it."

Before Aradia could respond, Javal was gone. Gage was silent as he lifted Liam's body onto his horse and remounted. Tears shone in his eyes and Aradia struggled to find something—anything—to say.

"Gage—"

He shook his head. "Don't." He stared stonily ahead. "You have no idea what that did to me back there." He looked down at Liam. "I want to rip his fucking head off, but instead, I'm going to find someplace to put him until I can cram him through the portal. I'm going to send him off to kill me, Aradia."

Aradia took a deep breath. "You don't have to do it. No one would blame you for trying to change it."

Gage looked down at the body and then over at her. "I can't do that."

"I wouldn't blame you, Gage."

Gage angrily punched the dead man's chest. "I can't do it because I love you more, Aradia! Okay? Are you happy now? I love you more than

I love them!" He growled, the sound a combination of frustration, grief and anger. "I don't want to change things because changing them would mean I never got a chance to know you." His voice softened. "I know how horrific that sounds, but I can't help how I feel about it."

Aradia was silent as they rode through the back gate. Somewhere along the ride, the blood falling from the sky had turned to rain and they were both soaked to the skin, the water mingling with the blood. She dismounted and sent the horse with a stable hand that ran out to greet them. Gage took her elbow and led her through the crowd of people.

"We'll deal with this later. Right now I need to find the others, and you need to get to Graciela."

Aradia shook her head. "No, I need to change into something more conducive to battle and find Garrick."

"We've got two days, Aradia. This is the beginning of a marathon. You need to prepare yourself for not facing him until the day of the Solstice."

Aradia pulled her arm free as they entered the castle. "I need to go change my clothing." She rose onto her tiptoes and pressed her mouth to his. "Stay safe, Gage."

Gage shifted the burden of Liam's body on his shoulder. "It's not me I worry about, Priestess."

Aradia grinned as she dashed up the stairs. "I'll be fine."

She hurried down the hall to her room, closing the door behind her. There was a tub of water in the corner, and she peeled off her bloody dress on the way to the cool water. She sank into the copper tub and scrubbed the blood from her skin and hair. She worked efficiently and exited the tub less than five minutes after submerging herself.

She took the time to plait her hair into a tight braid before pulling on the jodhpurs and riding boots she'd had brought up several days earlier. She shimmied into her only bra, the one she'd been wearing when the plane had crashed, and pulled a snug fitting blouse on over her head.

Aradia went back down the hall and into the throne room. Graciela and her personal servant, Atlas, were there. Graciela was pacing anxiously, and Atlas sat in one of the chairs, his knees bouncing nervously. They both jumped when the door slammed behind Aradia. She offered a tense smile and strode across the room.

"They'll be trying to get in to you, Graciela. We have to make sure that you, and the child, stay safe." Aradia took Graciela's hands in hers. "The two of you have to survive."

Graciela jutted her chin up defiantly. "I'm not abandoning my people. I need to go to the temples to pray. I'll assist from there."

Aradia shook her head. "This has started sooner than we thought it would. You need to get to the portal and leave now. They'll be expecting you to stay. I know you don't want to think about it, but you have to go."

"I'm not leaving my people."

All three jumped when there was a loud crack and Graciela's spirit appeared in the room. She went straight to Aradia and embraced her daughter. "You've done as much as you can. Allow me to handle the rest."

Graciela's hands flew to her throat. "What kind of sorcery is this?"

"I'm you. I am accessing the dream plane in order to project my consciousness here." She looked at the Queen, who was standing regally at the foot of the throne. "I had forgotten how huge I got while I was pregnant." She smiled wistfully. "You need to listen to me. Aradia is your daughter. Our daughter. My daughter." She shook her head. "This is confusing. The child you carry is Aradia. The monsters that have come here are trying to kill her because doing so would allow them to pry open the gates of Hell and loose Lucifer upon the Earth. Atlantis is going to sink. This plague is the end of our beloved city. That is an absolute certainty. This battle has been fought before, when I stood where you are now."

Graciela rubbed her hand over her bulging stomach and looked at Aradia, then back to the mirage of herself. "I'm dead, then, and soon, since you're no older than me."

"You die giving birth to me." Aradia reached out and laid her hand on Graciela's arm. "You've been in the dream plane since then, giving me guidance."

"Who sank the city?"

"We did." Graciela flickered out of sight for a moment before reappearing. "Aradia can handle doing it. She has the power to sink it."

Aradia nodded. "I'll take care of it."

Graciela looked down at her belly and then at Aradia. "You've been here for two weeks. Why have you not told me that I'm your mother?"

Aradia smiled and squeezed the Queen's hands. "We aren't allowed to change the past. This isn't the present, it's in the past, playing on some sort of loop. I think we had to come here because no matter what happens, as long as the city sinks, the timeline is preserved."

Graciela laid her hand on Aradia's face. "Apparently I have a beautiful, strong, courageous daughter in here." She chuckled. "Are you sure you can do what needs to be done here?"

"I'm positive." Aradia tugged on the Queen's wrist. "I can take it from here, Mother. It's getting confusing with there being two of you."

The apparition disappeared without a word. Graciela led Aradia to the temple and then to the secret tunnel where she had erected the portal. It was a low altar with a control panel holding several stone buttons. Graciela went to the portal and laid her hand against it to activate it.

"Where am I going?"

"You need to go to Greece. When you get there, you're going to look for a couple named Diane and Richard. They're the two who raise me. Diane is a midwife. She helps you when you're in labor. Whatever you do, you can't try and change things."

Graciela looked sad. "It's depressing knowing that I'm going to die, but at least I get to exist in some form. Do you see me often?"

"More often when I was little than now. You visited Diane all the time when I was an infant. You don't miss out on much. I know it's a horrible way to look at things, but compared to the alternative, I think it's making the best out of a bad set of circumstances." Aradia looked at the dial. "Are you sure you've got it programmed for the right place?"

"I'm sure." She looked back toward the city with sadness in her eyes. "What of your father?"

Aradia sighed. "His fate is worse than yours. He will rise as a vampire. It's because of him that Gage was turned."

"Everything really is connected." Graciela smiled. "It's amazing how every little thing brings you back to the same place. Your father and I. You and the vampire. It's meant to be, Aradia." She laid her hand on Aradia's face and looked into her daughter's eyes. "I know I'm not the mother you know, but I know she's proud of you. I've only just met you, and I'm proud of the woman you've become. You'll succeed here today because there is no other choice, and because the alternative is too horrible to speak of." She leaned in and pressed a kiss to both of Aradia's cheeks. "I have faith in you, Aradia."

Aradia smiled and hugged Graciela swiftly. "Go, now, before they catch up to us. We need this portal to get out ourselves, so I'm hoping they didn't see us going in."

Graciela stepped into the portal. There was a bright flash of light, and the Queen was gone. Aradia waited thirty seconds to make sure the portal had shut down before she turned and raced back down the tunnel, through the temple, and into the throne room. Atlas, the servant, still stood at the entrance, his face frozen in an expression of terror. Aradia grabbed his shoulders.

"Go home and be with your family for as long as you have left."

She ran past the man before he had an opportunity to answer. She could hear the crashes against the walls of the city, and she ran toward them. She saw Damon and Greer directing soldiers. Greer had a tent set up where she was administering field medicine, healing those she could and making comfortable those she couldn't. Already, less than an hour into the siege, there were a dozen bodies piled up, wrapped in sheets and waiting to be burned.

She grabbed Damon's arm. "Where are the others?"

Damon hugged her tightly. "Thank God. We didn't know where you were. Alaria is at the main gate. She's trying to keep them out. Braxton is taking a squad to the back gate to try and hold it from a breach. Gage is going after Javal."

"Where's Garrick?"

Damon looked around anxiously. "We haven't caught sight of that particular asshole yet. They brought thousands of vampires, Aradia. We don't stand a snowballs chance in hell. All we can do is try to keep them out until we kill Garrick and Javal."

"I'm going up to the rotunda where I worked with Graciela. I sent her through the portal already. I think that's where I'll stand the best chance of finding Garrick."

Aradia left Damon directing troops and raced into the castle. She turned left toward the stairs and ran up them. She burst into the stairwell at the top of the living quarters and ascended it as fast as she could. There were hundreds of steps leading to the peak of the castle where she'd spent days training with Graciela.

Before she was halfway, her heart was pounding in her chest and she was gasping for breath. She gripped the handrail hard and used it to heave herself up the steps in bursts. She had to stop once, leaning over and bracing her elbows on her knees, panting for breath. She allowed herself thirty seconds to take several gasping breaths before continuing to run up the stair case.

It took almost fifteen minutes to reach the top, and when she burst through the door and into the round room, she was breathing so heavily she couldn't have spoken had her life depended on it. She stumbled to the window and leaned out, scanning the horizon for any sign of the powerful warlock.

She knew from the potency of his power that he was close. She also knew that Garrick was not the type to want to be involved in a battle. He would be far enough away to avoid the hand-to-hand aspect and close enough that his power was still effective.

There. Standing on a knoll, a staff in his hand, was Garrick. He had long hair and a scraggly beard and wore flowing robes. Aradia absently thought that he looked exactly as one would expect a wizard in a fairy tale to look. There was a large crystal on the top of his staff, and it streamed a thick beam of magic up to the sky, keeping the clouds so thick that they filtered out every bit of sunlight.

She ran to the table and picked up the chunk of citrine that she'd been using for the spells. She clenched it in her hand, feeling its warmth in her grasp. Black magic pounded at the door that she used to keep it out, and she smiled grimly as she stared out the window.

She had once told Gage that she felt as if she'd been born to love him. In that moment, she knew that was a lie. Loving Gage would allow her to do what she had been born to do. She would kill Garrick and keep Hell closed.

Eerily calm, she pocketed the stone and left the room. She darted down the stairs, the muscles in her legs burning from exertion and her lungs straining to suck in enough air to continue fueling her flight. When she exited the stairs on the floor containing the living quarters, she dashed down the hall and onto the second staircase, taking it to the entrance to the castle.

Already the air was thick with smoke and smelled of blood.

Aradia made her way to the back gate, knowing both that there were fewer enemies there and that Braxton was more likely to let her out than Gage or Damon. Braxton was climbing a ladder to the top of the wall, a sword in one hand and a stake tucked into his trousers. He turned and looked over the wall, his expression grim. She waited for him at the bottom of the ladder until he came down.

"There're a couple hundred vampires working their way around from the main gate. It won't be long before they're coming at us from all sides." He sighed. "This is going to be a long thirty-six hours."

"I need a horse and for you to be quiet when I leave the city."

Braxton's brows drew together. "Why the fuck would I do that?"

Aradia glared at him. "I know where Garrick is. My mother's already gone through the portal, so they're not going to be able to kill me before I'm born. I have to kill the warlock. To do that, I have to go to him."

"I'm all for killing the warlock, but I can't let you go alone. If he kills you, they win. I know you have to do this, and no one is going to try to stop you, but you can't go by yourself. I'm not even sure it's a good idea to do it now. We can't get out of here or sink the fucking city until the Solstice. Gabriel said you needed the power from it to be able to kill Garrick."

"Brax, the longer it takes me to get to him, the worse off we're going to be. The battle has started. We have to assume that we have to take every opportunity we have to end it as soon as we can."

Braxton looked back at the wall. "I can't let you go alone." He kicked the brick half-heartedly. "Fucking hell. Give me fifteen minutes to get Damon or Greer over here and I'll go with you."

"I can accept that."

Chapter Thirty-Two

Gage had one purpose. Kill Javal. He elbowed his way through the crowd, pushing people out of his way. There were ladders positioned on the walls to allow archers access to the top. He used one of them to leap over the wall and landed on the other side. He cast a look from side to side and stood up.

Alaria was battling four vampires fifty feet to his left. He debated whether or not to help her before striding over and wading into the fight. He used the short sword on his belt to hack off two heads while Alaria used her stake to end the rest.

"Why aren't you inside the city?"

Alaria brushed dust off her bustier. "No sense in staying in there when all the fun is out here." She grinned. "Where are you off to?"

"Javal."

She sobered and put her hands on her hips. "You're planning to go after the big bad on your own with no backup and without telling anyone where you're going?"

Gage chuckled. "I'm telling you where I'm going."

She shook her head. "I'm going with you." When he started to object, she held up her hand. "Don't even think about telling me no. Even when Greer went into Hell, she had two of us in her head. We're meant to do this as a group, Gage. That means no sneaking off to exact revenge on your own. I'll come with you. I promise that I will let you kill him. I'm not interested in taking that away from you, but it's stupid and reckless to take off alone and go do this."

"What are the odds of me talking you out of this?"

Alaria glared at him. "Do you really need to ask me that?"

"I suppose not." He nodded sharply. "Come on then. We've got a lot of work to do."

They struck out into the woods, their gaits matching stride for stride. Alaria was a tall woman and strong enough that she could hike even the most strenuous terrain. She followed Gage for half an hour silently, watching him thrust his nose into the air several times, inhaling scent and changing direction to compensate.

"What are the odds they don't know we're coming?"

Gage looked at her with an expression of grim determination. "They know. I'm counting on them knowing we're coming."

Alaria drew to a stop and crossed her arms. "Why are we not at least trying to sneak up on them?"

"Because I want the fucker to know I'm coming to kill him. I want him to feel as much terror as possible."

She started walking again. "Fair enough." She wiped her hand over her forehead. "Any idea how many nasty things are with him?"

Gage smiled wryly. "Likely more than we would like to deal with, I'm afraid."

"I'll handle them."

"I don't doubt you will." He pointed at a steep hill. "Unless my nose betrays me, they're on the other side of this hill. Javal and about thirty vampires. Most are newborn."

"Why isn't he trying to get inside the city?"

"Javal isn't going to go to the gates and beat on them himself. He's above that. He's sitting in some swanky tent waiting until they get in. Then he'll go and wreak some havoc." He looked at her out of the corner of his eye. "How is it that you don't know Javal?"

"I don't know every demon in Hell. I know of him, but I hadn't ever met him personally until this." She heaved herself onto a ledge and extended a hand to help him up. "We need to get back in time to help Aradia go after Garrick. I like the idea of her doing that alone even less than the idea of you coming out here alone."

Gage shook his head. "She's guarding her mother. She isn't going to go after Garrick. He's going to have to go into the city to get her. With Graciela there, I'm not too worried about her. The two of them together are a hell of a combination."

"They're definitely powerful. It's never been Aradia's power that concerns me. It's her heart. I've never met someone so emotionally vulnerable."

Gage smiled softly. "That's one of the best things about her. You never have to wonder where you stand with her." He scrambled up the final slope and dropped to his stomach to look over the edge and down the other side.

Alaria scooted next to him, keeping her whole body pressed into the ground to make herself harder to see. She pushed up and out, going over the edge long enough to get an eyeful of what was going on. Once she had assessed the situation, she shimmied back down and waited for Gage to join her.

"Looks like you were spot on about the number of things we have to deal with. Javal has to be in that tent, and it looks like the vamps are on patrol. You think they know we're coming?"

"Javal has to know. He's stupid if he doesn't. I'd be willing to bet most of the vampires are too new to be able to trust their noses, but there are a few that likely know we're here."

"Think they're waiting for us to come down that hill?"

"That I'm not sure of. They could be banking on us being turned off by the sheer numbers or coming up with some complicated plan to go in there, or they could be listening to every word we say, if they're good enough." He lifted his shoulders in a shrug. "Either way, we have to go down there, and they're going to try and kill us. The only question is how we want to do it."

Alaria nodded solemnly. "I think I have an idea about that." She clenched her fist and snapped her whip through the air. "I have enough power left that I'll be a nice distraction. Give me sixty seconds to get their attention. You cut around and come at that tent from the back. By the time you get there, they'll be so preoccupied with me that they won't even notice that you're there."

"Are you sure you're up for this? It's not too late to head back to the city and let me do this alone."

She snorted. "Like hell I would." She took a deep breath and stared at him for a long moment. "Try to stay alive. Or undead. Whatever it is that you are."

"Either works." He smacked her ass playfully as she stood. "Don't die, Alaria."

Alaria spared him a reckless grin as she went over the edge of the hill and started down the other side, whistling. The vampires turned almost as one entity and Gage could tell from their eyes that they were caught in the spell of bloodlust. He shook his head and sent up a quick prayer that Alaria really was as good as she thought she was.

She scrambled down the side of the hill, whip in one hand and sword in the other. Her black hair flared out behind her, and her body looked long and lean in black and red leather. She planted her heels into the soft ground and whirled, swinging both her weapons simultaneously. She slashed through one vampire with the blade and wrapped the whip around the neck of another, jerking hard enough that the entire head popped off his shoulders.

Four down. Twenty-six to go. Gage didn't allow himself any more time to consider the odds. Instead, he headed back down the slope and cut through the trees, making his way toward the tent where Javal waited.

"I'm not in there, you know."

Gage turned when the voice rang out through the forest. In front of him was Javal, wearing a flowing blouse and tight leggings. His hair was long and lush, and his eyes were nearly black. Gage laid his hand at his belt, where his sword hung.

"So I see. Here is as good as in that tent. I'm here to kill you, Javal."

Javal shrugged carelessly. "Killing me is relative since the worst you can do is send me back to Hell. As soon as Garrick guts that witch, it'll be a leisurely vacation to go there before I come back out that gate."

"When Aradia kills your warlock, the gates will be closed permanently, and you won't be able to come back out."

Javal chuckled. "We'll see who comes out on top, I suppose." He shrugged, appearing bored. "Should we get this on the road, then? I'm growing tired of your constant need to chat before we fight."

Gage was ready for the demon when he charged. Javal didn't have as much magic as he had before, presumably unable to keep it because Garrick was actively using his abilities. Gage was able to dip his shoulder and send the demon flying.

Javal landed on his knees and stood slowly, his face contorting into a mask of anger. He held out his hand and formed a ball of fire, using what little magic he had left. He lobbed it at Gage, who dove to the side, slamming into the ground in an effort to avoid being burned. Javal used the time to draw his sword and drop into a sparring stance.

Slowly, Gage climbed to his feet and drew his own sword. "This is how you want to end this? With blades?"

Javal laughed. "I'll get great pleasure from running you through with this blade."

"That won't kill me."

"Neither will it kill me. The only way to send me back to Hell is to kill this body with me still inside it. The second you get a blow in, I'm gone and into another, healthy body. Unless vampires have some abilities I don't know about, you can't do that, son."

Gage shook his head. "You're right about that." He twirled his blade. "Good thing I had the sword smith engrave traps on my blade. The second I run it through, you're stuck. You won't be able to leave your host, and I'll be able to put you back where you belong."

Javal sighed. "Enough talking."

The two men clashed, the noise of blades colliding echoing through the clearing. Both were accomplished with a sword, and both knew the fight would not be easily won. Gage was quicker, but Javal had more brute strength.

Again and again their swords met. Sparks flew as the metal hit and several blows found their mark. Javal's sank deep into Gage's thigh. Gage blocked the next, parried it, and stabbed Javal in the arm, nearly sinking the blade up to the traps before the demon pulled away and swung his own weapon.

Gage spared one look over to Alaria, who was surrounded by vampires. She hacked her way through them with ruthless abandon. Blood trailed down her neck and there were several bite marks on her throat. Her mouth was set in a thin line and she used both whip and sword to battle off the mob of vampires. In that moment, Gage was thankful she was with him. If he had been alone, it would have been too much to handle.

She swung her sword and whip expertly, taking out two vampires in one swipe. She lashed out, kicking one away and elbowing another in the face when it got too close to slash at with her sword. She grunted when one vampire sank his teeth into her wrist, and she drove her sword through his head with one jab. It exploded into dust.

Alaria whirled and slashed with her whip, wrapping it around one vampire and bringing it close enough to slash his head off with her sword. She spat when dust got into her mouth and took a moment to count. Seventeen left. She gritted her teeth and waded back into the fight.

Sweat and blood dripped into her eyes and she swiped it away impatiently. The vampires that were left weren't quite as crazed by blood lust. They waited patiently as she fought each of them. It tired her more quickly than if she'd been taking on several at a time. When one burst into dust and another hesitated a half second before charging her, she spared a glance to check on Gage, who still fought Javal.

The two men were locked in a wrestling match. Their swords were on the ground, and they attacked one another with fists and feet. They rolled on the ground, kicking up dust and leaves as they grappled for the upper hand, neither willing to allow the other to emerge as victor.

Gage rolled Javal onto his back and slammed him into the ground, the sound of Javal's skull striking the ground echoing through the clearing. He fumbled for the sword, his fingers brushing the handle. He dragged it across the dirt inch by inch until he wrapped his fingers around it.

Lifting the sword, he held Javal to the ground with one hand. "I warned you back in Scotland that I would kill you. You messed with the wrong people. No one comes after what belongs to me and survives."

Javal opened his mouth to speak and Gage shoved the sword into it, driving it through his mouth, the back of his head, and into the ground. Black and red fog started to leak out the body's ears, but the traps on the sword kept Javal's essence from escaping. The eye sockets sparked and flashed with energy and electricity. Gage leaned down and pressed his mouth to the demon's ear.

"The beauty of being in the past is that the Gate isn't closed in this time. You're going back to Hell and you won't be able to come back out."

Gage wrenched the sword from Javal's mouth and climbed to his feet, watching as the ground opened up and swallowed the demon, closing where he'd been as if nothing at all had happened.

There was no time to celebrate. Alaria was still fighting off nine vampires. He swung his sword and waded into the battle. With two of them, the vampires didn't have a chance. Alaria slammed her back against his and they rotated, taking on the vampires that charged them efficiently. Within two minutes, the ground was covered in dust and no more monsters attacked.

Alaria dropped to the ground to catch her breath. She took stock of her injuries and groaned. "I'm going to have to see Greer before I dive back in to anything." She winced when she wrapped her hand around her opposite wrist to stem the flow of blood coming from the bite mark there. "Dare I say that wasn't as difficult as I thought it was going to be?"

Gage sat next to her, resting his elbows on his knees and looking out into the woods. "Enjoy a five minute break while you can. We need to get back to the city and help the others. There's no telling how long it'll take for Garrick to come looking for Aradia." He looked up at the thick black clouds. "It looks like he's still working, but soon enough, it'll be night, and then Garrick won't need to keep this spell up."

Alaria laughed. "He doesn't need to keep standing there like fucking Gandalf as it is. He could cast one spell and bring on the night until the spell is broken. He has enough power to do it. He's standing there like that because he wants to be seen. This warlock likes his theatrics."

Gage stood and extended his hand to Alaria. "We need to get back."

She let him help her to her feet. "Can we avoid confrontation until I've had a chance to let Greer take care of these bites?"

"We'll do our best." He held her shoulders until she gained her stability. "Ready to go?"

Alaria nodded. "Let's get it done."

They retraced the path they'd taken, running down the hill and jogging along the path back to the castle. What had taken them an hour to do the first time took nearly two the second. Gage gave Alaria a leg up, holding her feet while she scrambled up the wall before leaping over it himself.

Inside the walls was absolute chaos. Some people were bleeding in the streets, and others ran screaming. The sounds of the battle from the front and back gates were loud and overwhelming. Greer was barking orders to several men. There was a pile of bodies behind her and rows of injured waiting for her. Already, there were circles under her eyes and her skin was pale and clammy. She looked up when she heard Gage's voice and offered a tight smile.

"This is getting bad fast. There are too many. I feel like I'm in some old war movie. I'm literally deciding who lives and who dies. I have to allocate my energy to be able to keep doing this."

Alaria chuckled wryly. "Do you have enough to spare for me?"

Greer nodded. "As much as I hate to say it, I'd gladly sacrifice them for any one of us. They're all dead anyway." She shook her head and blinked back tears. "I hate this more than I can say. I'm patching these people up to send them back out there so they can die all over again."

Gage touched Greer's arm. "We knew it would be hard. We don't have a choice. This is where we have to be, and this is the battle we have to fight. You're doing everything you can. We all are." He looked around. "I'm going to go find Aradia."

Greer looked up from healing Alaria, her eyes filling with concern. "Go find Aradia?"

"She should be in the castle guarding Graciela."

"Shit. You don't know, do you?"

Panic rose within Gage. "Know what?"

"Aradia sent Graciela through the portal already. She and Braxton snuck out the back gate to go after Garrick. They've been gone, God, at least three hours."

Chapter Thirty-Three

WITHIN FIVE miles of the city walls, the sky turned from black to red. Braxton shifted uncomfortably in the saddle of his horse and looked over at Aradia, who stared stonily ahead, an expression of calm on her face. He cleared his throat.

"Are you sure you can handle this without your mother?"

Aradia looked over at him. "I'm sure. This is why I'm here, Brax." She smiled. "Don't you think I can do it?"

"I think it's going to be tough."

"If it was supposed to be easy, the fate of the world wouldn't ride on it." She chuckled. "Relax a bit. We've got a long ride. I don't believe for a second that Garrick doesn't know we're coming. He obviously likes the drama, so I would expect the show to start sooner or later."

"Show?"

Aradia nodded. "We're likely not going to be able to just ride right up to him. We're going to have to fight our way through."

"Through what?"

"Warlocks as powerful as Garrick can make you see what they want you to. That's how he changes and manipulates the dream plane. It takes a lot more energy, but it can be done in reality, too. I'd expect he's going to twist everything the closer we get."

"Could you do the same to him?"

Aradia shook her head. "Not if I want to have enough left over to fight him. He uses purely black magic. Any white magic that he had is eroded. I can hypothetically use all black magic, but the risks are substantial to do it that way." She reached down and patted her horse when the animal quivered. "I need you to trust me, Braxton. No second-guessing me."

"I understand." He twisted in the saddle to look back at the gates. "I can't figure out where all those vampires have been hiding. We've been here for two weeks."

"There's a lot of countryside. As far as how they're getting to the city now, they're coming in waves from the beach. They're blocking access to the water so people can't get out. They likely moved in through the night."

"I wish there was a way to get troops out to the beach to attack them there. It would give us the best shot."

"Of what? Winning?" Aradia shook her head. "Brax, we're not here to win. We're here to kill Garrick and Javal and get my mother out safely. As soon as those three things are done, I'm sinking the city and we're out of here."

Braxton sighed deeply and faced forward. "It's hard to fight a war knowing we're going to lose."

"We're not losing. We're winning. Atlantis lost thousands of years ago." She straightened and pointed to a tree several yards ahead. "Look there. What's off about that tree?"

Braxton looked at it and smiled ruefully. "Last I knew, trees don't bleed."

Blood dripped from the leaves and ran down the trunk, pooling into thin rivulets that tore through the dirt, boiling and steaming. The horses both jumped over the blood, but were both quivering and dancing, clearly uncomfortable with the situation.

"These horses aren't going to be able to take much more before they spook. We might be better off on foot."

Aradia surveyed the blood on the ground. "I agree. Should we tie them up or just let them go?"

"We'll tie them in that clearing just ahead. Worst case, they're not here when we come back, but if they are, they'll cut the trip by three-quarters."

They dismounted and tied the horses to trees in a clearing. Both tugged at the reins and whinnied out of concern. Aradia patted her mount's withers and murmured to the animal before checking to make sure her crystal was securely in her pocket and striking out down the path. Braxton stayed a step in front of her, one hand on his scabbard and the other clenching a stake.

"No offense, Brax, but I don't see vampires as our problem. They're all trying to get into the city. The only thing we're going to face out here is Garrick." She stepped over another trail of blood running down the path. "This is not going to be fun."

Braxton grimaced when he saw the body of a deer lying on the side of the path, gutted and with greasy entrails hanging out of the abdominal cavity. They both jumped when the dead animal lifted its head and parted its lips in a grotesque smile. Aradia took several breaths to calm her roiling stomach and laid a hand on Braxton's arm.

"It's an illusion. It isn't really there, or if it is, it's not doing anything other than laying there and rotting."

"That doesn't make it any less gross."

"This is just the beginning, Braxton."

They plodded in silence for nearly an hour. By the end of that time, Braxton had lost count of how many dead animals had grinned and sneered at him. One coyote had even been standing, eating its own intestines. Even Aradia had turned green at that sight.

The other constant was the blood. The closer they got, the thicker it flowed, until there were deep divets in the path filled with blood. The red, sticky liquid boiled as it ran down the hill, and after a while, neither Aradia nor Braxton even bothered stepping around it. It took less effort to walk right through.

After another thirty minutes, the blood stopped and the dead animals disappeared. Aradia smiled triumphantly.

"He must be running out of energy. He needs to conserve what he has for the fight." She looked around. "Now would be a good place to take a breather and get a drink of water." She pointed to a small creek flowing into a pool. "That pond looks pretty clean, and I'm dying of thirst."

Braxton looked around. "We'll make it fast, but I could use a drink, too."

Aradia walked to the pond and dropped to her knees, leaning forward to cup her hands and bring water to her lips. The cool water was clear in her hands. When she brought it to her lips, however, it had turned to thick, red blood. Before she could fling it away, it began to boil, scalding her palms. She shrieked and shook her hands, flipping blood.

She gagged when she looked back at the pond and saw that the entire thing was filled with blood. Chunks of animal flesh floated to the surface, swollen and slimy red. Several rats bobbed up, and as she watched, they split open and leaked organs into the bloody water. She closed her eyes and shook her head.

"So much for the drink."

As Aradia climbed to her feet, hands erupted from the water and latched around her feet, dragging her into the water. She screamed as she fell and dug her nails into the ground, clawing at it to keep herself from being completely submerged.

Braxton grabbed Aradia under the arms and heaved her out of the water, lifting her to her feet and steadying her. She clung to his arms until her legs were able to hold her before nodding and taking a step back.

"I should've seen that coming."

Braxton nudged her back onto the path, anxious to get away from the bloody pond. "You're fine. No harm no foul." He groaned when a figure appeared on the path in front of them. "This just doesn't end. What now?"

Aradia shook her head. "I don't know, but whatever you do, remember that it's not real. These apparitions only have the power you give them."

The figure became clearer as they got closer. Aradia saw herself, running, covered in blood, with her clothing torn to shreds. Behind her, chasing her, sword in hand, was Braxton. They stood in shock and watched the vision of Braxton tackle the one of Aradia.

He held her down, pummeling her with his fists. She struggled, kicking and biting. The apparitions fought and tangled until Braxton rose above Aradia and drove his sword into her chest, ripping it up and splitting her ribcage, organs and blood spilling out onto the dirt and soaking into the ground.

Aradia unconsciously rubbed her sternum before shaking her head and walking forward, determination evident in her stride. "It's not real and watching it is just wasting time. Come on."

Braxton watched her walk right through the apparition and smiled darkly. "This is the creepiest thing I have ever experienced in my life."

Within a hundred yards of the pond, there were bodies hanging from the trees. Aradia shivered when she saw that they were illusions of her and the others, over and over again. They saw Greer with her neck broken and her eyeballs hanging out of her sockets. Alaria had been eviscerated, and there was a still squirming fetus attached to the umbilical cord hanging outside of her body.

Damon was merely a trunk and a head, with all four limbs piled on the ground below him. Gage shrieked from pain as stakes were driven into his body from more than a dozen entries. They also saw themselves hanging with thick ropes around their necks. The sounds of their gasping breaths filled the path.

Aradia forced herself not to look, even as the cries of infants filled the air. By the time they made their way past the bodies, she was pressing her hands against her ears and humming loudly to keep the noise out. Braxton was stoically weathering the onslaught.

Aradia reached out and took Braxton's hand, holding it tightly. He squeezed her fingers in return, though he didn't say anything. Both could now see the top of the slope where Garrick stood, his staff in one hand with a stream of black and red magic pouring into the clouds. He seemed to be staring directly at them, and Aradia thought she could make out a smug smile on his lips.

"I wish I could tell you that was the worst of it, but I'm afraid we haven't seen half of what he's got yet."

Braxton cast her a quick look. "I think half of me wishes I'd stayed in Atlantis and sent Damon with you."

She chuckled softly. "There's no shame in turning around and going back." She squeezed his hand again. "I'll warn you, though, that with Garrick still alive, I think the odds are good that the way back is just as difficult as the way forward."

"I'm not leaving you to do this alone, Aradia. None of us were ever meant to fight these battles alone. We're supposed to do it as a team. There's no way all six of us could go with you to make sure everything that needed to be accomplished was, but neither do you have to be solo. It's much too dangerous that way."

Aradia looked over at him fondly. "You're a good man, Braxton. When we get up to the precipice, you have to stay back. I don't want you to get his attention. He'll know you're there, he already does, but you're not the focus. If you were to become the focus, he could incinerate you before I could get any magic out to stop him."

"I'm not interested in turning into a pile of bones, so don't worry about that. I won't interfere unless he's killing you, and then I'll step in. I fully understand that the odds are we'll both end up dead, but if one dies, we all fail, so there's no point in surviving anyway." He shook his head and muttered under his breath. "When all this is over, I'm going to make it my mission to punch God in the nose."

Aradia was already focused on the next apparition. She pointed up the trail where a woman with long blonde hair wearing jeans and a sweater had just run onto the path. She clutched a knife in her hand and had an expression of pure terror on her face. Braxton dropped Aradia's hand when he saw it and stared down at the dirt.

"Is that..." Aradia trailed off, not sure how to ask the question.

"That's Griffin. He's showing us the Choosing."

"It's not real, Brax. She's been dead a long time. It's not real."

He looked up in time to watch Griffin throw her head back and drive the knife into her chest. Her voice filled the forest, surrounding him and squeezing in on him, ruthlessly loud. He pressed his hands to his ears, but even that gave no respite from her voice.

. "After thirty years, the slate wiped clean, I stand here today, ready to claim my birthright. I accept my role as a voice for all the people, and I have made my choice. God in Heaven, Lucifer below, hear me! Today, I Choose."

They watched as she again held the knife out, both hands wrapped around the hilt and plunged it into her chest. When she spoke again, her voice was strangled and blood soaked through her sweater, dripping onto the ground and running toward them, a red river.

"I've paid the price for this privilege with my life, willfully given. As payment for my Choice, I demand the life of Alaria." She spread her arms and tipped her head back up. "Heaven take me home."

Aradia felt Griffin as they walked past. Braxton stopped on the path and stared down at his dead wife's body. As he watched, Griffin's eyes opened and she climbed to her feet, tearing at the sweater to show him the gaping hole in her chest. The apparition sneered at him, and her voice again echoed amongst the trees.

"You killed me, Braxton. You couldn't keep me alive, so I had to make a deal with Alaria. Now you want to fuck her. You're going to fuck the thing that made me die. I hope that every time you look at her face, you see what she did to me. I hope your cock goes limp, you son of a bitch! How could you do this to me?"

Griffin's face twisted into a mask of grief, but in her eyes, Aradia saw the look of pure glee that was reflecting Garrick's emotions. She retreated back down the trail and slipped one arm around Braxton's waist.

"It's not real. She's not here, Braxton. Garrick is using what affects you most as a weapon. Don't give it any power. He's feeding off your emotions. Come on!" She yanked at him until he broke out of his trance and allowed her to lead him down the path.

The blood receded again, and the apparitions faded so that all they saw was the forest. When, after ten minutes, nothing new had popped up, Aradia again chanced finding water. Braxton found a stream several yards off the path, and they were both able to take a long drink. While she waited for Braxton to slake his thirst, she picked some berries from a nearby bush and they ate those before returning to the trail.

"He's right, which I think is what hurt so bad about that."

Aradia's brows drew together. "What are you talking about?"

"The illusion of Griffin and what she—it—said. I knew it wasn't real, but it looked just like her. That was the same sweater she wore the day she died. Her hair was exactly right. Everything was perfect. It felt like Griffin, and what she said is true. I couldn't promise her that I could bring her through the Choosing alive. Alaria could, and she wanted her humanity in return."

Aradia reached out and again took his hand. "That wasn't Griffin's to give."

"She got to demand one thing of God as a gift for the Choosing. You heard it. She asked for Alaria's life when she could have asked for her own if I had been able to bring her through it. It's my fault she's dead, and it's my fault Alaria's a human, and I feel so mixed up about it all because I don't regret Alaria being human, but I do regret Griffin dying."

Aradia's voice was gentle when she spoke. "Did it ever occur to you that Lucifer would have still done this even if Griffin was alive, and that without Alaria on our team, we wouldn't be able to succeed?"

"Yeah, I've thought about that. I just wish I could know that she doesn't hate me."

"Braxton, she's dead. She can't hate you."

"Logically, I know that, but I think it's pretty clear that my emotional state isn't quite so okay with the whole thing."

Aradia linked her arm through his, bringing their strides in line. "I think you need to forgive yourself. You've forgiven Alaria for her choice. You need to forgive Griffin for hers and you for yours."

"I'm not mad at Griffin."

"Aren't you?" She looked up at him. "You don't have any animosity towards her for not telling Alaria no?"

Braxton didn't have a chance to answer. A fog rolled in, so thick it was impossible to see more than six inches through it. It started as a white mist, then darkened until it was black. The dark was so oppressive that it felt heavy against their skin. It rolled over them, hot and heavy, stealing their breath and curling its fingers around their throats.

Aradia dropped Braxton's arm to claw at the fog. It slipped through her hands like water before rearing back up and wrapping around her again. She fell to her knees, choking for breath. She was blind and deaf, unable to see or hear anything. The fog clouded all of her senses, blocking her from Braxton, whom she knew was only inches away from her.

Desperate, she reached inside of herself and flung open the door to the black magic. She concentrated on her crystal and on making the prism. She forced the black through the mirrors and thrust it out into the fog, lighting up the forest and driving it back. She threw out her arms and screamed, flinging as much magic as she could into the fog.

It disappeared as quickly as it had appeared. In its place was Garrick, a wizened wizard with long, scraggly hair. He was dressed in flowing black robes and he had crystals both around his neck and on the head of his staff. When he smiled, all of his teeth had been sharpened to points.

Aradia forced herself to her feet and faced him. "The fog was a nice touch."

Garrick held out one hand and formed a ball of black and red fire. "Don't insult me with small talk. I'm here to kill you, and you're here to kill me. Let's see which of us emerges the victor."

Aradia lashed out with a thick red stream of magic. It struck Garrick and left his robes singed and smoldering. He brushed the fire out with one swipe of his hand and reached out, curling his magic around her throat and clenching his fist, cutting off her air supply.

She gasped and fought, bringing both hands to her throat to hit the force strangling her. Gathering her energy, she focused on her magic, on using it to combat what he sent at her. She pictured a knife and hacked at the hands around her neck. They splintered and fell from her, the magic retreating into Garrick.

Aradia threw her head back and closed her eyes, allowing more of the black inside her. Her crystal darkened from red to black and she pushed the magic through her prism, strengthening the stream. She peeled open her eyes and Garrick laughed when he saw that they were black.

"You can't defeat me with black magic, little girl. You have no idea how to bend it to your will. It will control you well before you control it."

Aradia concentrated the magic and let it build up inside her crystal. "Don't be so sure." She spared a look at Braxton, who was standing several yards down the path. She forced her way into his head. *I need you to help me. His crystals are what makes him so strong. He uses them to magnify his power. Sneak around behind him and when I say, you go for his staff. Smash it.*

Braxton jumped when he felt the intrusion into his mind. He nodded. "On it. *Jesus fucking Christ this is weird.*"

Aradia turned her attention back to the warlock. She let him take the lead, reacting to his strikes. They danced in a circle, avoiding the blows of the other. Aradia calculated her opening carefully, waiting until they were perfectly positioned in front of Braxton. Garrick sent a fireball at her, which she deliberately allowed to hit her.

She hit the ground, a huge burned hole in her stomach. It hadn't penetrated deep enough to kill her, but she would need to get to Greer quickly after the battle. Aradia clamped a lid on the pain and watched as Garrick approached her. She waited until he was less than ten feet away and sent all the magic she had at him.

It hit him in the chest, sending him to the ground. His staff flew to one side. Before she could tell him to, Braxton lunged forward and grabbed it, striking the ruby on a rock until it splintered and broke.

Magic flowed out of the stone and Aradia opened herself to it, taking it in and meshing it with what she had. She forced it through her citrine, melding it and forcing herself to her feet at the same time.

She tackled Garrick, pinning him to the ground with both her body and her magic. She fought off his attacks, brushing them aside with his own magic. She formed a hand with it and thrust it into his chest, wrapping the fingers around his heart and yanking.

Her eyes cleared from the magic and she looked down at her own hand, finding it covered in blood and holding Garrick's still warm organ. She tossed it to the side and climbed to her feet, staring down at the dead body. The black clouds cleared to reveal a rising sun with a purple ring around it.

"Oh my God."

Braxton was beside her in an instant. "What is it? How badly are you hurt?"

"We've been up here for almost two days, Braxton. That's the ring of the Solstice. We have to get back to the city! The vampires will be inside and we have to find the others and get out of here. I have to sink it."

Aradia looked up and her eyes darkened once again. She brought the clouds back, darkening the sky until it was dark once more.

"We have to keep the time line from changing. If all the vampires turn to dust because it gets bright and sunny, people could get off the island that aren't supposed to."

Braxton pulled the strips of fabric around her abdomen and stared at the seared flesh. "This is really bad."

"I know. It hurts like hell." She leaned against him. "Greer can fix me up when we get back to the city." She winced as they started back down the path. "We're just gonna have to take it slow is all."

"I can carry you."

"It's miles back to the city. Let's just get to the horses. I'll be fine." She gritted her teeth and kept walking. "The longer we spend talking about it, the more time we waste getting there."

By the time they had gone an hour, Aradia's face was pale with pain and skin was peeling off her stomach where she'd been burned. Most of the blood vessels had been cauterized by the heat, but some still bled sluggishly. She leaned heavily on Braxton, one of her arms around his shoulders and his around her waist. Her other hand was pressed against her stomach in feeble defense against the pain.

The trek back to the castle was nearly fifteen miles, and a six hour walk at a good clip given the terrain. The illusions on the way up had messed with their sense of time, and the fog had clouded their senses for what had to have been hours, but on the way back, the sense of desperation and Aradia's slow pace made the trip feel longer than on the way up.

By the time they got to where the horses had been tied, Aradia was leaning the vast majority of her weight on Braxton and tears streamed down her face from the pain. They came around the last curve before the clearing, and instead of finding their mounts, they found two dead horses.

"Garrick."

Aradia's voice was weak and thready. Braxton stooped and lifted her into his arms, brushing away her meager objections and cradling her against him. He took five seconds to balance her weight before striking out down the path toward the city.

"I'm too heavy for you to carry all the way back."

"I'll manage. I'm strong, and you're not that heavy."

Aradia laughed weakly. "I'm not teeny like Greer and Alaria."

Braxton snorted. "Neither of them are tiny, either. Greer's got more muscle than I do, I think, and Alaria is five foot ten if she's an inch, and weighs at least as much as you do." He adjusted her slightly. "Besides, it's been a while since I visited the gym. This is good for me." He grinned down at her. "See? You're doing me a favor. You get a ride, and I get a workout. It's a win for everyone."

They were silent for the rest of the trip. By the time the walls came into sight, the smell of blood was thick in the air. The walls had been breached. There were wide holes in the stone, and they had collapsed in several places. Screams were easily heard long before Braxton lifted Aradia over the pile of rubble and into what had been a thriving city full of life.

He stuck close to the wall, trying to avoid detection. Vampires were roaming the streets, most with blood smeared on their faces or hands. Twice, Aradia mustered enough magic to shield them from detection when one of the monsters got too close.

The entrance to the castle was covered in blood and littered with bodies. Braxton stepped over them carefully and wound his way through the building to the tunnel leading to the portal. At the end of the hall, Damon stood with a sword at his side, guarding the entrance. The stone was coated with dust.

Damon rushed forward when he saw them coming down the hall, yelling over his shoulder. "It's them! Aradia's hurt!"

Gage bolted out of the temple and took Aradia from Braxton, running his hands over her face and pressing his mouth to hers in a desperate kiss. Aradia wrapped her arms around his neck and broke down, sobbing from both pain, and relief.

Gage carried her into the room containing the portal and laid her on the floor. Greer was there before he could call for her, ripping the shirt off her and pressing her hands to Aradia's stomach. Within moments, the burned flesh turned pink and the blood stopped.

"We have to sink the city and get through the portal." Gage cast a look at Liam's body, which was still laying on the floor, dead. "He'll be waking up soon. I need to put him through, but I'm not sure how to activate it."

Aradia climbed to her feet. "I do." She walked to the portal and pressed her palm to several of the panels. "Push him through."

Alaria cleared her throat. "How do you sink the city?"

Aradia looked up from the console. "I'll use the same spell my mother did the first time." She waited until Liam had disappeared and pressed several more buttons. "Be ready when I finish. We have to get out fast."

Gage nodded. "We're ready."

Aradia took a deep breath and tried to remember the words. They filled her head and she opened her mouth "Winds howl, waves crash. God of heaven, God of sea, heed my words, hear my plea. Free us from this endless night, raise the sun, bring the light. Walls crumble, city sink. God of sky, God of Earth, take the Beasts, free us now, preserve our worth. By the power given to me, as I command it, so shall it be!"

Within a heartbeat, waves crashed against the walls and rain poured from the sky. The screaming from outside got louder. The portal glowed bright green. One by one, they went through. Aradia went last, sending one last look back as the water coursed through the tunnel and into the portal.

Chapter Thirty-Four

Michael and Gabriel were waiting for them when they came through the portal. Michael stepped forward, a smile on his face.

"Congratulations. The second task is complete. You did very well."

Alaria looked at Aradia. "We all assumed you killed Garrick since you came back, but how did you do it?"

Braxton and Aradia exchanged a long look. Aradia shook her head and spoke. "I ripped his heart out of his chest." She reached out and squeezed Braxton's hand. "We did it together."

Michael laid a hand on Gage's shoulder. "Very nice work with the demon. You all battled impressively. We'll take you home now. The next task will begin in several weeks. There will be some time for you to heal and rest before we begin anew."

Alaria crossed her arms. "Can you tell us more about the next one? I know we have to cast out the demons on earth and that part of it is carving the wings from the backs of the original Fallen Archangels. The only problem with that is that I'm a human now. I don't have wings. Hell, none of them have wings."

"The roots of their wings are still deep inside their bodies. There is one weapon that can pull the remnants from them." Michael looked sad for a moment. "You share that fate, Alaria. Unfortunately, that is all I can reveal at this time. We're still waiting for several things to fall into place before we can make known to you the rest. The last thing I want is to give you inaccurate information." He held up his hand when Alaria started to speak. "I'm not purposely keeping you in the dark. I don't know anything else. I'd tell you if I did."

Gabriel stepped forward. "Allow me to transport you all back to your home."

He reached out and touched each forehead briefly. With one snap of his fingers, they were all jerked forward and landed in Gage's dining room. Gabriel grabbed Alaria's hand and snapped his fingers again, taking her to the white room he kept. As soon as they appeared, Alaria jerked her hand free and whirled on him.

"Did you know it would happen?"

Gabriel looked slightly panicked. "Alaria, let me explain."

Fury coloring her cheeks, Alaria shook her head. "No explanations, Gabriel. I ask, you answer. Did you know you would knock me up that night in the hotel?"

"Yes."

Her shriek of anger echoed through the room. She grabbed the pitcher of tea that sat on the coffee table and hurled it at his head. Only his Angel reflexes kept it from striking the target. Furious, she struck his chest with both fists as he grabbed her, and she punched him in the nose when he tried to hold her.

"Don't you touch me! You don't ever touch me!" She backed against the wall and wrapped her arms around herself, tears streaming down her face. "How could you do this to me? How? I thought you cared about me!"

"It's because I care that I did it." He looked grief-stricken. "If I hadn't, God would have found another Angel to do so. The birth of the child is ordained. It must be."

"It must be? That's all you fucking give me? You impregnate me on purpose and then only offer up 'God made me do it' as an excuse?" She screeched in frustration. "You are unbelievable! I should have gotten a choice!"

"Would you have agreed to carry the child?"

"Fuck no, I wouldn't have agreed!"

"Then there was no point in asking you." Gabriel shrugged. "I had no choice, Alaria. Just as you have no choice."

"You had a choice! You chose to deceive me. I'm the one who was robbed of choice." She slapped him across the face when he approached her. "Don't you come near me! I don't want you to touch me or look at me or—fuck—be in the same room as me! I hate you for what you did! I hate you because I loved you and I trusted you, and you betrayed my trust!"

"I did what I believed was best for both of us. You can believe that or not, but I'm telling you the truth. In thirty-four weeks, you will become a mother and I, a father. I believe it is in the best interest of the child for us to work together."

"No." Alaria shook her head. "If I'm going to have a child, you'll have nothing to do with it. You forced it on me, Gabe, but I'll be damned if I share it with you. You betrayed me, and you used me. You chose God over me. This child will not know what it is. You're not going to be involved."

Gabriel closed his eyes. "I understand that you're emotional. I knew when I did it that you would be angry with me. I am also aware that I will not be the one to raise the child. It would never be allowed, and for that, I am sorry. However, you will not keep me from watching over my child. I have known since the beginning that I would never be the one to be known to it as Father."

"Take me back." She turned her head and refused to look at him. "I don't want to be here."

Gabriel nodded. "As you wish." He faltered. "Will you go to him?"

Alaria's eyes sparked with anger. "Better him than you."

Gabriel snapped his fingers and sent her back to Gage's house. The lights were all off and only Braxton was left sitting in the kitchen. He stood when she appeared and crossed the room to stand in front of her.

"Did he hurt you?"

Alaria shook her head. "He knew he was doing it. He knocked me up on purpose because God told him it had to be done."

Braxton rubbed her shoulders. "One of these days, I am going to punch God in the nose."

"I hit him."

Braxton's eyebrows nearly met his hairline. "God?"

Alaria laughed despite herself. "No, no. Gabriel. I hit him. Twice."

"He deserved it." He perched on one of the stools. "Is there anything I can do?"

She met his gaze steadily. "Yeah. Get your shit together."

He pulled her to him. "I'm working on it."

"Work harder."

They were both smiling when he kissed her gently. He pulled back after only a moment and hugged her tightly. "Yes ma'am."

Aradia rolled onto her back and trailed her fingers over Gage's chest. Her skin shone with a thin sheen of sweat, and her hair was mussed. He reached up and stroked her curls away from her face, drawing her down for a gentle kiss.

"I should be furious at you for running off without me to battle Garrick."

Aradia laughed. "I should say the same about you for running off and taking on Javal without me."

Gage chuckled. "Let's call it even then." He sobered. "There's something I need to tell you."

Aradia looked into his eyes. "What is it?"

"Your mother and Michael have both told me about a prophecy. That when I am cleansed by fire and have experienced a love like no other vampire, then I'll become human again. They've also told me that if we succeed at the third task, then I'll get the choice whether or not to accept humanity."

Aradia worked hard to keep her face neutral. "What are you going to do?"

"For a long time, I've been telling them both no. That I didn't want it. I like my life, Aradia. I like not growing old, and I like having exactly what I want. I accepted my fate a long time ago, and I have not sat around pining for my old life or hoping to be like Alaria and get a beating heart. It's just never been what I want." He tipped her face up when she lowered her eyes, crestfallen. "Look at me." He stroked one finger down her face. "I thought I could do it. I thought I could let you go at the end of this. Then I thought I'd lost you today. When I saw Braxton carrying you in, I was scared, and I knew in that moment that, given the choice, I choose you. Every time."

"What are you saying?"

He stroked one finger down her cheek. "You've changed me, Aradia. You're beautiful and pure and innocent, and you make me want things I haven't wanted in more than a thousand years. You make me believe that I can be better because you think I am. I want to be who you think

I am. If I get a choice, I'd take one lifetime of being with you over a hundred more without you."

Aradia battered down a surge of hope. She maintained a serious expression. "I love you, Gage, and I've dreamed of hearing you say this to me. I want it, too, more than anything, but you need to know what that means to me. I want a life after this. I want a home and children and a life together. That's all I've ever wanted. If you don't want that, I don't want us to try and make something fit that doesn't."

Gage rolled her beneath him and nuzzled his face against her neck. "I want you to be happy. If marriage and kids is what will do it, then that's what we'll do. I loved being a father. I'll always miss my children and grieve their losses, but that doesn't mean I won't enjoy watching you grow with ours." He laid his hand on her belly. "I can imagine how you'll look swollen with child, how we'll raise them together." He pressed a soft kiss to her forehead. "There aren't any guarantees, Aradia, so I don't want you to think this is a foregone conclusion. There's a lot that has to go right for this to happen. I thought you deserved to know that there's a chance."

Aradia wrapped her arms around him. "A chance is all we need."

About the Author

Sirena N. Robinson is an author who lives and works in the foothills of the Appalachian Mountains. When she is not helping her characters defeat unspeakable evil, she spends her days working as a drug and alcohol counselor and as a court-appointed attorney in the local Juvenile Court. A firm believer in wearing many hats, she spends many weekend traveling the country with her husband, daughter and Bengal cats attending cat shows. On off weekends, she can be found with the rest of her family at a hunt-test or field trial helping shuttle dogs or holding down the fort at home, caring for the menagerie of dogs and cats living in her house.

Sirena writes in several genres, focusing primarily on novels with paranormal or supernatural elements. She has several other novels in various stages of planning, including a futuristic crime series. She writes both because she loves it and because she has no choice and is a self-proclaimed slave to her characters. She considers herself incredibly lucky to be the one chosen to tell their incredible stories. Keep in touch with Sirena via her blog at sirenanrobinson.blogspot.com or through her publisher Supposed Crimes, at supposedcrimes.com.